A
School
of
Daughters

A
School
of
Daughters

Kate René MacKenzie

RED LACE BOOKS

For Lucy Jeanne

My lifeline when I really needed a lifeline

Acknowledgments

Many have contributed to *A School of Daughters*. Here, in the order I drew their names out of my Alaskan hat with the earflaps, are those who share these pages with me.

My animal family—some are in my past, some in my present, but all are in my heart. During my darkest moments, they are my beacon. When the path is obscure, they lead the way. They teach me patience, perseverance, and gratitude, and make me the best of who I am.

Holly Doucette is nanny to my animals and an ever dependable friend.

With the help of author and friend-cum-editor Lena Hubin—and her admonishments of "too much" and "choose one"—my writing has lost the fat, kept the muscle. Not so with her fab vegan lunches and heavenly sherbet and cookies. Lena knows me too well. Which is exactly what I want in an editor and especially a friend.

Scott Gere of Gere Donovan Press taught me the publishing ropes so I wouldn't become tangled.

First responders Mari Klassert and Jeanne Dolan have the unenviable task of CPR and tourniquets. For 40 years, they've answered my calls.

My family. We're all doing the best we can with what we know how to do.

Jennifer Longworth, alchemist, created a book from a Word file.

My wagon-circlers (in first name alphabetical order): Cheryl Strenger, Diana Wold, Janice Royce, Lona Hammer, and Marcy Noren. In the rutted trail behind us are the broken wheels, campfire confessions, and discarded bandages from our shared prairies.

Accomplice and courtroom confidante Linda Rupp is always up for a good caper. But make no mistake—*she* pulled the string.

Sascha Darlington, blogger big time, reminds me that, when words escape me but rejections find me, I really want to do this.

Gretchen Brink, a woman of few adverbs but much insight, helped achieve clarity.

Alaska and Arizona are my constant companions, even when I'm elsewhere.

Allison Mendel pushed me toward the light.

Linda McQueary and Diamond H Ranch resurrected my childhood dream of belonging to a horse...and forever changed my life.

Preface

I would fail. Or so I was told. The MBA program was too hard for me. Never mind that I'd been a President's Scholar and had managed a respectable score on the GMAT. Even my undergrad GPA of 3.8 failed to impress my academic advisor. "How hard is it to get an A in Painting?"

Fast forward through two years of graduate school to the Friday night before graduation. The next day, in black robe, mortar board, and maroon and white hood, I would walk across the stage in the cavernous university arena—where the likes of Bruce Springsteen, Elton John, and Garth Brooks had performed—and I would receive my master's diploma in Business Administration.

Not only had I proved my advisor wrong—along with some classmates and a few professors who had raised an equally incredulous brow at my Bachelors in Art—I did it with a 3.7 GPA. I might've improved that had I studied more and not blown off an accounting midterm for a weekend trip to St. Louis and a Fleetwood Mac concert. But, barely twenty-three at the time, I rarely thought about consequences, and, c'mon, *Fleetwood Mac*.

But on that Friday night, it was water under the bridge. I partied with fellow graduates at the home of a friend, everyone contributing booze and food, celebrating our shared accomplishment. Sometime around midnight—I'm guessing—I slid behind the wheel of my 280Z. I whipped around the curves of Old Route 13 and ten minutes later hung a left on 127 South, a similar two-lane country road, passing the telephone booth beneath the streetlight at the corner of the intersection. Less than a half mile later, I turned right onto Carbon Lake Road, which would take me down a hill and past the lake to my rented home. Except that it didn't. I was 100 feet too soon and dived down a 30-foot embankment crowded with birch and alders. My Z lodged at the bottom between trees, headlights kissing the earth, my seatbelt saving me from harm. Gin-addled, I took a few minutes to grasp what had happened.

Thinking I would return for my car—did I mention *gin-addled?*—I left the headlights shining so I could find it. I grabbed my purse and stumbled out the door in my 2-inch platform wedges, twisting my left ankle. Staying low and fighting the alders, I clawed my way up the embankment. Headlights shown in the dark, coming down the road. Fearing anyone spotting me would call the sheriff, I pressed the ground until they passed. Then I crept along the slope toward the phone booth.

Given the late hour, there was little traffic. At the intersection of 13 and 127, I struggled to my feet and made a hopping dash across the road to the phone booth. As I fumbled in my wallet for coins, a car pulled up. The passenger side window was down and the car's only occupant, the driver, leaned toward it and peered at me, his face illuminated by the street light. He was about my age, nice-looking with dark hair.

"Do you need help?"

After crawling in the dirt through weeds and alders, I must've looked a needy mess.

"Can I give you a ride somewhere?"

Leaning into the open window, I asked to see his driver's license. I remember his "are you kidding" expression, but he pulled out his license. He said he was a grad student. I asked for his university ID. There it was again, that silent stare. Nonetheless, he humored me. Returning both pieces of ID, I got in his car.

Heading down 127, we passed my unseen accident, then turned onto Carbon Lake Road. He stopped in my driveway. I thanked him and got out. He waited until I went inside before driving off.

Saturday morning, I woke safe in my bed, my mind clear but my memory hazy. *Had I dreamt last night or lived it?* I opened my front door and checked the driveway.

Two hours later, a tow truck pulled my car out of the ravine, not a scratch on her. She needed a new battery since the headlights I'd left on had drained the old one.

That afternoon, in front of a packed arena that included my mom and sister, I limped across the stage and received my diploma.

I suspect we all have times when we're plucked from our native Kansas and dropped into Oz. Experiences that have us shaking our heads because we were strong enough, courageous enough, or just plain lucky to have survived them. Moments of craziness that read like fiction, but are all too real.

And so it is with this book.

Funny, I always knew that one day my life would come in handy.

September 30

She called them *a school of daughters.*

I assume Mom came up with that later because it doesn't seem like something a 6-year-old would think up. Then again, maybe it's exactly the kind of observation a *precocious* 6-year-old puts into words, unrealizing the truth she airs.

I haven't thought about the daughters in years, not since the last time Mom told me her story. I'm thinking about them now because of that awful woman I met this morning at the Garden Center. Her off-the-cuff confession woke a sleeping memory and I fled that woman the way a cottontail flees a coyote.

It's crazy how the past floats up.

So, I'm back a dozen years to the last carefree visit with my mother, when she rode her bike every day and grew her own salads, and her hair was thick and sunny. On this particular day, Brian was mowing her lawn. We were visiting from Alaska and there wasn't a lot to do, and without any prompting from me, Brian asked if he could cut the grass for her. Mom normally hired a neighborhood kid with his dad's riding mower, but she seemed to appreciate my husband's offer. Pointing Brian in the direction of her shed, she let him have at it. Which was no small feat. Her lawn was a rolling half-acre scattered with oaks, and her mower was prehistoric, and it was August in Southern Illinois.

I can't remember the last time Brian had mowed a lawn and I know he hasn't mowed one since. But he was out there, shirt off, flexed and pumped…a suburban gladiator, glistening with sweat, wrestling that beast of a mower and giving my imagination an invigorating workout.

The rattling baritone of the old mower swelled and faded. I glimpsed Brian through the kitchen slider as he passed and passed again, and I couldn't have loved him more. Men think women love them for the expensive stuff—the houses, the cars, the diamonds. But it's the everyday priceless moments that make our hearts go pitter-pat, that keep us wanting *him*.

That night felt like high school again, in my old room, locked in secret passion, with every word, every breath, every moan choked into silence so we wouldn't wake my mother who slept across the hall. And at the same time being completely lost in everything *us;* a velvet ache of heart for flesh that feels like the sensuous drizzle of a James Last sax and has me imagining the bayou and slatted shutters and a lazy ceiling fan.

And after, the two of us tangled in sleep, dreaming as one.

It all comes back sometimes, from just a glance, that split second when our eyes lock and Brian smiles as if he knows.

Some moments you want to stay in forever. But hours before I knew that would be one of them, while Brian mowed the lawn, Mom and I were in her kitchen peeling apples at the ceramic-top table I once needed the Sears catalogue to reach. Together, we made my favorite Dutch apple pie using a recipe with how-to photos she had cut from the Chicago Tribune in 1948 when she was a wife but not yet a mother.

Aged the color of brown sugar, that clipping is folded into a manageable square and tucked inside the cover of her tired and stained *Woman's Home Companion Cook Book*, now residing in my kitchen cupboard.

I haven't made that apple pie in maybe two years, not since the last time Brian's sister and brother-in-law visited. But I'm making it for Brian's dessert tonight even though he still has Rocky Road in the freezer. Unfortunately, I'm the one who'll eventually eat most of the pie since Brian's sweet tooth is not the nag mine is, but at least apple pie has the redeeming quality of being apples. As long as I don't dwell on all the ingredients that make apples a *pie*, life is good.

At eighteen and a college sophomore, I was Princess *Red Delicious*, and first runner-up in the Apple Queen Pageant held during the county Harvest Festival.

Last year, I had my first facelift.

And this is how one thought spawns another until they swim in your head like so many fish in a pond, impossible to follow one specific.

Today is Brian's and my anniversary...*twenty-two years*...and for the first time in twenty-two years, Brian has forgotten. *No*, he won't surprise me later. Right now, he's finishing eighteen holes. Then he'll sit at the bar with the guys and have a couple of beers. Three hours from now, the garage door will rumble. From the garage, he comes through the laundry room and into the hall where he pets Molly, who is forty pounds of frenzied adoration.

Then it's my turn. His kiss is convincing. He tells me *something smells good* as he peeks inside the oven. While making a Manhattan, Brian talks about his game—complaining about his putt—then he asks about my day. With drink in hand, he'll retreat to the couch, change my channel, and wait for dinner. After roast duck, and warm apple pie with a cheddar slice, when I give him his card and a pair of Lucchese boots, he'll have nothing for me.

So, I'm thinking...maybe I should ignore our anniversary. Simply say nothing and treat this day like every other. In a few days it might hit him. But if not, Christmas will be here soon enough. I can change the wrapping and put his boots under the tree.

Wouldn't you know, I don't have a frozen pie shell. I finger through my mom's cookbook.

Crust isn't hard to make; it's the fluted edge I'm dismal at. Mom would gently plant the sides of her thumbs in the dough, squeeze together, and twist two ticks. Her crust was a golden crown of peaks and valleys. Mine is thumbprints.

I begin peeling a tart Granny Smith and I'm in Mom's kitchen again, the drone of the mower in the background, flicking my eyes on Brian as he passes. Mom and I are chatting as we compete for the longest spiral, when something catches her attention—like that woman's confession caught mine—and trips a memory I know like my own.

But I listen, as I always do, and the years drift away until my mother is an adorable little girl in her favorite bright green dress—with starched pleats and a scalloped collar—and wearing the brown, button-up shoes passed down through two older brothers.

Mom presses against her mother, who cradles my aunt Kate, as they board the crowded sampan. In one small fist are a few inches of her mother's skirt; in the other is a coin to give to the boatman who powers their ride with the push of his pole.

Mom has returned to Hunan Province, to the banks of the Yuan River, and to the city of Changde. Here, in this ancient port of temples and cobblestone streets, she was born and for eight years lived, the first daughter of Christian missionary parents.

As the bow of the sampan ripples the water, Mom peers over the side. Innocently searching the shallows, she follows darting fishes... and comes face to face with the unfathomable.

I watch my mother who forever remembers these perfect babies... *rocked by gentle wakes...their umbilical cords floating like severed lifelines...*and I see the dead who haunt her still, seventy years past.

Barely a toe-dip into life after nine months of promise then returned to their maker, like a bad purchase, because of one fatal flaw.

Trying to purge what she cannot, Mom searches for understanding. She asks me again how someone drowns a baby, let alone *their* baby, and I know she's not questioning the mechanics...

A perfect spiral hangs from my naked apple. One final cut and the peel collapses on the counter. I take my knife to the green collar surrounding the stem.

So...how **do** you drown your baby daughter?

Do you put her in a burlap sack like an unwanted litter of kittens and sink her to the bottom with a rock?

Do you hold her beneath the surface until she is limp in your hands?

Or, do you simply drop her in the water and walk away...

Molly jingles past the kitchen as I start a new curl.

Molly jingles past the kitchen? But, the duck's not in the oven yet.

Nevertheless, that dog can hear cheese.

I peer around the corner.

Molly is in the carpeted hall outside the laundry room where she always waits—ears pricked, eyes focused on the door into the garage, wagging her tail, and starting to dance.

November 8

Last night, I was in Otter Bight, where none of this is happening.

Blissfully adrift in a lavender twilight, I woke to blinding darkness. I've been lying here since, dreading the dawn, while Brian sleeps with one arm locked around me. In our flannel nest, skin-to-skin, not so much as a word can come between us.

Outside, a *yip* pierces the quiet—followed by a second and a third—before multiplying into a raucous coyote chorus of yips, yodels, and howls that stops as suddenly as it started.

Responsibilities nudge me; last night's sex escapes the sheets. Brian pulls me back and we settle into our favorite lazy position. He swells inside me, taking his time, but clearly on a mission.

Billions of Brian's sperm have died, unfulfilled, in my womb; I imagine them gasping and flopping like spent salmon. Another fifty million attempt the impossible.

This is Brian's moment, not mine. But, it's enough that he's here, enough that he wants me. I hold that thought as he holds me, my hope in his happiness.

"Love you, Kate."

My heart swells, spilling a tear. "Love you more."

Brian drifts back to sleep, still in my grasp.

****

You would think, after all these years of sharing the sheets with Brian, I could come up with sentiment more inspired. But I don't know how to tell Brian that my world spins on his axis without sounding like a cliché from a 1950's Harlequin paperback.

Plus, I'm cautious about over-promising. When I was nineteen, I sent a love letter to my Air Force boyfriend after he wrecked his motorcycle. Borrowing from Nilsson, I wrote…*I can't live if living is without you.* Six months later when I broke our engagement, he pointed out that I obviously can.

Now, I stick to the basics. Whenever Brian travels, I pick the perfect card and inside I write…

I love you more. I miss you more. Hurry home to me.

But my world **does** spin on Brian's axis.

So sometimes I shake it up by adding… *You still make my heart go pitter-pat…*

Or… *I can't imagine my life without you.*

But I always anchor it with…

I love you more. I miss you more. Hurry home to me.

I don't know where they all are, these twenty-two years of Hallmark moments, but every now and then I find one holding Brian's page in a spy thriller or on his desk by the phone, scribbled with a message on the envelope back.

Are my words so familiar that he no longer sees them? Have they given him a false sense of security? Or, am I simply boring him with my vanilla sameness?

Perhaps I should write… *I can't imagine my life without your hot, throbbing cock.*

Or… *Your hot, throbbing cock makes my heart go pitter-pat.*

But I figure my actions speak that, so instead I write… *I love you more. I miss you more. Hurry home to me.*

After signing with a solitary **K**, I slip my card into its envelope and on the front write *Brian* with a little smile line beneath his name. Then, I swipe my tongue across the point and seal the flap.

And, finally, on the day before he leaves—as I've done for *twenty-two years*—I tuck my card into the outside pocket of Brian's leather briefcase.

****

I carry my catch from the cold, smoky shadows, away from the water trough, and through Quinn's stall.

What are the odds, I ask as Milton might, that I scoop a sinking packrat—*but a breath away from his last*—out of my horse trough on the same morning that I struggle to keep my own head above water?

Even so, not everything is a burning bush. With all due respect to the 17th Century poet, sometimes chance is chance and a lucky packrat is a lucky packrat.

Inside the barn, beneath the spray of lights, I get a better look at Providence.

"Oh-my-God…*Winston*?"

His resemblance to Churchill is unmistakable—as is the Cheshire nick in Winston's left ear.

With a nod to Milton, I'm doubly grateful for arriving at the barn early and on time. But fearing a *dead* Winston and *that* bush, I hurry toward heat, past the spigot where I keep a small pail of water with a chunk of wood leading out.

I don't know why some ignore the obvious and, instead, choose tragedy. But four or five times a year I get a lesson in humility when I grieve a mouse or a packrat, and a chipmunk once, who didn't make it home from their nighttime adventure. I always worry about a family waiting and I hope dominoes won't fall because of a bad decision.

Inside the warm tack room, I tip my net into an empty bucket. Claws, on his finger-like toes, catch the weave, but Winston frees himself from the net. He trembles against the molded plastic and his frightened eyes stare at me. I plug in the hair dryer I keep on the shelf for emergencies—wet outlets, cold feet, damp gloves, and now, a frosty Winston.

I know what I must look like, waving a hair dryer over a packrat. But, better someone who tilts at windmills than that awful woman I met a few weeks back at the Garden Center…

I was on my way to checkout with three bags of fertilizer when I stopped beside the shelf displaying the animal repellents. She was there, too, and since we're both at that mid-century pause where conversation with strangers is welcomed, we started chatting. We have packrats in common, as many people in Arizona do, and we shared our stories about these little dyslexic Houdinis who are forever getting *into* places they shouldn't.

We agreed on how adorable they are—with big, soft eyes and kind, generous faces harboring the sweetness of a toddler's main squeeze—then we talked about mothballs and dryer sheets that are supposed to keep packrats at bay. Together we wondered if commercial repellents work any better. I told her that sometimes I live-trap and she said that she does, too, and right about the time I felt warm and fuzzy at the discovery of a kindred spirit, she added, "Then I drown them."

My stomach turned and my face soured as if I had swallowed lumpy milk…and I couldn't lose that woman fast enough.

But, thinking about it now, apart from the obvious necessity of a stone-cold heart, how *do* you drown a packrat? Do you open the trap…*shake, shake, shake*…until his grip gives up and he splashes into the water like a passenger off the Titanic? Do you watch him frantically paddle and claw at the sides until his legs tire and his lungs fill? Or do you return later, a coward who won't witness your own dirty work? Perhaps you put trap and packrat into the water together, letting them sink to the bottom like a mobster in concrete boots.

Maybe I've experienced too many last heartbeats, after forcing death into the veins of innocent throwaways, to treat life so cheaply.

Besides, we live at the end of a long road, on a ranch bordering thousands of wild acres. We might as well be flashing a red neon *Vacancy* sign. Either we co-exist with nature—and the occasional frustrating encroachments—or this ranch becomes a killing field.

So here I am, drying a packrat. Knowing him is just extra incentive.

And I figure it can't hurt, depending on what comes later, to be thought of as someone with redeeming qualities.

I tuck a towel inside the bucket; Winston burrows into the folds.

Stepping down from my soapbox, I will concede that drowning isn't the cruelest of deaths, especially in winter, when the water is that piercing instant before ice and it so quickly numbs the brain. It's terrifying at first—like any last moments—then everything is peaceful.

But summer is tough when tiny feet *paddle, paddle, paddle,* with all that hope, just to end up at the bottom like their winter cousins. Still, like Winston, miracles happen, and I once rescued a mouse who didn't give up. But my joy was cut in half by the *other* mouse.

Amber sunlight thaws the air. One-by-one, I haul the three muck buckets from the stalls I've cleaned to the ends of their paddocks.

I look up the hill at our house where Brian is now awake but still in his bathrobe, his hair haphazard, sipping his first cup of coffee with hazelnut cream and finishing yesterday's *USA Today.*

His small carry-on backpack sits on our unmade bed waiting for last minute additions. Already inside are an emergency overnight kit, a pair of socks and black Calvin Klein's, and a novel. Inside Brian's briefcase, leaning against his desk in our office, is his airline ticket to Alaska. In the outside pocket of that briefcase is my card.

Paddle, Kate!

I take the blankets off our three horses and hug their heat, hoping to melt this chill I've had since yesterday.

Soon Brian will leave his recliner, go to the kitchen and refill his coffee mug. He shuffles into the bathroom, puts his mug on the tile counter—leaving behind a coffee crescent that I'll wipe away—then he takes his electric razor to his morning stubble.

He hangs his robe on the hook, opens the shower door, turns on the water. As the spray steams, Brian checks himself in the mirror. With both hands like Santa, he gives his tummy a contented pat.

I linger with Quinn who stands quietly beside me, shoulder to shoulder in solidarity. He's a big, handsome Belgian-Quarter Horse cross, born six years ago on a Premarin farm in Canada and illuminating proof that humble beginnings are not forever.

But I look back and imagine how scared and brave Quinn was, at only five months and barely weaned, making that long trailer ride to Arizona with the other lucky foals.

I think about Quinn's mother, separated too soon from yet another baby, and not so lucky, left behind with the other mares, then pregnant again—day after day after day in her stall, year after year, her value trickling away...until she is nothing but pounds and cents.

And I wonder about the women who pop the pills without thought to the suffering they swallow—

Kate! Paddle!

Quinn is safe beside me. Winston lives another day. My birthday is in June.

Two out of three…

I breathe in the honest scent of Quinn, like sun-dried sheets, wishing more than anything to think of nothing else, but instead I imagine Brian in Wal-Mart…swiping his Visa for $3.61…taking his purchase…walking away.

I kiss Quinn's nose, wrinkled in playful protest, then I return to Winston who has a worried frown. An hour in a bucket must seem forever when you live only three years.

I carry the bucket to a fallen juniper. Lecturing Winston about stupidity, I tell him that I can't always rescue him. I warn him away from the horse trough and remind him to use the pail with the wood. Tipping the bucket, I ask that he *please* be careful and then I bless his journey.

Winston sniffs at the opening, looks around, takes tentative steps. He makes a mad scurry for a tangle of gnarled branches…and disappears.

✶✶✶✶✶✶✶✶✶

From behind my sunglasses, I scrutinize Brian. I notice the silver lighting his temple and the squint lines meandering from the corners of his glacier blue eyes. At fifty-eight, he is even more handsome than the moment I fell in love with him twenty-four years ago in Anchorage…

Snow covered the ground. It was our first real date after scattered business lunches, one happy-hour drink, and a 2-year acquaintance. We were going to dinner at the Alyeska ski resort—an hour drive from Anchorage—and then to Brian's ski condo. I worried about leaving my dog for so long, so Brian put Lisa in the back of his Corvette and took her with us. *In his Corvette.*

And now we are in *this* moment, making the 45-minute drive into Juniper Verde so Brian can catch the shuttle to Phoenix Sky Harbor airport. From there he'll take the first of two flights to Anchorage where, for thirty years, he's been practicing law.

****

Crowded into that same outside pocket where I tuck my card, are Brian's business receipts. I part the slips and nest my card while always ignoring the detail at my fingertips.

I once felt pride having all this faith in my husband when so many women have so little in theirs. But in a few thundering heartbeats, my faith disappeared, and with it my pride.

Expensive dinners for two. Inexpensive lunches for two. An afternoon jeep tour for two.

A single birthday card purchased at the Wal-Mart Supercenter in Scottsdale.

****

We drive the same roads; we pass the same houses, the same fire station. We hit the same bumps, make the same turns, stop at the same lights. Everything is the same, except it's not.

Brian is happily chatting. He tells me to call Best Buy and get our new television calibrated; says he's thinking of buying a duplex rental that I could then manage; unnecessarily reminds me to send $100 to Angela, his oldest grandchild—and mine by love and marriage—who turns twelve in two weeks.

It's a long shot, but… "Did you buy her a card?"

"That's **your** job." Brian's smile is the same engaging smile as when he was four, sitting on Santa's lap. I see it every day, framed, on our dresser.

Brian will be back in two weeks, a few days shy of Thanksgiving; he tells me now what he wants for our holiday dinner—turkey, stuffing, mashed potatoes, gravy, and *absolutely,* pumpkin pie. The same Thanksgiving dinner we've had for twenty-two years. I always ask if he wants something different, but he never does.

Yesterday, when I spread the pocket to nest my card, a woman's handwriting caught my eye. Like finding a weevil in my flour, I didn't believe it, then I plucked it out.

Two weeks ago, Brian was three hours away in Scottsdale for a 5-day conference. I searched for the hotel printout. Not that I need it. The first line of *Dear Brian* is evidence enough…

Thank you for a wonderful week!

****

Half of my brain is on Brian; half is on yesterday's frenzy after the house finally landed. But it's the moment before that haunts me, when the tornado hit and the clock stopped and silent white nothingness engulfed me. A moment I barely remember but won't ever forget.

Then adrenaline surged, like a tsunami. After the wave, I trembled like the warning of the earth before it quakes.

I returned *Dear Brian* to my pocket in Brian's briefcase. A pounding heartbeat later, I took it out and pressed it against our very slow copier as I encouraged it along….

C'mon, c'mon, c'mon! Hurry, hurry, hurry!

I was in an espionage movie, trying to gather evidence before the evil genius walked into the room. I kept wiping icy sweat from my hands onto my jeans for fear of bleeding the ink. My thoughts bounced around like a pinball while that damn copier wheezed out the facsimile with the speed of an 80-year-old on oxygen.

Then, thinking I didn't want Brian to know I knew, I put her note where I found it. But I remembered something about copies not being admissible in court so I took her note back *again*. Which actually makes no sense; Alaska has faultless divorce. Brian can be fucking a dozen women and it won't matter. But given the circumstances, I can hardly be blamed for muddled thinking.

So…her note has no legal value, original or not. But I kept it anyway—the original scrap, the original ink, the original *feeling*—because it has value to me. It has cost me everything.

Now I have *Dear Brian* hidden in my purse, while I sit beside the man I've loved *forever,* who might now be in love with someone else.

How the hell did we get to this moment?

"New jacket?"

Brian takes his eyes off the road and flashes me a loving smile. "I've had it for a couple of months. I brought it down last time and left it in the closet." He checks the road, glances back at me with the same smile. "I got it on sale at Nordstrom."

Liar!

She gave it to him. I know because he put a *tail* on his explanation—and he's not a shopper. Then again, maybe not. Maybe he did get it at Nordstrom. But I don't think so…

A scream wells inside me for what 𝒟ear ℬrian has taken. Is this what I can expect for the rest of our lives together? Wondering if everything he tells me is a lie?

Knowing everything he tells me is a lie?

A month ago, before there was anything in blue and white, Brian casually mentioned that he had meetings in Anchorage and wouldn't be with me at our ranch for New Year's Eve. *Like the midnight screech of a smoke detector.* That fast I reacted. "The only reason a man's not with his wife on New Year's is because he's with his girlfriend!"

I really said that, in a blazing rush. It was a visceral reaction, but now I see how right I was, how much I *knew* even when I didn't know anything.

Brian took the offensive and berated me for not being supportive when he was "working his butt off" to pay the bills. That's when I knew he was lying. He always takes the offensive when I catch him in a lie, making me seem the bad guy. *Of course* he's working. *Of course* he misses me. *Of course* he loves me. He makes me doubt what's right in front of my own nose.

I should've seen this coming two years ago when he switched from blue boxers to black briefs. But he never lost weight. He has the same beginning of a Buddha belly that he's had for years. After dinner, he settles into the couch, unzips his jeans and out pops the belly, a little mound of marital contentment. Or so I thought. I've always heard that the first sign of an affair is weight loss—getting into fucking shape. Apparently, this is a myth, probably started by men to throw women off the scent. Men don't have to lose weight to share the sheets with someone new. The proof is right before my eyes.

Then there's his hair. It would be silver, but he dyes the evidence, keeping just a hint of time around his temples so he doesn't look like one of those 58-year-old men who pretends he's not.

Just for Men, #10, Sandy Blond.

I buy it.

****

While Brian checks in at the shuttle, I wait by the driver's door, with thoughts, like bumper cars, uncontrolled in my head.

When I said *I do,* I wasn't agreeing to the marriage we have now. This back-and-forth travelling and our separations—that have stretched into six years—were supposed to be for only twelve months until Brian retired. But, life colluded and conspired and kept us apart, and here we are saying good-bye again…but with one small, huge difference.

I've had *Dear Brian* for twenty-four hours. *Hurry home to me* is in his briefcase pocket. *It is you I love most* isn't.

Has Brian figured any of this out?

Brian comes toward me, acting as if nothing is going on. But then, I'm acting, too.

We hug. I hold on a few seconds longer than he does.

"Fly good," I tell him as always.

"See you soon."

"Not very. Two weeks."

"You've got lots to do. Remember to wash my jean jacket. I'll call you tonight. And don't forget to water the trees."

"I love you."

"Love you more."

"No…you don't."

Curiosity sparks his eyes but he decides against it and hugs me again; kisses me by habit.

Watching him walk away, I feel more alone than I can hardly bear. I'm sad for what I couldn't give him that he had to find with someone else. I think of all my shortcomings, and, believe me, there are many, and I wonder how I can save my marriage. How can I make Brian know that I love him more than anything? I assumed that twenty-two years implies that, but maybe not.

Maybe Brian wants reassurance, too. Maybe he wants me to know about Micky—that's her *too cute* name, *Micky*—so I'll do something about her. So I'll fight for him. So I won't let Micky steal my husband!

On the road home, I call my sister in Washington.

"Brian loves you. I know he doesn't want a divorce."

I am buoyed by what I want to believe. Buoyed by other people—even if it is Ellie—seeing what I've always seen, knowing what I've always known.

Brian loves me.

If I leave it alone, it will go away. *Micky* will go away.

Twenty-two years, I keep repeating as if the number holds magic. Like, after twenty-two years, this crap shouldn't happen. Or maybe it's the reverse; after twenty-two years this crap **does** happen.

I always thought of marriage like days of the workweek. Once you get over that *hump Wednesday* of eighteen or twenty years, you get to cruise to the weekend where you relax and play. Thursday and Friday are easy days—your reward for all the fires you put out on Monday, Tuesday, and Wednesday.

I figured Brian and I were past the fires, over the hump, and well into Thursday.

I think of the tapestry that *twenty-two* years has woven. Of the friends, the family, of the thousands and thousands of insignificant moments that create significance. That create a single life out of two. That create a bond. That create a union. That create a marriage.

And I think of the handful of carefully penned words that have it teetering. All of this *substance* unbalanced by a slice of paper and a dram of ink.

****

I get through the rest of the day. I feed the horses, wash their faces, brush their coats, pick up poop, then walk the dog, fill the bird feeders, clean the litter box. In between, I hug an old teddy bear. Actually, it's more than a hug. I cleave to my bear like a life preserver keeping me afloat against the waves of despair that threaten to drown me.

And…*finally*…I cry.

Sometimes I just stop what I'm doing, slump to the ground, and wail. It is the most awful, primitive sound and I can't believe it's pouring from me.

Molly comes to me, tail wagging, ears back, offering the comfort of her warm, soft tongue. I reassure her that it's okay, that *I'm* okay, and I climb up from the ground and soldier on.

Then there are merciful respites where the pain still exists but I'm too drained to express it. But the best moments are when numbness takes over and I simply exist. It feels like the aftermath of a funeral, when the anguish of death has subsided and all that's left are soft, graveside tears.

Brian and I have shared seven family funerals. Is *Micky* Brian's attempt to postpone the inevitable? Does she make him feel young and new while I remind him of death?

We've also shared the birth of seven grandchildren. Does each new life add to his making him seem that much closer to the grave?

I want *so much* to understand why he is doing this. I want to forgive him. But what I want most is to pretend it all away.

****

Brian called two hours ago to let me know he had made it safely to Anchorage. He told me he loves me; I told him I love him *more.*

I lie in our king-size bed, hounded by midnight doubts. One arm hugs Teddy while Alyx-cat curls beside me and Molly snores.

I've been alone before, but this is really *alone.* The photographs, the bed we share, the walls, the ceiling, the home we created…all of it becoming invisible. My life is emptying like trash from a dumpster.

My plan was to ignore *Dear Brian* and see what happens. Just wait and see.

I can't sleep; I haven't eaten, and there is a running dialogue in my head that won't shut up.

I've had four biopsies, owing to the legacy of a cancerous family. *Wait and see* sucks.

I reach for the bedside lamp. My heart drums and my hand quivers as I pick up the phone and punch in our Anchorage number. "Hi, Honey, did I wake you?"

"Almost. Why aren't you asleep?"

I try to force the words. *I know about Micky. I **know** about Micky.*

"Hon?" he asks my silence.

"I couldn't sleep. I miss you."

"I'll be back in two weeks."

"That's a long time."

"We have the rest of our lives."

My heart sighs. "I just really miss you."

"I miss you, too, but I'm beat. I'll talk to you in the morning."

"Good night, Honey. I love you."

"Love you more."

I turn off the lamp.

I lie here, bombarded by thoughts impossible to escape.

I turn on the lamp.

I know about Micky. I know about Micky. I **know***—*

I hear the question in Brian's hello.

"I know about Micky."

"What're you talking about?"

"I **know** about Micky."

"I don't know what you're talk—"

"I found her note—in your briefcase."

"You went through my things?"

"It was in **my** pocket where I always put your card!"

"…What do you want?"

The question catches me off-guard, but his callousness stuns me. His tone is venomous, holding no remorse, no guilt, no apology. "You're the one with Micky. What do **you** want?'

"Kate…"

I slam the phone on his patronizing tone, my whole body shaking. I wait for his callback, which I won't answer.

I wait for his callback.

Turning off the lamp, I snuggle into bed with my teddy bear while Alyx stretches beside me.

It'll be okay. **We'll** *be okay.* There is something about us that keeps us together. When I look into my future, Brian is there. Older, grayer, as am I, but always the two of us, holding hands.

November 9

The question crowns long before the sun and lures me from familiar flannel into frightening foreign territory.

On a normal day, I brew Market Spice tea then sit at my computer and knit scenes into my latest romance novel. Everything is peaceful except for the soft hum of the computer and the occasional yips and howls of the coyotes. This is my nirvana. A couple of hours just for me before responsibilities dictate my day. But now, along with everything else, my nirvana is gone.

Who is Micky?

Maybe another attorney? Maybe this affair is a once a year fling, like in a Neil Simon play. I want to think that, but there is something Micky writes to Brian that dashes my hope…

I value each day I am given and pray that we have many more memories to share.

While my stomach churns and my hands clam, I read *Dear Brian* again, each carefully crafted word written on a rip of paper.

She couldn't buy him a card?

Micky knows Brian is married; why else does she value each day she is *given*? And what is her prayer? *Please, dear God, make Brian leave his wife so we can share more memories…*

Micky is waiting in the wings. But what has Brian told her about our marriage…and me?

I know the half-truths and lies men say about their wives and marriages when they want an excuse to do what they shouldn't. So, why does Micky value each day and pray for more?

I sit at Brian's computer. It's 2:30 Sunday morning in Anchorage. I picture Brian soundly sleeping and wonder if Micky is cuddling next to him—in *my* bed, in *my* sheets—the way I do.

Paddle, Kate, paddle, paddle, paddle!

I quickly delete my last few thoughts. No woman could lie beside a man as he talks to his wife and then remain there all night… *could she?*

I sip my tea then start clicking keys.

I'm in Brian's business—and only—e-mail as if I am sitting at his office desk in Anchorage. It's quirky why I'm able to do this, why I even know his password.

But Brian doesn't expect me to be here. I've proven myself as trusting and trustworthy. In twenty-two years, I've never snooped in his business, never checked up on him. I've always trusted Brian completely and, a few friends have warned, *naively*.

A total of 1825 messages exist in his in-box. Starting at the beginning, I scour the e-mails for a name or something in the *Subject* line that hints of being personal. Quite honestly, I don't expect to find anything. Brian and I rarely communicate by e-mail. And he has too much legal savvy for incriminating words.

Even so, I scroll through time, open a few e-mails, resume scrolling…stop…click…

> *Good Morning!*
> *Hope you are having a fantastic Wednesday!*

…breathe.

Not the sizzling expose' I expected, this e-mail leaves me ambivalent. I'm torn between wanting to prove my husband's innocence and nailing him to the wall with his guilt.

But, this May 21st e-mail gives me information I didn't have before. *Michelle Wright* is a counselor with a school district in Juneau, a 90-minute commercial flight from Anchorage, and I suspect there is some kind of client connection.

Now I wonder if my sleuthing is a good idea. Like the Velveteen Rabbit, Micky is becoming real.

Okay…bad, **bad** analogy. But I can't fight without knowing my enemy. I open an e-mail here and there, but no Michelle Wright until August 19…

> *Hi! Having a great time in Hoonah (not), but lots to do. Still no phone, maybe later tonight or tomorrow. Hope you are well. My flight gets in Friday at 4:00. Will talk to you later in the week. MUMCUS. M.*

I'm sick and icy like I was when I stumbled onto her Scottsdale note. There is no question that *Micky* is *Michelle*. Thinking about the months between her May e-mail and this one, I imagine Micky and Brian together as I sweated out the summer in Juniper Verde, alone. I think about the double life Brian has been leading—all that pretense without a fumble, until, of course, her note.

I am slowly uncovering their past, all the bits and pieces that make up Micky and Brian's present. Will my next click reveal their future?

****

We have a song, Brian and I.

Once, when we were driving on a wilderness road, our song played on the radio. Brian pulled over. On the shoulder of the road, not another soul for miles, we held each other and danced to John Michael Montgomery *swearing* forever love with the same vows Brian and I said to each other when we married.

> *For better or worse,*
> *In sickness and in health,*
> *Forsaking all others,*
> *Till death us do part.*

****

I try not to think about Brian meeting Micky's flight and greeting her with a hug and a kiss as he does me. I try not to think about Micky staying at our house, eating off my china, sleeping in my bed, fucking my husband…

I've barely slept, haven't eaten, and I'm operating, the best I can tell, on pure adrenalin. And I still can't believe this is happening.

I read Micky's August 19 e-mail again then focus on the last line. **MUMCUS.**

A pet name? Some kind of code?

I close the message and move to her e-mail on August 20.

> *Hope your day went well. Wish I could check in. No phones. Will call tomorrow from Sitka. MUMCUS— Michelle*

There it is again—MUMCUS. *MUMCUS.* M-U-M-C-U— It slaps me across my face.

Miss you more. See you soon.

Along with everything else that was *ours*, this is now *theirs.*

And yet what I don't see gives me hope. There is no LUM.

I move to the next e-mail, dated August 25.

> *Good Morning! Here is a reminder to send the thank you to Trudy and Sonny! Have a great day! MUM!*

Who are Trudy and Sonny? And why is Micky—

Okay, this *Micky* shit has got to stop. I can't stomach this *too cute* name. It's as if she's a little, innocent kid…or a loveable mouse. I'm calling her Michelle, and putting her on adult footing with me.

The next e-mail is dated September 13. Subject: *Mile 619 Project.*

> *Please see attached folder. Let me know if you need anything more. M*

There is no attached folder. What is *Mile 619 Project? Six-nineteen.* A date? June 19? Or is Mile *six-hundred-nineteen* an actual place along the highway in Alaska? Or the miles *between* locations like Anchorage and Juneau? That sounds about right. But why this cloak and dagger?

I hit *print.*

I open an e-mail from Alaska Airlines, dated September 20. After scrolling through the usual blah-blah-blah, I stop on the reservation details for Michelle Wright.

Not only did she accompany Brian to Scottsdale, she came to Anchorage a few days early, undoubtedly to spend time with Brian, in our house, *before* they left together for Arizona.

I scroll down…

> *The amount of $817.90 was charged to the Visa Card **********3343 held by BRIAN WILLOUGHBY…*

Brian paid for Michelle's flight to Scottsdale—and the hotel and the dinners and God only knows what else. A birthday gift to go with the card?

Or maybe Brian was gift enough.

Michelle left Phoenix and returned to Anchorage on October 30. The next day, I drove down to Scottsdale and picked up Brian at the Scottsdale Plaza Resort.

I think about the hotel staff who saw me waiting in the lobby while Brian finished his last class. Had they seen him all week with Michelle? Did they wonder who the hell I was when Brian greeted me with a hug and kiss? Or did they have it all figured out?

And where did *Brian* find her note? Inside his book? Peeking out of his shaving kit? Was he moved by Michelle's last-minute attempt to love him more—*need* him more—than I do?

Or…*is it possible*… Is it even **remotely** possible that Brian didn't find her note? That her note was still waiting for him when I found it instead? That *Michelle* put 𝒟ear ℬrian in my pocket?

What about Michelle? How can she possibly believe I'm the only one hearing lies?

Then there is Brian, keeping his balls in the air while patting himself on the back.

The sun is rising, squeezing through the blinds.

I click on the next Alaska Airlines e-mail and discover Brian's itinerary. No surprise that it matches Michelle's except for his return to Anchorage a week later on November 8.

The final e-mail of interest is dated October 23 from Alaska Airlines.

> Good News! The Willoughby party has been upgraded to the first class cabin!

****

At 9:30 the phone rings down at the barn. A few minutes later, my cell rings.

Every minute feels like an hour, every step is labored as if I'm dragging a cross, but I get through my morning routine.

Incredibly annoying monologues run through my head—words I will say to Brian. Sometimes angry, sometimes biting, sometimes forgiving. Words that remind him of our twenty-two years married. Words of love, hurt, hope. Sometimes they're words of letting go…

*If you really want to be with Michelle, then go. If you think that she has the enduring power of twenty-two years; that she will stick by you and be there when you're eighty, then go; that she will spoon-feed you, wipe the drool from your face and change your diaper, then by all means, go, go, **go**…*

My cell phone vibrates. Back at the house our machine is blinking.

"Honey, you're not communicating. We need to talk about this. Call me back."

Brian is once again sweet and caring. I feel renewed hope. We love each other. Arizona is to blame. And once Arizona is no longer part of our lives, we will be as we were.

November 10

I step on the bathroom scale. I've lost six pounds in three days and now weigh 120. I suppose I could count that as good news in the absence of any other good news.

The bad news is I look like crap. There is nothing pretty about despair. My face is gaunt and hollow, a reflection of the way I feel. Inside and out, it's me in the Edvard Munch painting, *The Scream*, forever frozen in the moment of discovering *Dear Brian*.

****

Arizona wasn't even on my radar when Brian returned from a guys' Utah ski trip with a deed for thirty-six acres in Juniper Verde. We had been talking about wintering outside Alaska, had visited the San Juan Islands and the Oregon coast, but Arizona had never been mentioned. I can't recall my reaction exactly, but it was something like, *you bought land where?*

I do remember that we argued about my lack of involvement in his Arizona decision, but by that time, my career was Brian, and he cut to the chase pretty damn fast…

"I'm going to be in Arizona. If you want to be with me, you'll be there, too."

It's one of my shortcomings that I have never been sufficiently grateful for this ranch Brian loves so much. I've tried, and there are moments of connection, like when the sun sinks into the hills and a brilliant fuchsia washes the sky or when a small herd of deer drinks at our watering trough. And once in a blue moon, a blazing star steals my breath before I make a wish to win the Mega Millions jackpot. But mostly Arizona attacks me, as if I am some invading army it must defeat and expel. Every time I turn around, there's something else on the battlefield pyre.

My heart and soul are in Alaska. When I was twenty-six, I packed my dog, cat, clothes and art in a Ford truck and drove up the Alaska Highway from Illinois. I had no job, no place to live, and not much money, but I **knew** I would be okay.

I spent the next twenty-three years in Anchorage. And I loved it. Even in the darkest of days and the deepest of snows, I loved it. I have an MBA that I earned when it actually meant something, before the proliferation of on-line degrees. And I had a good career going when I married Brian. But Brian wanted a woman married to him and not her career, so thirteen years ago, I gave it up.

I'm re-thinking that decision right about now, but at the time, Brian's needs were mine. Besides, for our first seven years together, including two before we married, I supported Brian. Alaska was going through a recession and his real estate investments were taking a dive and he had four kids and an ex-wife to support. I gave Brian my home and my food, and I clothed him in expensive suits, ties, and shoes that made him look like the successful man he is today.

By the time I put my career on hiatus, I had already worked twenty-five years. I worked my way through high school, college, and grad school. Then I topped it off with fifteen solid years of professional experience and a salary to match. So I figured a break wouldn't hurt. With a small inheritance, I continued to pay half of the expenses even though Brian was making $300,000 a year as managing partner in his law firm.

It was lovely, our life together, full of exotic vacations to places like Hawaii and Kenya and Tasmania. We skied Aspen and lounged poolside at Acapulco. We rode the Royal Scotsman, swam the Great Barrier Reef. Summer weekends we spent at our beach house in Otter Bight, an hour south from Anchorage in Brian's plane. I took riding lessons and adopted my first horse. In the mornings, I wrote romance novels; in the afternoon, I cantered the trails. I walked the dog and tried to grow roses and took care of our home. I met

Brian for after-work drinks with our friends and made dinner for him and his son, Aiden, who lived with us for his last two years of high school. At night, I snuggled next to Brian on the couch and draped my legs over his lap as we watched television. We had sex most nights and afterward fell asleep cuddled together. When his kids had kids, I became *Grandminnie Kate*.

Mingling at parties or business functions, I looked across the room at Brian and my heart thumped. He was my beacon, my one and constant light, drawing me home to safe harbor.

It's easy to see now, when life is condensed into a few paragraphs, with little imaginary bullets, that *there's a mistake* and *there's another mistake.*

But life doesn't happen in paragraphs, or bullets, to spotlight foibles. Life happens in minutes, spread over years, and one decision doesn't necessarily touch another until decades later when everything screeches to a halt and all the mistakes crunch together and land in your lap and you realize that your husband has another woman and all you have are memories and a prenuptial agreement that pushes you overboard with not even a life vest to keep you afloat.

****

As the world around me sleeps, I return to Brian's e-mail. Staring at my options, I wonder where my husband has forgotten proof of his cheating. I go to the beginning of his **sent** e-mails, all the way to January. It takes a while before I find the May 21 e-mail from Michelle...

> *Good Morning. Hope you are having a fantastic Wednesday!*

Now I have Brian's response...

> *You too. See you soon.*

It's hard to pull my eyes from the screen, from the truth it is telling me. And of course, the inevitable question... *How long has this been going on?*

****

I should've added a fidelity clause.

But the week before our courthouse appointment, when Brian came home with an unexpected pre-nuptial agreement, I wasn't thinking my husband would twenty-two years later have a girlfriend.

"It's no big deal," he said when I complained about the maze of legalese that stretched across seven pages. "And it will protect your inheritance."

I didn't know that my eventual inheritance was already protected, that it was not community property. And the major provisions of the pre-nup seemed innocuous enough: his money was his money; my money was my money. As long as we didn't co-mingle funds, it would stay that way. Anything we bought together would be subject to split. Whatever assets we each had in our names before marriage would remain separate. There would be no spousal support. A divorce would fall under Alaska law.

However red Brian's bottom line appeared at the time, his income was three times mine. Eventually his children would grow up, graduate from college and support themselves. Alimony payments would end. The economy would improve. I loved Brian, not his money, but it was part of his attractive package that included boyish good looks, charm, and intelligence. Never mind that I sold my condo and bought a house so his Corvette would have a garage and his visiting children would have bedrooms; I feared any resemblance to his ex-wife, although I knew little about her. Brian's trust meant everything and I didn't recognize my own attractive package—income, inheritance, and gullibility. I focused on the future and the wonderful life Brian and I would build *together*.

I never saw this coming. I had a career; I had property; I had money. It was unfathomable that I could let that slip away, that I would ever be so blindly complacent. I never imagined I'd be at the mercy of Brian's money—not when I generously and unconditionally shared mine.

So, a week later, I signed the agreement, and on that same Thursday, I said *I do*.

****

I scroll to the August 19 e-mail from Michelle when she was in Hoonah. Steeling myself, I open Brian's response...

Miss your calls. Hope all is well, my schedule is still the same. See you soon

And then a follow-up e-mail from Brian a minute later…

Hope you got my e-mail

If Michelle didn't, I did. I guess I should be grateful there aren't phones in Hoonah.

I discover a reply from Michelle, unseen the first time around…

Still no phones. Miss talking to you as well. Will call you tomorrow from Sitka. Can't stop thinking about you. See you Friday. Wish I could say more.

And how much more could Michelle say? I fear, quite a lot. But probably no more than I already imagine.

On the same day, in the afternoon, Brian writes again—he's golfing and will talk to her soon.

The next e-mail from Michelle is the one from August 25, reminding Brian to send a thank you to Trudy and Sonny.

Suddenly my hackles rise at the nerve of this woman telling my husband to send a thank you to people I don't know! Who the hell does Michelle think she is?

I continue scanning Brian's **sent** file and land on the September 13 e-mail from Michelle referencing the attached folder that doesn't exist.

Her e-mail seemed harmless enough when I first saw it yesterday, but Brian's reply is anything but…

Password for AK airlines 12345. Credit card # 4126-3400-1515-3343. Visa. Number on back is 3343-409 Talk to you soon

I do a double-take-head-jerk at the unrelated response, but then focus on the meaning.

Michelle must have booked their flights so Brian's assistant, who normally arranges his travel, wouldn't know he was going to Arizona with a woman not his wife. In his effort to conceal his cheating—and Michelle's all-expense-paid trip—he has unwittingly exposed it to me.

The next e-mail from Michelle is the twin of her last. But Brian's reply changes…

Try my mileage number 05033555

Hit hard, I let it settle, everything lurking beneath the words. There is trust here, and collusion.

My husband is not having an *affair;* he's having a *relationship.*

****

In the high desert of Juniper Verde, we have tarantulas. I suppose there are tarantulas in the low desert of Phoenix but talking about "the high desert of Juniper Verde" sounds sweepingly romantic. It's not. Arizona is more an arranged marriage, a *taming of the shrew,* so to speak. I don't know how Providence matched us—not through e-Harmony—yet, we have our moments.

I love waking to snow. Bundled up, I shuffle to the barn in clear silence. Phantom tracks crisscross my path, reminding me of all that exists, unseen.

I'm in constant *aaahhh* of a night sky that has more sparkle than a Miss America pageant. I forgive summer because of fall, winter, and spring. But the binding tie is the wildlife.

However, you can't pick and choose, so you *really* have to love nature to appreciate the myriad of creatures living here. There isn't much I take exception to, but centipedes and scorpions give me the jeebies. I have no closed-toe slippers because I dare not get out of bed and slip my feet into a dark space where either of these bad boys might be hiding. I don't know how they get inside the house; through what minute breach they pass. But a chill shoots up my spine whenever I see them scurrying across my very expensive tile…

As I was saying, we have tarantulas. Sweet, hairy, docile creatures that tiptoe past our house and sometimes climb the stucco. They wander through the barn and occasionally settle among the hay bales, eliciting a small screech when I unexpectedly find them.

The cottontails like the hay room, too, and more than once, a mama cottontail has dug a shallow burrow and birthed her babies beneath a bale. Hoping for the best, off she goes to feed herself, returning for only a few hours each evening to rest and nurse her young until a mere four weeks later, they hop from the nest.

Truly, there is nothing more precious than a baby bunny. Nothing. So imagine the horror of seeing your dog—your sweet, adorable, *well-fed* dog who curls on the couch and licks your face—imagine the horror of seeing your dog devour a trio of these babies as hors d'oeuvres, lickety-split, leaving behind nothing, not even a tuft of fur as testimony to their brief existence.

It makes me realize how close to the surface the baser instincts really are; how *domestication* is only a hope; how the cave is still home.

When it gets down to it, Arizona is a pretty brutal place, kind of a 24-7 nature program without happy endings. Slowly, it's stripping my soul the way my horses strip the bark from junipers…

But, I was talking about tarantulas.

I don't see them much except during August migration, when they leave the safety of their ground holes and make a perilous journey across open fields in search of love.

Enter the tarantula hawk.

This is not a majestic feathered raptor, but a large, black venomous wasp with burnt-orange wings who gracefully cruises the air with the attitude of a Great White.

And it is freakishly strong.

One evening, after I'd finished my barn chores, I started up the path to the house. Twilight blended the surroundings like an artist's charcoal, but I saw slow, steady movement across the trail ahead.

"Oh my God," I mumbled when I reached the spot and saw the paralyzed tarantula being dragged by the wasp, inch by inch, across the path. I was as paralyzed by what I witnessed as the poor tarantula and I wrestled with trying to save him from his ghastly fate.

Once inside her ground nest, the wasp burrows into the belly of the tarantula and lays her eggs. As the larvae emerge, they eat the paralyzed, *but still living*, tarantula.

Quite literally, eat him alive.

Like that innocent tarantula, I'm being consumed from the inside—by my husband's love for another woman, by the words I hear him saying to her, by visions of skin against skin. By his lies and betrayal. By the larvae of his deceit nibbling away at my core.

I have been dragged into some dark hole where I am completely alone and no one can save me and all I feel is the sharp stab of each lie and the dull aftermath of emptiness and all I see is the slow death of twenty-two years, shriveling and dying beneath the scorch of a July sun.

I wish someone would stomp on me, one heavy, crushing blow, to put me out of my excruciating misery.

I think about that tarantula, being dragged across the path, alive but not really, into hell, and I wish beyond all that is rational, I had somehow saved him.

Screw nature. Screw the wasp. There is no justification for this kind of suffering. I question the God who would allow it, let alone *create* it, and I wonder if maybe there is no God and I fear that all my prayers are empty words into the air, plummeting to the ground, unheard, unanswered.

Like that poor, tortured tarantula, I'm hopeless for anything but death.

****

Darkness falls as I trudge up the hill with Molly trotting in front. The horses are fed, their blankets are on, and now I have to make it through the worst part of my day—that tunnel of despair between 6 and 9.

Albert calls.

Nearing the back deck, I stop. Perched on the ridge of the roof, Albert is a shadow in the dying light. Close by, but unseen, Victoria answers.

Albert and Victoria are most chatty at dusk and in the dark before dawn. I've lain in bed at four in the morning, listening to Albert's masculine drawl…

Whoooo…Whoooo…Whoooo.

And Victoria's sweet, snappy comeback…

Ah who-who. Who-who. Who-who. Who-who.

Their 3-mile territory includes our house. Built on a hill, our home is taller than the surrounding junipers and pinions. Considering Albert's keen eyesight, I imagine he can spot the twitch of a mouse's ear from up there.

Molly waits at the garage side door while I eavesdrop on a conversation as poignant as the verse of Elizabeth Barrett Browning.

Monogamous and mates for life, Albert and Victoria are courting even though they're an established couple. In January, eggs will be in their nest.

Regal and austere, my great horned owls are the monarchs of birds; in short, no one messes with them. Fierce predators, they will eat pretty much anything they can sink their talons into, including hawks and other owls, dogs and cats; they'll even take down eagles. Their middle claw is razor sharp and they wield it like a Ginsu. In spite of being large and robust, these owls are phantoms. Thread-like feathers on the leading edge of their wings muffle their flight; not so much as a ripple disturbs the air to betray their presence.

Albert calls; Victoria answers.

Mother Nature puts a great deal of genius into her offspring. Each, it seems, has at least one trait—speed, stealth, camouflage, or defense—that helps level the playing field. And if all else fails, an ace—that older-than-Adam, miracle-conjuring instinct to fight Death, who is not as determined as we think. With a well-executed twist or a perfectly-placed bite, you can land in a soft tuft of grass, a little wiser, a lot grateful, and free, while Death flies off searching for another who won't put up such a fuss.

On Anchorage hillside, I once watched a bear give up when a moose didn't. Refusing to surrender her wobbly newborn, the cow kept Death at bay with jarring, *second*-thought-provoking kicks and 800 pounds of steeled resolve. After a short stand-off, the bear ambled away, unwilling to risk a broken jaw when an easier meal was down the road.

Albert calls; Victoria answers.

When I was a college art major, an image came to me. Like Richard Dreyfuss in *Close Encounters of the Third Kind,* I was driven to get it out of my head. Today, that self-portrait in oil hangs in the office. An owl hovers over my left shoulder, face forward and wings spread, as if he will fly off the canvas…and light on my roof.

The east is dark and brooding; the west is a blood-orange sizzle.

These few minutes with Albert and Victoria have been like morphine after surgery, but as I leave, the relief fades, and the larvae chow down with a vengeance.

I open the door. Molly hastens into the garage; she doesn't like being outside at night.

Albert calls.

Reliable as a Rolex, Victoria answers. *I'm right here, Honey. As always.*

Inside the house, I flick on the lights and turn on the television. I feed Molly and Alyx-cat, lower the shades, check phone messages.

"Hon, it's me…again. At least call so I know you're okay."

I haven't talked to Brian for two days and now I feel guilty for making him worry.

But if Brian really cares, if he's really worried, he would be here. He would've been on the first flight to fix this mess, to beg my forgiveness, to make promises for our future. He would do whatever he must to keep me.

But, that's not Brian.

If my husband has one flaw—cheating notwithstanding—it's his inability to admit his mistakes. For all our years together, Brian has apologized only twice. Two times, in twenty-four years as Brian & Kate, he actually said the words "I'm sorry" for *his* behavior.

The events were so extraordinary—like Halley's Comet—that I vividly remember each one.

Usually his apologies are *non*-apologies—"I'm sorry you're upset"—which don't account for *his* behavior at all.

Of course, he's sorry I'm upset; I'm sorry I'm upset, too. He's probably sorry I'm upset **now.** But is he sorry he lied, cheated, and took Michelle to Scottsdale?

Men know when it's time for serious groveling. If that's not happening… I've got to assume…he's plain *not* sorry…*for anything.*

November 11

I squint at the flashing red light through tender, swollen eyelids then turn away from Brian's message.

I don't bother with the bathroom scale; I avoid the mirrors. I'm cold all the time in spite of the layers of clothes I've piled on to compensate for the weight falling off me like meat from the bones of a boiled chicken. Last night, shivering uncontrollably, I did the unthinkable—I turned up the heat.

The kitchen lights push back the outside dark. After setting the kettle on the burner, I put canned food in Alyx's bowl although she's probably wondering why she's getting breakfast at 4:30 in the morning. Molly still sleeps, curled in her bed.

Retreating to the couch, I wait for the whistle.

Five days into this hell and I still can't believe this is happening. It's all a mistake. *It's all a mistake…*

I glance around the room…at the 15-foot ceiling and the sculpted carpet; the cherry wood wainscot; the stone fireplace filling one wall.

My eyes drift from one framed memory to another, poor substitutes for an absent husband.

Has Michelle put their Scottsdale photos in a new album? Has she tucked away her birthday card in a special drawer? Are the vases from Brian's roses collecting in her kitchen cabinet? Are the fallen petals pressed between Keats and Yeats? Is Michelle's toothbrush in our holder? Is she sleeping on my side of the bed?

Who the hell is Michelle Wright?

****

I have three bears and four bunnies.

Big Teddy is twenty-four and knows all my hurts. He goes back to my therapist who told me, "When you dig inside your head, you should hug something." So, for two years, as I plowed through muck and shoveled through mire, I hugged Teddy.

The tiniest of my seven is a 16-year-old "clown" bear dressed in purple plaid and lace ruffles. *Sunny* came with daisies and tears from co-workers turned best friends, Marlene, Candace, and Nina, after my cat died.

Sitting upright, with soulful eyes, lopped ears, and velveteen noses, my two fluffy white bunnies and one fuzzy brown bunny are twins to those I've given to grandkids.

My small, yellow bunny is not attractive at all. But who else would have her? Made of felt and posed in a crouch, she's not soft or cuddly, and on her left side is a round patch where Mommy sewed up a hole after my sister tortured her with scissors.

And the first of my menagerie, at a diminutive eight inches, is *Teddy*. A gift from my Aunt Kate, for whom I was named, Teddy arrived when I did and for fifty-three years has never been far away.

But his metal button eyes are dulled to blindness and his brown coat is matted in spots, bald in others, and his stuffing has shrunk just like mine. No longer firm and plump, when I sit him upright, everything goes south, and he droops empty-headed.

****

With tea mug in hand, I return to the computer and start Googling.

Huh... My husband is in bed with a Country-Western singer, Canadian, no less.

Modifying my search, I include the name of the Juneau school district and get a more believable result.

I scroll through a school newsletter, stopping abruptly at page five, where the article "Faces at the District Office" includes a photo. Unfortunately, it's a group photo, so each of the twenty-seven faces is about half the size of my little fingernail. Still, there she is in the second row, a smiling blond, Michelle Wright.

I could've picked her out of a line-up.

*How soon did they hit the sheets? Is Michelle divorced? Does she have kids? What's she like in bed? What's Brian like **with her** in bed? Does he call her Hon?*

After the printer churns out the photo, I move on, dragging my questions.

I wander through more newsletters and scroll through pages, stopping on a little box titled *Staff Birthdays*. Here I find Michelle's name with her birthday of October 27.

Brian couldn't remember our anniversary, let alone get me a card, but he managed to buy Michelle a card, not to mention the trip to Scottsdale.

That's more information than I care to think about. Although…I sure would like to read what Brian wrote on her card.

Actually…no.

There isn't a year attached to October 27, but I know enough about men to know she's younger than I am.

I continue scanning but no additional photos come up until I click on a newsletter from last year. Oddly, I feel like I've hit the jackpot…although…I never imagined I'd be looking at this particular photograph.

Sarah Palin, Alaska's former Governor and the 2008 Republican candidate for Vice-President, is standing beside my husband's girlfriend at some sort of gala.

I don't know how long I stare at this sweet, angelic face framed by blond ringlets, because time has again stopped.

Michelle is certainly younger than I—late thirties maybe?—which is no surprise. I've yet to hear of a man leaving his 53-year-old wife for his 53-year-old girlfriend.

Men don't make lateral trades. They always trade up by trading down.

****

The summer before I moved to Alaska, when I was twenty-six and still living in Illinois, I fell madly, passionately, head over heels in love with Garrett. I was so foolishly enamored that on my drive to Alaska I stopped at a Canadian tattoo parlor to have his name permanently inked on my fanny.

Garrett was forty-four. Today he's seventy-one, assuming he's still alive. That's kind of…unsettling. To think the man I was fucking in every room, in every position, in every orifice when I was twenty-six…could be dead.

Garrett was a psychologist. Probably still is, *assuming…*

Fortunately, he wasn't *my* psychologist. He was the business partner of my psychologist. When our eyes met for the first time as he strolled past me in the waiting room, it was instant recognition. He recognized my need for a *bad boy*, and I recognized Garrett as just the bad boy who could fill that need.

Not only was Garrett a bad boy, he was a married bad boy with two pre-teen kids. But before the lynch mob storms the ranch screaming *karma,* that situation and this situation are not the same for several reasons, with one most important—Garrett's wife knew all about me. Not only did Regina, who was also a psychologist, *know* about me, she *agreed* to me. Not only did Regina agree to *me*, she agreed to Garrett's other occasional women as well.

I may have been only twenty-six, but I hadn't just fallen off a turnip truck; I checked out Garrett's story with my therapist. With a sigh, and a slow shake of her head that told me she didn't get it either, Joni corroborated her friend's version of his marriage. Which didn't mean she thought my involvement with Garrett was a good idea, only that I wouldn't invoke the wrath of the fidelity gods by having a fling. Since Regina and the kids were in Sweden visiting with her family for the summer and since I was leaving for Alaska in August… I saw no harm.

****

Armed with the truth, I finally call Brian.

"Hi, Hon. It's about time," he says cheerfully. "Why haven't you called me back?"

"I didn't want to talk to you."

"We have to talk. Why didn't you bring this up when you found the note instead of waiting until I was three thousand miles away?"

"Because I didn't know what I wanted to do."

"So what do you want to do?"

"Tell me about Michelle."

"There's nothing to tell."

"Brian…I have her note. You took her to Scottsdale."

"I certainly did not."

"*Thank you for a wonderful week—*"

"You're jumping to conclusions."

"Are you telling me…Michelle was **not** with you in Scottsdale?"

"That's right."

"Michelle was **NOT** with you in Scottsdale?"

"No, she was not."

My heart is deafening. I can barely hear my husband's lies. It's unfathomable that Brian is sticking with his story. I'm outraged, not only by his lies, but because he thinks I am a complete idiot!

"I have a copy of her plane ticket!"

"You have a copy of her plane ticket?"

"So **now** tell me she wasn't with you!"

"I was perfectly happy. **You're** the one making a big deal out of this!"

****

I don't remember how Garrett and I started. I vividly recall that first spark of recognition, but then there's a blank and the next thing I remember is being in the middle of the affair. Maybe we knew our time was limited so we skipped the dating preliminaries and got right to it. What I do remember is the sex. There was lots of it and it was good. Garrett had accoutrements, most notably amyl nitrate, otherwise known as *poppers*. One of Garrett's occasional, but long-time lovers was an MD, and she supplied him with a prescription for these fabulous little bedroom gems. It was like shooting to the stars…

And I remember our last night together before I got into my green Ford pick-up with my dog and cat and all my worldly possessions and drove to Alaska.

But most memorable is the epiphany I experienced owing to one particular moment that taught me how expensive our choices can be.

November 12

"*Why* isn't this a big deal?" I finally asked Brian.

Brian wouldn't answer other than to say, yet again, that I'm jumping to conclusions.

My brother, Taylor, an Air Force colonel who works for the Department of Defense and has spent much of his diplomatic career negotiating missiles away from the Soviets, tells me during our telephone conversation…"in the absence of a plausible explanation, you must go with the evidence available."

****

"She's worried about my feelings for you," Garrett told me after his overseas conversation with Regina.

Fifteen minutes earlier, I had gotten "home" and found Garrett with the phone to his ear. Hearing long silences punctuated by consoling murmurs, I realized this was a very personal call. I left his house for the humid summer evening on the front porch steps.

As I waited, I considered what it must be like for Regina, so far away in Sweden, imagining me in her house, eating off her dishes, sleeping in her sheets, fucking her husband…

I felt what it must be like, after fourteen years and two kids, to have your 44-year-old husband smitten with a 26-year-old "bimbo."

"You said she didn't care about me," I challenged Garrett about his marriage when he finally joined me on the steps.

"This is why I love you so much, because you worry about Regina."

And *that* was the moment I realized I cared more about Garrett's wife than Garrett did.

That was the moment I understood that agreeing to something and *liking* something are entirely different.

That was the moment I saw the high price Regina paid for *allowing* Garrett this—for lack of a better word—*polygamous* lifestyle.

That was the moment I recognized Garrett as the selfish ass he was.

I would like to say I took my epiphany, walked off the steps onto moral high ground and never looked back.

But, hey, I was nuts about the guy and it wasn't like he was cheating on *me*. So, Garrett got out the poppers and we had great sex.

The thing is, I was not the referee between Garrett and Regina. I was simply a pawn in their marital games.

I haven't thought about Garrett in years, but now I wonder if he and Regina have stayed married or if Regina finally decided that the cost of keeping Garrett was too high.

It's a horrible assault on your self-respect and status to know your husband can't keep his dick out of other women and that hurting you takes a back seat to his desires, and that your only choices are to live with that or live without him. Just because you agree to something and put up with it, doesn't mean it doesn't hurt or even that it's okay.

I saw Garrett for the last time a few months after I moved to Anchorage. We rendezvoused in Chicago and spent the weekend at a Marriott. The weather was freezing wet and I had a miserable cold, which I doused with gallons of NyQuil. I really wanted to be in my Anchorage bed, **alone**, with a hot water bottle. In short, the bloom was off the rose.

Saying good-bye to Garrett for the last time, I was grateful—very, *very* grateful—that the tattoo parlor where I stopped on my move to Alaska was closed, and thus nothing is permanently inked on my fanny as a reminder of this folly.

It's chilling to think what his name would look like now, but when you're young and believing that a borrowed love will last the ages… sagging and blurring don't enter in.

When I look back on that moment, waiting in my truck for the tattoo parlor to open—and waiting and waiting until I gave up—I'm convinced that Providence intervenes to keep us from doing really, *really* stupid things.

****

"Brian's having an affair." My delivery has taken on the mundane, matter-of-fact tone of weather reporting.

Across the miles in Atlanta, Lucy's response is leaden. "Oh, no."

"I found a note from his girlfriend."

"Oh, no," my friend repeats, this time with dread—and a spark of surprise lacking in her first *Oh, no.*

Giving her the details, I finish with…"Her name is Michelle, but she signed her note *Micky.*"

"…That's cute."

"Yeah. And, actually, she is."

"Wait—you know her?"

"No, but I went into Brian's office e-mail—"

"Wait, wait—you have access to his e-mail?"

I explain the quirky, fortuitous details.

"Does he know?"

"He doesn't seem to."

"He has *so* underestimated you."

"I'm sure when he thinks about it, he'll change the password. But anyway, I Googled Michelle…" I share what I discovered.

"Where'd you find her note?"

I tell Lucy about my habitual cards and the outside pocket of Brian's briefcase.

"God…that must've been awful."

"Thing is, I can't decide whether he wanted me to find her note or not. I mean, it's the one place he knows I go."

"Yeah, but you said he puts receipts in there so it's kind of a natural place to stuff it. I doubt he was thinking about your card going in a week later. In a way it shows how little value it has; it's not like he put it in his wallet."

"No…but he didn't throw it away either. And of all the places he could've hidden her note that I never go, including his wallet—"

"You don't suppose *she* put it there?"

"And it sat for a week until I found it? Believe it or not, I considered that. It just seems to be stretching coincidence. Anyway, only two people know the truth and neither one will likely tell me so it's a question that won't be answered."

"Does Brian know you know?"

"Oh, yeah. I told him. And he accused me of going through his things—"

"Oh my God!"

"Tell me about it. He denied taking her to Scottsdale—twice—and then I told him I had a copy of Michelle's plane ticket, and then he said—get this—*I was perfectly happy; **you're** the one making a big deal out of this.*"

"You have got to be kidding! What an ass!"

Feeling oddly ambivalent about Lucy's assessment, I say nothing. I have to admit, and it's weird, that one of the hardest things about this is having the people I love, think the man I love is an ass.

"So… What'd her note say?"

I'm not sure how long I talk to Lucy, but by the time we hang up, she knows everything I know and, like me, is guessing at what will happen next. Lucy offers plenty of understanding, but no advice. Whatever decisions I make, she won't hold them against me. And if the decisions I make today end up being a mistake next month, she won't remind me of them next year. For over twenty-five years, whatever the attack—a misogynist boss, suspicious lumps, my mom's death, and now my cheating husband—Lucy is beside me, pulling out arrows, loading bullets, bandaging wounds, sharing her canteen, keeping me alive. She's a *wagon-circler.* Like the pioneers of old, crossing untamed prairie in their wagon trains, Lucy and I travel this life apart, but together, ready to circle in times of crisis. It may not seem like much, but it's everything when my wagon is down to its last spoke and rib, and vultures are low in the sky.

November 13

"Are you still seeing Michelle?" This is the first question I ask when finally, after two days, I take Brian's morning call.

"Noooooo," he answers as if my question is ludicrous.

He's lying, of course. I suppose I asked the question to see if he would. The thing is, Brian doesn't know that I know what I know... *Men don't break up with women to whom they've given their credit card number.*

"I'm thinking of coming to Anchorage for New Year's," I tell him.

"That's fine."

"*Fine?* So...you don't care whether I come or not?"

"Who'll take care of the animals?"

"Remember Glenda, the Scotts' caretaker? She can do it."

"It's up to you."

"Up to *me*? That's encouraging."

"I'm not going to be where you think I'm going to be."

"Do you want me to come or not?"

"We can talk about it when I get home."

My grip on the phone tightens. "Either you want me to come or you don't."

"I'm not discussing this now."

I let it go, afraid to push. Afraid if I do, his answer won't be what I want...or worse, he'll not come back for the holidays.

"Barry and Felicity invited us for Thanksgiving dinner. Do you want to go?"

"I think we should, don't you?"

"I wasn't sure."

"I think we should be as normal as possible," Brian adds.

Suddenly I have hope, as if I'm standing in a field where wild flowers have miraculously, unexpectedly bloomed, obscuring the elephant.

"I'll tell Felicity we're coming."

"So, what're you doing today?"

"Same ol', same ol'."

"Are you taking Quinn out?"

"Probably."

"Call me if you do."

"I've gotta go," I tell him.

"Okay, hon, I'll talk to you later. Have a good day."

The wild flowers are wilting; the elephant is in sight. Our *normal* conversation has a glaring omission. There is no "I love you."

I load the poop buckets onto the back of the Gator, then drive over the hill to the other side of the ranch where I dump them. Living on thirty-six acres in Arizona has its advantages—there are lots of places out of sight to spread manure, it dries out fast, and in a few weeks, a good wind blows most of the remnants away.

I fear the elephant dung will be less accommodating.

I ready Quinn, but I don't call Brian. It's horrible, this not calling Brian. This being normal, but not really. I always call Brian before I go out on the trail.

But, I'm caught between two worlds.

Still, I'm practical. If something happens and I can't make it back to the ranch, no one knows where I am. Without a cell signal, I could lie injured among the cactus, junipers and range cows for who knows how long, life draining from me, at the mercy of the ants, coyotes, and the freakishly large, scarlet-head vultures, another piece of carrion to get picked at and nibbled on...

I call my sister.

****

That damn squirrel!

I rap on the window. The squirrel looks up from the birdfeeder where he is stealing sunflower seeds.

I rap harder. He looks my direction then stuffs his cheeks.

I exit through the slider, onto the deck, and yell at the squirrel. He scampers down the juniper and runs under the deck I'm standing on.

Between him, his relatives, and the growing chipmunk family raiding the feeders, there's hardly anything left for the birds.

It's not so much that the squirrels and chipmunks eat the seeds, it's that they *hoard* the seeds.

Early in my Arizona adventure, I stuck my foot into the right boot of my working Wellingtons. From heel to toe, it was filled with sunflower seeds. Somewhere on this ranch is a humongous stash.

In the meantime, I keep filling the feeders.

With the squirrel gone, the birds are back…along with my mid-afternoon despair. I can't think of anything to help that, but maybe hot tea will melt the frost off my perpetual chill.

I set the kettle on the burner. Through my kitchen window, I see chipmunks around the courtyard fountain. They start and stop and jerk as if caught in a strobe light.

In summer, they lie on their tummies atop the cool flagstone slabs of the fountain perimeter as if they're on vacation, poolside. When they're not relaxing, they defy Newton by chasing each other around the outside walls of the house in a haphazard pattern, like an Etch-a-Sketch gone amok.

Unlike the intellectual squirrels and the introverted packrats, chipmunks talk incessantly to anyone, everyone, and no one, in sharp, explosive barks.

One Sunday, as fall crept in, I woke to a barrage of barks. Outside the window where the birdfeeders hang was a chipmunk at attention, his tail waving, sounding the alarm. Three feet away was a coiled Diamondback.

Chipmunks are nature's little sparklers, but they've got the courage of a Chinese New Year.

I watch my guys play hide-n-seek-tag over the chaise lounge. *Give me a double of whatever they're having.*

****

"Why didn't you call me?"

"I didn't see the need," I tell Brian that evening, feeling some gratification that he noticed.

"Well, you should call *someone*."

Someone…but not him?

It's horrible, this dissection of everything he says, trying to determine what it portends. It's like seating guests at a wedding—bride or groom? But here I ask myself what his words mean—marriage or divorce?

I ignore the missing "I love you" and park the conversation on the marriage side. It's a bloody miracle we're even talking and that should count for something.

Yet, lying in bed, the glow of the full moon frosting the room, I cannot help but wonder if the words I'm desperate to hear are being said to someone else.

November 14

I stare at a face I barely recognize.

"What are we doing today?"

Shifting my eyes from my reflection, I look at Ronnie, the perennially happy, mid-thirties alchemist who does my hair. "Same ol', same ol.'"

Lifting my highlighted strands, she assesses the ashen roots. She leaves but soon returns with a bowl of white paste and a stack of foils, which she hands to me.

She partitions off the first hair strand. "What's new?"

I hand her a foil sheet. "Nothing."

She brushes on the paste. "Is hubby here?"

After six years of every six weeks, Ronnie knows about my back and forth marriage. "He'll be here next week."

"Any plans for the holidays?"

"Same ol', same ol.'"

Every chair in the salon is occupied. Conversation ricochets around the room and laughter follows. It's all so wonderfully simple, this moment, and *normal* that I almost breathe.

We're all here, singular in purpose, fighting the future. It's a losing battle, of course, but aging is rarely graceful so we soldier on against an enemy we can never defeat.

Growing old isn't quite so bad when you age with someone you love who loves you back, but it's a tougher battle when there's no one by your side. It's one thing to start with someone young and journey into time loving, as Yeats wrote, *the sorrows of your changing face*, but quite another to fall in love with sorrows already there.

Some men will love a woman for her sorrows and her *pilgrim soul*, but most, given the choice, will opt for smooth skin and buoyant breasts, even if they, themselves, look like a Shar-Pei.

And herein lies one of the biggest differences between men and women...

Men don't mind *looking* older; they mind *getting* older. Women don't mind *getting* older; they mind *looking* older.

Which is why my 58-year-old husband has no problem doffing his clothes and sharing the sheets with a woman twenty years younger, while I cringe at the thought of rubbing skin with a new man my own age, let alone twenty or even five years younger. Regardless of all the talk about *cougars*, women are not Dinah Shore.

Men hate losing their strength, which is why men who don't need Viagra, take Viagra and why a man with money will always find an unwrinkled woman to cast a youthful light on the shadow of his years.

This is why women spend time in salons and why mature women with even a little money are on a first name basis with a plastic surgeon.

Maybe it's about attitude and bravura—you are what you think. But this is a very shallow world and while it's life-sustaining to be loved by sisters and daughters and friends, we also want to be swept off our feet into strong arms and if a marble staircase is involved, so much the better.

I scrutinize my reflection as the foils multiply on my head.

It's awful to be of so little value to the man I value so much and it's that much worse seeing the sorrows of the last seven days nest on my face, adding to my depreciation. How can my hollow countenance possibly compete with Michelle's youthful radiance?

I am a woman of sorrows and soul, competing against raging pheromones and a Viagra hard-on.

My multiple orgasms have given way to multiple epiphanies.

I am *sooo* screwed.

November 15

I want my life back.

The good, the bad, the ugly. I don't care. I want my life the way it was *before* Michelle.

I feel like I've been dragged across the desert by a herd of javelina, who scatter and tear my body, pulling in this direction and that, over rocks and cactus and a dozen different kinds of prickly bushes, until I've been tenderized enough to gnaw on.

I think about those who suffer through so much more than a cheating husband, who have *real* pain, and I wonder how anyone survives, let alone triumphs.

And I am scared. So scared that I tremble—or maybe I'm just shivering from cold. I pile on the clothes, but the shivering continues.

I'm scared. Scared of the known. Scared of the unknown.

And I cry. But the wailing has given way to that near silent, bowed-over torment that escapes through my face in grotesque contortions. Yet, it never escapes to the point of emptying.

I try to live in the here and now, to be grateful. For the roof over my head, the food I'm not eating, for the animals who force me out of bed each morning and keep me in a routine, who keep me alive. Breathe in, breathe out. One minute at a time, sometimes one second at a time.

I live for the phone calls from my sister, from Lucy, and from Faith, another wagon-circler. And my brother, Taylor, the arms negotiator, calls to check in.

"I'm thinking of going to Anchorage for New Year's," I tell him.

"In a wig and sunglasses?"

I smile. "Actually, I told Brian I might come."

"Ahhh. And what did he say?"

"Not much."

"Ouch."

"So…what do you think?"

"Maybe you should talk to an attorney."

Ouch.

****

carrots

bananas

tomato soup

Sunflower seeds !!

Kleenex

grape juice

****

I love photographs. I suspect I inherited that obsession from my father who always seemed to be lining us up in front of something and clicking the shutter. Wherever we travelled, the camera came with us. But my father didn't take photographs; he took *slides*. After they were developed, out came the projector and up went the silver screen for a sleep-inducing evening of memories. I still hear the hum of the projector and the *click-clack-shoosh* of the revolving tray.

(Do slides exist today?)

Yet, for all the images frozen in time, there wasn't one framed photograph in our house. Really, not one. I never thought about that until right now.

When my father died, he left boxes and boxes and boxes of little celluloid memories, none of which my brother, sister, or I wanted.

But I have memories I love and the photographs to prove it. I have framed photographs of Brian and me; of Brian in Otter Bight; of the kids; of the grandkids; photos of my sister and brother and niece; photos of my mom. I have photos of the animals, of Brian and me with the animals. I have one particularly adorable photo of us with Molly sitting at our feet.

It was taken seven months ago.

Then I have memento photos from cruises, safaris, and luaus. The oldest framed photo of us was taken on our first trip to Hawaii by a restaurant photographer. My face is surrounded by a mass of permed curls. Brian is thirty pounds lighter and his hair is thick and blond without a hint of silver.

And I cherish that black and white photo of Brian on Santa's lap. I can see that sweet, little boy in Brian's face today.

Every five years or so, a professional photographer updates our life and I place the new photos over the old, keeping the frame. But some photos stay, like breadcrumbs, leaving a trail to our past, and reminding me how far we've come together. I can look at each photo and remember what was happening in our lives when the shutter clicked. Not every smile reflects a happy time. But they reflect commitment. I am surrounded by framed promises for our future. I cannot believe this is where the camera stops clicking…

Two summers ago, I walked into our cottage on Kachemak Bay in Otter Bight. Brian had opened the cabin six weeks earlier, but this was my first visit of the season. Eight months had passed since I was there and for this trip my Anchorage trail buddy, Paula, and her husband Eddie, came with us.

As usual, we flew from Anchorage in Brian's Cessna. We landed at the Otter Bight airstrip, loaded up the Jeep we keep there, and drove seven miles down the overgrown country road to the spot where foot access to Otter Beach begins. Paula and I hiked down the trail through the brush, one eye out for bears, while the guys transferred gear from the Jeep to the John Deere Gator, left chained to a spruce alongside the road.

Brian and Eddie rumbled past us on the beach. They had the cottage open by the time Paula and I climbed up the old, uneven plank steps from the sand to the grassy yard of our cottage. Then another few steps onto the deck and through the back door of the house.

Inside, I gazed through the expansive front windows at the majesty of Kachemak Bay and fifty miles beyond to the snow-capped Alaska and Aleutian Mountain Ranges. I snuggled into the moment like a kid snuggles into his bed on a snowy night.

Our husbands unloaded the gator and put everything inside the back door. Grabbing my bag, I entered our bedroom. And that's how fast I sensed the emptiness. With my heart pounding, I checked out the living room—the tables and the walls where I should be, where I *used to be,* but nothing, literally. That's when I knew and the *knowing* landed like lead in the pit of my stomach.

How I made it through the weekend acting perfectly happy, I haven't a clue, but I suspect the presence of Paula and Eddie kept me from confronting Brian and making *our* problems *their* problems. Plus—and this was probably the main reason I said nothing—it was humiliating having my husband's infidelity exposed like a cadaver at an autopsy. Let's plunk my husband's lies and deceit into the middle of the living room and have everyone render an opinion.

It didn't take much searching to find my photos, dumped in the bottom drawer of my nightstand. When the weekend was over and we were leaving, I took all the framed photos with me, carrying them in plain sight.

I will never forget that look on Brian's face when he saw the photos in my hands—that *oh, shit* moment in his cool blue eyes when his gaze met mine.

I said nothing, which gave Brian some recovery time; in other words, time to come up with a story, which he did by the time we got back to Anchorage.

Seeing me come out the back door, Paula asked about the photos I carried. Taking her aside, I confessed the situation. She knew, like every woman knows, and undoubtedly every man knows, that there is only one reason a man hides photos of his wife, **only one**, and it's not because he wants the cabin to be a "guy place," or that he doesn't want to look at photos of dead pets. It's not because he's worried about an earthquake rattling them off the tables and breaking the glass.

There is only one reason and there it is again, that stinky cadaver.

We had a huge fight when we got back to Anchorage yet Brian never admitted to anything. Brian's self-confessed mantra has always been *lie and deny*, and he did, and he did, and he did.

I didn't want to believe what my husband was doing, what I *knew* my husband was doing. I wanted a reason to believe in him. A reason to think I was the one jumping to conclusions. It was easier to believe *I* was crazy and paranoid than to believe what I knew was true.

Denial is not a river in Egypt. It is a pristine tropical isle with white sand beaches and dolphins frolicking in the surf, where the sun warms you but never burns, where pina coladas make you mellow but never give you hangovers, where you still look good in a bikini and where your husband has eyes only for you.

It's a place we go when truth is not an option. It's survival gear for the storms of life that you can't avoid or change.

So I lounged on the beach and convinced myself that if we could get past Arizona and this separation; if we could just hunker down and get through this storm… Everything would be all right. *We* would be all right. The cadaver would magically bury itself beneath that perfect white sand, never to re-surface.

Besides, I didn't have a warm body with a name, or a love letter, or a flight itinerary. I partly blamed myself for being absent so much, even though I didn't want that.

Would I, *could I*, really walk away from Brian over something as tenuous as hidden photographs? Over something as unsubstantial as suspicion? I only had the tip of the iceberg.

So, like the captain of the Titanic, who thought his ship unsinkable, I ignored whatever lurked perilously underneath, and stayed the course.

November 16

"Hey, how's it going?" Candace is cheerful and breezy.

"Not great." Thankfully, this is a phone conversation and my Anchorage friend can't see me. "Brian has a girlfriend."

"Oh, Kate. Are you sure?"

"I found her note. He took her to Scottsdale."

"Oh, gawd. What're you going to do?"

"I'm thinking I should talk to an attorney. I figured you would know a good one. I was going to ask Brian who he'd recommend, but that might be awkward."

"Y'think? I'll talk to Joe and let you know."

I've known Candace for over twenty years; I used to be her supervisor at work, but we quickly became friends. Joe is her attorney husband. They've been married longer than forever.

The rest of our conversation is filler. I connect the dots, color in the shapes, and tell Candace what I know. She is part of my wagon train.

****

"I got you a Santa Claus cookie jar. You don't have one, do you?"

"You got me a cookie jar?"

"I think so." Brian hedges. "I was at a party last night and there was a silent auction. I put in a bid, so we'll see if I get it…or if you get it."

I have a collection of seven cookie jars that started with an original Shawnee *Puss-n-Boots* that sat on our kitchen counter when I was a kid.

"I'll bring it down with me next week."

"That's sweet, Honey." I think about the party and wonder who Brian was with.

"So, how was your day?"

"Good."

"Anything exciting?"

"Same ol', same ol'."

"How're the horses?"

"Good."

"How's Molly?"

"Good."

"Nothing new to report?"

I could mention the callback I got from Joe with the names of attorneys. But, in light of the cookie jar, maybe I'm rushing things. "No, Honey, we're just getting through the day."

"I guess I'll hang up then. See you soon."

"Not very."

"Pretty soon."

"Bye, Honey."

"Bye, Hon, talk to you tomorrow."

Just like that, there is again nothing. It's weird that you can *have* nothing. But without *I love you*, our words are vapor.

****

I stopped dead in my tracks. Spinning around and then back again, I searched for the unrecognizable buzz, like a distant airplane or a chainsaw, but less mechanical.

The buzz grew louder. My heart instinctively thumped, as if I *knew* I should be afraid.

Then I saw it. A black cloud, but opaque like a woman's stocking, zoomed toward me, shifting and breathing as a single organism instead of the thousands of bees I feared it was…

In neighboring Mesa Verde, an angry hive attacked three horses outside their barn. When the fire department responded to the frantic 911 call, they discovered the horses crumpled on the ground in a shroud of stinging bees.

Firefighters described it as the worst call they'd ever been on.

But a moving swarm isn't supposed to be dangerous; searching for a new hive location, they're not defending territory. Unwilling to test that theory, I grabbed Molly and dragged her behind a small juniper off the trail where only seconds earlier we were walking without worry.

As the swarm headed for us, I remember thinking, *we need a bigger juniper…*

I watched, terrified, and yet, mesmerized by the power of small things. The cloud passed a hundred feet in front of me, maybe five feet off the ground, sounding much like a speeding motorcycle. It stretched into a ribbon as it flowed over a ridge before ballooning once again. Then it disappeared into the landscape and faded into silence.

✸✸✸✸✸✸✸✸✸✸

Coincidentally, Brian's last gift to me was from an auction, three years ago.

We were in Kodiak where Brian attended a professional conference. At the closing dinner, there was a fund-raising auction. Among the items was an ivory bracelet made by a native artist and etched with Alaskan wildflowers.

Brian placed the winning bid. "For our anniversary."

I love that bracelet, but it's a fragile piece of art, and I've worn it so much that the dyes coloring the wildflowers are fading.

Now, instead of thought, I get money. A one-hundred dollar bill stuck inside a card.

The first time Brian did that, for Valentine's Day, I went ballistic. But nothing changed. For my birthday the following June, I got $100. Now we've settled into a routine. He gives me money; I smile and thank him.

Last Christmas, he gave me $1,000. Yep, that's a lot of money without any thought. And in some weird way, the more money, the less thought.

Over the years, I've received wonderful gifts from Brian, some expensive, some not so much. My favorite gift is my first manuscript that he had professionally bound like a hardcover book. That was the moment I knew Brian understood what I was about. That gift was for *me* and could never be for anyone else.

But cash is what you tip the waitress or the cab driver.

I know there are wives who would rather get money while there are husbands whose gifts get exchanged. But it seems that once or twice a year, attention should be paid to the person you love; some effort spent bringing a little spark of joy to the woman who scrapes the dinner dishes…even if it's one red rose and a few slow spins around the kitchen.

But if a man gives more thought to the scent going into his car when it's detailed than he gives to a gift for his wife, no one should be surprised when the marriage goes down the disposal.

November 17

With Molly in the lead, zigzagging from scent to scent, I take Quinn and Teena for a walk so they will stand quietly for their hoof trim when the farrier comes this afternoon. Petunia, the *boss mare* of my little herd, stays home munching hay.

At twenty-two, Petunia is too arthritic for long walks; her left front knee is so badly knotted and bowed that every day is a gift. Eventually something will give way. Either a bone will break or her kidneys will succumb to the harshness of her pain medication. Or maybe she will simply tire of each difficult step. But, for now, she is still the boss of our little herd, as demanding and determined as the day I met her.

She practically raised Quinn, and now, at six and a half years old, he is bigger, stronger, faster, with an attitude to match. But Petunia doesn't see it. She will swing her rump around and threaten a kick or nip his flank if he doesn't yield.

In nature, there are no mirrors. Reflections are self-created. Petunia sees Queen Elizabeth—the *first* one, who beheaded her cousin, Mary.

I'm sure there are some who, watching Petunia, would tell me to *put her down,* which is the sanitized version of telling me to kill her. It's a bit jarring to think of it that way, but maybe if we stop whitewashing the horrible things we do, we'll stop doing horrible things.

And while we're in the neighborhood of whitewashing, let's scrape off the black-tie veneer we give to the word *affair* and call it what it most often is—a back alley rut. Few *affairs* come with a 40-piece orchestra, Dom Perignon, and caviar. They are scraps and leftovers, served with pretense. They are the *haggis* of relationships.

But my darling Petunia cares not about my side thoughts, unless they interfere in her 4-squares and twice-a-day rice mash she loves so much. She is happy to be here, crooked leg and limp. I'm sure there's a lesson in that, because with animals there often is, but I'm too focused on my husband's haggis to see lessons so I'll leave it at this. I'm not going to kill Petunia because Petunia is not ready to go. She'll tell me when she is. Until then, we will bear the pain together.

No one likes to see loved ones hurting, even a little. It was excruciating watching my mom fight but lose to cancer. It's easier to suffer yourself than to be a helpless bystander.

Just ask my sister, Ellie, who begs me to take Prozac as she does. But I fear Prozac as much as I fear my circumstances. Do I really want to be *okay* with what's going on in my life right now? Or will I be better off experiencing every splinter of pain, every shard of anguish? If I numb my pain, how will I know when it subsides?

How will I know when I'm better?

****

My ob-gyn gave me a prescription for Zoloft when I moved to Arizona. It was the only way I could leave Alaska. It was the only way I could convince myself that it was okay, that **I** was okay, to be in a place I didn't want to be, seven miles from my mailbox, twenty-five miles from town and 3000 air-miles from Anchorage—without my friends, with only a part-time husband, but with full-time isolation.

Zoloft worked. I wasn't happy, but I wasn't miserable, even when I gained fifteen pounds.

And when, nine months later, my dog, Nick, unexpectedly died from a heart attack while Brian was in Alaska and I was here alone, it was *okay*. That's when I knew something was very, very **not** okay.

I quit Zoloft cold turkey and turned into a raging bitch for about eight weeks. I was the Incredible Hulk with PMS, but finally I found the grief Nick deserved. By Christmas, I was back to "normal," just in time for a loss so painful, no drug could dull it.

****

Rush Limbaugh heckles the world from the radio of our farrier's truck. I stand in the barn aisle with Quinn, smooching his velvety-soft nose as Allen trims his hooves. Allen's wife stands by, trying to sweep up the hoof crescents before Molly snatches them.

I can't imagine what hoof tastes like, but Molly sits in wait to grab an errant sliver. If she succeeds, twelve hours from now I'll see these hoof pieces again, on our carpet, where Molly will deposit them undigested, in a stew of stringy, yellowish-green goop, because her stomach is no match for a substance so resilient it can carry a thousand pound horse over rock and sand, 24-7, with barely a scratch.

If I understand this upheaval will happen, why doesn't Molly? Then again, maybe Molly does understand. Maybe she does, but the taste of hoof is so irresistibly sublime that she will have it no matter the consequences. Even if the consequences include me getting out of bed in the middle of the night to clean up her mess. Because that's when this stuff happens, when I'm all cozy and warm, snug and safe, blissfully sleeping…until the sound of a heaving stomach jolts me awake.

Women have an internal alarm for messes, and then we clean them up. The little ones and the big ones. And, it seems, we stand by our men as we're doing it. Just ask Hillary.

So here I am, smooching Quinn's nose, watching Allen trim and file while his wife sweeps up the by-product of his work, otherwise known as "the mess."

Women are the sweepers, the scrubbers, the moppers, the organizers, the folders, the put-things-away-ers. While there are special men who share this, we know who does most of the *mess-making,* and who cleans up the mess-makers' messes.

Women are the Band-Aids and, if necessary, the sutures that close the gaping injuries of life, and more often than not, we're the ones who bear the scars.

We are amazing in our ability to pull our marriages from the dumpster, clean them up, glue them back together, and recycle them. We do it out of love, or so we tell ourselves. But it's a dirty, thankless, underappreciated job. And I'm thinking…

If what we have created with the man in our life has less significance than a fleeting hard-on, why the hell are we trying to save it? Come on, is Michelle's vagina all that different—or better—than my vagina? Since Brian and I are still sharing bodily fluids, and all that implies, this isn't about sex, or lack thereof.

But maybe men, like Molly, want that fresh piece. Maybe men, like Molly, simply don't anticipate the inevitable mess that someone else will be cleaning up. Or maybe, like Brian, who is **not** down on *his* hands and knees scrubbing the carpet, men simply deem the mess as no big deal.

November 18

I flick on the courtyard lights and jerk open the front door. Heaving, Molly rushes out. At the courtyard gate, she expels the trouble-making contents of her stomach onto the stone. Following Molly, I open the gate and she disappears into the morning night.

Checking out the yellow goop at my feet, I spot what look like hoof parings. Somehow Moly has thwarted my diligence. But at least this byproduct of her fun can be easily washed away with a spritz from the hose. Not at 4:30 in the cold, dark morning, however. In my long underwear with only a fleece jacket, I feel the winter chill, but the fountain still sprinkles and the water in the shallow chipmunk bowl isn't frozen. In fact, it ripples. A moth frantically swims in circles; I scoop him out. It is way too early for any of this.

Leaving the bright courtyard, I shuffle down the drive into darkness, calling Molly. I stop, check out the sky, and easily spot the Big Dipper, but the North Star is candle glow and requires a search. In Alaska, it radiates, drawing the eye.

In the distance, maybe two hills over, Albert calls.

I wait for Victoria's reply.

He calls again.

I listen anxiously as he beckons with a third series of hoots.

Finally, Victoria answers.

A shadow approaches and materializes into Molly who is all smiles.

Albert calls.

Victoria answers. *I'm right here, Honey. As always.*

****

"I've been thinking about this, Brian…"

"What, Hon?"

Brian and I have managed to sneak back into our routine of two calls a day, without a single mention of our elephant. But this morning, I'm going rogue.

"…I love you. What's happening between us is the most painful thing I can ever imagine going through. And the thing is…" I take a breath as my heart speeds. "Michelle loves you. And I assume you've given her reason to believe you love her…" I give him two heartbeats. "I want our marriage. But I'm not willing to wait around for the other shoe to drop, for you to decide six months or two years down the road that you want a divorce so you can marry Michelle. I'll have nothing and be two years older. I guess, if I have to start over, I might as well start over now. If you want our marriage, if you want **me**, you're going to have to change the pre-nup."

The second hand on the barn clock ticks away time. "Brian?"

"I heard you."

"What do you want to do?"

"I'll think about it."

"You'll *think about it*?"

"You know me, when I'm unhappy, I make changes."

"So you want a divorce."

"I didn't say that."

"It's not a hard question, Brian. And it's not like you **haven't** had time to think about it. Do you expect me to go back to the status quo and pretend this isn't happening?"

I imagine Brian on the other end. I can see his stony visage at my ultimatum. Calming my emotions, I speak in business lingo—words he can relate to. "You've put me in a very insecure position. You have to share some of the risk. If you're not willing to, then I guess that tells me how you feel. So…what are we doing?"

"I'm not going to talk about this over the phone. I'll be home on Saturday. We'll talk about it then."

I have no voice. Everything is on Brian's terms. He's got the cards, the chips, the deal. Or as Brian says, *he who has the money has the power.* Helpless and ineffectual, I'm afraid to take charge of my life. I've become a scavenger in this marriage, accepting whatever carrion Brian leaves in his wake. When did I become so small? How did I become so lost?

****

Hearing anger, I hid in my bedroom. I was about ten, I think. I remember the house we were living in, so that would make me about ten.

My mom screamed.

I grabbed my shiny, silver baton, the kind every girl in the 1960's twirled, and wielding it above my head, I charged into the living room.

My father had my mom against the wall—six feet, 220 pounds of him against my mom, eight inches shorter and 100 pounds lighter. Arms crossed in front of her face, she tried to protect herself from my father's fists.

"Daddy, you leave my mommy alone!" I remember my words exactly, as if I were yelling them now.

Daddy, you leave my mommy alone!

My interference shocked everyone; there was an eerie calm, like right before a tornado hits.

It's ludicrous, as I picture the scene, this little sprite against the giant. What was I going to do, pummel him with the rubber bulb of my baton? But there isn't always time for a well thought out plan.

My father turned from my mom and stepped toward me. I was so scared, so scared; I still feel the drum of my heart.

"Go back to your room!"

"No!"

"Kate René, go back to your room!"

I drew back my baton. "No!"

My father charged. That's when my mom escaped past him into the kitchen. I watched in frozen horror as my father veered from me and stormed after her. She grabbed a butcher knife from a drawer. With the 10-inch blade pointed at my father, my mom warned him to "stay away" as she eased toward the back door and fled the house…leaving me behind.

****

It's jacket weather in Juniper Verde. Sunny and cool with a light breeze. Another perfect winter day in paradise.

I put Teena on a lead while Quinn follows along, free from restraint. Molly runs ahead as we start our walk, past the front gate into open space. We'll walk for an hour and we'll see no one. We have a better chance of meeting a range cow than another person. Letting Teena browse on the scrub, I call Quinn, who is nowhere in sight. Seconds later, I hear his thundering hooves and then he appears, blazing toward me in silver screen magnificence.

His hooves churn dirt as he slams on the brakes. I give him a carrot for coming back. Then he trots off until the next time. I spot Molly under a juniper and tug on Teena to continue our walk. All the while, I'm re-thinking my conversation with Brian.

When it comes to being told what to do, Brian is like a 6-year-old who plants his feet, torques his face and shouts, *You're not the boss of ME!* I know better than to make demands when I have so much to lose. What the hell was I thinking?

I was thinking he'd agree. I was thinking he would understand what he's done to our marriage. I was thinking that twenty-two years meant something. I was thinking I had value, that losing me *mattered*. I was thinking he loved me more than money—and would prove it.

I was **not** thinking Brian would have to *think about it.*

****

One December day three years ago, out of the blue, Brian asked if I would like to live in Oregon. He'd read an article in a flying magazine touting the Columbia River Gorge and The Dalles as an oasis of sun and fair weather in an otherwise dreary world known as the Northwest.

After three years of desert, I was easy to convince. So in January we flew to Portland, drove east, and spent two days looking for land along the Columbia River. Two days was all it took to convince us that *sun and fair weather* meant different things to different people. We then travelled north to Seattle and took a right on I-90, over the

Cascades and into the valley of Ellensburg. It looked like Arizona, but without the green.

Back over the Cascades, we continued west, making camp at my sister's home in Gig Harbor. Then we travelled north for an hour, crossing the Hood Canal Bridge into Port Townsend and, it seemed, entering a time warp. It was a blend of the new Millennium and the innocent 1950's where Seattle millionaires owned waterfront weekend homes, and yachts crowded the docks; historic Victorian homes dotted neighborhoods; exclusive boutiques mingled with quaint shops, and jukebox diners competed with *haute cuisine*. Restrictive building codes limited housing and kept prices high while the closest Supercenter was in the next town. The Visitors' Guide touted this particular strip of coast as the *Banana Belt*. The annual precipitation for Port Townsend was listed as thirty-six inches, which was only three inches more than what Juniper Verde claimed. But here it was carpeted with grass, trees stretched to the sky, and ocean permeated the air. Here I could imagine *home* and growing old with Brian.

We talked about how Brian could fly his plane down from Alaska on weekends; talked about how much shorter the commute to Anchorage would be from Seattle; how much easier it would be to bring Molly to Alaska so I could stay longer in the place I really called home. We would find land; we would hire caretakers. We would put Arizona behind us, forget the loneliness and the loss, and start over *together*.

****

I'm on my third phone call to find an attorney. The first two attorneys know Brian and don't want to represent me.

For the third time, I give my name and tell the receptionist why I'm calling. She puts me through to Sid.

Sid knows Brian, too, but then "who doesn't," and she agrees to represent me.

Finally, I have a champion. I give her the nutshell version of my marriage. She questions me about the pre-nup.

"I don't remember much about it, other than Brian gets everything, and I can't find my copy. I signed it on the way to the courthouse, the day we got married."

"Well, you can throw that out!"

"Really?"

Sid hedges. She tells me to find the pre-nup and send it to her, along with $5,000.

"I don't have $5,000."

"I'm not a bank."

"I have annuities, but it will take a couple of weeks to get money out and it's all the money I have."

"A divorce like this could cost a hundred thousand. If we go to trial, it could be another fifty. Do you have that?"

$150 thousand? Trial? The market is a disaster; my annuities have lost half their original value. When I factor in taxes and penalties for early withdrawal, $200,000 is about all I have. Now I have to spend that on something I don't even want.

And if I lose this battle with Brian…? "Won't the court make Brian pay for my attorney's fees?"

"No." Sid softens…a little. "You'll probably get it back in the settlement, but that could be a year or two—"

*A year… **or two?***

"—You'll have to pay my fees yourself. Don't you have access to any joint accounts?"

"Only a checking account that Brian puts money into once a month."

"I don't think I've ever had a client who didn't have access to *something*."

If I didn't feel like a fool before, I certainly do now. The phrase "barefoot and pregnant" comes to mind.

I tell Sid I'll get the $5,000 and find the pre-nup. I tell her that Brian is coming home in a couple of days and we're supposed to talk. I'll call after Thanksgiving and let her know what's happening.

****

In June, six months after we began our search, we bought eighty acres in Port Townsend, Washington. Eighty acres of trees and pasture on a gently sloping hill near the shores of Defiance Bay. We settled on a builder, found someone to fence the perimeter, and started clearing trees to let sunshine onto the spots where the house and barn would be. After three plus years of detour in Arizona, our lives were finally back on track.

A few weeks later, when I was in Anchorage, Brian handed me a paper to sign. I was waiving my rights to the Port Townsend property.

"I bought the property with my money," he said. "It should be in my name."

I loved, I trusted, I believed.

I signed.

****

I call my brother who offers the money without hesitation. He doesn't chastise or berate; he doesn't even question. I start to cry and promise to pay him back as soon as I cash out my annuities.

"Let's not worry about that now."

I am so grateful, but at the same time, I am so embarrassed and so humiliated and so *ashamed* that I need my brother's help. I'm fifty-three; I have an MBA; and I cannot believe the financial and emotional mess I'm in. I cannot believe I allowed myself to be at Brian's mercy. I simply cannot believe any of what is happening in my life right now.

Like Icarus, who ignored the dangers of tenuous wings, I am in a free-fall back to earth.

November 19

"I should have left him a couple of years ago, but it's hard to think of starting over again, especially at my age."

Charlotte is sixty-two and this is her third divorce, although she doesn't really count her first one after a six-month marriage when she was twenty.

Charlotte and I last had lunch together in May. She wasn't wearing her wedding set then, but she said nothing and I didn't ask. Today the diamond solitaire is on her right ring finger.

Browsing the menu, I listen to her situation, but I don't mention Brian's back-alley rut. I'm amazed she wants to give marriage another try. I'm even more amazed at how *upbeat* she is, considering the challenges before her.

The man Charlotte is divorcing is ten years her senior. While Charlotte is active and interesting and looks a decade younger than her years, the pool of available men for her is pretty much a puddle compared to the ocean of women her 72-year-old ex gets to swim in.

"My friend Jayne who's sixty-three just started dating this man who lost his wife of thirty years to cancer," Charlotte tells me later in the conversation.

I pity the woman who has to compete with that. And I marvel at the resiliency of men who never skip a beat as they forge ahead in life, leaving the women they have loved—sometimes for decades—in the grave…but not necessarily dead.

****

I was stopped at the red light when Rob drove across the intersection in front of me, a mattress lashed to the roof of his car, a brunette in the seat beside him. I saw the laughter on their faces, could almost whiff those "new relationship" pheromones. REO Speedwagon, *Can't Fight This Feeling,* was playing on my truck's radio.

Two weeks earlier, Rob had been living with me in my Anchorage condo.

Before Brian, there was Rob. We were together two years when we started talking marriage. One conversation led to another and within a few weeks I was paging through bridal magazines while he told his family in California about our engagement.

I don't know that we were ever *officially* engaged because we never got around to looking at rings, but his parents sent us the sweetest crystal boudoir lamp that threw prisms of light, and I remember thinking that I could get onboard with these people.

Then one day, not too long after the arrival of the lamp, Rob said he didn't think he could marry me. He didn't say he couldn't *marry*; he said he couldn't marry *me*. A week later, Rob moved out.

I went through the usual break-up tears and contortions, but kept eating, and was secretly happy to be rid of his stuff, especially the cumbersome wood bookcase that dwarfed the small dining nook in my 900 square foot condo.

Nonetheless, I felt the loss, especially at night in bed after I switched off the light and all was quiet and I was once again *alone* and starting over. But I had my dog and cat, my career, my friends, my home, and most important, I had Alaska, where everything *righted itself*, like a Weeble.

A few months after the break-up, Rob called and we had a few dates. Then one autumn night in his car, with the engine humming and the heater blowing and the dash lights softly illuminating our faces, he told me he had been fantasizing about our getting back together.

Truthfully, I had been waiting for—and maybe even plotting—that moment, when he realized what a ghastly mistake he had made by leaving me, but by then I knew I loved the breathing space in my dining nook more than I loved Rob. I gently declined the reconciliation and we went our separate ways for good.

But before all that happened, I was waiting at the stoplight when

Rob went by. I thought about how easily and quickly I had been replaced. Then I experienced the churning ache of *seeing* how very expendable I was; he had probably given more thought to his mattress than he had about me.

I was two weeks in the grave and Rob had moved on.

Sometime during our brief reconciliation, I told Rob about the intersection and the brunette and the mattress and that it hurt to realize how fast he'd gotten over me. He looked perplexed as if he wasn't quite sure what my complaint was, but then he said something so simple, and yet profound, I remember it still today.

"I was lonely."

That's when I realized how bad men are at feeling bad.

Asking a man to experience a painful emotion is like asking him to hold a woman's purse. Oh, sure, he'll do it for a moment and kind of hold it in one hand away from him, but he won't ever get comfortable with it and will certainly **never** sling the straps over his shoulder or clutch it under his arm, and he'll rid himself of the burden at the earliest opportunity.

Painful emotions, like purses, are a woman's property.

Which is why men forge ahead and smother bad feelings with a warm body or work or gin.

Women mourn; men move on.

But women have a knack for disassociating pretty, sparkly things from sentiment, which is why we keep the crystal lamps…

And the diamonds rings…and simply wear them on a different finger.

****

"This is the first time Jayne has dated since her divorce," Charlotte further explains. "And that was like ten years ago. She wasn't looking. I think Richard caught her by surprise. The problem is, Jayne's not the only woman he's dating."

"Let's face it," I tell Charlotte. "The pool for men is a lot larger than the pool for women. And most men like to swim in that pool for a while…"

…before they get out, find a lounge chair, and get cozy with a

waitress twenty years younger.

"I know," Charlotte says. "And Jayne's having a tough time with it. She's so sweet. I hate to see her go through this."

"I think it's bloody amazing she's dating at sixty-three."

"It is tough, but what else can you do? I don't want to spend the rest of my life alone. I miss the companionship; I like having someone to share things with. You've just got to go forward."

I nod understanding, but I have no words. I don't want to go forward. I want to go back…to the Isle of Denial, before Michelle, before the missing photographs, before Arizona.

I eye the dessert menu. I might as well take advantage of the one good thing about all of this.

"So what's new with you?" Charlotte asks. She passes on dessert while I order a Napoleon to go. "You look like you've lost weight."

****

My mom's mom died of ovarian cancer on Valentine's Day.

To be honest, I don't remember a lot about my grandmother. Most of my recollection comes from old photographs and my mom's memories, but I do remember her German accent, robust contours, and her kind, dark eyes.

And I remember her two little fingers that bent inward at the last joint. I see them every time I look at mine.

I was only seven when Grandmother died. Our visits before that were infrequent since we lived in Viet Nam, where my parents served with the US Agency for International Development. But a few months before that Valentine's Day, when we were temporarily living in Carbondale, Illinois, we made the daylong car ride to Milwaukee.

Weakened by cancer, Grandmother spent most of our visit in bed. During our stay, she asked to see each grandchild alone. When it was my turn, I sat in her bedroom, on the corner of her bed, breathing in air of lilacs and antiseptic. There, just outside the spray of light from her bedside lamp, I showed my grandmother how I had recently learned to snap my fingers.

Snap, snap, snap. First my left fingers, then my right. *Snap, snap, snap.*

Her dark eyes melted over me…and she smiled.

November 20

Lilly, my aesthetician, brushes melted wax over my clipped hairs. She pats a strip of paper over the wax and then—

Oh my God!

The pain sucks my breath and sears my eyeballs. All those protesting hairs ripped out at the roots, leaving behind a patch of smooth, soft skin.

I breathe deeply as Lilly applies the next strip of wax then I clench my face as the ripping repeats.

"Oh my God!"

"Sorry," Lilly says as if it's her fault that I've made the desperate decision to remove what nature intended. "But your husband is going to love it."

It's a gift for my husband, I told Lilly when I came for the appointment. She understood completely. The porn look is quite popular apparently and women do it for their men. *Once in a blue moon,* she gets a man on her table, but usually it's a woman.

That's a shocker.

I relax at the momentary respite then suck air and brace myself for the next harvest. After the front is tidy, I roll over on my stomach for the Brazilian part of the wax. Lilly now knows me better than my ob-gyn.

After thirty torturous minutes, the waxing is complete; all that remains is an unobtrusive island triangle amidst smooth, exposed skin.

I leave the salon feeling strangely naked. After a few errands, I walk the aisles of Safeway, harboring my secret.

At home, I check myself in the mirror.

That little tuft of hair has me thinking of a Chinese Crested.

A Chinese Crested...porn princess.

But Lilly's right; Brian is going to love it.

But will he love it enough to choose me over Michelle?

****

Providence is the power that erring men call Chance.

So wrote the English poet, John Milton. Three centuries later, that's why Call Me Diablo became known as Chance.

I wasn't looking for a horse when the "for sale" flyer featuring a "Quarter horse gelding with show experience" appeared on the bulletin board at the Mountain High Stables in Anchorage. I had been taking riding lessons for a year and my waif of an instructor, Leigh, pointed me to the flyer.

I knew the obligations that came with a horse and for me, this commitment would be *'til death do us part.* So, even though I had yearned for a horse since I was a little girl—after giving up on *becoming* a horse—I wasn't completely sold. Nevertheless, my heart fluttered on that Saturday morning when Leigh, Brian, and I walked through spring snow for our first look at the handsome sorrel in the flyer photo.

It wasn't love at first sight.

For one thing, Diablo was BIG. At sixteen hands, much bigger than any of the school horses I'd been riding. Astride him, I looked down at the ground and considered a parachute. When I took him for a test ride, it was like driving a truck without a steering wheel. I was way over my head with this guy, but Brian liked him, probably because he was man-size. So, with Brian's encouragement, I put *Chance* in a stall at Mountain High and together we began our odyssey.

That first year was tough. Chance was smart and knew way more than I did. Our maiden trail ride ended with me battered and bruised in the dirt while Chance happily cantered down the road in a cloud of dust. I limped back to the stables, one minute hoping Chance would get hit by a car on nearby O'Malley Road so

I'd never have to do this again, and the next minute praying he'd be safe at the barn waiting for me.

Finding no Chance, I enlisted a couple of horse owners to help me search. It wasn't long before we spotted him, coming down a side road with someone on his back. To add insult to my injuries, the man riding him did so without the reins, which must have been trampled during Chance's getaway. There this stranger sat, cool as a cucumber, bringing home my horse while I stood there like wilted lettuce.

That evening, I phoned my mom in Illinois and told her my adventure. She sounded worried. "Can you give him back?"

"Why would I give him back?"

The next day, I returned to the barn. Bridget, the trainer whose personal attributes easily explained the 3-carat diamond sparkler on her left hand, looked surprised. "You came back."

Why is everyone surprised I'm sticking with this horse? What am I missing?

But I didn't need answers. What other people thought didn't matter. Chance was mine and I was his. It was, as Milton wrote, *Providence.*

November 21

Brian's Cessna barreled down the runway. The 182 caught air and flew past where I stood by its hangar on the tarmac.

Ten years disappear quicker than a finger snap; I'm *there*, chilled by an autumn breeze, and grounded, as Brian sails into the pale blue afternoon sky, heading north toward Palmer where his father is in the hospital, dying.

Arriving too late at Anchorage Merrill Field, I'm left behind. As the distance between us grows, my heart sinks. But I watch a little longer, as I always do, and, unexpectedly, the Cessna dips its left wing then banks into a one-eighty, slowly descending toward runway seven.

My heart soars.

Brian is returning *for me*.

****

Tomorrow Brian comes home.

Tomorrow when I see him, when I pick him up at the shuttle in Juniper Verde, when I get out of the car as he walks toward me and I'm standing there as he reaches me, he will take me in his arms. Closing my eyes, I'll breathe him in and we will hold each other so tightly that not so much as a word can come between us and everything else—everyone else—will be squeezed out, and there will be, once again, only the two of us, and we will affirm that we have chosen each other.

November 22

The day drags and speeds with annoying inconsistency. One moment, the whole day looms before me, then in a blink, the hands on the clock have advanced at an alarming rate.

I am horrible at judging time. Everything takes longer than I plan. Even when I gauge correctly, the unexpected happens, like a packrat or a flat tire or a garage door that gets stuck halfway up. All these little time stealers have me racing down the road fifteen minutes behind schedule.

But I have **no** excuse.

Late for pick-up, is #1 on Brian's hand-written list of eleven complaints squeezed together on a notepad taken from the Alyeska Prince Hotel. Along with his complaints, on a separate sheet, are changes he wants. He handed me both small pages—now tucked away in a drawer—during my performance review last spring.

I looked at the lists like a crowded elevator I didn't want to get into.

"What is more important in your life than picking me up?" he asked, none too kindly.

I defensively recited the list of all my ranch chores, followed by the other variables—the 45-minute drive into town, the uncertainty of the precise moment the shuttle from Phoenix arrives in Juniper Verde, the packrats, flat tires, stuck doors…

But he's right. Picking up Brian **on time**—meaning when he gets off the shuttle, I am **there**—is part of my job as Brian's wife and I should be able to master that, not 80%, not 90%, but 100% of the time. I have an MBA, for Chrissake.

I took his complaint seriously. Each time the shuttle pulled into the drive, I was there, even if I had to pack a lunch. From that moment on, he never waited, not even a heartbeat.

Of course, by that time, I was too late.

****

Rain sprinkles the windshield and the drops glisten like little mirrors when oncoming headlights hit the glass. The wipers whisk away the rain and the next batch of drops splatter the windshield.

I plow through a pond of water and my heart races. I check the clock on the lighted dash, panicking, but unless I have a flat tire or hit a deer—

I slow down, confident I will reach the shuttle terminal before the van.

Brian called after his plane landed and then as the van left the airport. Just as he always does but once again with that glaring omission. The missing words are as obvious as downtown Las Vegas at midnight. It's odd that something missing can be so present.

I make it through town and turn into the parking lot. With the engine off and the radio on, I wait.

It's been two weeks since I last saw Brian, two weeks since I said good-bye to him in very nearly the same spot I'm in now—literally and figuratively. It has been the longest two weeks since the Battle of Britain.

I know the Battle of Britain and the ensuing Blitz lasted ten months, but the last two weeks *feel* like ten months.

When the last bomb hit, did the British know it was the last? Or were they fearfully waiting for the next one? Watching the skies, listening for the drone of the bombers and the howl of the warning sirens, waiting, waiting, but not knowing what would happen next.

Would there be more destruction, more lives lost? Or would they finally be able to dig themselves out of the rubble, bury their dead, and start rebuilding? What is it really like, waiting for the last bomb to hit?

The outside lights surrounding the shuttle office drift into the car. I check myself in the rearview mirror. My hair has wilted from the rain and my face has wilted from despair. I've done the best I can with the wreckage, but it's been a tough two weeks. Part of me wants Brian to see the destruction, part of me doesn't. When he looks at me and thinks of her, why would he choose rubble?

The van pulls into the lighted drive and my heart pumps. Doors open; people congregate at the rear to get their luggage. Brian hands the driver a couple of bills and takes his small backpack. Smiling, he comes toward the car. I get out of the driver's seat.

"Hi, Hon." He pecks my lips—barely enough time for me to breathe him in—then he opens the back door and tosses his backpack inside. "Where's Molly?"

"I left her at home. You know how she hates thunder." The skies drum. "I figured she'd be happier hiding in the closet." I open the front passenger door and the elephant pushes in, hogging the console between us.

Twenty-two years and it's more awkward than our first date.

"Has it been raining a lot?"

"Off and on."

"Everything okay at the ranch?"

"Meaning…?"

"Any flooding?"

"A little pooling, but nothing bad. You can play on your tractor and fix it."

He flashes me a smile. A few silent miles down the road, he sighs. "It's been a long day," he says, which is his usual pronouncement after a day of travelling. "Hey, I talked with Shannon. She wants to come down the day after Thanksgiving. Wants me to fly up to Salt Lake and get them. What do you think?"

Shannon is Brian's youngest. Her husband, Paul is working on his Doctorate and in October, they had their second child.

"I'd love to see the baby, but, I don't think that's a very good idea, under the circumstances."

"Yeah, okay, I didn't really want to fly up there and get them.

And who knows what the weather will be like."

I glance at Brian, illuminated by the dash lights. I can't decide whether it's good he wants Shannon here or bad. Is he trying to make things normal or put a buffer between us?

"Maybe I'll take a day and fly up to see them."

Brian will be here ten days and he's already thinking of being gone one of those. I don't have to question on which side of the aisle to seat that.

We are down to nine days. Nine days to fix this marriage. No apologies. No hugs at the shuttle. No *I love you.* Nine days to rebuild all that Michelle has destroyed.

I cannot help but wonder, in this Battle for Brian, has the last bomb hit?

November 23

I wake early but stay in bed next to Brian. The waning moon dusts the bedroom with silver.

Brian and I barely touched each other last night and there was no sex. We always have sex the first night Brian is home. Then we fall asleep cuddled together. But last night, we brushed lips and went our separate ways, which was really noticeable with only six inches between our naked bodies.

My little Chinese Crested is undiscovered. And there is no Santa Claus cookie jar. Brian said nothing and I didn't ask, but I wonder what happened to it. I wonder what happened to the thought behind it. I wonder if Michelle got it instead.

Brian has his back to me. I swallow my pride, roll over and cuddle up against him, my left arm hugging his little Buddha belly. He kind of wiggles into me so that we fit together like a pair of spoons. It feels so good, this moment, that I think of nothing else and hope comes flooding back. I close my eyes, breathe him in, and drift back to sleep.

****

Brian is a pilot.

I am a white-knuckled flyer.

I've taken ground school; I've taken flying lessons. I even spent eight weeks in behavior modification therapy to get over my fear of flying. Which, as everyone knows, isn't fear of flying, but fear of *crashing*.

After all that effort, I am still a white-knuckled flyer—who now knows how tenuous flying really is.

Sometimes, you can know too much.

Give me a glassy flight with clear skies and I do pretty well, but turbulence is the bane of my flying existence. And I'm not too keen on fog, low ceilings, and flights over water. I guess I not only have a fear of crashing, I have a fear of drowning.

I suspect *that* fear stems from one weekend when I was six and we were living in Saigon. On a whim, my father drove us to the beach and marched me into the South China Sea. When I was up to my neck in water, with the salt waves smacking my face and burning my eyes, he ordered me to swim…as if I had some innate ability.

After four hours of fighting the waves and the undertow and my father's rage, drowning felt like a blessing. Before my next thought, a giant wave folded over me and pushed me below the turbulent surface and into the calm, silent depths where I floated, suspended in the peaceful darkness of eyes sealed tight against stinging salt as the ocean embraced me…

It would be another twenty years before I learned to swim, after I took myself to the pool at the University of Alaska and let go of the past. But those 6-year-old moments can still pull me under.

The problem is, most Alaska flying involves turbulence, fog, low ceilings, and water. Sometimes there is snow, rain, and ice, as well. Those glassy flights under clear skies are few and far between.

Adding irony to the mix, I don't like heights. But it is a rule of flight that the higher you are in the sky, the better your chance of surviving should something go wrong. That is, there is more *correction time* before you meet the ground and your maker. Of course, if a wing falls off, it doesn't matter what your altitude is… unless you consider "screaming time" a plus.

One bit of good news—I don't get sick. In adverse conditions, I simply hunker down and try not to move so I don't upset the plane.

Instead, I watch the instruments. Or the horizon, if there is one. Or the ground—unless it's the ocean. Or I keep a lookout for radio towers if the ceiling is really low.

For twenty years, I've flown with Brian in spite of my fear, logging a thousand hours in the right seat. For someone who can't get on a

737 without lorazepam, that's a lot of air time. We've flown across Alaska to Bethel and Nome, but mostly it's been 1-hour flights to our beach house in Otter Bight, during which we have to cross Cook Inlet where the winds funnel through the passage and slam the plane making it pitch and buck.

That I fly at all is a testament to love. I will do the one thing I most hate—and *mostly* without complaint—to be with Brian doing what he loves. In my mind, I have been a real trouper.

Yet for those same twenty years, Brian has taken my fear of flying as a personal affront. It isn't enough that I fly to be with him, I'm supposed to **stop** being afraid; I am supposed to **love** flying.

Sadly, I'm not alone in this half-empty glass. Many of my friends have experienced the same lack of credit for the years they've put in beside their man doing what **he** wants to do. Repeatedly, I hear men complain that their wives no longer share their activities. They add, "when we were dating," or "when we were first married," they shared all these things. Implicit in that is the accusation that women only do these things so we can *get our man* and once we walk away from the altar all bets are off. Even Brian says, "You used to fly with me *all the time*."

Well, I never flew with Brian *all the time*. And Brian has forgotten that I told him **up front** I didn't like flying, and flying in a small plane was worst of all.

Whenever he brings up his lament, I remind him of our first flight together—a short half-hour trip from Anchorage to Kenai under near perfect conditions.

After Brian landed his Cessna at the small airport, I got out and walked into the bar where I downed a vodka tonic…and then another, so I could get back in his plane, cross Cook Inlet, and land in Anchorage.

When I recount that story to Brian, I ask, "What about that moment made you think I would ever love flying?"

But Brian doesn't get it. He doesn't get my fear; he doesn't get my courage. He doesn't get how enormously much I love him to climb into that small plane and cross Cook Inlet *knowing* that I will be tossed around like a mouse in a cat's paw. And I don't get how he doesn't get that. I don't get how he gives me no credit for being in that plane, why being beside him isn't enough.

In his eyes, I'm a disappointment. *That*, I get.

****

I give up on sex for this morning and leave Brian sleeping in bed. He's probably having so much sex with Michelle he has no interest in me. Or maybe he thinks I have no interest in him since he's having so much sex with Michelle.

Whatever. The point is, neither of us risked rejection. Now I'm standing on the tarmac as Brian takes to the skies, getting smaller and smaller as the distance between us grows…

****

One night, a couple years back, we were having dinner with Brian's long-time friend, Archie and his wife, Jill, when after a few drinks Archie started ragging on Jill. "She used to play golf with me *all the time…*"

Jill and I shared the look. But, this time—owing to the wine—instead of silencing her defense, Jill picked up the gauntlet.

"I played golf for *ten* years," she began, as much to us as to Archie. "And I never really liked the game. But I took lessons, bought the right clothes, bought golf clubs. I hit that damn ball, week after week after week. I shared my Saturdays with people I didn't like and then after the game I had to sit and listen to the replay of their hits and misses. I pretended that I cared whether they got a bogie or a birdie. And I pretended to care if **I** got a bogie or a birdie. When we weren't playing golf, I had to watch it on television. And I did this for *ten fucking years*. For God's sake, Archie, even felons get paroled!"

****

For all the complaints men have about women trying to change them, men try to change women with equal fervor—they just don't see it that way.

Brian told me early on that what I like to do isn't fun. In essence, he was telling me that he would not be sharing in those activities. And since there wasn't enough time to do what he wanted *and* what I wanted, I did what he wanted.

Fortunately, we have common interests. We both like shopping for antiques and going to the movies. And we vacation great together. We love exploring new places or simply lounging on the beach. I love foreign destinations, probably a carry-over from my childhood overseas. It's not that easy travelling under the stress of a different language, different customs, different foods, different currency, and a different driver's seat. But we are two peas. Even long hours in the air are bearable with Brian beside me.

Whenever the plane starts jerking and bouncing, Brian, without prompting, offers me his arm. I bury my face against his muscles and close my eyes until the ride becomes smooth again, but until that happens, Brian does whatever he was doing, single-handed and without complaint.

Ironically, I have never felt so safe and comforted as I do at these turbulent moments.

I wish I had Brian's arm now.

****

"When are we going to talk?" My barn chores are done and I'm back at the house. I sit on a stool at the island counter and watch Brian. It's Sunday morning and he's making waffles. He always makes waffles on Sunday morning.

"What do you want to talk about?"

His question doesn't surprise me. Brian doesn't like talking about unpleasant things, especially if his behavior is linked to the unpleasantness. He treats our problems like a dead skunk in the road; he does whatever it takes to avoid the carcass and gets away from the stink as fast as possible.

"What do you *think* I want to talk about?" I don't do well talking about unpleasant things, either, especially if I sense bad news. Unfortunately, this is a skunk we can't drive away from.

****

Last spring, late one night as I turned out the lights for bed, Molly told me she needed to go outside. I tried to convince her she didn't, but she wouldn't be dissuaded. Flipping switches, I set the courtyard ablaze and cautiously opened the front door. Seeing nothing worrisome, I widened the gap.

Dashing through, Molly turned the corner out of sight. I quickly followed then stopped dead in my tracks. I screamed at Molly, but it was too late. She got a face full of tail, and since we were close to the front door, we got a houseful of pungent skunk with a dog to match.

That night, I learned two things about skunks. First, they are varying sizes. Some are small, like cats, but this guy (or gal) was closer to beagle size.

Second, their fresh spray is much more obnoxious—and caustic—than the diluted stench we all recognize as "dead skunk on the road." Fresh from the sac, it smells like burning rubber and it attacks the eyes, nose and throat with ferocity.

I hoisted Molly into our large Jacuzzi tub, but not before she had raced around the house, frothing at the mouth, rubbing on everything, trying to alleviate her discomfort.

Unfortunately, the bath did nothing except maybe make the stink worse. Although I opened windows, we slept under a heavy blanket of skunk that night.

The next day, I called businesses that specialize in home restoration and odor removal, like smoke from a fire. That's when I learned the third thing about skunks. You cannot artificially get rid of their smell.

"Skunks and cat urine," the woman on the phone told me. "The best you can do is air out the place and wash everything you can. Throw away stuff that can't be cleaned. And eventually, if you're lucky, the odor will fade."

Eventually, it did, **months** later. But every now and then, in a corner, or when I walk into a rarely used room, there is a history that tenaciously lingers. Just enough to remind me of that moment when I collided with the unexpected.

****

"I'll change the pre-nup when you get a job."

Getting a job is #8 on Brian's list of eleven complaints from the same Alyeska Prince Hotel notepad, although his actual written words are *you're under-employed.*

"I have a job and it's called taking care of this ranch. But I don't get paid for it!"

I have just spent three hours at that job while Brian slept late, leisurely rose, drank coffee, read magazines, took a shower and dressed. But Brian did make breakfast.

"And I've been looking for a job, and you know it. I've applied for four jobs and didn't even get an interview. I don't know what you want me to do. Wave a magic wand?"

I consider my barely-eaten waffle and two strips of turkey bacon and suddenly haven't the stomach for any of it.

"Maybe you should move to Phoenix."

How is it, when you think you're prepared for every eventuality, there's one eventuality… *"Phoenix*? Are you out of your frigging mind?"

"If you can't find a job in Juniper Verde, you need to go where you can."

"I hate Phoenix and I'm sure-as-hell not *moving* to Phoenix. But just out of curiosity, what would I do with the animals?"

"We can hire a caretaker and you can come back on weekends."

"We've advertised for a caretaker and nobody good wants the job because the ranch is for sale. I'm not leaving the animals with one of the felons who applied, *hoping* they'll be taken care of and *hoping* the house will still be here when I get back. And how much do you think it's going to cost for a decent place in Phoenix? Or am I supposed to live with the drug addicts? How much money am I going to have to make to cover my expenses and come out ahead? I've been out of the job market for thirteen years and I'm fifty-three. There aren't eighty thousand dollar jobs out there for me, Brian."

"Then move to Seattle."

"Seriously? What about the horses?"

"We can put them on the Port Townsend property."

"Am I supposed to take care of the animals and commute two-plus hours to Seattle every day? And what about this ranch? You can't just abandon it. We might as well drop the price to something ridiculous and sell it now. Honest to God, I don't know what you're thinking."

"We need to get you employed," he says emphatically. "I'm fifty-eight, Kate. I can't work forever. And I don't have enough money for us to retire on."

My mind flashes on Michelle's plane ticket paid for by Brian's Visa. And the hotel room. And the dinners. And the Jeep tour. And the birthday card. And God only knows what else for how long.

"I don't have a problem going back to work, Brian, but finding a job isn't easy. And up until this year, you haven't wanted me to work."

"I disagree with that."

I jerk back. "When did you ask me to get a job?"

"We talked about it last year."

"We talked about my working part-time after we move to Port Townsend when we're closer to town and have caretakers again. And I'm happy to do that."

"We talked about you helping out with the expenses around here—"

Was that before or after Brian spent $280,000 last February for another Cessna?

"—I thought you were going to take money out of your annuities."

Over the years, Brian has periodically pushed me to spend my annuities on this or that, but I've always resisted. I don't know why exactly since doing what Brian wants seems to be my calling. But all sorts of bells and whistles go off in my head whenever Brian mentions my annuities.

"I'm not taking money out of my annuities. It's all the money I have."

"Then you need to get a job."

"I'm trying to get a job! And you can disagree 'til the cows come home, but until this past spring—" *and Michelle* "—you've been perfectly happy with me stuck down here by myself, taking care of the ranch."

Brian leaves the counter and takes his plate to the sink.

I breathe, settling my emotions. "What about the pre-nup?"

"I'll change the pre-nup when you get a job."

"Brian…I love you. But, I'm not staying in this marriage without some security."

"And what about my security? I change the pre-nup and you divorce me."

"Welcome to *my* world. I moved to Arizona for you and now I'm down here by myself while you live the single life in Alaska—"

"I'm not living the single life—"

"Oh, please. You've been screwing around for years."

"It hasn't been that long."

"That makes me feel so much better."

But Brian merely gives me his signature head shake and eye roll as if I'm being ridiculous.

"I'm not the one who brought Michelle into the equation, Brian. And if you're not willing to take some risk to keep this marriage, that pretty much tells me all I need to know."

I listen to the silence and wonder what's going on in Brian's head.

"I'll think about it."

November 24

Another night passes without sex. Is Brian thinking about Michelle as he sleeps beside me, missing her, wishing she were here instead?

I know what that's like, wishing someone was someone else. I haven't wished that for twenty-two years. But now I wish Brian was someone else. I wish Brian was Brian. The Brian *before* Michelle. At this point, I'll settle for the Brian who was *just* hiding our photos in drawers…

****

Brian was married when I met him. I didn't know that until weeks later when we were having drinks. Although I had Garrett on my relationship résumé, I was still young and naive enough to be surprised by Brian's unapologetic admission and his apparent expectation that having his wife in our bed—figuratively speaking—wouldn't be a problem for me.

In therapy circles, that moment would be known as a *red flag*.

(In nature, it would be recognized as a *rattle*.)

Unfortunately, there's something seductive about a man who confesses his unflattering secrets. Years removed from that, I now know it would be better to find a man who doesn't have unflattering secrets to confess.

But there I was, sitting across from this bad boy who had my name stamped all over him, with just enough vodka swimming in my head to dull my judgment. I leaned into the table toward Brian and said, "I don't do married men. Call me if you ever get unmarried." Then I walked away and hiked up the hill to moral high ground.

So…how did I get from that hill to this desert?

****

I start for my cell phone on the counter where it has been re-charging all night. Brian's phone is next to mine, also re-charging. Nothing new about this. What *is* new—I change directions and reach for his phone instead.

Brian has an iPhone; I have no clue. The screen is dark. Leaving it plugged in, I check the sides for buttons and press the one on the upper right side. The screen illuminates. Where are the icons? This isn't like my outdated flip phone that fits neatly in my pants pocket and doesn't break when I drop it. Brian's phone has bells and whistles, and I don't know how to get information on his incoming and outgoing phone calls.

The toilet flushes.

I press the power button and the screen goes black.

"What are you doing?"

"Getting my phone."

Brian shuffles toward me in his slippers and robe, his hair haphazard. "Off to feed the horses?" He moves around me to retrieve the filters for the coffee maker. Normally, he would hug me, being this close…

"I'll be back in a couple of hours." I stuff my phone into a pocket, leaving his on the counter.

****

After my hike up the hill, I didn't see Brian for more than a year. Anchorage was green with summer and flowers bloomed all over the city. I hung geranium baskets off my deck, put away the mukluks and took my winter coat to the cleaners.

I reveled in the long days that never really became nights, ran my seven miles each day with my dog, Lisa, and without ice cleats, and fell in love all over again with my home. Anchorage winters can be brutal—long, dark, cold—but the summers are proof of what my mom said: *the pendulum always swings back.*

One day I looked up from my desk; Brian stood in my office doorway, unexpected and unannounced.

My heart went pitter-pat.

He was still boyishly charming and still badly dressed. He wore this horrible brown suit that had family ties to the polyester 70's. I remember thinking...*this guy needs someone to help him dress.*

"I filed for divorce," he told me. "I'm legally separated. Will you go out with me?"

Atop my lonely hill, I looked at all the pretty, twinkling lights that beckoned me from the valley below.

"When you actually *are* divorced."

"It will be awhile. I've got a complicated financial situation."

"I'll think about it."

Summer gave way to autumn and soon *termination dust* frosted Flat-Top Mountain. The winter fog rolled in. The next thing I remember is putting Lisa in the back of Brian's Corvette and going to his Alyeska condo. We saw each other naked for the first time.

On the drive back to Anchorage, well past midnight, an avalanche delayed us and we waited while the highway crew cleared the road. Somewhere in there, with the radio playing and the dash lights frosting the interior, Brian turned to me and said, "I could really get used to having you around."

Before I knew it, his awful brown suit was hanging in my closet next to the very expensive Hickey-Freeman I had bought him at Nordstrom's.

∗∗∗∗∗∗∗∗∗∗

"Do you want to go to a movie tonight?"

I consider Brian's question, shrug and say, "Sure."

All we have to do is get through the next eight hours.

There are over 3200 square feet in this house, 36 acres on this ranch, and it feels like we're living in a closet.

We spend a couple of hours riding the horses—an activity where we can be together without saying much. Back at the barn, we go our separate ways. I groom the horses and feed them lunch. Brian moves dirt with the tractor. We *act* normal.

Alone in the house, I call Lucy in Atlanta.

"He's thinking about it," I tell her after a quick update on our latest pre-nup negotiations.

"I'm sure he is. He's arguing both sides; figuring out the best scenario for *him.*"

Ignoring Lucy's cynicism, I wistfully turn back the calendar. "I just wonder what would be happening now if I hadn't said anything about Michelle's note."

"Okay. Try to remember he took her to Scottsdale. Try to remember he was going to spend New Year's with Michelle while you sat on that ranch by yourself. *Alone.*"

"Yeah, okay."

"Look…I don't know if he wanted you to find that note or not, but he didn't try very hard to hide it. Even considering his giant ego, he could've made some effort to conceal Michelle. Really, *really* think about this. *He brought her to Arizona.* It's not enough that he has her in Alaska, he practically brought her to your doorstep. Then he had you come down to Scottsdale and pick him up at the place where he had been *with Michelle.* Think about all the people who saw him with *her*…and then saw you. It's a wonder Brian could fit inside the car, being so full of himself."

"You're right."

"You say that, but I can hear in your voice that you're not convinced."

"No one willingly goes to the guillotine."

"Believe me, I know what this feels like. Detaching from Hazel was brutal. But you're not losing your head, you're gaining your self-respect and losing a person who treats you like crap."

"Brian wasn't always like this."

"I don't care! Although I'm not sure he wasn't always like this and you just didn't want to see it. You're seeing it *now*. And for the last six years you've been banished to Arizona where you never wanted to be. You're isolated and alone and completely dependent on him—which is exactly what he wants. In the meantime, he fucks around in Alaska, leading the good life. You don't have to be beaten with a two-by-four, Katie, to be a battered wife."

I recoil at the unflattering description.

"I don't think Brian cared whether you found her note or not," Lucy says. "I don't think he expected you to do anything about it even if you did."

"How could he not?"

"Because you didn't do anything about the missing photographs."

Nothing stings like getting slapped with your past. Lucy is not going to let me out of this conversation unscathed...or maybe... *unchanged.*

"The thing is… I don't know that I really care about his screwing around."

"Do you not care, or do you just think you can't do anything about it…short of leaving?"

I take a breath, thinking I might say something, but release it without words.

"Denial is a great coping method."

I audibly sigh as Lucy paints a portrait of someone pathetic and unappealing.

"I think," she begins with some hesitation. (Yeah, *now* she hesitates.) "I think you are so blindly in love with Brian that you can't see what's in front of you. I know how it is. I thought Hazel would take care of me and keep me safe and I closed my eyes to everything else. But I learned the hard way that expecting someone else to keep you safe is the most dangerous place you can be."

"I just feel...guilty. Like if I hadn't been in Arizona…"

"Stop! You didn't move to Arizona—Brian *moved you* to Arizona. He's given you about as much thought as someone who chains their dog in the back yard and walks away. He's forgotten about you, while he does what he wants. Don't take responsibility for Brian's choices. Taking responsibility for your own choices is bad enough."

"We're talking twenty-two years…"

"And when was the last time you were happy?"

****

Nothing is all-bad. The Titanic was the greatest ocean liner for five days, before it hit an iceberg. Then it became the greatest sea disaster of all time, even spawning an Oscar.

For sixteen years, I was pretty damn happy. Sure, there were rocky moments. Like every marriage. Right now those rocky moments are flashing in my mind like one of my dad's slide shows, but, under the circumstances it's human nature to go back in time looking for clues that portend an iceberg.

So what if there were signs? As my sister says, "It doesn't matter. You were happy."

Of course, when you're scrambling for a lifeboat, it's hard to focus on the great meal you had last night.

Before we were married, Brian told me, "When I'm unhappy, I make changes."

He said that while talking about his first marriage. When people tell me something, I believe them. I don't second-guess or look for unspoken symbolism or think their words camouflage what they *really* mean. I don't try to change what I hear to what I *want* to hear. However harsh, however unyielding, I believe them.

So when Brian told me his *unhappy equals change* motto, I took him at his word. He left his first wife; if unhappy, he would leave me.

If I'm completely honest—and what's the point in lying now—I've spent twenty-two years watching Brian for signs of unhappiness, wondering when the needle on his happiness meter would slip into the red zone of change.

Constant vigil is exhausting. It's impossible to be on alert 24-7 without eventually ending up in the loony bin.

So last spring when Brian handed me his list of eleven *Complaints*, followed by his list of six *Changes*, I admit, I was none too keen, but I saw that quivering needle.

However, now I know that Michelle was in the picture when he handed me that list. So I have to wonder…*why*? Was he giving me one last chance to make him happy before he went full-bore with Michelle?

I'll never know what Brian was thinking, but I know enough to know this… For months, maybe even years, as he juggled me with other women, Brian was *king of the world.*

****

Brian is in the living room, watching television, waiting for me to get ready. With my hair in hot rollers, I slip into the office and sit down at my computer. At the Google prompt, I type: *How do I get a list of phone calls off an iPhone?*

****

"I don't want you to go anywhere."

We're on our way to the movie and Brian's statement comes out of the blue. We weren't talking about anything of consequence, just acting normal, driving along, and without any transition whatsoever, he says…

I don't want you to go anywhere.

What do I say? I'm not even sure a response is required. I mean, twenty-two years with this man and that's the best he can do? It's not exactly Yeats, is it?

It's not as if I require much. I would settle for those three little words I haven't heard since I confronted him with Michelle.

I love you.

Why didn't he lead with that?

I love you. *I don't want you to go anywhere.*

Why **didn't** he lead with that?

Honestly, I'm a pretty cheap date. All I want to know is that Brian loves me, that he wants our marriage, and he'll give up Michelle. That's all. Just those three little words and I'll go back to the Isle of Denial and be happy again. "You've brought Michelle into our marriage," I tell him.

"I understand that."

"I don't think you do."

We drive on in silence, crossing an intersection. I look out my window as dusk steals across the desert.

"When men get older, sex becomes less important."

I turn to Brian, disbelieving what he has just told me, trying to decipher what he means. It sounds like—

Am I his...*back-up plan?*

"I'll give you a life estate on the Port Townsend property. We'll build you a little house and if you ever get tired of living with me you can go there and you'll always have a place to live."

I listen to his silky tone, but what I hear is what he doesn't say. There is no *I love you...our marriage is important...I'm sorry I hurt you.* No feeling that this moment between us is anything more than a settlement negotiation. Brian wants the least risk with the least investment that offers the greatest return...*for him.* He wants Michelle for pleasure and me for picking up poop...and eventually, for changing his diaper. Brian wants it all.

The truth is, he's had it all. He exiled me in Arizona so he could fuck around in Alaska and I would be too far away to see it and too scared to leave if I did.

As Lucy said, I'm the dog in the back yard no one cares about, kept alive with food and an occasional pat, but who is otherwise left in the shadow of the house while everyone inside goes on with their life. I'm forgotten, neglected and abandoned but I'm too stupid, trusting, and dependent to change it.

Apparently, that's Brian's assessment, too.

"So I get to live in this *little* house while you move Michelle into the big house? But I am stuck on this property because if I leave I have no home and I can't sell the property because I don't own it so I have no money to buy another home. What a deal."

"It wouldn't be like that."

"You have Michelle. You have a pre-nup. Why don't you want a divorce?"

"Because I'm not going anywhere!"

But you've already gone somewhere, I think, before hope smothers my senses. Out of this semi-conversation, I cling to his last proclamation.

I'm not going anywhere.

Maybe Brian **does** love me. Maybe he **isn't** going anywhere. What if Michelle **is** just a flash in the pan? What if I **am** making a big deal out of this?

I cling to these possibilities by a thread, fearing that if I challenge Brian, if I push my cause, the thread will snap and I will fall and fall and fall and God only knows where I'll land. So we drive on in silence. Pretty soon, we pull into the parking lot. Now we're in the popcorn line. Before I know it, we're sitting beside each other, sharing popcorn, intently watching the screen as if we're on the worst date of our lives. After the movie, when we walk to the car, we keep our hands to ourselves, neither reaching for the other as we did for twenty-two years.

On the 45-minute ride back home, I am quiet. From time to time, I feel Brian's eyes on me, but I keep my focus out my window, on the homes encrusted with little twinkling beacons of hope. It's not even Thanksgiving and people already have their Christmas lights glowing.

Christmas arrives earlier each year it seems. And maybe it's a good thing to extend the season of love and hope for those extra weeks. But for me, it just allows more time to visit with my *Ghosts of Christmases Past*.

November 25

I wake before dawn; Brian sleeps with one arm locked around me.

Last night he discovered my Chinese Crested, and he seemed pleased with something different.

But there were no words of love and I settled for his arm around me as we drifted to sleep.

I wonder if he thinks about the missing words. Is he too proud to say them, or will they make him feel like a hypocrite? He has lied for so many months, looking me in the eyes without flinching, you'd think he would be able to say *I love you* whether he means it or not. But whenever the opportunity presents itself, Brian lets it slip by.

Lying here, in the dark of a moonless night, I wonder what Bill said to Hillary when the *Blue Dress* surfaced. Did he profess love, beg forgiveness, and promise the sun, moon and stars? Or did he offer Hillary a cottage behind the White House? Tell her he'd be back when "sex was less important," but in the meantime, she can wash his underwear.

Yeah…I don't see that. But then, Bill *needed* Hillary. He was staring down the barrel of impeachment, and, if he survived that, two more years of his presidency. Imagine the First Lady filing for divorce. How *lame* would Bill be?

But Brian doesn't need me for anything. There, I said it. *Brian doesn't need me.* And for men, *need* always trumps *love*.

So why is Brian here? He has money. He has Michelle. He has a pre-nup. Why is Brian here?

I think about his offer of a life estate. It feels like a Cracker-Jack prize. I can't wrap my mind around how little I am worth.

Pounds and cents.

I inch away from Brian, intending to start my day. He pulls me back and soon he is rocking inside me in a hazy, lazy, pre-dawn penetration we have done for *twenty-two years*. No preamble, no fireworks, just familiar, comfortable, reaffirming sex.

Afterward, I close my eyes and think of nothing except Brian cuddled around me, the rise and fall of his breath…and the slow slipping away of our connection.

****

Dawn glimmers on the horizon as I steal into the garage with Brian's iPhone, a pen and notepad.

I scan the list of his most recent connections—calls made, received, and missed, some with names, others not. I don't have time to think about any of them, except to disregard the few I recognize. I quickly jot down each one in sequence, including the ones that repeat.

I return his phone to the counter then tuck away the list of phone numbers to deal with later. I check on Brian, still asleep in our bed.

****

My grandfather was a minister with a large church in Milwaukee, which, as an aside, is where my father, an Air Force pilot, met my mother. I don't know why it's important to this story that my grandfather was a pastor, but somehow it is.

The summer after my grandmother died, my grandfather visited. He brought with him two quilts for my mom, exquisitely stitched by her mother's hand, and nine Indian-head pennies. Three at a time, he placed these in my brother's palm, then my sister's, and finally mine. My grandmother had saved these for each of her grandkids before we even existed.

I looked at the three deeply burnished coins and read the dates. 1901. 1898. 1905.

I couldn't imagine anything that enduring.

On December 22nd, after forty-five years of being married to my grandmother and only ten months after her death, my 68-year-old grandfather married his 50-year-old secretary.

My mom did not attend their wedding.

I still have the pennies.

****

"He said he's not going anywhere," I tell Lucy from my flip phone. The horses have been fed and groomed, the stalls cleaned, and now I'm reporting to Atlanta on the latest developments.

"I can believe that."

Her answer is unexpected. "But her note... And Scottsdale."

"He's cocky. Pushing the envelope. Might even be totally infatuated. But maybe he's smarter than we give him credit. We know he's done this before."

I glance up the hill again. It's almost 9:00. Brian should be coming to the barn to get Molly for their walk. "But Michelle loves him."

"Well, yeah, but that doesn't mean **he** loves *her*."

"You don't think he loves her…and has told her?"

"Probably, but that doesn't mean he loves her enough to turn his world inside out."

"He hasn't said he loves me since I confronted him with her note."

"What can I say? Proud men, stupid decisions."

"Last night, out of the blue, as we were driving to the movie, he said…*When men get older, sex becomes less important.*"

"Geez. It sounds like you're his back-up plan."

"You heard it, too? Damn. I was hoping it was just me."

"No. That's what **I** heard. What'd you say?"

"Actually, it caught me by surprise. Before I could say anything, he offered me a life estate on the Port Townsend property."

"Huh. That's interesting."

"You can't seriously think this is a good deal."

"Well, would he pay for everything…utilities, upkeep…?"

"Who cares? I want a husband, not a house. Besides, if I leave him after that, he loses nothing. In the meantime, he can screw around all he wants and my only choice is to stay on the property and put up with it or leave and go where? He risks nothing and gets everything. And what happens if he brings Michelle or whoever on the property. I get to sit there and watch because if I leave, I have no home. And if I stay, it would be like the War of the Roses. Brian didn't say anything about him not living there. He would make my life soooo miserable. And don't tell me that wouldn't happen. I never thought *this* would happen. I'd have to be an idiot and a masochist to take his deal."

"You're probably right."

"Brian's trying to get out of this mess the cheapest way. And the only way cheaper is *free*."

****

"Are we going for a ride?" Brian asks when Molly and I return to the house. He's dressed and in his recliner, reading a magazine. Apparently, he changed his mind about walking Molly.

"We can. I was going to make a turkey so I should put that in first."

"Turkey?" Brian acts happy like a little kid.

Thanksgiving is two days away. The one objection Brian has to Thanksgiving at friends' is no leftover turkey, so I'm making a turkey today so he has leftovers for the week.

"You don't really want stuffing, do you?"

"Yes."

"You never eat the leftovers."

"Don't make so much."

"Okay. But it's going to take a little longer to make the stuffing and get the turkey in."

Brian uprights the recliner, tosses his magazine on the coffee table. "Maybe I'll play on the tractor until you're ready." He gets his jacket then comes my way. "Give me a kiss."

I wait for the words that used to come after…

Seconds later, I hear the door into the garage shut.

Why won't he tell me he loves me?

Words are cheap. But some are priceless. Ironically, Brian could get out of this mess so *cheaply* with a few *priceless* words.

I chop onions, chop celery, and start them sautéing in the skillet. I open the slider onto the deck and hear the tractor's rumbling engine.

Using our home phone, I punch in my sister's direct line at the school in Washington where she teaches.

"I need you to call some numbers." I look at the list taken from Brian's phone, at the first series of numbers that waterfall down the list again, and again, and again.

"Start with this one…"

****

From my earliest memory, I wanted a horse. I have a book about horses given to me when I was five, and still on my shelf today, with pages worn and ragged from constant wishing, its cover layered with yellowed tape, testifying to my dream. On a middle page, in the white space, my faded words still linger. *I hope I hope I hope I hope I hope I hope I hope I hope I hope I hope I hope I hope I hope I get a horse.* His name was Black Diamond, this dream horse of mine, and we would spend all our sunsets together.

I never thought about the time I might spend in the dirt, battered and bruised, after I'd been unceremoniously dumped from my dream steed's back. Pain was never part of the dream. Neither was fear. But I have to admit, as Chance and I negotiated the rocky road of our early relationship, I was plenty afraid. He was 1200 pounds; I was 125. I don't care what the horse gurus say, when the scales are tipped like that, there is no *control*…except for the horse.

My every thought and emotion were reflected in Chance's behavior. The harder I pulled on the reins, the harder he resisted. The tenser I was in the saddle, the bumpier the ride. The louder I yelled, the more he ignored me. The *more* control I exerted, the *less* control I had.

I dreaded our rides. My stomach churned and my palms pooled. Disaster reigned in my thoughts. My dream horse was a nightmare.

Then one day, exhausted from the battle, I gave up. And a miracle happened. If I wanted to go left, Chance went left; if I wanted to go right, he went right. If Chance refused a request, I trusted his judgment—even if I didn't see the reason for it. No anger, no frustration, no worry. I enjoyed the ride, wherever it went.

I lost the saddle and gained balance. I tossed the bit and found freedom. I loosened my reins and tightened my bond with Chance.

Sometimes I'd drop the reins completely and Chance meandered wherever he wanted, through the woods on moose trails, across open marsh, while I was clueless as to our location. But then I saw the main trail and soon we were cantering home.

On days we didn't go out on trail, we played in the large outdoor arena. He chased me around the jumps and I squealed like a little kid when he brushed past me. As he cantered straight for me, I forced myself to stand there and not dive out of the way, trusting he would stop. He always did, sometimes so close I smelled the carrots on his breath.

Focusing on our relationship, I got the best rides of my life. As I trusted Chance, he trusted me. No matter what we might encounter on the trail, I *knew* we would be okay. Together, we could handle anything.

****

"It's the first number you gave me," Ellie blurts out before I finish my hello.

"Did she answer?"

"I got her voicemail."

"How does she sound?"

"Perky."

****

Horses and Life.

While nothing is ever 100%, men, it often seems, are in it for the ride while women are in it for the relationship.

When the ride gets old or boring, uncomfortable or just plain not fun, men dismount…and look for fun elsewhere. But women stay with their horses, even when they are too old and arthritic to carry them, and are not quite the *fun* they used to be.

Women understand age and change. While it might sadden us to watch a fiery steed sail over fences, knowing we will never do that again, it doesn't make us crazy. So we brush our horses and kiss their soft noses, and reinvent our passion, even if it means watching them laze in the pasture from our rocking chair on the porch. And we are content.

Because it was never about the ride.

November 26

My little Chinese Crested is getting regular visits from the Dachshund. Wow. How silly is that? It just popped into my head. Amazing, how weird analogies and euphemisms clutter the brain when the bricks and mortar are crumbling.

Brian and I have settled into something of our old routine—at least where sex is concerned. Other times, it feels like we're in plaster casts.

I don't dare tell Ellie or Lucy or Faith I'm having sex with Brian because they would yell at me for screwing my husband when he's fucking his girlfriend. If my situation were their situation, I'd yell at them, too. But, at the moment, sex is the only connection I have with Brian and I cannot—*will not*—give it up.

Yet, lounging on the Isle of Denial is how I ended up on this River of No Return, so I force myself—*I force myself*—to look at what I don't want to see.

While the sun still sleeps and Brian, too, I take his phone into the garage. The screen illuminates. I click the icons. The numbers appear...

****

I was about eleven...and crying. But trying so hard to stop. Because if I didn't stop, my father was going to hit me. Never mind that I was crying because he had just hit me. I guess my father didn't want to see, on the face of his daughter, the consequence of his cruelty.

I don't remember what offense I committed. Truth is, I don't remember any of the provocations that caused his violence. He struck, without rhyme or reason, and he was particularly fond of snatching my hair in his fist and jerking me around. And when the inevitable outcome was tears, he threatened to hit me again.

Do you know how hard it is to stop crying on demand?

Nonetheless, I summoned all my strength, and clamped my jaw and held my breath and I was so close, *so close*…

I sniffed and audibly gulped breath. But I made one last ditch, pitiful, whimpering effort to stop the inevitable…

"I'm sorry, Daddy."

"I'm sorry, too." Then he slapped me hard across my face and started my ears ringing.

Miraculously, I stopped crying.

Which proves that my father's "hit them and they will stop" approach to behavior modification did sometimes work.

I dug deep and clenched my gut and steeled my jaw and balled my fists and replaced whatever hurt I had with pure and simple *hatred*.

And I prayed that he would die. I didn't care how. Truth is, I didn't even think about how many people might die with him, like in a plane crash; I just wanted *him* to die.

That hate sustained me and I thought I was beyond his reach, no matter how many times he hit…

Until my 13th Christmas, when I learned that cruelty is a shape-shifter.

****

The sun is up. Brian is in his bathrobe, lounging in his recliner, drinking coffee and reading yesterday's *USA Today*. His phone is on the counter, charging.

I'm at the barn, in the utility room, wedged in a corner where walls meet floor, and tucked in a ball, alone and crying.

****

"Michelle called me back!"

I'm stunned by my sister's news, said in a rush, halfway into my *hello*. "Oh-my-God—" I stop my afternoon barn clean-up.

"When—"

"Just now at school! My direct line. I answered and she said…*this is Michelle Wright. Your number came up on my phone yesterday.*"

"Oh-my-God, what'd you say?"

"I scrambled. I told her that I had dialed her number by mistake, that I was calling applicants for a job and realized I had gotten a wrong number when I heard her voicemail."

"Wow. Good save. What'd she say?"

"Well…she sounded kind of disappointed. Said she called me back because she *didn't want to miss anything.*"

"*Didn't want to miss anything*? Like…a job? You think she's applied for jobs in Washington? Did you give her your name?"

"I answered the phone *this is Ellie.*"

"Do you think she told Brian? That she got a call from Bremerton Schools?"

"I don't know," Ellie says. "But, you know what's weird? I called her on her cell phone, right? But she didn't seem surprised that I had the number or confused about the call, even before she knew it was a mistake. Know what I mean?"

I pose the implied question. "If this was school business, why didn't you call her work number? So…she's expecting calls on her cell."

"Maybe…maybe not. Maybe we're reading too much into this."

"You mean, *jumping to conclusions*?"

My cell phone to my ear, I stare at the dirt beneath my boots. I pace…as my brain percolates. The horses munch hay; Molly is intent on something hiding inside a culvert. My eyes drift up the hill to our house where I left Brian in the courtyard sun, reading a book and sipping a Manhattan. He could be talking to Michelle right this minute.

Ellie breaks the long silence. "I cannot believe Brian is doing this."

Thanksgiving

Thoughts crowd my head, milling about, bumping into one another—what I know, what I suspect—along with those uninvited flashes of the past. If my brain were on fire, my thoughts would trample themselves fleeing to the nearest exit.

But there is no rush to leave. They linger, impossible to forget, impossible to ignore—sometimes shouting, sometimes whispering—but always reminding me of the very, very bad place I am in.

The question repeats like heartburn…*what am I going to do, what am I going to do…***what** *am I going to do?*

Nothing.

At least, not yet, not until I know *for sure.*

Besides, we have Thanksgiving to get through. If I think too much, I won't pull off dinner at Barry and Felicity's with their other guests. I won't be able to act the loving wife in a loving marriage with a loving husband. I will take my plate of turkey, with all the trimmings, and dump it on Brian's head…

Or worse. My despair will show.

****

I am the daughter of a mother who never aired dirty laundry, who never confided in family, let alone friends. What is private doesn't go public.

I don't know how my mom suffered through my father without a confidante. But maybe that's exactly how she did it. If you don't have someone holding a light to your life, it's easier not to see. Not unlike the Jewish tradition of draping mirrors while sitting *shivah*. It's easier to go about the business of mourning if you can't see how bad you look.

Maybe Mom never wanted to see how bad she looked.

****

Before me, there was Rae-Lynn.

I learned about Rae-Lynn years into my relationship with Brian, after our vows. And, as often happens, by *Chance*.

We were at our beach house in Otter Bight, where so many revelations seem to occur, with Archie and his wife, Jill, who had come for the weekend.

After dinner, with half a bottle of wine and a couple of Manhattans down his gullet, Archie started waxing sentimental about the good old days, before Jill and me, when he and Cathy, Brian and Rae-Lynn—

Rae-Lynn?

Archie happily divulged the ins and outs of Rae—the dates, the parties, the trips…the co-habitation—while Brian sat stone-faced sipping his drink, only once flicking his eyes at me.

Yes, Brian was living with Rae-Lynn when he started dating me. As Archie rambled on, pieces of the puzzle fell into place…which is amazing since, until that moment, I had no idea there was a puzzle.

Wedged between Brian's first wife and me was Rae-Lynn.

That's when I realized the New Year's Eve Brian said he spent with his buddies in Alyeska—three months after our first date—had actually been spent with Rae.

That's when I knew the *Cosmopolitan* I found at the cabin about a year into our relationship bearing the subscriber's name *Rae-Lynn Rogers*, didn't belong to the girlfriend of Brian's buddy, as Brian had claimed, but to *Brian's* girlfriend, also known as Rae.

Brian had juggled us, lying as he did, and after the pieces fell into place, I questioned the business trips and the weekends he supposedly spent with his kids. And I wondered…how long were we a threesome and when did Rae-Lynn depart?

I thought about how comfortably the lies slipped off his tongue, slick as silicone.

I questioned my own blindness, my own complicity. Because, going back to the *Cosmo*, I remember it disappeared. The next day, when I wanted to read the magazine, it was gone, nowhere in the cabin. The *evidence* was missing. But, I just sort of ignored the gnawing in my gut. How could there be another woman without my knowing? How could this man, who cuddled after sex; who brought my dog with us on our weekend trips to his cabin; who always thanked me for the dinners I made; who called me when he was away...how could this same man be a liar and a cheat?

I had no capacity to understand Brian's deceit. I simply could not fathom the duplicity and the subterfuge that shared his existence; that IS his existence.

I understand violence. But emotional manipulation is unrecognizable when it comes wrapped in a sweet, seductive shell and a charming, boyish smile. I couldn't believe such cunning existed in a man I loved so much.

So I turned a color-blind eye to the red flags and pledged my allegiance to a different banner...

Love. Trust. Believe.

I stayed true to that standard instead, even as it started to fray.

****

I am pathetic in my attempt to act normal, but I hope no one notices. Smiling and chatting at Felicity and Barry's Thanksgiving dinner, I wonder what everyone would do if I tossed my holiday punch in Brian's face and announced that he is a lying, cheating rat-bastard.

But that stuff only happens in movies; no one in real life gets to do that. We don't like to make other people uncomfortable, especially innocent bystanders who are only here to enjoy the holiday and not to witness the meltdown of a marriage.

So, for a few hours I pretend, and almost believe, that Brian and I are okay. But I catch Felicity watching me with a critical eye and I see the occasional shared look with Barry and I suspect they suspect, but I am too exhausted to care.

Brian, however, is amazing. He wears pretense like James Bond wears a tuxedo. Which makes me wonder how many times he has done exactly this? How many times has he *been with me* after being with someone else?

****

Arizona has snakes.

Some might think that snakes are the worst thing about Arizona. But snakes don't bother me, not even the bad boys, rattlesnakes.

Alaska has bears, mostly the black and the brown, otherwise known as the Grizzly. They don't bother me much, either, although I'd much rather run into a rattlesnake than a bear.

Arizona has bears, too, little black ones, but people pretty much shoot them on sight, even when they're minding their own business, which is yet another reason I'm at odds with Arizona.

There are, of course, other differences between Arizona and Alaska—the weather, the terrain, the people—but for me, the most striking difference is the *orientation*.

In Alaska, when I'm communing with nature, my eyes are up, in a constant scan of what's around me. In Arizona, my eyes are down, careful of my feet, because that's where the snakes are. More than once, I've had to suddenly stretch my step to avoid a crushing hit.

A few months after I adopted Molly, I scheduled her for *snake avoidance training*. In Arizona, it's common to teach your dog to recognize rattlesnakes and to stay away from them.

(As a comparison, Alaska has *bear **encounter** training*. For people. And the inevitable.)

Snake avoidance training is pretty basic. There's a rattlesnake, a dog, and a shock collar. Supposedly, the dog associates the pain of getting shocked with the rattlesnake and from there on out, stays away from rattlesnakes. It isn't pleasant to watch. I can only imagine what it's like for the dog. After Molly got shocked the second time, I stopped the training, much to the anger of the trainer, who ordered me to stop interfering, and actually called me *Ma'am*. (As in *Ma'am*, *step away from your dog.* I'm thinking I should offer *Ma'am avoidance training...*)

Ignoring the idiot trainer who liked pressing the button a little too much, I scrambled to get that damn collar off Molly who was cowering and quivering. And that poor snake, out in the open with no place to hide, wanted nothing more than to escape.

The problem is, I'm not sure the training works as it's supposed to. I've known two dogs who endured the shocks but were later bitten. I think we're teaching a lie. We instill so much fear that when the dog sees a snake he thinks he must strike first.

People act according to that same lie. We feel justified in killing a snake, not because of its actual behavior, but because of its *potential.*

Snakes get a bad rap. Even the non-venomous ones like Garters and Bulls. Mention *snake,* and people reach for a hatchet. Which, ironically, is when most snakebites occur. Too many people have the arrogant belief that nature hasn't the right to defend herself.

In our barn, a cute Checkered Garter about 18 inches long has taken up residence. I call him Willie because he looks like a Willie— cute, sweet, little.

One evening I was closing the barn doors and I reached for the handle only to be surprised by our little guy draped around it. Whoever said snakes don't climb, don't know Willie. I once spotted Willie on the ledge over the hay room slider. How he got there? Hell if I know. But he was happy as pie, and I was happy as pie to let him be.

Still, I'm not an idiot about snakes, or a charmer, or a Dr. Doolittle. I give wide berth to anything I don't trust that can kill me. Which is why my heart stopped this past summer when I saw my visiting 6-year-old niece, Natalie, playing a lazy game of hopscotch within the strike zone of an Arizona Black, coiled at the foot of our barn.

My sister, Ellie, found me in the grain room and wanted me to see this "big black snake."

Fifteen minutes earlier, it had not been there.

"Natalie, come here," I said calmly, but sternly. When she was out of harm's way, I grabbed my PVC pole and noose, along with a lidded bucket.

The Arizona Black hadn't moved. I slowly extended my pole toward him with the soft noose open. As the rope came near, he raised his head and flicked his tongue. The noose eased over his head and he started to uncoil. After guiding the rope a foot down his body, I pulled the noose taut and slowly lifted him off the ground. The hollow PVC pipe curved from his weight. I lifted him up, and up some more to clear his 40-inches over the top of the bucket. As he rattled, I gently deposited him inside.

With him safely in the bucket, I loosened my noose. The snake slithered out of the rope and I withdrew the pole as Ellie clamped the lid shut.

"That was pretty neat," Ellie said. "What kind of snake is that?"

"It's an Arizona Black." Her face was blank. "Didn't you hear the rattle? It's a Western rattlesnake. Why do you think I'm moving him?"

She shrugged, unaware that rattlesnakes come in a dozen different varieties. Being from the Seattle area, where snakes are harmless and few, she assumed I did this with all snakes, venomous or not. But now I needed to release him. That meant going down the road about two miles to state land where no one lives, and tipping the bucket.

I was driving and Ellie offered to hold the bucket in the front seat with Natalie.

"Are you nuts?"

She looked at me, clueless.

"Let's pretend we're watching a movie. Two blonds have a rattlesnake in a bucket. They're in the front seat; the snake is in the front seat; an adorable little girl is in the front seat..."

I gave her a minute to imagine the scene.

"What do we know is going to happen when they swerve to miss a cow? And what are we saying about these two women?" I allowed my stare to penetrate. "*How dumb ARE they?*"

I put the bucket holding the unhappy snake into the trunk and we eased on down the road.

****

It's 7:00 and we're home from our Thanksgiving dinner. With my stomach knotting and my heart racing, I sit beside Brian who is on the couch watching television.

"Honey, can we talk?"

He flicks his eyes my direction. "What, Hon?"

"I've been thinking about our conversation the other night, about Port Townsend and the life estate."

His eyes stay on the television.

"The thing is, I can't keep doing this while Michelle is in the picture. It just hurts too much to think of you with her. When we're together, I wonder if you're thinking of her."

Brian sits there stoically, his eyes on the television.

"I love you, but I can't work on this marriage as long as you keep seeing Michelle. I can't imagine my life without you. I **don't** want a divorce. But I have no idea how you really feel. It's been weeks since you told me you love me—not since I found out about Scottsdale."

Still staring at the television.

"I've spent the day wondering if you'd rather be with Michelle. When we're in bed, I wonder if you're thinking of her…

Brian flicks his eyes at me and then back to the television.

"The other night you made a comment about older men and sex not being important. I don't know what you mean. It sounds like I'm your back-up plan. Do you want to explain…"

Eyes still on the television.

"…Or shall we call it a day?"

I wait. One heartbeat, two heartbeats, three heartbeats…before I realize there is no pulse. I'm halfway to the kitchen when…

"Older men don't run around so you don't have to worry about it."

"Older men don't run around? What are **you** doing?"

Brian shrugs as if I just don't get it. Or maybe he doesn't think of himself as an *older* man.

"You're having a relationship with another woman."

"I'm not having a relationship."

"What are you having then?"

Again with the shrug.

I throw up my hands, turn away.

Finally, as if it's an inconvenience, he spits, "Yes, of course I love you."

"*Of course* you love me? *Of course…?*"

Brian joins me in the kitchen. "You're jumping to conclusions."

"My conclusions are based on what I know. If you want me to know something else, tell me."

"I don't know what you want."

"You don't know what I want? Did you hear anything I just said? I want my marriage back. I want you to stop seeing Michelle."

"You act like I have something to give up."

"Look, I can understand how you got involved. I'm not blaming you. Arizona hasn't exactly brought out the best in either of us. I'm lonely, too."

He rolls his eyes and looks disgusted.

"You're right," I say. "Screw it. I'm always the bad guy."

"There are no good guys or bad guys—"

Like hell!

"—Maybe it hurts me to think about all the money you spend on the horses."

"I don't think that's the same thing."

"You love the horses more than you love me."

"Oh, please."

"You just don't get it, do you? I'm not the one who needs to change here. **You** have to change to make **me** happy. All I'm asking is that you not be a dependent."

"I'm working on that and you know it. But I can't stay in this marriage if you keep seeing Michelle."

"I'm not seeing Michelle."

"You're not *still* seeing Michelle?"

"No."

"You're not in contact with Michelle?"

"What do you mean *in contact?*"

I glimpse Bill—*I did not have sexual relations with that woman*—Clinton. "Do you have contact with Michelle, of any type?"

"Well, she might be e-mailing me, but I don't think so."

"Why would she be e-mailing you?"

"I don't know. I'm just saying she might be."

I have a split second to decide—

"You talk to her every day on your cell phone! Her number is there *every fucking day!*"

Brian reacts with his trademark shrug and a roll of his head as if Michelle is a figment of my imagination.

****

My grandmother sat on the foot of my bed...*glowing.*

Never mind that she had been dead for twenty-four years and I was now living in my Anchorage condo. I woke to see her looking at me, much like the last time I saw her when I was sitting on the foot of *her* bed. I thought for sure I was dreaming, especially since I wasn't particularly frightened. And it seems this would be something frightening so I told myself to *wake up,* as is possible when you're having a dream you don't want.

Nothing changed.

So I pushed up on my elbows and curiously looked at her, wondering how long she'd been there. She stood up, as if she had been waiting for me to see her. I sat up in bed, because this was something I should be sitting up for.

She moved gracefully, in what I would later think of as a *bridal glide.* I watched her pass along the foot of my bed and along the other side toward the bedroom door. But before she reached it, she faded, taking the glow.

****

Brian is reading his book when I come to bed. It's a little weird that we're still sleeping together, but Brian will not give up ground because of a little war, and I'm here because...

"Can I say something?'

Without taking his eyes off the page, he says coldly, "You can always say something."

Why I say what I'm about to say, I don't know. Maybe it's the deathbed effect. When your last breath is imminent, you want to make amends. Maybe I recognize that I've run out of time and chances, and I don't want to part angry.

"Thank you for the twenty-two years we've been married, most of them pretty good. Thank you for the times you've supported me and the animals. I'm sorry I've disappointed you. I'm sorry for the times you've felt unappreciated and uncared for. I know how that feels, and I'm sorry if I've made you feel that way. I'm sorry if I've hurt you. Except for Arizona, which, let's face it, has been disastrous, I've been happy. And I owe that happiness to you."

Brian keeps his eyes on the page.

I don't wait for something I know isn't coming. I roll over and close my eyes and, for the first time since *Dear Brian,* I drop the reins.

The Day After Thanksgiving

"I want you gone! I want you out of here! I want you off this ranch!"

It's morning, and Brian's bombs explode around me.

"We'll sign a property settlement now and get a divorce later!"

Brian quivers as if he might explode, too, and take me with him. Stunned and speechless, I'm grateful the kitchen island is between us.

"Just tell me how much money you'll need and I'll pay it—I'll borrow it if I have to."

"At the moment I have no place to go." I hear my words, but someone else is speaking.

"What's your plan?"

"I have no plan."

"Shouldn't you have a plan before you make accusations?"

"Until last night I thought I still had a marriage!"

"Well, you're going to have to go somewhere. I don't know what you're going to do for health insurance. I guess you can stay on my policy, but you'll have to pay for it. Come up with what you need to get out of here. Write it down. We'll get this settled **today**. I want to get it signed and done! And we can move on with our lives."

****

Brian writes the most wonderful cards. I have them all, from the beginning, probably a hundred cards, even the tiny ones that came with roses. Bundled and tied chronologically, with the most recent on top, they are in the bottom right drawer of my dresser along with other treasures. Nick's collar. My mom's pearls. A lock of Chance's mane. My father's Air Force wings.

I live for the words Brian pens in his cards. Words of love, words for our future. He's much better at writing his feelings than speaking them. Maybe for that reason, I've always cherished his cards. I anticipate them with the eagerness of a bride opening gifts.

Mostly they have been the frosting on my cake, confirmation of my wonderful life with Brian. But in Arizona, they have been the bread and butter of my existence, giving me hope that we will survive this desert and make it to our promised land, that we will not end up like Moses.

My last card from Brian was postmarked 9/22 and mailed from Anchorage. The front has a stick figure with arms wide; below the drawing are the words **A Big Hug.** Inside is printed **from me to you.** He included a check for the monthly expenses and signed it, *Love you more.*

Last June, for my birthday, he gave me the cutest card ever. On the outside are a pre-teen boy and girl standing at an ice cream counter. The girl says **He'll have the nonfat, sugar-free sorbet.** The inside reads **Loving you is always 100% good for me.**

Then Brian adds…*I like the inside of this card. 100% good you are. A good wife and partner. Love you more.*

I suppose that card is so cute because it's true. I've spent years taking care of Brian, trying to limit the booze and the cigars, forcing vegetables on his plate, secretly buying decaf coffee, surreptitiously filling his SPF 4 suntan lotion bottle with SPF 30, demanding seat belts around his tummy. Doing everything I can to keep him healthy—in spite of himself—so we will grow old *together.*

It's torture thinking of those cards now. When Brian bought my birthday card, did he also choose a card for Michelle? Has she started her collection? Does she keep them in her dresser drawer bundled with a ribbon? Are they signed *Love you more*?

For all these years, I have saved each and every card Brian has given me.

But I can't find our damn pre-nup anywhere.

****

I have to do *something* to get through this day. I log onto *Realtor. com* looking for property in Port Townsend. It's ridiculous, of course, since I have no money to buy anything, but I have to *do* something…

I look up. Brian is standing a few feet inside the office. "I shouldn't have yelled at you."

I stare at him.

"I don't want to talk about Michelle," he adds. "I don't want you checking up on me. I don't want you asking me where I'm going or what I'm doing or who I'm with. You aren't allowed to go through my things. We either put this behind us and forget about it, or we move on."

What comes to mind is *Monopoly* and the *Get out of Jail Free* card. For Brian.

"I **have** to talk about Michelle. I can't pretend everything is okay."

"I won't be questioned. I don't want to be watched and scrutinized. I won't put up with your suspicion."

"Then I guess we move on."

Brian storms from the room…and I panic. My heart races; my head explodes. What the hell did I just say? It was a knee-jerk response to his outrageous terms. But outrageous or not, he offered me a reprieve. I'm drowning in the deep end of the ocean and I just said no to a dinghy. Do I think a yacht will come by? *Really, what am I thinking?* Oh my God, it was a mistake. I'll put up with anything, *anything*, to stay Brian's wife…

****

Anchorage has a lot of woods…and a lot of bears. Some years back, Fish and Game released a statistic of something like 200 black bears and 50 brown, or Grizzly, bears living in the Anchorage bowl. Amazingly, for what seems like a large number of bears in close proximity to people, we don't see them that much.

One summer day I found a black bear standing upright on our deck eating the birdseed from our feeder. I actually did a double-take. Then I grabbed my camera. But I guess I wasn't the only one who had bears eating birdseed, because around that same time, the city council passed an ordinance requiring people to take down their feeders in the summer.

This is one of the many reasons I'm in sync with Alaska. We treat our wildlife as if they vote and pay taxes. Instead of shooting bears for being bears, we remove temptation. But unless food is involved, we rarely see our citizen bruins.

On my daily walks with Nick, we kept on the narrow, seldom-travelled side roads that cut through our neighboring woods like a maze, linking homes hidden from view. I strapped bear bells around my ankle and I *jingled* down the dirt road, letting the bears know we were in their home.

Bears are benign predators. As long as they see you first, you don't need to see them. Humans are not part of their diet. They may kill us in defense of their cubs or to keep their moose dinner, but they rarely chow down on people.

So I follow this rule—let the bears know I'm visiting and then pretend they don't exist. And I *never* look too deeply into the woods, because I don't know what will be looking back.

I don't *want* to know. Kind of like, what you don't see won't hurt you. During the twenty-three years I walked and hiked in the Anchorage woods, I'm absolutely, unequivocally convinced that I passed unseen bears, watching me and listening to my *Good Humor* bells, but who made no effort to try the ice cream.

This is how I choose to live, trusting in the inherent *saneness* of life, believing that *goodness* lurks in the woods. I have to say, I think my philosophy has worked really well…*with bears.*

****

I stare at Brian's briefcase. The same briefcase where I found *Dear Brian* exactly three weeks ago today.

Ten minutes ago, Brian told me he was going into town for a newspaper. Mellowed since our last encounter, he was pretty much back to his congenial self.

I, on the other hand, feel like a lab rat who hears the *ding-a-ling* and doesn't know if she'll get fed or zapped until the mere sound of the bell drives her crazy with uncertainty.

Does Brian love me; does he not? Am I married; am I divorcing? Do I have a home; am I homeless? Do I trust? Do I believe? Do I look into the woods...?

I sink to my knees. I memorize how the briefcase is leaning against the side of Brian's desk. Gently opening the soft leather, I expose the two main, unzipped compartments. One holds papers and files that I quickly sort through and dismiss as work, leaving them in place.

The other compartment contains a faux-leather portfolio and a personal-size checkbook. I memorize their positions before taking them out. I open the portfolio; inside are checks printed with *B. Willoughby*, three to a sheet. There are no carbons, but there is a check register.

The beginning entry is dated 6/27 to his elder son for $100. Quickly going down the list, I recognize some of the entries, others not. I see a check made out to me for Arizona; a check to Bank of America for $5,360; a check to Dorothy Willoughby—Brian's stepmom—for $75,000 with "loan" next to the entry. Scattered among the smaller checks is one into his business account for $226,000. On the same line is a deposit for $231,000. There's a check to pay off the Port Townsend loan for $310,000 and on the same line is a deposit for $314,000. I flip to the next page and discover checks from $20 to $20,000, but also find one for $101,000 to pay off the mortgage on our home in Anchorage; a $111,000 check to New York Life, noted as "pay-off"; and another check to Dorothy Willoughby for $150,000. Additional deposits include $13,000, $20,000, $10,000, $275,000, and $300,000. The last check written is dated 11/20 for $50,000 and is *again* to Dorothy Willoughby.

Since June, Brian has deposited about $1.2 million into his personal account. And he has written checks for the same, most of it going to pay off loans or mortgages.

I know my husband. He would not pay off loans unless he has more money where that came from. And $1.2 million in and out, over six months, is a pretty fair chunk of change. So the question arises...

Why is Brian so hot on my getting a job? Why now? And don't tell me we suddenly need the twenty or thirty thousand I might bring in. What has changed that makes getting me employed so urgent that he wants me to move to Phoenix, for Chrissakes?

Of course, any fool knows the answer.

If I'm working, if I'm supporting myself even a little, there's less risk that Brian will have to pay spousal support. Even though our pre-nuptial agreement excludes support, Brian wants to hedge his bets. But the real gut-churner is that Brian has been planning *for months* to divorce me. He's simply been getting his ducks in a row.

I get off the floor and take the register to our copier where I wait while the magic happens with the speed of cookies baking. But I am grateful I have a copier. Down on my knees, *Thank you, Jesus!* grateful. In this moment, I see how a decision made a few years back is a blessing today. To sell investment property Brian had bought before the real estate heyday, I got my realtor's license, set up a home office, and bought a copier.

Weird, how a past thread ties to your present in the most unexpected ways.

With the copies made, I return to my spot on the floor by the briefcase and lay the faux-leather portfolio aside. I open his *WILLOUGHBY ENTERPRISES* checkbook. This isn't his business, but his *side* business. He's had Willoughby Enterprises for as long as I can remember and it always shows up on our tax returns; beyond that I haven't paid attention.

The check register is blank so I go right to the carbons and flip through. Nothing strikes me as odd; most check amounts are small and obvious. I flip, flip, *stop* on check #1368, dated 8/4… *Michelle Wright*.

The check isn't large—$700—but I suspect it's enough to pay for a couple of plane rides between Juneau and Anchorage.

I flip a few more carbons to check #1372, dated 8/25…*Michelle Wright*. Again for $700. And then again, *Michelle Wright*. only seven days before our anniversary—and eight days before my last card. This one is for $2,000. Then another, *Michelle Wright*, dated 11/9 for $1,750.

Wait…**11/9**?

Oh, God.

I check the calendar.

November 7…Friday…I find Michelle's note.

November 8…Saturday…Brian returns to Anchorage.

November 9…Sunday…Brian writes Michelle a check for $1,750.

Oh, God.

Was Michelle *there,* with Brian, when he wrote that check? Was she there when his plane landed Saturday night? There, when he called me? There, when I called Brian back and confronted him about Michelle's note? *There,* in my bed, in my sheets, with my husband?

I considered it before; decided against it. But now, our conversation that night makes sense. Of course, he was cold and non-responsive. What could he say with her lying next to him? How could he placate me without betraying her? He had a split second to decide who was important and who was expendable—

I jump at the ringing phone.

"Hi, Hon," Brian says to my *hello.* "Do you need anything from town?"

"I'm going to the store tomorrow, so I guess not."

"What's for dinner?"

"I took out a steak for you."

"Sounds good. I'll be home soon. Bye, Hon."

Maybe it wasn't about *expendable* and *important.* Maybe it was about who could be more easily manipulated, who was more gullible, who would be less likely to leave.

****

I was in my office, two years on the job, cleaning out the bottom drawer of a large lateral file cabinet. Piles of past audits were strewn on the carpet and I was on my knees, saving and tossing. Among the records were old proposals for professional services: CPA's, attorneys, architects, construction contractors. I found a spiral-bound proposal from Brian's firm.

I was eighteen months into my relationship with Brian when I picked this up and turned the pages…

This doesn't happen much anymore, but way back then, it was common to include personal information in staff profiles, especially when it came to the partners of the firm. Clients like to know to whom they're paying money, that the person is a pillar of the community, contributes to good causes, volunteers with worthwhile organizations.

I started reading Brian's bio with all his impressive professional qualifications and then his affiliations and finally his personal information…

Mr. Willoughby is married with four children…

My brow furrowed.

Yes, it definitely said *four* children.

But Brian told me he had *two* children.

Taking the proposal with me, I left the floor for my desk and dialed Brian's work number. After his happy greeting, I casually asked, "How many children do you have?"

"Why?"

"Just tell my how many children you have."

"Two."

"Are you sure?"

"Who told you I have more?"

"I'm looking at an old proposal. *Mr. Willoughby is married with four children.* You might want to fix that typo."

We hung up and I went back to my sorting.

About ten minutes later, the phone rang. It was Brian. 'Fessing up to four kids. And apologizing for omitting the other two.

(*Yes*, this is one of his two apologies.)

But, rather than being incensed by his lie, I was flattered.

There is something endearing about a powerful man with vulnerabilities, especially if one of them is you. As Brian put it, he was afraid I wouldn't be interested in him if I knew **all** his baggage. I was a single, unencumbered woman with the 4 C's—career, condo, credit, cash. And I was easy on the eyes. I had choices. His lie made sense. I understood. I forgave.

But the really crazy thing about that discovery? Until Brian confessed, I actually believed it was a typo.

****

One by one, I place the check carbons against the glass. Slowly, the copies emerge from the belly of the copier.

I am numb, lost in the labyrinth of Brian's lies, not knowing what path to take or how to escape. I am in a moment not unlike the gutting moment of Michelle's note.

But this is worse.

I might have believed that his back alley rut was one-sided, that Michelle's love was not returned, but the one thing I know about men—and Brian, in particular—when money starts leaving the bank account, it's serious.

The divorce will be serious, too, and expensive. What did Sid say? *$100,000? $200,000?* And I don't have Brian's money—*but I could.* Or, at least, a start. I can write a check to me for $50,000 and have it in my bank account before he knows it's gone.

I carefully peel off the next check in the book. I stare at the blank carbon before peeling that from the book, too. Since Brian doesn't write down the checks, he won't notice the absence of number 1388. At least, not right away.

But now comes the really hard part; the Everest of hard. Even as I remember what our marriage was, even as I still love Brian, I have to see what is around me. I can no longer jingle my way along the side roads. I must **go** into my woods.

November 29

"I'm going back on Tuesday," Brian tells me. "I'm stopping in Port Townsend to check on the property."

Brian is leaving a day early. I can't really blame him, but still...

"I'm not staying with your sister."

I glance at Brian, surprised he thinks I would expect him to. *Yes*, he always has before, but that was *before*. "I doubt she'd have you," I say as I continue cleaning up the breakfast dishes, wiping the counter, doing something to get me through this latest blow. In spite of all the evidence... *in spite of **all** the evidence*...I simply can't believe my marriage is over. I can't believe that Brian doesn't love me.

*Brian **doesn't** love me.*

If I were in the audience, I would be annoyed at my inability to accept what is so obvious to everyone else. But it's so much harder when you're in the script. I could never have imagined how hard it is to just...stop. If this is addiction, I have newfound sympathy. I may need the 12-step program.

****

We descended out of the sky, floating down, down, down, toward Otter Beach, as we'd done a hundred times before. In the next blink, the front wheels of Brian's Cessna 180 mired in the mud. The tail lifted and arced in a slow somersault.

Everything tumbled upside down. From the back seat, my dog, Lisa, landed in front of me, inside the roof of the cockpit, while Brian and I hung suspended from our seat belts.

Brian yelled, "Get out! Get out! It's going to explode!"

I pulled the handle but it wouldn't budge. Brian reached across me and pushed the handle *down* instead of up. My door swung open and Lisa got out. I released my seatbelt and hit the roof. I crawled from the plane as Brian did the same from his door.

Still in a daze, I scrambled through the sand with Brian until we were a safe distance from an explosion should fuel escape and hit the hot engine. As my senses returned, I hugged Lisa and checked for injuries. Brian stared at his Cessna, belly-up on the beach like a dead fish.

"Look at my plane," Brian lamented, when the risk of explosion had passed.

My arms still around Lisa, I looked up. "We're alive and we're not hurt. Let's try to be grateful."

"Yeah…But look at my plane."

"But it didn't explode. It's still in one piece."

"Oh, shit. The tide's coming in. We've got to flip her."

We?

Suffice to say, it takes a village to flip a Cessna.

Within an hour, there were enough people on that beach with boats, four-wheelers, and rope to leverage Brian's plane back on her wheels and push her up the beach, away from the encroaching tide.

Once she was righted, we got a good look at her. There was a small gash in the leading edge of the right wing; the tail was crunched and the propeller looked like a curly Q. But she was in good shape otherwise. She still had fuel in her tanks, and the engine, except for some infiltration of salt water, appeared in working condition.

One of Brian's Anchorage friends flew down in his plane and brought another nose cone and propeller. For the remainder of that weekend, Brian and Brad worked to get *Alpha Delta* flying again.

Never will I doubt the miracle of Duct Tape. That, and one-half of a plastic bleach bottle covered the gash in the right wing. More Duct Tape and cardboard reconfigured the crunched tail. They drained and cleaned the engine, added fresh oil, and then started her up with the new propeller. I have to say, it felt a little like *Flight of the Phoenix*.

Everything that wasn't welded came out of the plane to lighten it. Lisa and I and all our stuff would fly back to Anchorage with Brad in his twin engine Baron.

On Sunday afternoon, I kissed the nose cone and said a little prayer. Brian and I kissed, and exchanged *I love you*s.

"Fly good," I told him as usual.

He kissed me again. "I'll see you in Anchorage."

The engine rumbled, the propeller spun. Brian maneuvered his patched plane to the end of the beach giving it as much ground as possible to become airborne. He revved the engine, lowered flaps. With a lump in my throat and tears in my eyes, I watched the plane come toward me, full throttle. My heart pounded, swelling pride, as Brian passed and I saw him in the cockpit. Then the wings caught air and the tires left the beach and *Six-Four-Zero Alpha Delta* rose above the spruce and into the blue of an Alaskan sky.

I watched from that beach until Brian faded from my sight. And then I watched a little longer.

****

Brian is reading, as usual, when I sandwich between the covers, wearing my long johns.

"Do you want Ellie to come for Christmas?"

I roll over and look at him. Hard.

"I just thought maybe you'd rather have her here than me."

"If you don't want to be here for Christmas, Brian, don't be here. But don't pretend you're doing this for me."

I turn my back to him, tears pressing my eyes. My whole being contorts to prevent this show of pain. Mercifully, Brian turns out the light and we are back to back. I wait until he snores. Then, taking my pillow, I steal from our bed for the sanctuary of the sofa.

Lights from the courtyard sprinkle through the windows allowing easy passage. On the sofa, I snuggle under my mom's afghan and let the sadness escape. I don't know where it comes from, this endless ocean of tears.

Alyx mews at me from the floor. Gulping breaths, I calm myself, then pick her up and place her on my tummy.

My little black cat is now seventeen. She was an anniversary gift from Brian when she was six months old. My last cat had died the year before and knowing how much I missed her, he gave me a gift certificate to Anchorage Animal Control and told me to get a cat. Since Brian isn't a cat person, I consider Alyx a monumental expression of his love.

Alyx used to stalk Hobbes, the ferret that came with Brian's son, Aiden. But Hobbes, only half Alyx's size, was no pushover. She would turn on Alyx and keep her at bay with admirable ferocity. Our little ferret lived about eight years, which I think is pretty good for a ferret. I remember when she died, in Brian's lap. I remember the single tear that escaped from Brian's right eye and meandered down his cheek.

****

"Kate?"

In the fog of my sleep, I hear Brian's voice.

"Kate?" He is standing in the shadows next to the sofa. "What are you doing out here?"

"I couldn't sleep in there."

"If I'm this upsetting to you, maybe I should leave."

"I don't want you to leave and that's why I'm upset. And I know you want to. I know you don't want to be here for Christmas, and that's why I'm upset."

Brian says nothing.

"Go back to bed," I tell him.

By the illuminated oven clock, it's after four when I drag myself back to our bed. Exhausted, I crawl between the flannel sheets and curl in a fetal position, inches away from Brian.

I am back on Otter Beach, dizzy and disoriented, my world upside down, but trying to get out, frantic to escape, but alone, unable to unlatch the door, and it's going to explode, this nightmare I'm in, and I cry, as Brian scrambles up the beach, leaving me behind...

November 30

I look like an old washrag that's been through the wringer a dozen times too many. And I feel worse.

I scrutinize my reflection in the bathroom mirror. Do I try to fix my face knowing my competition is younger, perkier and glowing with love, or do I let Brian see the havoc he's wreaked?

Who am I kidding? He doesn't care either way.

While Brian sleeps, I quietly dress. I grab a couple of ibuprofen for this splitting headache and go into the kitchen. The first glimmer of sunrise dusts the room with orange. Molly trots out of the bedroom, smiling and happy. Clearly, we did not have the same night.

I ignore Brian's cell phone and grab mine.

I bundle up in my coat and hat, and Molly and I go to the barn.

****

Once upon a time, there was a little red dog...

Thus begins the first of only two fond memories I have of my father.

...Little Red Dog lived on a farm with his family—a daddy, a mommy, and a baby. While daddy plowed the fields and mommy cleaned the house, Little Red Dog watched baby and kept her safe. If baby headed for trouble, Little Red Dog would grab her by the diaper and carry her to safety. Little Red Dog loved his family and his family loved Little Red Dog.

Then one night it was storming. Baby was sick and had to go to the hospital so they bundled baby up and they all got into the truck. It was raining so hard they could barely see in front of them. And when daddy started the truck, the windshield wipers didn't work. So Little Red Dog jumped onto the roof of the truck and wagged his tail across the windshield to keep the rain off so that daddy could see the road. They drove like that all the way to the hospital.

The next day was sunny and baby was all better. Mommy gave Little Red Dog a great big pork chop for saving baby's life, and Little Red Dog was very happy.

I loved my father's Little Red Dog stories. There were different tellings, but Little Red Dog always saved the family and his reward was always a pork chop.

I don't know where these stories came from—were they remnants from my father's childhood or from some spark of goodness inside him? But in Little Red Dog's world, everyone was kind and loved each other, and Little Red Dog lived with his family forever.

Ironic, when I think about little dog Ben.

✳✳✳✳✳✳✳✳✳✳

Waffles are waiting when I get back to the house. It's Sunday. Brian always makes waffles on Sunday.

"Hi, Hon, I made you a waffle."

"Thanks," I answer with feigned cheer, mistrusting the *ding-a-ling*. Yet, at the same time, I'm trying hard not to be a shrew, not to drive Brian away.

"I'm sorry you were upset last night," he says as I sit at the counter with my waffle. "Have you thought about what you want to do?"

"About what?"

"Moving off the ranch. I'll help you if you have a plan."

"At the moment, I have no place to go."

"Well, why don't you think about it today, figure something out."

"I'm not leaving the ranch."

"You can't afford this place on your own…unless you have money somewhere that I don't know about."

"That's my point. The money I have is in this ranch. Until it sells, I can't move."

"You can't maintain this place by yourself."

"That's what the yellow pages are for."

"I'm not supporting you on this ranch."

"The only reason you want me gone is so **you** can be here, with Michelle. For now, this is my home, and I'm not leaving."

His expression hardens, but he says nothing. He leaves the kitchen for the living room and clicks on the television looking for a game.

Cutting up a few pieces of waffle, I put them in Molly's bowl, dumping what's left in the trash compactor. Then I put on the rubber gloves and clean the kitchen mess.

****

The listing on the ranch expires today. Thankfully, it gives me something to do. I take my time on the computer, making changes to extend our "for sale" listing another six months.

I can't fathom the next six minutes, let alone the next six months.

"I'm going to take Teena out. Do you want to come?" Brian is standing in the doorway.

"No. But take Molly." I hear the jingle of her tags as she follows him out the door.

I call my brother and update him about the money into and out of Brian's bank account, about the checks written to Michelle. Then I tell him, "I took a blank check."

"Why?"

"Well…I was thinking I would write a check to myself so I have money."

"Your plan is to write yourself a check from his bank account and forge his name?"

"I guess."

"So, forgery and theft—twin felonies."

My brother's deadpan reality check makes me smile. "Hey, I wasn't thinking clearly, okay?

"Well, y'know, you need to be thinking clearly."

"All things considered, I'm doing pretty damn good."

Taylor softens. "Yes, you are."

"So, do you think he'll notice the missing check?"

"Did you take the carbon?"

"Yeah."

"Then probably not right away. But don't take another one."

I laugh. I didn't know I could still do that.

"You really should be careful," Taylor says. "Do you have a place to go if you need to get out of there?"

"I'm not leaving the animals. But I did hide the gun. But Brian wouldn't hurt me. He'd hire it done."

"Really?"

"Brian doesn't leave fingerprints." Then I seriously consider what I flippantly said.

Brian doesn't leave fingerprints.

December 1

Brian sleeps as I ease out of the covers in the dark.

I cannot believe we're still sharing the bed. But, why not? It's a king.

For twenty-four years, Brian is the only man I've had next to me. I can't imagine what it would be like having someone else here. I can only imagine emptiness.

Sneaking past Molly in her bed, I shut the bedroom door behind me. In the kitchen, I flick on the lights. I feed Alyx-cat and put the kettle on the stove. I wash the few dishes from Brian's turkey sandwich last night and pick at the carcass. Christmas is twenty-four days away and I've done nothing—no cards, no gifts, no decorations. Standing at the kitchen island, I thumb through a couple of catalogs, looking at all the *things* that mean absolutely nothing.

Albert calls. Nearby, Victoria answers.

Hoping to see them, I go to the living room slider and raise the large woven shade that covers both the stationary and sliding sides of the glass. I'm startled to find Albert, in the flannel light, perched on the deck rail. Facing away, he rotates his head 180 degrees toward me for a quick look. Then he gracefully spreads his wings and takes off, chasing the night. My eyes are still wide when a second phantom sails past. This must be the elusive Victoria, following her mate.

As a new day flickers, I feel excruciatingly alone.

How does Nature decide who will mate for life, who will be monogamous, who will be a passing fancy? The blue-footed booby mates for life but isn't faithful. If the female lays an egg that her mate hasn't fathered, the male rolls it out of the nest. How does the male booby recognize his offspring when a human male would need a DNA test? And humans think they are the superior species.

Wolves, swans, voles, beavers, angelfish, skinks, eagles, owls, even termites are a few of the many who are monogamous and mate for life. Others, like gibbons and the blue-footed booby, keep the same partner but aren't monogamous. The serial monogamists, like penguins, stick with their mate for one season and may or may not hook up with the same mate in the future, although many do. Humans run the gamut of relationships, including the passing fancy and *the harem*, common among horses, gorillas, and Fundamentalist Mormons. We are the only species that has no specific *instinct*— except, it seems, *whatever works.*

Maybe what works for Brian is a harem. In many parts of the world, including Colorado City at the Arizona-Utah border, this is an acceptable lifestyle. Perhaps I should've given Brian's offer of a "little house" more consideration. Surely, playing first wife and second fiddle to Michelle beats living in a trailer...

With tea mug in hand, I check e-mails. Two more wagons join my circle.

Nina and Marlene, Anchorage friends for over twenty years, have responded to my e-mail of last week where I *mentioned* that Brian is having an affair and *hinted* of dire consequences. Each is uniquely qualified to offer her 2¢.

Nina is chattier, providing not only sympathy, but websites for Alaska jobs and suggestions for boarding the horses. She wants me back in Anchorage. She confesses that, in August, she saw Brian and "some blond" at a bar; they were dancing and "very much a couple." At first, she thought the woman was me.

I struggle to pinpoint the last time Brian and I danced then I imagine the interaction and nuances that make two people *very much a couple.*

Nina writes that she didn't know what to do with the information. And there it is, one of the oldest dilemmas.

What would I have done differently had I known in August? Could I have grounded Michelle's plane and kept her from getting to Scottsdale? Or was it already too late? Even if I had temporarily thwarted her, what then?

You can't keep someone from cheating who wants to cheat and you certainly can't police someone who's 3000 miles away.

When I told Lucy I didn't care that Brian was screwing around, I really didn't care—about the sex. What I care about is exactly what happened. A man who hunts will eventually find a trophy he wants to mount and display. But this is where Lucy is right—I couldn't do anything about that.

A wife cannot compete with a girlfriend and it doesn't matter how many verses of the *Enjoli* perfume commercial she Streisands, it's just whistling in the dark.

****

I finish reading Nina's e-mail. Then, before I take on the day, I read her last paragraph again….

> *I know it's hard right now, but think of this as an opportunity. Write a book, taste a new wine, cry, give all the emotion you are feeling validation and write it down. Take something away from this marriage that Brian can't take away from you. Write a book, write a bestselling book—you have the talent—after all, the best revenge is living well. You are a bright, beautiful, delightful woman and, in my mind, Brian never did understand just how intelligent you are and never did fully appreciate you. Take care, my friend. We all love you.*

****

So far, I've re-located six rattlesnakes—two Diamondbacks and four Arizona Blacks. I've left seven rattlesnakes untouched and I suspect there have been dozens who slithered through my territory unnoticed.

A few months ago, an Arizona Black was coiled near the bird feeder. Spotting her from the window, I weighed whether I should relocate her. Then she rubbed her face against her body as if satisfying an itch and this behavior was so *cute* and so un-snake-like that I let her remain.

Over the next several weeks, I saw her out and about maybe three times. She was voluptuous and I recognized her by the white spot below her right eye and the eight segments of her tail that crooked to the left. I named her Cassandra.

Then one evening, Cassandra surprised me in our courtyard where I let Alyx-cat sun. I decided that was a little too close, although she had likely been there many times without my knowledge.

But I knew it now, and it's one thing to be charitable, another to be stupid. I got my pole and bucket. She was heavier than expected and I imagined the chipmunk or baby bunny who had met its fate.

Down the road we went.

Weeks passed. One evening I was walking up the drive to the house after locking the front gate for the night. Molly was stopped up ahead, her nose pointing in the weeds. I called to her, which is my usual response any time Molly's nose gets blindly curious, and she pulled back. As I came near, I recognized the long black form as a snake and after a closer look, I recognized Cassandra.

****

My morning chores done, I return to the house. Brian is in his recliner reading a magazine. Molly makes a beeline for him, her rear in happy contortions. Avoiding the living room, I stay in the kitchen.

"Hi, Molly-wally," he says, laying his magazine aside and petting her.

Brian is upbeat, probably because he has only today to get through and then he gets to leave me and go back to his perky girlfriend.

"I think I'll fly up to St. George and see Dottie," he announces.

St. George is in Utah, only an hour away in Brian's Cessna, and Dottie is Dorothy Willoughby, Brian's stepmom. She was twenty years younger than Brian's dad, Aaron, and married him a few years after Brian's mom died.

For over twenty years, Dottie took care of Aaron. For the last ten of those, Aaron suffered from Alzheimer's. By the time I met Aaron, he was well into the throes. Each time we visited, I had to introduce myself. Every time I left the room and came back in, I had to **re**-introduce myself. We'd go through the same questions again and again. When Aaron asked me where I was from, I'd say "Illinois." And Aaron would always answer "the boys from Illinois," pronouncing *Illinois* like *Illi-noys*...

Brian rises from the recliner and comes into the kitchen with his coffee cup.

Moving to the island, I tell him about standing water in the corral. It's been drizzling off and on for three days—winter weather for Juniper Verde. I ask if he'll drain the corral before he goes.

"You should probably learn to operate the tractor."

For six years, we have had the tractor. For six years, the tractor has been Brian's personal domain. Not once in six years has Brian suggested I learn to operate the tractor.

"I'll do it this afternoon after I get back," he says to my silence.

Leaving the kitchen, I go into the living room with my banana.

"Have you thought about what you want to do?"

"About what?"

"Moving off the ranch."

I look at my husband's evil twin. "At the moment, Brian, I'm just trying to make it through the day."

"Well, let's try to come up with a plan."

I stare at him. I don't know if he's purposeful in his callousness—trying to wear me down to surrender—or just plain clueless.

I'm still on the couch fifteen minutes later when Brian leaves for the Juniper Verde airport where he parks his Cessna.

I breathe and go into the kitchen, tossing my banana peel into the trash. I put dishes in the washer and wipe the counters. I try not to think of anything but this moment and just getting through it. I feel lifeless and empty and yet I have plenty of tears, which spill at every opportunity. I wonder if Brian has even a single tear...

The truth is...*the truth is*...Brian stopped caring when he stuck me on this ranch and forgot about me, when he demoted me to *back-up plan*. And yet, I can barely believe it.

While I'm barely believing that, was I ever anything more? Twenty-two years... *Twenty-two years of being a back-up plan.*

I put on my coat and then my hat with the earflaps that my friends in Anchorage always teased me about. But there is no one here to notice. I walk with Molly on the road, avoiding our cross-country trail and the mud that would stick to my boots like setting concrete. The day is sunny and not too cold, but clouds are gathering. A breeze cuts through to my bones.

When we get back to the ranch, I let the horses out of their paddocks to roam the thirty-six acres and then I dump the poop buckets. I fill the wildlife trough with water. I hike up the hill toward the house, veer off the path to the bird feeders and fill those.

Inside the house, Molly picks up her dish and prances. I find a smile and momentary anesthesia. A few circles around the couch and I manage to get it from her. I give her a cup of food and she eats half.

Now what?

I'm sure Brian is now in St. George and lunching with Dottie. What is he telling her? Not much, but probably enough. Brian isn't much of a talker. What I know about his first marriage and subsequent divorce can fit on a postage stamp.

I turn on the burner for tea and go to my computer, checking e-mails again. I don't know what I'm hoping for, maybe just a connection.

Nina comes through…

> *Food for thought… Do you still want to be married to Brian? If so, fight for him! My brother was having an affair and my sister-in-law marched up to the woman and said "You are only a fling and not the first," and she stood her ground. That affair ended shortly thereafter when the "other woman" realized that he wasn't going divorce his wife so she could become "the wife." Same with Harry's sister, Rhona. She caught her hubby, Javier, and her best friend on their couch, but she's found a way to deal with his multiple indiscretions. She travels, paints in France, enjoys her life and is still his wife. Rhona's mother-in-law once told her of Javier's father who also loved the ladies… "he is charismatic and he thrills me, and I will put up with his indiscretions to keep him."*
>
> *As odd as it sounds, you might want to broker a compromise with Brian where you still have access to the kids/grandkids,*

and you still spend time with Brian as his wife. A wise man I dearly loved said to me, "My relationship with Susan doesn't have anything to do with my feelings for you. But, I'm 45 and you're 27 and when I'm 60, you'll still be young…." I wasn't willing to accept those words then, but we have remained friends throughout the decades so in a way it did work out. This 38-year-old won't stay unless she becomes the wife; you have time on your side. And perhaps Brian loves you as much as he's loved anyone. I believe that, and if you accept him for who he is and are willing to fight for your life with him, you may find that "the other woman" will fade out of the picture in a year or two; eventually Brian's age becomes an issue. Anyway, just another thought.

Do what is right for Kate! Your friends are behind you whatever you do. N

Nina's e-mail simmers for a moment, then I type…

You know, it's funny you should say these things because I've thought them myself.

The teakettle whistles. I stare at the screen, at the words I've written.

When did I become Regina?

December 2

"Are you coming back for Christmas?" It takes all my courage to ask the question.

Smiling, Brian diverts his eyes from the road to me. "Do you want me to?"

"You know I want you to."

"I think my being here upsets you. Half the time you barely speak to me."

It's my husband's evil twin. What does Brian expect? Champagne and confetti? "You're in love with another woman…" I give him a heartbeat. "It's tough to wrap my head around that."

"Just because this is going on doesn't mean we can't talk about other things."

"Under the circumstances, it's a little hard to be chatty."

"Well, you're not much fun."

I can barely breathe. I turn away, gaze out my window at the passing landscape. Every now and again, my reflection flashes in the glass. It's not pretty, but I stare back the way passersby gawk at a car crash.

"Are you coming for New Year's?"

I turn to him. He smiles and looks expectant.

"Why would I come for New Year's?"

His smile dies; Mr. Hyde returns. "Have you come up with a plan yet? How much money you need to get off the ranch?"

"No."

"Why don't you come up with some numbers and we can work on this when I come back."

"You're coming back for Christmas?"

"Well, yeah. You may not like JV, but I love it here. It's cold and dark and miserable in Anchorage. By the way, Aiden might be coming."

"When did that happen?"

"A couple of weeks ago. I just forgot to mention it."

I feel like I'm at 30,000 feet in severe turbulence. I'm powerless to change anything so I hunker down, tighten my seatbelt, and pray that things will get smooth before I start screaming.

We arrive at the shuttle. Brian takes his bag and checks in. I'm standing by the driver's door when he returns.

"Okay, Hon," he says brightly. "I'll talk to you tonight."

I linger…hoping, hoping…

As Brian walks away, I slip behind the wheel, a death grip on this moment.

I glance in the rearview mirror as I ease into the garage. My face looks like it's been mobbed by angry bees. That's what forty-five minutes of hard crying will do. It's a miracle I made it home.

I walk into the house and the emptiness bears down on me. Molly greets me, her tail churning happiness, and the heaviness lifts.

I drop my purse, take off my coat, and call my attorney.

Sid has my check and the pre-nup from the attorney who drafted it. Omitting most of the details, I simply tell her that Thanksgiving didn't go as I had hoped, and then I ask her opinion of the pre-nup.

"I haven't had a chance to look at it."

"We may be on the fast track. He told me to get off the ranch. He wants me to negotiate a property settlement."

"You didn't sign anything, did you?"

"No."

"And the ranch is in your name, too, isn't it?"

"Yes—"

"Then he can't do anything."

"He can stop supporting me."

"You have money, don't you?"

"In annuities."

"You'll need those. In the meantime, we need to get you an attorney."

"I thought **you** were my attorney."

"Oh no, I don't have time for this."

"Two weeks ago you had time."

"That was two weeks ago. I've gotten busy."

Sid gives me names of attorneys I've already talked to. She gives me a couple more. "Do you still want me to look at the pre-nup?"

I wish she could see the incredulous expression on my face. We hang up; I call Joe and tell him what happened with Sid.

"That's weird."

"Y' think?" I ask him about the attorneys Sid suggested.

"You can do better than that."

"Apparently I can't!"

Joe is calm in the face of my hysteria. "Let me make a few calls."

****

I first met *Stubby* shortly after his brush with death when what remained of his tail was crusted with blood. I wondered from whose jaws he had escaped, what bobcat or coyote had ended up with an appetizer instead of dinner. Although I know it's all a balancing act, I was glad Stubby was here to tell his story.

Over the following weeks, his tail healed, but a bald spot remained where it had been severed and was only half the length of the other chipmunks' tails.

But it was somehow nice to tell Stubby apart from Chip and Chip and Chip. I looked out at my bird feeders and there would be Stubby, stealing seeds, and I smiled...*It's Stubby!*...and along with that came the glow of knowing this little spirit.

But chipmunks live maybe two years in the wild and although this ranch is a little more upscale than that, there's danger beyond the birdfeeders and fountain. It's been awhile since I've seen Stubby.

While I still have Chip and Chip and Chip and Chip...and Chip and Chip...and a dozen Little Chips for company...I miss Stubby.

****

Alyx-cat purrs on my stomach, which is where she wants to be almost every time I sit down. I'm not sure if Alyx is seeking comfort or hoping to provide it, but there is something reassuring in her gentle hum, something life-affirming with the in and out of her breath.

It's dark, but not late. The horses are fed and blanketed; Molly snoozes in her bed a few feet from the sofa. We have one more trip to the barn and then I can crawl under the covers and cross off another day.

The phone rings. I gently move Alyx to the sofa cushions. After introductions, Beth gets right to the point. "Joe says you might need an attorney."

"That's probably an understatement, but yes, I need an attorney."

"What's going on?"

"My husband is Brian Willoughby…"

"Uh-huh."

I pause at Beth's ominous *uh-huh*. "A few weeks ago, I found a note from Brian's girlfriend…"

I tell Beth about Scottsdale; about the checks Brian has written to Michelle; about the e-mails; about his long absences this summer. I tell her about living together before marriage; about the pre-nup; about Brian's edict to leave the ranch; about his suggestion that we sign a property settlement and divorce *later*.

Beth interrupts here and there with questions. "Any proof that Brian lived with you before you were married?"

"Where else was he living if not with me?"

"Did he give you money for rent or food? Use your address for his mail?"

I answer slowly, the brilliance of my husband dawning. "No. And he's never used his home address for his mail, even during our marriage. But I continued to pay the mortgage, utilities and food for five years after we married, before we built our house on hillside. I also bought all his suits—"

"Why?" Beth sounds bewildered.

"Believe me, he needed someone to help him dress. Then, when his ex-wife moved to Washington, his son, Aiden, came to live with us for his last two years of high school."

"What was the mortgage payment on *your* house?"

"About nine-hundred dollars."

There is silence and then Beth says, "Over seven years, that's about seventy-five thousand. Add in utilities and food and clothing…**and** later you took care of *his* son? Brian had a good deal."

It's painful to see my husband through cynical eyes. "Y'know, Beth, Brian has done some wonderful things. Last year we fostered a Shar-Pei that needed eye surgery and Brian paid for that. And this past summer I fostered a horse that had been starved and abused and Brian paid for her food and vet bills and never complained."

"You mean, this past summer when he was with his girlfriend?"

Paddle! Paddle! Paddle!

"Kate…a lot of people do good things to feel less guilty about the bad things they do. It's wonderful Brian helped those animals. But don't give that more weight than it deserves."

I'm deflated and limp and feel more stupid than words. I can imagine what Beth thinks of me—what I would think if I were hearing my story.

I'm the blond in the front seat, going down the road, holding the bucket with the rattlesnake. I'm fine and dandy until that elephant appears. Then everything tumbles and the lid is off the bucket…

I tell Beth about my working, my quitting, my inheritance—

"You were a full-time wife **and** you depleted your inheritance to pay half of *everything* while he was making what? Three or four hundred thousand?"

Idiot flashes in my mind like a red neon *vacancy* sign on a midnight highway. I'm sure Beth sees it. But I believed Brian and I were forever. I never foresaw that once my money was gone, Brian would be, too.

Stifling my lame defense, I tell Beth the Arizona story. I tell her about Port Townsend. I tell her what property is in my name, what isn't, and why. I condense twenty-two colorful years into ninety black and white minutes.

"Are you taking my case?"

"Truthfully, I've stopped doing this kind of divorce. I'm doing collaborative divorce now…"

"You might've mentioned—"

"…**but**, *your* case I'll take."

I breathe—really, *really* breathe.

Beth asks about my money situation; she says she'll put in motions for support after we file for divorce.

"Brian is coming back for Christmas. I'm not sure I want to file until I see how things go."

"Once you file, the court puts a freeze on the marital assets so they can't *disappear.* The longer you wait, the more time he has to move stuff around and hide assets."

"I don't want to file until I know for sure."

"Know *what* for sure?"

"Until I know for sure…that our marriage is over."

Silence, then Beth says, "Kate, your husband has a reputation for having a new girlfriend every year."

As if I didn't hear her… "I still love him, Beth. I'm not ready to file."

December 3

From my little document nest, I've found my latest annuity statements. ING allows me to take a loan of $26,000. I start my raid with that.

****

Where our ranch sits, there are no woods. Arizona **does** have woods, however. In fact, forests and state parks overflow with majestic pines. Flagstaff, at 7000 feet, has trees all over the place. Even Juniper Verde has a vast area of tall pinions aptly called *The Pines*.

But the biggest trees on our ranch are the junipers, which aren't trees at all, but bushes, really humongous bushes that pretend to be trees. And if the lower branches are cut off, they actually look like trees. Some of the junipers are hundreds of years old and so expansive they have a stately oak silhouette.

Junipers flourish in an environment that would kill unattended roses in a week. If that weren't amazing enough, the berries they produce, and eventually drop, feed every animal out here, including my horses and Molly. The horses scrape the firm, blueberry-size berries from the branches directly into their mouths, that's how much they like them. Juniper is the common ingredient in all gin, which might account for its popularity. I once tasted a berry just to see what the poop was about, and all I have to say is, *thank God for Safeway*.

Around here, unless a hill gets in the way, I can pretty much see for miles, not that it really matters since the only large animals I'm likely to encounter are semi-wild range cattle. And while they can be dangerous, especially the bulls, I've never known one to stalk or attack. I don't wear cow bells; I don't stick to the roads.

Once in a blue moon, I'll round a hill and find a big, black bull lounging under a juniper. As long as I keep my distance, he lets me pass without a challenge.

No, out here, it's the small, camouflaged stuff I really have to watch for, like the fallen branch that unexpectedly wiggles or the cow pie that suddenly uncoils. I've come within inches of a rattlesnake hidden among the rocks before realizing the threat.

In Arizona, I live in a world of disguise. But, maybe Alaska is the same and I simply never saw it that way. Maybe I've been living in the same world of pretense and camouflage, but in different locations. Perhaps I've been too preoccupied with everything on the outside to see the danger in my own bed.

December 4

It's good to hear Jill's voice, distracting me from my evening tunnel.

We start out the conversation as usual. She talks about her volunteer work at the Anchorage Animal Control Center and about the elderly basset hound she recently adopted. She asks how Arizona is doing.

"Not good. Brian's having an affair." Instead of disbelief and outrage, there is conspicuous silence. "Do you know about it?"

"Yes, I do."

My heart drops to my stomach. How many times will I have this reaction to the same damn news? I ask Jill how long she's known.

"About a month. Darla told me."

Darla is the wife of Jason, a partner in Brian's law firm.

"Brian took Michelle skiing and they stayed with Darla and Jason at the condo—"

That would be the same condo where Brian and I first shared the sheets.

"Darla was pretty upset at having Michelle there. She told Brian she was going to tell you and he just smiled and said *you wouldn't do that.*"

I try to imagine Brian introducing Michelle to our friends. I try to imagine what I would do if Jason was with another woman and I was witness. I like to think I would read them both the riot act. I like to think I wouldn't be party to such betrayal. That's what I like to think.

"So when did Darla tell you this?"

"We were having dinner at their house. Darla took me aside and spilled the news, then told me that Archie had been with them in Otter Bight last spring! I was so pissed. I went straight to Archie and he admitted it. He didn't know Michelle was going to be there when he showed up at the airport and then he didn't know what to do so he went along. How did you find out?"

I tell Jill about Scottsdale, the e-mails, the checks Brian has written to Michelle. I tell her everything and feel sicker and sicker with each recount. Finally, I ask, "What does Archie think?"

"Well, he thinks it's terrible what Brian is doing."

"I mean...about Michelle. This is serious, right?" With that question, I know what I'm thinking, what I'm *hoping,* and I can't quite believe it.

"Well, yeah. Brian hasn't introduced her to me and Shawna, but he sure isn't trying to hide her. Actually, I met her a couple of months ago in Sea Galley."

"He's taking her into Sea Galley?"

"He introduced her as a client then."

I stop breathing.

"I'm really sorry, Katie...."

I clamp my jaw, unable to speak, and do my best not to cry.

"I've always thought Brian is an arrogant ass-hole incapable of loving anyone but himself."

But he loves *me.* He loves **me.**

My life with Brian flashes before me in little snippets. Then I see Michelle in The Sea Galley. Michelle in Otter Bight. Michelle at Alyeska. Michelle meeting Brian's friends.

The e-mails. The checks. The Scottsdale trip. *Dear Brian...*

I think of the insignificant moments that create significance. That create a single life out of two. That create a union. That create a bond. That *destroy* a marriage.

All this triviality adding up to a life for Brian and Michelle, a life without me.

December 5

I wake with excruciating cramps. I pop four ibuprofen then listen to Brian's messages from last night.

"Hello, Hon. You're probably in the shower. I'm home. Give me a call."

Then his second message.

"Hi Hon, where are you? It's late. I'm going to bed. If I don't talk to you tonight, I'll talk to you in the morning."

All like nothing is going on, except for the same glaring omission. I am, it seems, waiting for Godot.

Second by second, I get through the day. I never realized how much time I spend preparing and eating food. Without that, I have all this extra time to struggle through.

I'm down to 115 pounds…in *winter* clothes. I haven't seen that on the scale since I was a go-go girl at the Peppermint Lounge, a little retro, college bar in Carbondale, Illinois named after the 1961 song, *The Peppermint Twist.* I made $20 a night and danced four nights a week in twenty-minute shifts with three other girls, all of us college students. There were about twenty dancers in total and the Peppermint Lounge, with its go-go girls, was THE spot for years, even garnering a visit from *60 Minutes.*

I earned about $300 a month, which was a fortune and better pay with better hours than the student work jobs offered by the University. Wearing the same style of white bikini, we danced, two at a time, in little cages on opposite sides of the dance floor. We shimmied and shook to the beat of the fifties and sixties.

My hair was to my waist. I looked good in a bikini and had no problem being the object of public scrutiny. There were certainly girls who had more to offer, but I held my own, and as I think about it now, I didn't really think about it then.

Yvonne was one of those girls who had *much* more to offer but, in spite of that, we became great friends. Resembling Raquel Welch, she was an anthropology major who spoke fluent Spanish. When she graduated, she found a job in Alaska. A couple years later, I visited.

I couldn't imagine anyone *choosing* to live in Alaska. Although it was finally getting press with the oil pipeline, it still had a reputation for being cold, dark and remote.

I remember the flight from Seattle to Anchorage and the first time I saw those endless snow-capped mountains. The sky was an intense cerulean blue and the snow atop those sharp peaks was neon white by comparison.

That was the moment.

From the window of the plane, I stared, falling deeper and deeper under her spell. When my plane landed in Anchorage, I was home. It was that fast, that certain. It was love; it was destiny.

But it would be a few more years before I packed my dog and cat in the truck and moved to Alaska. I had my MBA to finish and after that, I owned a women's weight-lifting gym, which I named The Body Shop.

Sandwiched between the gyrating and the lifting, I volunteered at the Humane Society of Southern Illinois. Every two weeks, I put an adoptable dog or cat in my '64 Chevy Biscayne and drove thirty miles to the ABC network affiliate where I appeared on a local kid's program, *Cactus Pete and the Funny Company.*

But eventually I was where I belonged and, ironically, Yvonne left Alaska soon after.

I can't remember the last time I thought about any of this, but there is something about feeling lost that makes me want to retrace my steps and find my way home.

I don't know if it's possible to have moxie and not be a dame in a Humphrey Bogart movie, but if it is, that's what I had. I leapt with flair from stone to stone without any thought to the crocodiles, and it was easy, or it seems that way now, years removed from the jumps.

Somewhere I took a leap and left me behind. Because, as I look at me now, I'm remembering that I was once someone else.

****

"This shows how little regard he has for you."

I just told Ellie about last night's conversation with Jill. I suppose if I didn't want the truth I shouldn't have undraped the mirrors.

We decide Brian is mentally ill. A narcissist, maybe a sociopath. What other excuse could there be for his callous behavior? His inability to feel the pain he is causing? His total disregard for me after *twenty-two years*?

"What could I find out that would be worse than this?" I hope Ellie has no answer; I hope I've hit bottom.

"That she's pregnant?"

"Well, yes, I suppose that would be worse."

"That they're building a house in Port Townsend?"

"Well, yeah…"

"That he's bought her an engagement ring?"

"Okay, you can stop now."

"I can't believe he would do this to you. I hope he falls into a pit!"

My sister's final hope causes a smile, but nothing more. I don't want something bad to happen to Brian. I wish I did because the anger behind such a wish would goad me through this horrible, horrible, *horrible* moment.

I hang up the phone, shaken from yet another blow to my reality. I'm being buried alive by my collapsing life, the bricks and mortar raining down. There is no place to hide, no way to stop it. I double over with the agony of not being loved by the man I love so much.

When Brian calls that night, I vow to tell him not to come for Christmas. I'll tell him to stop calling me. But when the phone finally rings, I simply don't answer. When it rings later, I don't answer again. I hear Brian's voice on the message machine, but I don't listen.

I sit here in the rubble, like a kid with a dirty diaper.

December 6

After several messages from Brian, I finally called him back. I told him about my conversation with Jill and that he doesn't need to call me anymore.

I cannot believe how *blasé* he was. He didn't deny anything; he didn't try to explain. He simply didn't care.

But that's not why I'm thinking of the gun.

****

"You only have to be brave for a few seconds..."

That's what I said to each and every one as we played for the last time.

"When you wake up, you'll be in God's hands."

The puppies licked my face; I smelled their sweet baby breath. Light as air, the kittens climbed my sweater and burrowed into my long blond hair. I cuddled them like babies.

It's hard to find a vein in an animal this small so the needle always goes into the heart. I pushed the plunger as fast as I could.

I held them, lifeless and limp, trying to find peace in their peace, telling myself that they were free from abuse and suffering when I knew I was really doing the dirty work for those who were indifferent and irresponsible.

Yet, as heartbreaking as the puppies and kittens were, the older animals haunted me. How do you abandon your dog or cat after eight or ten or twelve years when you know what the outcome will be?

"Drop her off and leave," Brian's friend, Mark, told me. "You don't want to be there."

Mark didn't know how many times I had already been there, wielding the needle. And he was right, no one *wants* to be there, but that's not the point.

Mark had recently *put down* his retriever and I was facing a similar moment with my dog, Lisa. But unlike Mark, I couldn't fathom **not** being with Lisa when she passed from this life into the next. From my arms into God's hands.

****

I've just hung up the phone after talking with Jill. Michelle is flying to Anchorage and Brian is taking her into Sea Galley. He's officially introducing her to the rest of the world. In fact, they're likely sitting at our table right this minute.

It's excruciating to imagine—but I can't stop. The pain roils in my gut and multiplies until I am nothing but pain, contorted and wretched like images of people in hell.

I **am** in hell. It's inconceivable that I can be this tormented and still be alive. But I don't have to be…

****

He was standing by the side of the road. His dark eyes brightened and his tail slowly wagged when I stopped my car. How many others had passed him by?

His belly was hugely distended. At first, I thought *he* was a pregnant *she*. I could only imagine how he had been forced to survive.

Sitting in my car, he looked hopeful.

I don't remember them all, individually, but some have been my companions for thirty years. Like the white cat who purred in my arms while maggots ate from a wound in her side. She went quickly, as if she had little life left to take.

And this sweet hound who deserved so much more than expediency. As sick as he was, I wish I had saved him. I wish it again and again and again.

****

Doubled over at the foot of the desk, I drench the carpet with my tears. I wail until no sound remains, but still the pain attacks. *I only have to be brave for a second.* That's all it will take to pull the trigger.

Molly comes into the room, tail wagging, ears flat, trying desperately to get me past this moment with a frenzy of licks and paw jabs. I push myself up from the carpet and settle against the desk, trying to calm her.

How long will it take before someone finds me out here with a bullet in my heart? What will happen to Molly in the meantime? I must leave food and water.

Or…I can call someone and tell them I'm shooting myself so please come for the animals.

Or…I can shoot all the animals and then kill myself.

I think about that for a moment, about the news stories where a father shoots his kids then turns the gun on himself. I used to wonder, *how does someone do that?*

Molly isn't a people dog. She will bark and growl and snap at those trying to rescue her. The cops will have to use the pole-n-noose to drag her away from my corpse. They'll stick her in a kennel and she'll be alone and so afraid.

My brother and sister will come and, I suppose, Brian, too. Someone needs to identify my body. Ellie will be an absolute basket case. It will have to be Brian or maybe Taylor. They might both be there, with me sunken and grey on the slab, except that Taylor might beat the crap out of Brian if they're in the same room together. Or, given his years of diplomacy, Taylor might pummel him with words.

Will Brian take the animals? Molly adores him. But Brian will never alter his life for a dog, so who will take care of her?

Michelle?

Yeah…I don't see that.

Quinn has such an attitude. He started out as the by-product on a Premarin farm—a candidate for slaughter—but now he is the golden horse, all the circumstances of his birth invisible.

He is a handsome, *handsome* guy and really smart. But he is so strong-willed that he can be a handful. And he's big—16 hands and 1100 pounds. He bucks, but not maliciously. It's more of an exclamation point at the end of an uphill canter. I ride him with the same bareback pad and hackamore I rode with Chance, so if Quinn wants to unseat me, he easily can. All that exists between the ground and me is my balance and his kindness.

I've been offered thousands of dollars for Quinn by persons who want a dressage saddle on his back, steel bruising his mouth, and shoes nailed into his hooves. They tell me that Quinn is not living up to his potential wandering these thirty-six acres with an occasional trail ride thrown in. They tell me he could be *more*.

More than a *horse*?

I fear that the person who comes after me might actually believe in *control* and *potential*, and won't see Quinn as I see him—*fully realized*—and won't share his heart as I do.

Animals are resilient. They adapt. They survive. They get by. I'm not the only person who can take care of these guys. They'll do fine.

****

"We might have to keep her."

Her was Natasha. Five weeks earlier she had been eking out an existence at an abandoned trailer in Otter Bight with her two buddies, Cody, a large, handsome black and brown dog maybe a year old, and a nameless geriatric orange tabby. Their owner had moved to California, leaving them behind. Cody had wandered down the beach begging for handouts; we asked in town about him and the locals told us about the trailer. None too soon, either. It was mid-October; in another week, Brian and I were closing the beach house for winter. We would fly the two dogs and cat in Brian's plane to Anchorage where I hoped to find homes.

The first storm of the season was early and furious. In a matter of seconds, the weather wrapped around us like a down parka. The ceiling dropped to 300 feet and clouds settled on our wings. Snowflakes turned into ice on our windshield. Crossing Turnagain Arm into Anchorage, we skimmed whitecaps.

I didn't breathe until the Cessna touched down at Merrill Field.

"We made it," Brian said, taking off his headset. I couldn't have loved him more. Reaching over from my seat, I hugged my hero until he said, "Enough."

I found Cody a home within a week. My vet, Ginny, kept Cat at her clinic with another office cat. But it had been five weeks and Natasha was still with us.

Seeing Natasha for the first time, Ginny cried. Natasha looked like she might have once been a Sheltie, but her fur was matted into clumps and she walked with arthritic stiffness. Hard of hearing, she was also in dire need of dentistry.

"How do people do this?" Ginny asked. I knew she wasn't questioning the mechanics.

A week later, after repeated grooming, and minus a few bad teeth, Natasha looked like a new dog. But she still had her old issues. She was going deaf, stiff with arthritis, and ten or twelve years old.

One morning, Brian looked at Natasha, sipped coffee, and said, "We might have to keep her."

I couldn't have loved him more.

Then a few days later, I got a call from a rescue group. A retired couple in Palmer was looking for an older dog who needed them; their 16-year-old poodle had recently died. That weekend, amidst two feet of snow, Natasha tottered into their log home, said hello, then made a bee-line to her bed by the fire.

"Why are you crying?" Brian asked as we drove away. "Natasha will be loved and taken care of. You couldn't have found better people."

"I know," I squeaked, gazing out my window at falling snow.

****

Molly pads after me into the living room. Grabbing Kleenex, I sit on the couch. Molly curls on her bed, intently watching me.

Alyx utters a tiny note, asking for my help. Her 17-year-old legs have lost their spring.

Numb and blank, with Alyx on my lap, I click on the television.

In half an hour, Molly and I will tuck in the horses. I'll tell them I love them and remind them, *I'm only a whinny away.*

Back at the house, I'll give Molly her bedtime cookie. I'll take a hot shower to dull this chill that's been my shroud for thirty days.

I'll watch television until my eyelids drop, then crawl under the covers while Alyx stretches beside me and Molly curls in her bed.

I will find the faith to click off the lamp.

Years from now, when I can see clearly from a distance, after all the rubble crushing me has been rebuilt into something I now can't even imagine…I will look back on this moment, rescued from the water *but a breath away from my last.*

December 7

The message light doesn't blink; the phone doesn't ring.

I imagine Brian curled beside Michelle; I imagine him rocking inside her. I see them sitting on the couch together, drinking coffee and reading the morning newspaper.

I am a ragged, starving misfit in a Charles Dickens' novel peering longingly through the window of an expensive restaurant which I have no hope of entering.

And I am seriously worried about my health. If this weight loss continues, I won't need a gun. I think about electrolyte imbalances and kidney failure and heart attacks. I think about Karen Carpenter.

I'm grateful I'm here alone where friends and family can't see me. My misery would spook them; I would see alarm in their faces. They would whisper among themselves, shake their heads, and wonder how to help. When they hugged me, I would crumble like a chocolate Easter bunny with nothing inside but air. Soon I will have holes in my skin where despair has eaten through.

But I can't stop the destruction.

What are Brian and Michelle doing today?

****

My trail buddy calls. Hitching up her wagon, she joins my circle.

Paula is the only woman born after World War II that I personally know who's made a career out of her family. A nurse by profession, she quit work after the birth of her first son, and never looked back. Soon she'll be adding to her resume with the birth of her second grandchild.

Today is Paula's anniversary. She and her husband, Eddie, have been married thirty-five years and neither has ever betrayed the other. I'm sure I would know because Paula—God love her—is chattier than my chipmunks.

As we rode the Anchorage trails, Paula on Kiki and I on Chance, we talked. This was when I couldn't have been happier. I had the best marriage, the best husband, the best horse. Any bumps in my life were just that, *bumps*.

While Paula kvetched about this or that, I had no real complaints. I had my life figured out. I lived my nirvana.

One day, we landed on the topic of men and the universal things they do that are so annoying, like channel surfing or forgetting something at the store because they won't use a written grocery list. Paula told me how she dealt with Eddie whenever he really pissed her off.

"I make the most fattening meal I can think of. Something he really, really loves, with lots of gravy or cream. I watch him eat it, scraping the last bite off his plate. Then I give him seconds. And I imagine his arteries clogging and his heart sputtering and I smile, thinking how I've taken a couple of days off my life sentence."

I laughed so hard I slid off Chance. I thought about my daily effort to keep Brian alive and healthy. The salads, the fruit, the decaf coffee; my constant vigilance about booze and cigars; my insistence on seat belts; and the SPF 30 suntan lotion. Every morning, I set a ginkgo tablet alongside his multi-vitamin and breakfast oatmeal. To lessen the chance of Alzheimer's, I bought drinks in plastic or glass instead of aluminum. I thought about all I did both openly and surreptitiously to insure that Brian has a long and active life.

"You've just got to kill them with kindness," Paula said.

I think about that now, as Paula castigates my husband for being shortsighted and choosing a new, younger woman at this stage in his life.

All my loving care benefitting Michelle.

If only I had taken Paula's advice then, maybe today, instead of planning my divorce, I'd be planning Brian's funeral.

****

I log in to Brian's Alaska Airlines account. My heart pounds as I click on his flight reservations for upcoming trips. It seems forever before the screen appears; when it does, my heart steadies.

December 8

No phone calls; no blinking message light.

I put away all the photos with Brian in them. Blank spaces are everywhere. I rearrange things so the emptiness is less empty. Some spaces I fill with old photos of animals I have loved and lost—an adorable picture of Nick with a favorite squeaky toy; a portrait of Chance and me.

Our wedding photos are stuffed in a drawer as is the photo taken on our Mexican cruise with Brian in a tuxedo looking very James Bond-ish. Twenty-two years of photos shuttered away behind the cherry wood in this beautiful house, now a mausoleum for memories.

Looking around this cavernous room, I think about all the packing I will do to take my stuff to no place. Where will I send my mom's china?

Mid-afternoon, I call Lucy who has become my daily lifeline. She encourages me to eat something. I'm managing tomato soup.

"Try to eat a grilled cheese sandwich along with the soup."

"I've thought about it; I'm just not there yet."

"This too shall pass."

"When?"

"Give it a year."

"A *year*?"

"Actually, you'll have feelings longer than that, but it'll take a year before you start acting normal again."

"What's normal?"

"When you don't spend every waking moment thinking about Brian. When you don't have a running monologue. When you forget about getting him back. When you have that split-second realization that being without him **isn't** the worst that can happen. When you can talk about something else."

"Sorry."

"I understand. And I'll listen for a year. After that I'm cutting you off."

"Jesus, you're going to listen to me for a year? You are a really, really, *really*, good friend."

"But only for a year. After that, it'll be tough love."

"I thought about killing myself."

"Yeah. That's turning your pain inward," Lucy says unconcerned. "I thought about killing Hazel. I imagined running her down with my car."

"Really?"

"Oh, yeah. I totally connected with my dark side. I joined an art therapy group and you should've seen my paintings. All black and red and outside the lines."

"I don't want anything bad to happen to Brian."

"You haven't tapped into your anger yet."

"A year of this. I can barely get through the next minute. And now I've got Christmas and New Year's."

"But Brian wasn't spending New Year's with you even before you found her note."

"Thanks."

"You're going to get through this. And afterward, you'll be better and stronger and smarter. You'll spot the men who are bad for you and you won't make the same mistake."

"I'm not making the same mistake because I'm not doing this again. Ever."

"I went six years before I found Abbie."

"In six years I'll be fifty-nine. I can't imagine sharing the sheets with someone new at fifty-nine. Hell, I can't imagine sharing the sheets with someone new **now.** Did I mention that my thighs are drifting to my knees?"

"It happens to the best of us. But you might discover that what's inside is more important than drifting thighs."

Lucy allows me to disagree and then she asks, "So, why didn't you kill yourself?"

"I couldn't leave the animals."

I sense her smile and then she says, "Want my opinion?"

"Why stop now?"

She laughs, but says, "Brian's not worth dying for, but the animals are definitely worth living for."

After that, I let Lucy escape. I feel better, but it isn't long before I'm lonely again.

The phone rings.

Beth tells me that she's sent a retainer agreement, along with forms I must fill out listing all the joint and individual assets. She needs copies of recent bank and credit card statements. I must write a history of our relationship for my affidavit, necessary for the divorce petition.

Still ambivalent about filing, I agree to everything she asks.

Beth has a copy of the pre-nup and asks me what I think it says.

"I get nothing."

"That's not what it says."

"Not in those words. But I haven't worked in thirteen years and I have no money. The pre-nup says I don't get any of Brian's money. So, essentially, I get nothing."

Beth gives me a legal discourse on *marital assets* and *transmutation* of individual assets, then asks about Joe, *my* attorney who drafted the pre-nup.

"But Joe isn't just *my* attorney. Brian and I used Joe for other stuff before the pre-nup. Before we married, when we thought we were buying a house, Joe worked on an agreement for us to live together."

"Do you have a copy of that? How did you pay him?"

"If I have any of that, it will be in our Anchorage house. Assuming Brian hasn't tossed it. I don't know if I paid Joe or if we paid him from our joint account."

"*What* joint account?"

"Brian and I had a joint account before we were married."

"You did?"

"Yeah. Does that matter?"

"You bet! Are you coming to Anchorage any time soon?"

"I'm not sure."

"Well, you should. Not just to go through the house, but so we can meet."

We talk a little longer and I'm drained when we hang up. I never thought I'd have to *prove* my relationship with Brian; that I would need evidence for a divorce.

Ironically, the only proof I know I have is twenty-two years of cards and notes—plus anything before marriage—that Brian has given me. Twenty-two years of his written word expressing love and commitment and a future. And none of it is worth the paper it's written on.

December 9

Early, early morning. So early, it's still night. I'm bundled in long underwear and two layers of fleece. I sit at Brian's computer and log-in to his e-mail.

I'm both grateful and amazed. I thought for sure, by now…

I scroll through his in-box without knowing what I'm looking for. I click on an e-mail from Alaska Airlines confirming a reservation change.

After half a box of Kleenex, I'm back at Brian's computer with a mug of hot tea. One of these days (I pray) I'll take a hit without landing on the mat.

I'm at the very beginning of Brian's in-box, all the way back to January. I look at the subject line and who sent the e-mail. Most mean nothing to me, but I open and read anyway…

> Brian—The market looks very weak. Your IRA has a large bond position so you are buffered…

I print.

> Net income so far is $76,756. Passive loss carryforwards are $62,866 for Willoughby Ent plus $81,815 for Borealis West, so a total of $144,681…

I print.

> Good Afternoon, Brian—I am working on a note and deed of trust regarding the money you loaned your son for the purchase of property in Homer. Loan amount of $219,000…

I print.

Here is the updated quote for the 4320 Tractor with the canopy and post hole digger. This price also includes you picking up the tractor and taking it to the Port of Tacoma. $27,561.45…

I pause.

Brian is buying a tractor? For…our Port Townsend property? More e-mails follow between Brian and his friend, Dale, who has a business in Alaska, a wife in Washington, and a maid he's *doing* in Anchorage. I know Dale, but not his wife. He once helped me choose a set of golf clubs for Brian.

It looks like Dale has done research for the tractor. I print every e-mail. Then I return to the in-box.

I slowly scroll when I spot an e-mail that stops me…

Hi Brian! Hope you did not think I had forgotten you and your generous time spent to include me on your 2 days of fishing at Otter Bight in July. I'll always remember the gentle tides, the breaching whale, good company and a stern captain. Thank Michelle for me as well.

As Sonny and I had promised, I have today ordered what are Sonny's favorite cigars and shipped them to your office in Anchorage. Let me know if you don't receive them by mid-month so I can do a tracer. When you do receive them… Enjoy!

Best Regards,
Trudy

I read the e-mail again and again, each time stopping at the words **Thank Michelle for me**—like an old 45 stuck in a groove. I remember the e-mails from Michelle reminding Brian to thank Trudy and Sonny. And now, finally, I know why.

I still don't know who Trudy and Sonny are. But what I do know is that Brian presented Michelle as the woman in his life; she was the hostess for Trudy's two days in Otter Bight.

Who else was there for those two days? Who else was I invisible to?

This e-mail has an arrow; I click on Brian's reply…

Thanks. Maybe see you guys next year.

****

Once *haggis* gets shared, everything changes.

It's one thing to carry hurt where only you feel it; it's another when the world is in on the secret. It's a fine line, I suppose, but it's walked by women everywhere, every day.

You can try to salvage your marriage, but that's exactly what it will feel like—*salvage.* No matter how much time and energy is put into banging out the dents, filling in the cracks, spraying on paint… underneath it's still a wreck…that all your friends and acquaintances and your husband's receptionist know about.

For some, this is perfectly fine. I know a woman in such a marriage. It's too damn expensive to get a divorce; she doesn't feel like fighting for half the assets; her husband likes the excuse of marriage. So they live separate lives and their only connection is legal.

Really, this is no different from working a job you hate.

I suspect I might have had this option, briefly, when Brian offered me a life estate on Port Townsend. The problem is…can you trust a man to keep his word when you know him to be a liar? Even assuming this is the marriage you're willing to settle for. And how can you be certain that your husband won't screw you over next month or five years down the road when the woman he's shagging refuses to do one more blow job without a ring on her finger?

If your husband cares so little about you now, why do you expect him to treat you better when whatever guilt of the moment has faded?

I suppose it's possible, as Brian contends, that sex becomes less important, common sense prevails, and men return.

But return to what?

****

I get through my day on autopilot with that damn running monologue I can't turn off. This evening, I sob inconsolably during the movie *Love Actually* when Emma Thompson realizes her husband has given the gold heart necklace to his much younger secretary and his Christmas gift to her is a Joni Mitchell CD.

That, however, is better than cash.

I pop more ibuprofen for cramps as stubborn as my despair and I curl on the couch with my blanket and Big Teddy and search for a sitcom that will move me past this moment.

My mom would say I'm wishing my life away. She would remind me that we learn more from ten days of sorrow than a lifetime of happiness.

If that's true, I'm going to end up an Einstein. Hell, I'm even starting to *look* like Einstein. But the trick, I think, is to keep ten days from *becoming* a lifetime.

The phone rings and hope rises, but it's Aiden, Brian's son, calling to say he's not coming for Christmas. He asks for his dad and I tell him to call Anchorage. He updates me on his life and I pretend everything is fine. I tell him we love him; I say good-bye.

Finally, I crawl into bed. But I can't turn off the light. I'm staring down the barrel of Christmas and I sense my ghosts.

Picking up the phone, I call Anchorage…

Six years older than I, Faith was my first Anchorage friend. I had been in the city only a month when I was hired in the Sears Personnel department where she was working. Already a wife and mom with two pre-teen kids, she taught me the essentials of Alaska living like having the right outerwear—bunny boots and an overstuffed coat that, worn together, made me look like the Michelin man, but kept me toasty in sub-zero weather. She welcomed me and my dog, Lisa, into her home and for the first few years, until I started dating Rob, we spent every Thanksgiving and Christmas as family. Beyond that, Faith introduced me to books by Florence Scovel Shinn which inspired our long discussions on metaphysics, spiritualism, and my random ability to know what will happen before it does.

But tonight, I get Faith's voicemail—which I didn't foresee. I hesitate then try another number.

I'm surprised when Brian answers; I intended to leave a message. It's only 8:00 in Anchorage and I figured he'd still be drinking at Sea Galley.

Sounding cheerful, he asks how I'm doing. *Not great.*

I ask if Aiden reached him. *Yes.* I ask if he's coming for Christmas; he hesitates, says no. Even though I already know this from the Alaska Airlines e-mail, pain courses.

"Have you told the kids?"

"Told them what?"

"That we're splitting up."

"No."

"Well, would you, before Christmas, so I don't get any calls looking for you?"

More hesitation. "Yes."

"So…we're done then."

"I'm not going to confirm that."

"Not going to *confirm?* You've gone public with Michelle so clearly you've made your choice. And in the absence of any other evidence, I can only assume you want a divorce."

"I'm not going to confirm that."

"Honey, I'll say this one last time. I love you and I still want our marriage—"

"I don't want a dependent."

"Okay. I'll file for divorce."

He asks me how much money I need. *I don't know.* He says he'll send the regular. He asks about the real estate market. Any sales? *No.* Any lookers? *No.*

"What are your plans?"

"I'm going to get through Christmas."

"I'm willing to help if you have a plan."

He asks if I want him to call and check in. I say we can talk on an as-needed basis. He reminds me that I'm the one who told him not to call. I remind him about Michelle.

He tells me to call any time. "Say hi to Molly for me."

It's funny about hope, how it lives even under the most inhospitable conditions. Then how devastating it is to discover it has died. Like a canary in the mineshaft. *Singing* only seconds ago, she's fallen off the perch and her little nothing legs pierce the air.

I suppose I should get out of this hole before whatever killed her, kills me. Instead, I stare at her stiff body and dull eyes.

I've heard that hope can keep a person alive, even in the absence of anything else.

So if hope is dead, what is left?

Where do I find a new canary at 10:00 at night?

December 11

I resurrect photos of Brian and me and put them in their old spots.

****

I used to be a runner. In my twenties, I competed in 10K's. I never placed, but I always finished. During the long Alaskan winters, I often ran indoors on the University track; one mile equaled sixteen rotations. It was not fun.

During *break-up*, when the weather had improved, but the trails were still slick with melting snow and ice, I walked a few blocks to the outdoor track at the neighborhood middle school. Lisa tagged along as I started my rotations, but after twice around she realized we weren't going anywhere. She waited by the side of the track. An hour and seven miles later, we walked home.

I'd been in Alaska three months when I heard about the Glacier Marathon. Named for Portage Glacier which was along the route, this race was an "out and back." It started at Girdwood, went south thirteen miles along the Seward highway then turned around, finishing at the start.

The course is pretty flat and the race occurred in May, but the Seward Highway borders Turnagain Arm. While the scenery is spectacular, the wind can be vicious, and May in Alaska can be like February in Chicago.

This particular race day wasn't bad, a little overcast and cool, and the winds were reasonably well-behaved. What I remember most about the marathon is the mid-thirties man in the wheelchair—he passed me on the outbound leg; I passed him on the way home.

I earned a fifth place purple ribbon in my 26-30 year age group at a mediocre time of 4 hours, 48 minutes.

The organizers of the Glacier Marathon were a husband and wife team, John and Marcie Trent, so physically opposite each other they made *Abbott & Costello* look like twins. Marcie was the runner, petite and wiry, with so much energy she practically sparked. She was already in her sixties when I met her, and proof that age is just a number. She was, in short, *a force.*

One day in 1995, she and her son, Larry, ran up McHugh Peak, a popular hiking trail south of Anchorage. The best anyone could tell, they silently came around a blind corner and ran smack into a Grizzly with a moose kill.

Marcie was seventy-seven, her son forty-five.

I sometimes wonder about all the events in Marcie's life that led her to that Grizzly. Like the day she bought her first pair of running shoes.

I wonder about the forks, the decision to go left instead of right. The insignificant moments we never think about that eventually create significance. I think about the small, pivotal choices we rarely notice that set us on our path and keep us there.

If we choose differently, if we start over and go right instead of left, if we decide to run McHugh Peak tomorrow and not today, will we instead get hit by a bus or will the Grizzly be at the end of our trail tomorrow?

What if we wear bells…?

✳✳✳✳✳✳✳✳✳✳

I call Beth and tell her about last night's conversation with Brian. "He couldn't *confirm*? That's cold."

"Yeah, well, I guess that's it. I can't think of any reason not to file."

I keep it together until I hang up the phone. Afterward, I dry my tears, blow my nose, pick myself up, and blaze trail.

December 12

Out of the blue, I decide to go. I scan the itinerary selections for flights to Anchorage.

I thought about being there for New Year's Eve, and advertising in the Anchorage Daily News or maybe on Craigslist, for a date…

Reasonably attractive 50-ish woman needs reasonably attractive 50-ish man for New Year's Eve fun. No strings; sex possible…

Then I realized that sex *isn't* possible and I started doubting the "reasonably attractive" tag I'd given myself and I remembered a college spring break trip to Biloxi, Mississippi, with my best friend, Faye.

The week before, she had broken up with her fiancé and she wanted to be bold and put him behind her, and I just wanted to be bold, so on our second night there, we hooked up with two off-duty Harrison County Sheriff's deputies, still in uniform.

At the end of the evening, Faye went with her deputy and I went with mine, and the next morning we met back at our hotel.

I had a wonderful time with Robbie—not to be confused with Rob, my former fiancé—doing all those things that "the pill" allowed, when penicillin was a cure-all for any misjudgments, while Faye, by her own admission, cried most of the night.

I fear that's exactly what *I'll* be doing—grieving and crying—and it seems cruel to drag some man along to my pity party when all he really wants is to get laid.

Besides, it crossed my mind that I might be singing Auld Lang Syne with a serial killer. Having my body parts strewn along the

Seward Highway doesn't seem like a very auspicious start to the New Year. Or worse, what if no one answers my ad? What if I'm too pathetic for even a serial killer?

Going back to Faye, she had her happy ending…eventually. She re-united with her fiancé and I was a bridesmaid in their July wedding. Then they moved to Manhattan, Kansas to attend graduate school at K-State, where she met husband #2.

But since I'm not looking for husband #2, I've decided to skip New Year's and go to Anchorage on January 25th, returning home on the 30th.

It's been over two years since I was in Anchorage and I'll be there looking like the main course for the Donner party.

It's a bold move, but I don't feel bold. I feel scared. And cold.

I add another layer of fleece and purchase a first class ticket for 80,000 frequent flyer miles. Borrowing from the male philosophy, the more money I have—or appear to have—the less attractive I need to be.

I look at the last professional photo of Brian and me. I'm fifteen pounds heavier and six months past a facelift. I look good. Not thirty-eight, but good. I promised Brian that as he got older, I would get younger, and that facelift was my down payment.

Eighteen months later, my cheeks still tingle where the feeling hasn't completely returned. But I *look* good. Or did…until the bombs hit.

I worry about the pity I will see in people's faces. I know the comparisons that will be made.

I put *inner beauty* on my to-do list and call the surgeon who lifted my face.

December 13

The information available on the internet continues to amaze me as does the discovery of my husband's name attached to several lawsuits including one for paternity and child support. But delving deeper, I see the Brian Willoughby on the screen has a different birth date than **my** Brian Willoughby. As much as an illegitimate child would help my case, I'm relieved there isn't one…or isn't a *public* one. I already know enough.

What I haven't found are Brian's divorce records, probably because they're too old to be available online. I leave my husband's name and on a whim, type in Michelle Wright…

June 19…complaint for divorce…with children. Michelle Wright, Plaintiff. Kevin Wright, Defendant.

So…Michelle was married when she met Brian but has since filed for divorce. And she has children.

The papers were filed in Juneau, where Michelle is now, but Kevin lives in Anchorage. Was Michelle living and working in Anchorage when she and Brian met?

As I scroll through the events of the case, questions explode like popping corn. *Is Brian the reason for the divorce? Was Kevin surprised? Did he have someone, too? Does he know about Brian? How long have Kevin and Michelle been married? How many kids? How old? Have they met Brian? Are they a family-in-waiting?*

Then, the big question…

Did Brian and Michelle plan this together?

December 14

I order Molly a new bed. Since the skunk encounter, when I had to toss out the bed I couldn't wash, she's been one shy. Besides, someone around here has to have a merry Christmas. I wonder what I can get Alyx and the horses. For my niece, Natalie, I browse the on-line kids' catalogs looking at holiday dresses.

I take care of the horses, go for a walk, get through the day. But my suspicions niggle.

Did Brian and Michelle plan this together?

I imagine them at a candlelight dinner or cuddled after sex, deciding how to get rid of their deadbeat spouses. Who will file first? Kind of like the way clandestine couples leave a bar separately, ten minutes apart.

I remember Brian told me I was *jumping to conclusions* and that he wasn't *going anywhere.* I remember again and again and again.

****

The first time Chance spoke to me, I thought my heart would burst.

I arrived at the boarding stable as usual; when I got out of my truck near his paddock, he greeted me with a deep, rolling *hello.* I had been waiting a year for that possessive nicker.

By the time I got Chance, when he was thirteen, I was his fifth person. I'm amazed he gave me a go. But there he was, telling me that he'd thought about it *for a year*, and maybe I was worth the effort.

Sadly, most horses don't have that voice. They exist like bastard children—part of the family but not really. Relatively few people spend time with their horses beyond sitting in the saddle; there's no playing, teaching, or learning. Their protection under the law is equally limited. While we kill our unwanted dogs and cats—which is bad enough—they don't end up in a can on grocery shelves or on our plates. We immortalize horses in books and movies, gather to watch them in sport, yet turn our backs on the old, the injured, and the broken as we did with Kentucky Derby champion, Ferdinand, butchered in a Japanese slaughterhouse. Every year, 10,000 racehorses suffer a similar fate.

Where is our sense of responsibility? Our compassion?

During his lifetime, the average horse has seven different homes. That's like starting over with someone new every four years and not by choice. Because they're big and people are often afraid, horses are treated harshly. The word *control* is used an awful lot. And many horses start over in the autumn of their lives, abandoned by those who don't see value in age.

Their stoicism worsens their plight. Horses suffer in silence. Perhaps if a horse yelped with each sting of the whip, or moaned with each tug on the bit, people would be more compassionate, more respectful of his *sentience*. But a horse expresses pain through his heart, undetected without a stethoscope.

One morning, I came down to the barn as usual and found Quinn standing quietly in the corral, reluctant to walk. His right front hoof had found an old construction nail, which had pierced and lodged in his sole. I pressed my scope to his heart, drumming at 70 beats per minute, twice the normal rate, and the equivalent of the 1963 Good Friday Earthquake on the Equine Richter Scale for pain. Yet he stood there, enduring.

In the 1800's, English social reformer and philosopher Jeremy Bentham unpopularly advocated for the humane treatment of animals. In one treatise, he asks the heartfelt question Quinn so eloquently answered...

The question is not, Can they reason? nor, Can they talk?
but, Can they suffer?

In Alaska, during my beginning lessons with Chance, my trainer told me that for Chance to be obedient on the trail, he had to be more afraid of me than of what we might encounter.

Because I was inexperienced and Chance was really, really big, I remember thinking *okay, if that's what I have to do,* until I saw someone put this philosophy into action with whip and spurs. Her horse complied, eventually, but it reminded me too much of the South China Sea.

I tossed the crop, removed the bit, gave up the saddle, and tried patience, kindness and humility. I wanted him to trust me beyond whatever he feared.

Some days, it was a war of wills. Chance backed me into trees; he twirled around; he planted his feet. Once, at the trailhead, we disagreed for an hour. Luckily, I didn't have a pie in the oven.

I waited, without hitting or yelling, while periodically suggesting he might want to go through the gate before snow fell. After he decided to go, the rest of our ride was wonderful.

That day I learned two things. First, you don't need to be a raving lunatic to stand (or sit) your ground. You just need to know where your ground is and stay there.

Second…patience, patience, patience.

And as I think about it now, maybe I learned something else.

In the early months with Chance, everything was frightening—to both of us. A plastic bag blowing along the trail caused my heart to thunder, and a moose in our path was pandemonium. But as our trust grew, Chance's reactions diminished into not much more than a *Fred Astaire*—a soft-shoe, side step—then on he trotted. The same things were happening on our rides, but trust minimized our reactions like the Riddikulus spell transformed *boggarts* into the laughable.

Once, as we were cutting across tundra, Chance sank belly-deep into unseen bog. As he plowed his way to solid ground, I hung on to his neck for dear life. My thoughts didn't catch up with me until we were cantering home.

Some might argue that Chance was saving himself and I was incidental. I know better.

There is a reason women love their horses. I doubt most women look too deeply into those woods for fear of what will be staring back. We just know there is a trust that exists like no other.

Chance came to me from a woman who was giving him up to appease her husband. Chance was too expensive and too time-consuming, her husband told her. He was really saying he didn't want the competition.

Men know when women have other loves. But few men can handle the truth of their own insecurities so they camouflage them into practical concerns like money and time.

Women know that's all bullshit. But we love our men and we somehow allow their notion that loving a horse (or dog or cat or bird or turtle) is wrong and we feel guilty and even a little crazy if we occasionally choose our animal companion over our husband. When push comes to shove, we prove our love by sacrificing what matters most. Yet, deep in our woods, we know that *real* love would not want that sacrifice.

As much as men say they desire interesting, independent women, men aren't mushrooms.

Yet, for twenty-two years, I've lived in the shadows of Brian's career, his business, his plane, boat, beach house, and his friends—along with their big boy fun like fishing, hunting, skiing—and I've rarely felt the sun.

Once, when we were dating, Brian went skiing for the weekend with his buddies and sent me flowers as compensation. His card read, "With boards on my feet, I'm thinking of you." I sent the flowers back to his office with a note that said, in more genteel language, he was full of crap.

Now look at me.

A few short weeks ago, Brian accused me of loving the horses more than I love him. I've thought about that, **a lot,** and with guilt. That translates into **my fault** for Brian finding another woman.

Maybe Michelle **is** my fault. Maybe that 1% I *didn't* give to Brian is my undoing.

But the horses…the dog, the cat…are the last vestiges of who I am, or who I *was* before I morphed into Brian's wife. After I've sacrificed everything else, they are all that remain.

Here I have stood my ground and kept a vow I made to myself some forty years ago in the wake of my father's cruelty.

In relationships, there is always compromise and sacrifice. But how much is *love* worth?

If you pay for love with *yourself,* what are you really buying?

December 15

"Where do you want Brian served with the divorce papers?"

My stomach somersaults. "I don't know. I suppose I can ask him where he wants them."

My hands clam after I disconnect Beth and tap in Brian's cell number. "My attorney is filing divorce papers. Where do you want to be served?"

"The office," he says as if stating the obvious.

"Are you sure?"

"Yes."

I call Beth.

"Really?"

"That's what he said. But maybe we should catch him at home before he leaves for work."

"If he said the office—"

"I know, but I don't want to embarrass him."

"The process-servers are very discreet. They're dressed in suits and ask to see Brian. It's all very low-key."

"When will he be served?"

"We'll likely file the papers with the court tomorrow, so... maybe late tomorrow or Wednesday. We'll let you know."

I clamp my jaw and try to keep the tears from my voice.

"I know this is hard," Beth says kindly. "But you'll get through it and it will be fine."

****

I cry. I take the horses for a walk and cry. A cold wind assaults me. In between sobs, I call Molly so she doesn't wander too far, and I resume crying. I hunker into my coat and hat. Back home, I hug Quinn, crying into his mane. Then I remove his halter and release him, along with Teena and Petunia, for the rest of the day.

I go through my routine, tears draining the life from me, but there is no tourniquet for this type of loss. Only when my eyes are swollen to slits and my nose is stuffed up like the worst cold do I force enough calm for feathered breaths.

Inside the house, I shiver, add more layers, and still shiver. After putting the kettle on, I go to the couch. The fireplace moans from a blast of wind. Alyx looks up from the carpet and opens her mouth with a silent mew. As I pick her up, she purrs.

When I brought Alyx home from the Anchorage Animal Control Center—no longer a kitten, but not quite an adult—she was super-kitty, able to leap from floor to counter in a single bound. Now I have stools of graduated heights pushed together to form a staircase to the kitchen counter where her food is safe from Molly.

The last distance is only twelve inches—an insulting challenge for a younger cat—but Alyx pauses as if convincing herself that she is capable.

My face gargoyles as I birth more pain.

I keep thinking, hoping, praying…that Brian will call and tell me that this is all a huge mistake; that he didn't mean for any of this to happen; that he loves me; that we'll work it out…

The teakettle whistles.

December 16

Dear Kevin:

I can't imagine you ever expected to get a letter like this and I can honestly say I never expected to write a letter like this, so it seems we might both be in unfamiliar territory. Given that, I hope you will be understanding as I muddle my way through it.

I'm Kate Willoughby, and my husband is Brian Willoughby, who is currently in a relationship with your (soon to be ex?) wife, Michelle, although their involvement started months before divorce papers were filed. I discovered their relationship in November when I stumbled onto a note Michelle wrote to Brian after they spent a week together in Scottsdale. I'm filing for divorce this week.

I have no idea what your circumstances were... whether the decision to divorce was mutual or whether you knew about Brian at the time or even if it mattered. And I truly apologize if I am dredging up events that you have put behind you and would rather forget. Believe me, I understand.

On the other hand, you and Michelle may be on the best of terms and none of this is of any interest to you. I just don't know.

I've been married to Brian for over 22 years and Michelle was a surprise (something of an understatement, actually). Now that the initial shock has worn off, I'm just trying to fill in the blanks and I'm hoping you might have some of the answers I'm looking for. I would like to connect with you in whatever way you are most comfortable. I'm currently in Arizona and for now you can write to me at 18345 Silver Strike Road, Juniper Verde, AZ... or you can e-mail me at KateRene@gmail.com. My cell number is (907) 898-1612.

I asked my friend, Jill, to deliver this letter just so I know you got it. Otherwise, if I sent this by mail and if you decide not to respond, I would always wonder whether or not my letter reached you.

I imagine I've caught you by surprise, but I didn't know how else to do this. Let's face it—there's just no etiquette for this type of situation.

In short, I will welcome any kind of communication, but I also understand if you choose not to respond.

In gratitude,

Kate Willoughby

December 17

Hi Katie!

Thanks so much for the super cute things for the kids. Jolie loves presents and she will love seeing Jonah get bunches of stuff. I am excited to give him his ball because he is just now starting to like toys so it will be fun to see him play with it.

Also, I talked to Dad today and he mentioned that he is not going to be in AZ for Christmas and I wanted to tell you that you are in my thoughts and that we love you a lot. I hope everything gets better really soon. You are such a wonderful part of our family. Jolie is dying to come and see you and your horses and talks about feeding Teena carrots almost daily (apparently, that made a big impression on her!) Anyways, we love you and we'll talk to you soon.

Merry Christmas.

Love, Shannon

Brian has told his kids something, but clearly not everything. Or maybe Shannon doesn't want to mention *divorce* any more than I do. I simply cannot bring myself to say the word in the same sentence with either *Brian* or *I*…

I've filed for…

Brian and I are getting a…

Nope, just can't get the word out.

I'm grateful I live at the end of the road where I don't have to see anyone; where I don't have to explain anything; where I don't have to pretend; where I can cry whenever I want. And I do cry, all the fucking time. Where do these tears come from? How can there be an endless supply? Doesn't the body eventually run out and dry up?

Apparently not, as I read Shannon's e-mail again.

****

At night, after a summer rain, I hear them—the baritone belches of Arizona toads. Those unlikely voices soothe me into believing everything is exactly as it should be.

The first time I saw a toad, it was hopping through the barn. Moving closer, I bent over and stared. So many things about Arizona I don't expect. Like snow…and poppies…and toads.

Yet, here they are, like *Brigadoon.*

So much of a toad's life is spent in patience, waiting for those life-creating, life-sustaining drops of water. Then for a few weeks, toads do all the things they're supposed to do and when the rains subside, they retreat underground and wait, invisible, until the next time.

Then, rising from earth, floating to stars, a hallelujah chorus.

****

A Christmas card arrives from my Aunt Kate, addressed to *Mr. and Mrs. Brian Willoughby.*

My aunt is eighty-four and in *her day,* this is how married women were addressed. Although I should probably cringe at the salutation, I don't mind. I guess I am, at heart, an oxymoron—a modern, old-fashioned woman.

Or maybe I'm just a plain old, garden-variety *moron.*

I know that once everyone knows we're divorcing, it will be easier to go forward, and…I hate that. But I'm on a mountain path that crumbles behind me.

I've already decided I'm never going to tell my aunt about the divorce. I want one place where I can keep the illusion of my marriage alive. I want her to die with my fantasy in her head.

I want her to think of Brian and me as married, not just for twenty-two years, but for twenty-five and then thirty, maybe even forty, assuming I can limit Brian's indulgence of booze and cigars and red meat. I want my aunt to slip into the afterlife thinking her namesake is as committed to marriage as she has been—sixty-three years married to my uncle.

I want my aunt to know that I will be there for Brian as she has been there for Carl, even when Alzheimer's has stolen Brian's memory and he keeps repeating *boys from Illi-noys* like his dad.

December 18

It is a cold, dreary day, everything in shades of gloom. It's too wet and muddy to take the horses out so Molly and I walk down the road without them. Freezing drizzle pricks my cheeks. Snuggling into my jacket and hat, I pull up my scarf and walk against the wind.

We're almost back to our front gate when my cell rings. Zoe, Beth's paralegal, tells me the process servers have the divorce papers.

"I thought that happened two days ago."

"We filed in court, but didn't get them served."

"Y'know, I'm re-thinking this—"

"Everyone goes through that," Zoe assures me.

"But maybe we shouldn't serve them at his office."

"Isn't that where he told you he wanted them?"

"Yes, but—"

"Look, I know this is awful. But everyone goes through this last minute remorse thing. Once it's done it will be okay."

Feeling tears, I get off the phone as quickly as possible, even though I know Zoe, like Beth, is wrong.

****

Brian is dodging the process servers.

"Why would he do that?" I ask Beth.

"I have no idea. He knew this was coming. But every time they go to his office, he's not available."

"Well, maybe he's not." I imagine two burly men in cheap suits standing in the expensive lobby of Brian's office.

"They've left messages on his phone and he's not returning their calls."

"He's probably busy."

"Anyway, they'll get him served today," she assures me. "I just want you to know what's going on."

I cry for the next hour. What if I **am** jumping to conclusions? What if Brian **does** love me? What if he **doesn't** want a divorce? What if he really **wasn't** going anywhere?

I picture myself in the audience and see all the events leading to this moment. I think about Brian's decision not to come for Christmas; his decision—long before I knew her name—to spend New Year's Eve with Michelle.

Her note, the checks, the e-mails, even Scottsdale, pale against that one choice Brian made months earlier. A choice *he knew* would set off an alarm. I remind myself of that over and over and over.

****

The left rear tire on the John Deere Gator is low again. I slide into the driver's seat and flick the ignition. Dead silence.

As if things aren't hard enough.

After a couple of back-and-forth, heart pumping rocks, I get the Gator rolling a hundred feet toward the tractor barn where we keep the air compressor and battery charger and where there is electricity for both.

It rains.

After the battery clamps are on, I head back to the house.

I used to shop at Nordstrom's. I used to have long, manicured nails and wear gorgeous suits to work. I used to call people to fix things. I used to read financial statements. I used to attend Board meetings where people valued my opinions. I used to be…more.

Now I pick up poop and shop at feed stores and get engine grease under my shabby fingernails.

No wonder Brian abandoned me.

****

The ringing phone jolts me out of an exhausted sleep.

Brian is sweet. He asks how things are going. I tell him about the lights not working in the den, about the problems with the Gator. He tells me who to call and then, like flipping a switch…

"By the way, Kate, what's the deal with process servers following me around all day? Are you trying to embarrass me?"

"I have bent over backwards trying NOT to embarrass you! I told you I was filing. I even asked you where you wanted to be served and you said the office. And isn't this like calling the kettle black? How about how you've embarrassed me with Michelle…taking her to Otter Bight with Archie and skiing with Jason and Darla. But embarrassing me is perfectly fine—"

"That's personal, this is business—"

"So, it's *okay* to embarrass me?"

"If you want a fight, I'll give you one. I can hire the best lawyers and they'll be the only ones making money! Have your attorney call me. There's no reason we can't hash out a property settlement. I don't need another attorney telling me what to pay. Now I have to hire an attorney to answer your complaint…"

His harangue continues and I listen, and as I listen, I wonder why. There is actually a moment when I realize that I am *choosing* to listen to Brian threaten and berate me.

The switch flips again. "I wish I was there to help you. But call Rich and he'll fix the lights. Will you call Rich?"

From somewhere inside me, a little voice pushes words past my lips. "I'm done."

I hang up the phone.

December 19

*...There exists an incompatibility of temperament
between the parties, such that it has become impossible
for them to live together as husband and wife...*

My copy of the divorce complaint arrived in today's mail. I hold
the pages in my hand and think...*legal rice cake.*

****

What surprises me are the many friends who have suggested I
might want to forego an attorney and work directly with Brian on a
settlement. Warning me about the expense and the emotional toll of
a long battle, they say that it's better to get what I *need*—apparently
different from what I *deserve*—and then get on with my life as soon
as possible.

Nina, my divorce-experienced friend, sends an e-mail.

> *...Personally, I think that is the adverse nature of
> the beast we call divorce. Boys want to keep the toys
> they perceive they've earned. When I consulted with an
> attorney, he recommended that everything be appraised.
> Harry went bonkers. After that, I decided that I could
> spend $60,000 fighting Harry and arguing about soap
> dishes, or I could decide what I wanted Harry to "share
> with me" and not care about what he was hiding and
> move quickly to my "better tomorrow."*
>
> *My philosophy? The best revenge is living well. And
> believe me, it's true. As I look back, Harry just outgrew
> me. I don't fault him, I fault ME for staying so long and
> being so unhappy that I almost lost Nina trying to be*

someone I wasn't. I opted for getting what I needed because of my kids and my fear that Harry could squash me like a bug if we got too sideways.

I also knew I didn't have the strength to fight a prolonged battle with Harry; I just wanted to be happy again. You may want to fight tooth and nail to break the pre-nup, but that's a tough road; I wouldn't have the strength. So, in my mind, your big task will be to figure out what road you want to travel...

****

In addition to the divorce complaint, Brian's check for the monthly ranch expenses arrived inside a generic Christmas card. He signed it...

love, Brian.

It's the first time he's used *love* since Thanksgiving night when he spit out the word. But from the position of *love* and *Brian,* it looks like *love* might've been added as an afterthought—

Jesus...does it really matter?

If that's not bad enough...*these damn tears!*

I fear my face will freeze in this horrible contortion of pain and I will forever look like this divorce.

The rain pelts the windows and the wind moans. What a perfectly miserable afternoon! I drag myself from my latest puddle and bundle up for the barn.

The horses are waiting. They have no interest in Brian's Christmas card. They want their mash; they want their hay; they want their stalls. Thank God for the horses!

Molly and I head back to the house where that hopeless tunnel awaits, made even more despairing by the weather.

Reading Brian's card again, I wonder why he signed it *love,* searching for hope in that one word. Brian mailed the card *after* he told me he wasn't coming back for Christmas; *after* I told him I still loved him; *after* he told me he didn't want a dependent; *after* I told him I would file for divorce.

So why is there love now, when love has been so obviously missing for the last six weeks?

December 22

I string Christmas lights around our courtyard trees. At night, when all other lights are off, they are beacons of hope in my winter desert.

I hang stockings for Molly and Alyx. At the barn, I hang stockings for Quinn, Petunia and Teena.

On the raised fireplace hearth is a small pile of gifts. What I want is not in any of those boxes. But I'm grateful I have friends and family—including Brian's kids—who remember.

When I had a regular paycheck, I bought everyone gifts. I started shopping months in advance, stashing purchases in my Christmas closet.

I bought gifts for staff, for my boss, and for the mail carrier. I bought for the *Tree of Lights;* I bought *Toys for Tots.* I bought gifts for friends and gifts for family. I bought gifts for the animals. I loved shopping for Brian's kids, and later *our* grandkids, and of course, for Brian. Beneath the branches of our dazzling tree, the gifts spread out like a glacier. I spent almost the same amount of time shopping for paper and ribbon and then wrapping the packages as I had in finding the perfect item to place inside.

After a childhood of miserable Christmases, I wanted to be merry. I wanted everyone else to be merry, too. I didn't want a single ghost lurking about. Whatever it took, I would banish them to my past.

And I did, or so I thought, until our second Arizona Christmas when a new haunting began.

****

A long, gold foil box with a red ribbon is at our gate. I find the box as the setting sun tints my world orange. From the size and shape, I know what's inside. Cradling hope, I walk back to the house with Molly.

****

The first time I read *The Gift of the Magi,* the ending surprised me. I don't know what that says about me; maybe I'm not self-sacrificing enough or maybe I've never been without a credit card. But it's a story that makes me feel warm and fuzzy and *hopeful,* and now it's Christmas and I'm divorcing and it somehow seems appropriate that its message is floating around in my head.

****

I slip off the ribbon and open the box. Roses, daisies, carnations, lilies. I read the card inside and my heart sinks just a little.

The flowers are from Carolyn, who, with her 10-year-old daughter Charity, adopted Roxanne, the horse I took in this summer when she showed up at our gate, starved and abused.

At the time, I had no idea how I would care for another horse, but I couldn't turn Roxanne away. I chronicled *The Rescue of Roxanne* into a short story that I submitted to *Equus* magazine only a few short days ago.

Now I have Carolyn who is my reward for fostering Roxanne. Carolyn is ten years my junior and a survivor of her own divorce from a haggis-loving man.

I put the flowers in water, trying to ignore the bitter-sweetness of this moment. It takes all my strength to focus on my blessings, to believe in a happier tomorrow.

I remind myself of the faith I had when I took in Roxanne, having no idea how it would all work out, but going forward anyway.

And I think of the pilgrim souls like Carolyn, who stop on their own journey, reach back, and hold out a hand to me.

Christmas Eve

A few days ago, my brother returned from *The Hague*, which, Taylor had to tell me, is a city in Holland. Today his Christmas card arrives.

On the front of his card is a cute kitten hugging the star at the top of a Christmas tree. Inside is the sentiment…

Jij staat bovenaan mijn lijst!
Prettige Feestdagen en een Gelukkig Nievw Jaar!

Below the holiday greeting, Taylor writes…

Boy—count on the Dutch to have a Christmas card that says… "Even though your husband turned out to be pond scum and your Christmas is ruined, you'll rise above it because you're a star!" (They can say that in so few words because they're a frugal people and it's a frugal language.) They also had a card that said "I'm still worrying about you" ("Juyk nievhr geglegge knickt das naar") but that didn't seem quite as Christmassy. So, I hope this card was worth the hour-and-a-half drive to your mailbox. I love you!

Taylor

I'm still laughing as I get a cookie from the tin my sister sent.

For as long as I can remember, my mom made cookies at Christmas. After I moved to Alaska, my mom sent these same Spritz cookies. Ellie continues the tradition.

But these aren't Christmas cookies; that is, they aren't trees and camels and wreaths. They are big, round cookies with clock faces. Numbers in pink frosting hug the perimeter and the hands indicate the hour and minute.

When we were kids, Mom made "clock" cookies to teach us how to tell time. That was when clocks only had faces. Now, for Christmas and birthdays, I get my mom's clock cookies from my sister.

I give the last small bite of this cookie to Molly, intently watching me, and I'm reminded of my first Christmas in Anchorage. While I was at work, my dog, Lisa, knocked the tin of cookies off the kitchen counter and ate the whole batch. I returned home to an empty tin on the floor and not a crumb anywhere. That year, Mom sent a second batch, which I kept in the cupboard.

I indulge in another cookie, breaking off a piece for Molly.

****

Everyone is tucked in for the night and I'm in my jammies. But because I don't feel bad enough, I read Brian's old cards. Last year's Christmas, last Valentine's, birthday cards he gave me this year. I read the cards he mailed in August and September, knowing he was with Michelle when he dropped these in the mailbox. I go into my head visualizing that so I won't linger in pretense.

I am so sad I can barely stand it. I miss Brian with gut-wrenching longing. It scares me to think what I would concede if he called, what I would do, what I would forget just to be with him on my sunny isle.

I snuggle beneath the covers; Alyx curls at my feet; Molly snoozes in her bed. The glow from the lights on the courtyard trees spills into the bedroom and illuminates my loneliness.

It's a little late to be grateful, I suppose, but I am. I'm grateful for the roof over my head and the food in my fridge. I'm grateful the animals are well and particularly grateful for Molly and Alyx who have been my constant companions through these horrible weeks. And I'm very grateful that I made it through, not only one more day, but *this* day. Last, I ask God to bless Brian.

The house is silent except for Molly's soft snoring. There is something infinitely comforting about a snoring dog. It takes me back to Nick and then Lisa. I wonder if I instinctively choose dogs who snore.

I feel like the phone should ring, as it did for so many years at this time of night.

Instead of sugarplums, I have visions of Brian and Michelle, cuddled beneath the covers. I imagine their words of love, their happiness at being together. It doesn't take much imagination; I was once there.

But now I'm here in a very large bed with my cat and my teddy bear...and my ghosts.

Christmas

I scrutinize my check register, examine my credit card statements, sort and separate expenses for my financial declaration. I put a "garage sale" value on our possessions.

I remember when all my *stuff* fit into the back of a Ford pick-up. I remember when I happily lived on $4,800 *a year*…

Now, the horses alone cost $1200 *a month*. I panic at the realization of supporting three horses when I haven't drawn a paycheck in thirteen years.

I think about my mom's china that I rarely set; about the Noritake *Blue Hills* collection my aunt Maisie gave me when I married. Both patterns cloistered in my cabinets because they are impractical for daily use, but I cannot part with either. I look around this house, at the Breyer horses I've had since childhood, now on my adult shelves.

I have artwork from college hanging on these walls—three prints I bought for $5 each during a fund-raiser. The artist is a professor who surely has passed on, but he lives through his art. I took the prints with me to Alaska, brought them to Arizona. They were my first pieces of "real" art. Now I have more art than I have walls, each piece attached to a moment in my life. And none can love me back.

Brian doesn't get attached. He couldn't care less about things except for comfort and functionality. He let me decorate our home as I wanted and I have to say, as I look around, this place is mostly me. Ironically.

Brian has possessions, but he's not attached. He upgrades when it suits him. A better car, a better boat, a better plane, a better…

That said, Brian is attached to one thing—his 1980 Corvette. It lives in the tractor barn, unlicensed and disconnected from its battery, powdered with dust. I fell in love with Brian in that car which is why **I** would keep it. I have no idea why Brian keeps it.

Maybe it reminds him of a time before funerals and grandchildren.

Now that he has Michelle, maybe he'll abandon the car.

****

"I will never do this again."

It's Christmas, five years ago. There is a mound of dirt in the corral and Chance is five feet under it.

Our Thanksgiving hosts, Felicity and Barry, have trailered over one of their horses so Petunia won't be alone…

After eighteen years in Alaska, stuck in a stall and paddock, Chance was supposed to enjoy many years of sun and warm and wide open spaces in Arizona. Truth be told, the main reason I moved to Juniper Verde was so Chance and Petunia could finally *be* horses. Chance's life in Arizona wasn't supposed to end after only fifteen months.

Felicity and I stood in the drizzle, watching Petunia and Sabrina get to know each other.

"You'll get another horse," Felicity said.

Numbed by my sudden loss, I knew better.

Felicity looked at me. "You love too much."

I heard Felicity's accusatory assessment and felt…anger.

How is it possible to love *too much*? How can you put limits on love, miserly rationed in appropriate doses? Love is nothing if not everything. It's every tick, every beat, every breath.

Love is…what love is. It shouldn't be controlled, like a simmering pot, fearful of boiling over.

Love done right has no regrets. There is grief, certainly, at loss—sometimes overwhelming grief that empties you. But while sorrow hollows, love comforts and eventually… *eventually*…fills us with gratitude for having the courage to love with such abandon, with such *hope,* when we know the future is uncertain.

Not loving doesn't insulate us from pain, it robs us of joy. We should all love *too much*, knowing that love's loss will absolutely devastate us. If we don't know that, *feel* that, then we don't love *enough…*

All that defiance ran through my head, but I knew I never wanted to hurt like that again. I would absolutely **not** get another horse.

With the help of my Fairbanks friend, Kay, I crawled through those dark weeks following Chance's death. I don't know how Kay did it, taking my phone calls day after day, listening to my sorrow, sharing my pain. But having suffered a similar loss when her horse, Domino, died, she was the only one who truly understood my despair.

One day I woke up, tired of being sad, knowing that if I didn't do something life-renewing, I would shrivel beyond revival. I had lost my dog; I had lost my horse. I was separated from Alaska and apart from Brian, who didn't seem concerned except for my rumblings about returning to Anchorage.

But Brian was adamant about Arizona, assuring me that he would be there more, insistent that our home was on this range.

So I turned to the one constant in my life.

****

It has rained most of the day. There was a brief break late afternoon and the sun beamed golden, Michelangelo rays, but then black clouds crowded together and heaven disappeared.

The horses rolled. Everything about them was muddy. But they are finally tucked in for the night, safe and dry in their stalls, in clean blankets, unless they decide to leave the barn and roll in mud again which horses like to do for reasons I don't understand.

I roasted a duck for dinner, knowing I will burn in hell for eating such an adorable creature, and mashed potatoes to go along with it. Most of it is in the refrigerator.

My brother called. My sister called. Brian didn't call.

Rain splatters the windows and the wind howls. The lights flicker.

Molly snoozes in her bed while Alyx paws the pile of cards and letters from Brian that I've pulled out from the bottom drawer of my dresser. These are my *receipts,* my *paper trail.* They are the proof of my relationship with Brian, but the courts view them as irrelevant.

There simply isn't room in the law for love.

Women keep love letters; men keep cancelled checks.

In the wake of that thought, I discover a business-size envelope lodged amongst a pile of early cards. On the back of the envelope, below the unsealed flap, is my handwriting...

> Check # 4203 Brian Willoughby $3963.35
> The Borealis Mining Company
> B Willoughby $10,000.00

Inside the envelope is a carbon of a cashier's check for $10,000 made out to Brian, a year before we married. In addition, I find an agreement for the "sale" of the Otter Bight beach house from Brian to me—collateral for the $10,000—but there's a caveat. I can't sell the property to anyone but Brian, and I have to sell it back to him when he wants it. Also in the envelope is a Xerox copy of a check written to me buying back my stock in The Borealis Mining Company for $463.01. I invested almost $4,000 in The Borealis Mining Company, which Brian owned. Three years later, I got back less than $500. That's called *being in love and going broke.*

But it's the cashier's check that surprises me—actually, it all surprises me. How could I have forgotten the $10,000? Not only did I give Brian a place to live, with food and clothes, I also gave him money.

And our agreement? Even back then, I knew "buying" property I can't do anything with is not a real sale. Obviously, Brian didn't trust me to return Otter Bight to him. Why didn't I see the inequity in our relationship? All of that trust going out, none of it returning. I'm trying to remember...*when did I give Otter Bight back?*

I set that question aside and return to my cards. If I have forgotten all of this, could I have forgotten something else?

Starting at the beginning, I slide card after card from its envelope and read what Brian wrote inside. Each promise of *forever* stabs my heart. I grab a handful of tissues and keep going. I open a card from our anniversary ten years ago and my heart pounds...

> Normally, I write lots of words to say "I love you"
> but this time I need to put down in words my future

actions which show I want you beside me. Why don't I start fully funding the household account? You take care of the animals and pitch in when you're able, but if not, when we are old, just take care of me! Naturally, if the pets need help, I'll assist. Love you more. B/W

I knew it wasn't my imagination that Brian offered to support me so I wouldn't go back to work, but I didn't remember that he put it in writing.

Now he doesn't want a dependent.

I return the card to its envelope and set it aside. I finish reading the remainder of the cards. When I'm done, I have six cards with paperclips and potential—promises Brian made to me that will now be used against him.

I think of Christmas…and crucifixion.

None of this is merry.

Returning to my question about Otter Bight, I sit at the computer and Google *Alaskan deeds*. Minutes later, I'm in the website for the Department of Natural Resources. After I type in my maiden name, several deeds come up. I find the quitclaim deed when Otter Bight was put in my name, and then I find the deed when the beach house went back to Brian, **four years later**.

I owned the property **during** our marriage.

I'm stunned by my amnesia. I remember the *exact moment* when our eyes first locked, but I didn't remember the $10,000 or the length of time I "owned" Otter Bight?

Quirkier still, I have that check carbon.

Had it been up to me, I would've written a personal check, but as the moment returns, I vaguely remember that Brian wanted a *cashier's* check, probably because they don't leave a trail—*unless you keep the carbon*. The irony is, had I written a check, I doubt I would have it today. In fact, I doubt I have any of my bank account records going back twenty-plus years. But for some reason, I stuck this information in an envelope and put it with Brian's cards.

Then I forgot about it.

I don't care what anyone says, there are angels who guide our hands, angels who whisper, *put the check carbon in with your cards.*

Beth will be thrilled with all this evidence supporting my story. But I'm not kidding myself. This is just a chip in the pre-nup wall.

Back at the *search* prompt, I type in Brian's name.

****

Every life has a destiny.

It's hard to grasp that sometimes, when one destiny is woven into another destiny and it's difficult to tell which is which. But, months after Chance died and the fog of my grief began lifting, I had an amazing revelation.

Life is not always about me.

That's not easy to accept when it *feels* like it's about me, when my tears are drenching the pillow, and the suffering is mine. But sometimes we are the ship and not the waves. When the seas calm, we sail on.

Chance taught me many wonderful lessons but his last, and maybe most important lesson is this…

Sometimes we do everything right and stuff still happens.

It should be embroidered on a pillow…

Sometimes we do everything right and stuff still happens.

Whatever my emotions after Chance died, I didn't have regret. Oh, sure, there were a few *what if* moments, but they never became sunflower seeds nor I, a squirrel. I loved Chance and did everything right, not only that night but for the seven years prior.

Which doesn't mean I did everything perfectly. It simply means, when I look at the whole of our time together, I was there.

Even with bubble-wrap and a crystal ball, we don't have the power to prevent another's fate.

The vet called it a *catastrophic colic,* and beyond help. As I knelt on the cold ground that night, stroking Chance's head, pleading for a miracle, I felt the unraveling of our weave.

Chance went out on the trail without me, in the darkest of hours on the holiest of days, and I could not stop him.

However much we love, however long we love, eventually we come to a fork.

Conventional wisdom says, if we have loved well, and without regret, our loss at that fork will be immense, but we will let go and walk our future path in peace.

If we have **not** loved well, we will be forever tethered to that fork with *what ifs*, unable to make peace with our mistakes, hoarding the past, fearing the outcome might have changed had we done something differently.

We can't change what is not ours to change, and those forks are unpredictable, but until we reach them, our task is simple…

Cut our hair, sell our watch, and love *too much*.

****

I can't believe my computer screen and the dozens of deeds in Brian's name. Before our marriage and during. Deeds with only his name; deeds in partnership with others. Some names I recognize, others I don't. Property transferred and property sold, most of which I know nothing about. *Money* I know nothing about.

How do I reconcile this man on the screen with the man who writes my cherished cards?

And yet, I'm not sure whether I'm more shocked at Brian or at myself for being so totally clueless and trusting. All the years I housed him, clothed him, fed him because I thought he was struggling; all the years I drained my inheritance trying to be a contributing partner in this marriage while being the wife Brian asked for; all the time thinking we were travelling this path together while believing he was taking care of me, only to discover that he was just plain *taking* me…down the *garden* path.

How do I accept the sharp edges and broken parts hidden beneath a synthetic softness when all these years I loved someone I believed to be *Real*?

December 28

The front door opens; Abbie peeks in and asks for a hairdryer. My electrical wiring is wet and that's why my courtyard fountain isn't sprinkling.

Lucy and Abbie arrived yesterday and leave tomorrow. On a quick tour of Arizona and New Mexico, they stopped to see me.

"It must be wonderful having someone who knows how to fix stuff," I tell Lucy after Abbie is back outside with my hairdryer.

Lucy giggles like a teenager.

Abbie and Lucy have been "Abbie and Lucy" for two years; they met at a Goodwill in Atlanta when they simultaneously dropped off donations. Lucy is a yoga wisp with cascading spirals of silver hair that I envy. Abbie is statuesque and ten years younger. I guess that makes Lucy a cougar.

"I had a hard time with it at first," Lucy says of the age difference. "Abbie is in such great shape and, let's face it, fifty-eight years of gravity take a toll. I didn't sleep with her for months because I didn't want her to see me naked."

I laugh. I don't know why, but I just expect *more* from a lesbian.

✱✱✱✱✱✱✱✱✱

My mom left my father on the Saturday before Thanksgiving.

Retired from his job with USAID, my father had been home for about six months and was now a university professor. Taylor was away at college; living at home, Ellie was a freshman at SIU where my father and mother taught.

Having given up all hope for a divorce and thus an escape from my father, I was totally shocked when my mom gathered Ellie and me and told us she was leaving.

The minutes after were frenzied; there wasn't time for questions. My father was at the hardware store and would be back shortly. Mom packed clothes and personal items in a manageable cardboard box then tied it with twine. Agreeing on the story to tell *Daddy,* we hugged good-bye. Using the knotted intersection of twine as a handle, Mom picked up her box and walked out the door.

She didn't take a suitcase or a car, afraid that doing either would somehow contradict what we were to tell our father. We had no idea where she was going or what would happen next. More like a younger sibling than a parent, Mother had never provided protection; for that reason, we didn't consider that we would now be alone with the man who made our life hell, but were instead jubilant at the prospect of our freedom once Mom came back for us. Which we thought would be soon. Ellie and I repeated our story then went about our day waiting for the inquisition.

I was fifteen and a sophomore in high school.

My mom was forty-eight and had been married twenty-five years.

****

I'm at the barn when Leigh, my former riding instructor, calls from Anchorage to wish me a happy new year. "I assume Brian is there for the holidays."

I have a nano-second to decide my answer. "No. We're getting a divorce."

Silence. I wonder if Leigh's going to tell me about my husband dancing with a blond.

"Well, I can't say I'm surprised."

Oh, great. Can't one of my friends be just a little shocked? "Why aren't you surprised?"

"Well, Brian seemed pretty content to have you down there and he didn't appear in any hurry to be there with you."

Leigh's assessment of my marriage simmers in my mind as I finish my late afternoon horse chores; it's there as I head back to the house. Still there when Lucy and I talk after dinner.

Giving Lucy and me time alone, Abbie is reading in the larger guest bedroom while we make Toll House cookies as we did a lifetime ago in Anchorage when we were young, unattached career women. I met Lucy at an interview; we'd applied for the same job. And thus began a beautiful friendship. She helped me move my meager possessions from a rental into my new condo. Wrestling my king mattress up two flights of stairs to my first mortgage, we couldn't stop laughing; I was "Ethel" to her Lucy.

By the way, Lucy got the job. But it worked out. Soon after, I was hired as controller for a large psychiatric hospital. *Willoughby Wickham & Steele*, Brian's law firm, served as legal counsel. One morning, Brian walked into my office. And yes, time does stop. Twenty-six years later, that eye-locking moment is as perfectly preserved in my memory as a photograph in a frame.

While the cookies bake, I tell Lucy about Leigh's phone call. "All these years I've been walking around with spinach in my teeth and everyone saw it but me."

"How could you, and survive? You had to be in some state of denial to be way out here, alone. You couldn't think about what might be going on in Alaska or you'd go crazy."

"But I knew…when the photographs were missing."

"You had the horses to think about. You had no job, no money, no support group. You're no different from a woman with kids. It's not like you could abandon the animals. Truthfully, I don't know how you managed all by yourself."

✳✳✳✳✳✳✳✳✳✳

I never really thought about what my mom went through that night after she walked away from our home; never considered all the thoughts that crowded her head as she rode the Illinois Central from Carbondale to Champaign and back again. She didn't go to a hotel or rely on friends. There were no women's shelters, although, knowing Mom, she wouldn't have admitted her problems to strangers, let alone sought help. She just rode the train, alone, until dawn.

After her round-robin, she walked to her office at the university where she stayed until she rented a room from Mrs. Tenofsky.

I can only imagine now, forty years later, the fear that drove her from that house; the torment she felt leaving her kids behind with a violent man, knowing she had abandoned us and worrying what might happen because of her escape.

I can imagine her guilt as she defied her parents, her faith, and even her God, to save herself.

I can only *now* appreciate how scared and *desperate* she must have been to close that door behind her.

New Year's Day

Pouring the last of the eggnog into my coffee, I sit on the sofa and watch *Leave it to Beaver* while I wait for the sunrise, an hour away. Beaver has the lead in his 3rd grade school play—

I cock my ear toward the windows then mute the television.

Whooo...whooo...whooo.

Albert.

Ah-who-who. Who-who. Who-who. Who-who.

And Victoria.

I've been listening to Albert and Victoria for three years. In the wild, great horned owls live an average of twenty years; the oldest known was twenty-eight. In captivity, they can survive much longer. The San Francisco Zoo had a great horned owl who lived fifty years. But, if the choice was hers, would she have traded those extra thirty years to be free, like Albert and Victoria? Is the moon on your wings worth a missed meal? Even with all the uncertainty outside the cage, is independence better?

I hope so, but it's too early for anything profound. I unmute the sound, sip coffee, and return to the carefree Fifties.

Ward comes home, as Ward always does, and joins June in the living room where she is sewing Beaver's costume. "What's this?"

"Beaver's bill," June answers.

"His bill?"

"Oh, Ward, you knew he was playing a bird."

"What kind of bird?"

"A canary."

"A *yellow* canary?"

"A **yellow** canary."

"Huh." Ward is obviously disappointed. "Why couldn't he play something with a little more meat on his bones, like an eagle…?"

In the end, Beaver is neither a canary nor an eagle, but a mushroom; he trades costumes with Whitey. Turns out, being a canary is more challenging than being a mushroom; no one expects a mushroom to fly or sing—or risk life and wing for miners.

Although I tried to avoid profundity, profundity has found *me*. We accept our assigned roles as if they are real, when all we have to do is swap costumes. We can choose who we will be—canary, mushroom, or something else. We soar or we dwell in shadow—our decision—although we too often think we have no voice. It was a young Queen-to-be Elizabeth who said, "I should like to be a horse."

As Beaver climbs up the billboard in the next iconic episode, then falls into the giant bowl that's part of the canned soup advertisement, I try to live in this moment, in *only* this moment, where I am okay. For each second of each minute, I live in just this moment, then, after the fire department rescues Beaver and he is once again in everyone's good graces, I dress and head down to the barn with pears for the horses.

Three hours later, with dark clouds rolling in, I'm back at the house.

I put away all the photos of Brian.

My brother calls; my sister calls; Brian doesn't call.

I finally answer Shannon's e-mail from two weeks ago.

Hi Shannon:

Well, your e-mail made me cry (I'm doing a lot of that lately). This is really hard and every day my heart breaks a little more. I love all of you so much and I feel like I'm losing my whole family. I love your dad very, very much, but sometimes things aren't fixable and I fear this is one of those situations. I do believe something good is waiting at the end of the darkness. I can't quite see that far ahead (and I can't find my flashlight), so I just have to believe.

I hope you guys had a wonderful Christmas and here's wishing you a happy new year. Hugs to all. K

****

My father didn't call the police.

Again, one of those puzzle pieces I never saw until now.

Returning from the hardware store with a new shovel, my father asked where our mother was. Ellie and I told him we didn't know; she said she was going out, but didn't say where. We didn't see her leave, didn't notice she hadn't taken a car.

If my father thought we were lying, he didn't let on. As the hours passed into days and Mother never returned, he repeatedly questioned us. He must have suspected we knew something because, although we appeared worried, we never suggested calling the police, either.

That Thanksgiving, we had Swanson turkey dinners in front of the TV.

January 4

Monogamy-challenged.

This is the term I've chosen for my husband's philandering. Now when asked what happened to our marriage I will say, "My husband is monogamy-challenged."

Or, I suppose, when asked the question—and I'm always asked—I can lean into the person and say in a confidential tone, "My husband is a *philanderist.*"

Either way, I will no longer have to be crude or tactful about his wandering dick or his affair.

I'm expecting the American Psychiatric Association to declare *serial cheating* a legitimate mental disorder now that celebrity sufferers like Tiger Woods and Jesse James scurry into rehab after their affliction becomes public.

Philanderists will likely become a protected class.

January 5

Brian and Michelle were in Port Townsend over Christmas, but returned to Anchorage for New Year's so Michelle could see her kids.

"She didn't see her kids on Christmas?" I ask Jill after her update.

"I'm pretty sure the kids are living with her husband. But I'm getting that second-hand, you realize. I've never talked to the woman and I have no intention of doing so."

I bask in the loyalty of my friend, but... "Archie is one of Brian's oldest friends. At some point you may need to socialize with her."

"I absolutely **refuse** to be in the same room with either Brian or Michelle. And Archie knows that. Nothing is going to change my mind."

"Well, okay…and bless you! But, if something happens, I'm okay with it."

Jill repeats her assurances and I let it go, grateful that, for the moment, her wagon is still in my circle.

****

About two weeks after my mom's *disappearance*, two police officers came to our front door and served my father with divorce papers.

When my parents split, vanilla divorce didn't exist; *blame* had to be assigned. The complaint cited my father for mental and physical cruelty.

So, when a 15-year-old girl looking like a Jehovah's Witness answered the door, what did the officers think?

Did I mention that my father made his daughters wear boyish, button down shirts and long skirts, and that, when we became teens, he forbade make-up and demanded that we keep our hair long and pulled back?

If ever there was a moment I might've asked for help, *that* would've been the moment. I could've begged the officers to *please, please, please* take me and Ellie with them.

But I couldn't leave Max, our dog.

****

"And to think I was feeling sorry for him, all alone on Christmas, walking the land. I hope he falls into a really deep pit!"

I *still* haven't tapped into, as Lucy says, my dark side, so I'm grateful Ellie has tapped into hers.

"I was feeling sorry for him, too. I should've known better," I say.

I think of Brian and Michelle in Port Townsend; I know the hotel they stayed at. I imagine them on *our* land, walking the trails Brian and *I* were supposed to ride with Teena and Quinn. I wonder if they met *our* builder and discussed *our* house.

It's really humbling to be so easily replaced…like a burnt-out light bulb.

"Something good is going to come out of this," Ellie assures me. "I just know it."

January 7

"You need a hysterectomy."

Still disbelieving my next *something good* that Ellie promised me, I'm driving home after my annual smear, me and the Bee Gees in my own little pity-party. I hadn't even processed *cervical polyps*— which explain my recent excruciating cramps—before Melanie, my doctor, recommended surgery.

I think about losing my uterus at the same time I'm losing my husband.

It's not that I'm overly attached to my uterus—I mean, it's never harbored life—but somehow this *change* seems poignant.

Or perhaps Providence is testing my sense of humor.

I dread the hospital stay and weeks of recovery. Then I see the silver lining. What every great love story needs—a crisis to re-unite the hero and heroine.

****

I called the number several times only to get the same generic recording.

Seven months had passed since Nick died, three since Chance, and I was grasping for a lifeline. But why would someone advertise Border Collie puppies using a disconnected phone? Certain the Juniper Verde Times incorrectly printed the number, I called the Classifieds' desk.

"Are you looking in the animal section or the free section?" the woman at the newspaper asked.

"I'm looking in the *free* section…but…there's an *animal* section?"

As the woman checked the phone number, I turned the page past the jobs and the houses-for-sale and found the pet listings. *Duh.* But finding no Border Collies, my eyes drifted from the dogs to the livestock…

GELDING UNREGISTERED. 2 year old Belgian/QH cross, big & gentle, suitable for 4H project…

The woman came back on the line. "That's the phone number in the file. I don't know why it's disconnected."

I thanked her and hung up. I let my thoughts simmer…

****

At home, I press the blinking message light.

> *Hi Hon. Hey, it's me…in Alaska. We need to talk about how much money you need for January. Give me a call at the office or on my cell. Talk to you soon. Bye-bye. I hope you have a nice day.*

Brian sounds cheerful, like nothing crazy is going on between us. I don't call him back at his office or on his cell, but instead leave a message at the house and discover that my outdated greeting is still on our voicemail…

You've reached the home of Brian and Kate, Nick, Alyx, and Chance…

I tell him I'll call when I know what the bills are. I quickly mention the Gator and the estimate for fixing it. I tell him about the new pain meds I need for Petunia. I don't sound cheerful. I don't wish him a nice day.

I change clothes and head to the barn for afternoon chores. The left rear tire on the Gator is halfway to the ground. I slide into the seat, flick the ignition, and…nothing.

****

"He's a PMU," Sally told me about the Belgian in her ad.

I knew immediately I was in trouble. I was very familiar with the plight of the PMU or *Premarin* foals, a *by-product* of a process that collects pregnant mares' urine as the main ingredient in the menopause hormone drug. Most of these foals had been sent undetected by the public radar to overseas slaughter until two decades ago when animal-rights groups began making a stink about the inhumane horrors of the pharmaceutical industry.

Because of ongoing bad publicity, some Premarin farms were allowing adoption of their foals, instead of selling them for butcher. Years ago, before I had a single thought that I might ever be without Chance, I knew that if another horse came into my life, it would come from a Premarin farm. Sally was part of one rescue group who had trailered foals from Canada.

But unlike the rest of his buddies, this guy hadn't found a home. Now, it was a year and a half later.

I made an appointment to see Sally's *almost* 2-year-old Belgian-Quarter Horse cross on Friday, four days away, but I warned her that I was just looking.

"Will you call before you come? Then I can clean him up before you get here."

"Sure. But, you don't need to clean him up," I told Sally. "I can see through dirt."

****

Brian is playing poker tonight. I'm reading the e-mail with the time and place and Brian's reply that he'll be there.

I scroll down and open an e-mail from Alaska Airlines confirming Brian's flight to Seattle on January 11, with a return on the night of January 13. *That's odd.* I assume he's going to our property in Port Townsend, but he does that over a weekend, not during the week. This time he's going on a Sunday, returning late on a Tuesday. Weirder still, he was just there over Christmas.

I open the last new e-mail. Michelle will be in town on Friday.

****

I ask Molly to come and eat the scattered morsels of her food I've spilled on the pantry floor. She looks at me like I'm asking her to jump off a cliff...into quicksand.

"Molly, come here **now**."

She gets off her bed and eases closer, but not enough to see the spilled food.

"Molly! Come here."

She lowers her head and wags her tail, but keeps her distance.

Incensed by Molly's defiance, I drag her by the scruff across the tile toward the pantry. She growls at me and then snaps.

I smack her across the mouth. She bares her teeth in a frenzied warning and I jerk back. Insane with anger, I'm about to kick her.

Her warning escalates. She advances toward me in a quivering dance of fear and courage…

This dog who loves me, who shares my life, who depends on me for survival, will fight tooth and nail to protect herself from *me*.

All that's missing from this moment is a baton.

Tears flowing, I collapse to my knees. Molly speeds to me, ears back, her tongue lapping my face. I hug her and hold her, begging forgiveness, promising never again to hit.

It's alright, she tells me. *Shit happens.*

She smiles and forgives, relieved to have me back. She happily wiggles and twists within my arms while her tongue cleans up the mess of my life.

It's okay, she tells me again. *It's okay. But just because shit happens, doesn't mean you become that shit.*

January 8

The needle pierces the delicate skin beneath my eyes. Dr. Conner presses the plunger on the syringe, filling the hollows. He pulls out the needle, barely moves it, and pricks again.

"Breathe," he tells me. "It hurts less if you breathe."

He wipes away the blood that beads at each prick as he continues down my tear track. Then he plumps my smile lines.

I wipe the icy sweat from my palms onto my jeans.

Dr. Conner hands me a mirror. "You might get some bruising but that should be gone before your trip."

I look past the blotches and the pricks and see a face that looks better than it did a half hour ago. Still fifty-three, but less tortured and hollow.

"Are you ready to do your lips or do you need a few minutes?"

I take a deep breath. *Needles in my lips…this will be fun…*

Maybe one day, what's inside will be more important than what's outside.

But not in two weeks.

****

A snow-white spot was on the top of her head. The rest of her was salt and pepper with random patches of black. A mask surrounded her bright, caramel-colored eyes and the tips of her ears casually flopped.

But it had been over thirty years since I'd had a puppy and this little girl was only twelve weeks old. I thought about the chewing and the accidents on the carpet and all that growing energy I would have to exercise.

Yet, her unbridled joy was impossible to resist. After losing Nick and Chance, I desperately needed that joy.

In late February, two days before my appointment with Sally and her Belgian-cross, I took Molly home from the Juniper Verde Humane Shelter and life began anew.

****

The ringing phone wakes me from my evening nap on the couch. I steel myself as Brian asks about the monthly expenses and the money I need.

"Did you get the information on where the fifty-five hundred was spent?"

"It went to the same place it always goes."

"That's not a lot of detail, Kate."

"Well, I'll see what I can do."

"I don't think that's asking too much."

"Well, Brian, it goes to the same place it always goes. There's nothing new...on the monthly stuff."

"It would still be nice to get some detail, Kate—"

"Okay—"

"It's **my** money, isn't it? So...don't you think I deserve some detail? What were your personal expenses? Don't I get a detail on that either?"

"I don't think I had much in personal expenses."

"Well it would be nice to know. It doesn't seem too much to ask—"

"O-kay!"

Seconds silently tick. Then Brian says, "I have to talk to an attorney since your attorney won't talk to me without one. It's ludicrous that I need an attorney. I AM an attorney! This is going to cost me six hundred dollars, which is the same as you want for Petunia. I'm glad you've had a course in economics. Anyway, I'd like to have some detail on the money you're spending."

"Anything else?

"No."

I wait for the good-bye…

"Did you actually come up here?"

"You mean over New Year's? No. I thought that was a little silly under the circumstances."

"I was wondering why you didn't call me and come over to the house and get some of your stuff, so I guess that's the reason."

I think about Brian and Michelle celebrating New Year's Eve.

"Okay, that's fine, just e-mail some detail, some information, a list of the payables. You said you're going to fix the Gator? I thought you said you were going to get a battery for it."

"I'm going to fix the tire on it. I put air in and it goes flat."

"Did you take it over to the tire shop?"

"I can't get it off the Gator, so I guess the answer is no."

"How're you going to get it off the Gator?"

"I'm **not** going to get it off the Gator. I'm going to have them come out and replace the tire."

"You think that's the most economical way—"

"YES, it's the most economical way of doing things, Brian."

"Why is that the most economical way?"

"I'm sitting down here and I have to deal with that tire every day. I've used that fix-it gunk at least three times and it's not holding air. And I'm not dealing with it anymore."

"Well, I really don't think that's the most economical—"

"I don't care! I'm down here, alone, doing everything—"

"Kate, I'd switch places with you in a heartbeat."

"Yeah, fine, let's not do this, alright?"

"I'm just saying we're both in places we don't want to be. You can move any day you want and I'll help you. So if you find a better place to go, just tell me. I'd love to have you outta there."

"Well, talk to my attorney. I'm sure we can work something out."

"I did try to talk to your attorney and she's not even in Anchorage. Do you know that? She's in Ireland."

"I'm sure she's coming back." I breathe. "I'll send you some detail on the expense. Anything else?"

"I'm warning you, the well is not that deep. We don't have the kind of money you think we have. So I ask you to be as economical as possible."

"Well, we certainly have enough money for Michelle."

"Okay, Kate, if that's the way you want to be."

"The way **I** want to be? You take no responsibility for anything you do—"

"Kate— I'm talking about two different things. I'm talking about economics and personal relationships…personal desires—"

"So…paying for Michelle's trip down to Scottsdale—that's *personal*. But paying for the Gator is *economic*."

"That's exactly right."

"Interesting. Why don't you pretend you're getting the Gator fixed for *her*."

"Why don't **you** figure out some way to get off **my** property? You're not doing anything good for that property. So take your little animals and go! You don't want to be there. I don't want you there. There should be a compromise to get you **out**. You're the only one who can come up with that idea. I can't—"

I hang up, then click the *off* button on my tape recorder.

January 9

Equus magazine wants to publish my short story, *The Rescue of Roxanne*. And the cherry on my sundae? They're paying me $50. That will cover 17 minutes of Beth's time.

I also get an e-mail from Brian, responding to my long e-mail with the detail on the monthly expenditures. Paragraph after paragraph of detail, after which I thanked him for paying the bills.

He writes back asking for *more* detail: A cash disbursements journal; an accounts payable list; a detail of the credit card by expense category. He wants me to board the horses and move off the ranch. He thinks the cost of fixing the Gator is too high. He tells me to send all the bills to him.

I am so pissed I could spit nails. Phoning Beth, I rant about what a jerk my husband is. She agrees, then tells me to send the bills to Brian.

****

"He likes you," Sally told me. "See how he stops beside you?"

I stood outside the round pen; inside Sally worked her Belgian-cross. "He probably does that with everyone," I said.

"He doesn't. He knows he's supposed to keep going, but with you he stops each time."

I looked at the almost-2-year-old, his rear jacked up like a hot rod because of still-growing, uneven bones. He looked back at me with soft, come-hither eyes.

"I'm really not in the market for a horse," I told her. "I was actually looking for a dog when I saw your ad. The truth is, I lost my horse on Christmas and I'm not sure I'm ready."

Sally didn't push. There was a teenage girl also considering him so I shouldn't worry.

I stood by the sorrel who had a blaze and three white socks. "Does he have a name?"

"Well, we had to call him something, so we named him Quincy. Quinn for short."

Like… *Quinn the Eskimo?*

****

"He didn't recognize Brian's name," Jill tells me. She's in her car, having just delivered my letter to Kevin Wright, Michelle's husband. "He said he had put all this behind him and really didn't want to dredge it up. But he'll read your letter and think about it. He was very nice."

"I'm sure he didn't see this letter coming. That's gotta give you pause, I would think."

"Like I said, he's very nice."

"What's he look like?"

"Tall, slim, dark hair…early forties. Good looking man. I doubt he's lonely."

****

I found Ben in the alley behind our Illinois house right before my 13th birthday. He was one of those hound pups with no distinguishing characteristics other than being a sweet, loveable guy who didn't have a lot of expectations. I'd had him for seven months when my father, on his last assignment for USAID and home from Ecuador for a month at Christmas, raged against my mother for allowing me to have Ben without asking his permission.

Like the Gestapo in *Sophie's Choice,* he made me choose—whom do I forsake? Ben? Or Max, our German shepherd, whom we'd had for two years.

Pick one or lose both.

Tears streaming down my face, I held Ben tightly as a shelter worker tried to pry him out of my arms while my mother told the receptionist that Ben was a stray we'd had only a few days.

Yet, I held onto the hope that my father would relent and bring Ben home. He'd made his point—I, and those I loved, were at his mercy. How deep did he need to drive it? But as each day ended and still no Ben, I cried myself to sleep. When my father discovered my bedtime tears, he gave away Carmen, my cat.

I'm haunted by that 13th Christmas—by my helplessness; by the *insane* cruelty of my father; by my mother's cowardice. That's when I vowed, *never again* to abandon an animal.

After that—for over thirty years—no one saw me cry. I simply endured like the wounded horses who break my heart.

When I was seventeen and a college freshman, I went to the Humane Shelter in search of a happy ending for Ben, hoping he'd been adopted. I didn't find the records I needed, but I found purpose. Two years after that, living with my college boyfriend, I picked Lisa out of a large litter that came into the shelter on a day I was volunteering.

A shepherd-collie mix, Lisa was my best friend for seventeen years, outlasting all the men in my life but Brian. Two peas, that dog and I.

During my last semester of graduate school, while I was interviewing for jobs in Dallas, Lisa escaped from the boarding kennel. After returning home, I scoured the area, put ads in the paper, cried myself to sleep. For three days, she was missing and then, on the third night, I had a dream so real, it was. Lisa was home, sitting on the little grassy knoll outside my front door. I woke, opened the front door, and there she was, *exactly* as I had dreamed. To get home, she had crossed a major freeway and the Little Muddy River, but there she was.

When I moved to Alaska, I planned to leave Lisa with my mom until my Christmas visit, not wanting to drag her along on a two-week road trip. Together, we would fly back to Anchorage. But every time I opened the door of my truck, Lisa climbed inside and curled on the seat. Every time. We drove the Alcan together.

Lisa was my mirror and my shadow—a relationship I'll have forever.

Nick was a big powder puff who loved everyone. If a lap was available, he was there. Never mind that his eighty pounds hung over the sides, he wanted to be close. An adoptee from Anchorage

Animal Control, he looked pedigreed, with a thick black coat accented by caramel markings on his face and paws. Just plain handsome. He lived by the motto *if you throw it, I will fetch.*

I knew of only one person Nick didn't like. One Saturday I took Nick with me to my Anchorage office where he barked and growled at a maintenance worker. The guy turned out to be a thief, later stealing tools and equipment from the business.

In Arizona, Nick's hind legs gave out. When surgery wasn't successful, I had braces custom-made for his legs and he was once again a dog. While chasing a rabbit, he suffered a heart attack. I will always remember his last moments, the soft fading of his eyes telling me he was sorry, but he had to leave.

Now I have Molly, a dog so independent, I feel like *she* adopted *me*. But every now and then she does the heroic, like chasing coyotes from her territory and refusing to leave my side when I'm sick. Accepting no substitute, she forces me off the couch to take her outside so she can piddle.

And she is exceedingly kind to Alyx, allowing her to curl in the middle of her large dog bed while Molly hugs the edge so as not to drive Alyx away.

After Molly had emergency surgery to repair a hind leg gored by a javelina, the vet called. I had to take Molly home early; she wouldn't let anyone near to care for her. When I arrived, she happily came to me and I carried her to the car. But for all that attachment, she isn't a cuddler, preferring her own space. She will join me on the couch, as long as I don't crowd her.

I marvel at Molly, meeting every challenge, going beyond her forty pounds. She owns the world, this dog, and she will fight to keep it. In the next instant, she is lapping my tears, telling me to get up, pity time is over; life won't wait.

Here they are, the seasons of my life.

With Ben I was born; he showed me my path.

Lisa was mine and I was hers; we lived simply, from one adventure to the next.

Nick was (almost) everyone's buddy, happily part of a large extended pack.

And now, in autumn, I have Molly who belongs to no one but herself.

The funny thing is, I thought I adopted, again and again, the same dog.

So, in winter, should I live to see it, who will I be then?

January 12

The computer screen prompts me for Brian's online ID. I take a few stabs, but no cigar.

I scroll down to the *passcode* box, sip my morning tea, and try my guesses there. Hesitant, I tap my fingers as I consider the consequences, then click the prompt for resetting the passcode.

The screen asks for the last four digits of Brian's social security number. Then his credit card number. *Thank you, Brian* for e-mailing it to Michelle.

It asks for the three numbers on back, the expiration date, and billing zip code. After the information is accepted, the security question pops up.

What high school did you attend?

A smile and seven keystrokes later, the screen reveals Brian's online ID, *KateRene930*—my first and middle names *and* the name on the side of his 30-foot boat—plus our anniversary date.

Will he re-name his boat *Michelle*?

The screen wants a new passcode. After I oblige, it displays my options.

I don't scrutinize each *Visa* statement now; instead, I *print* before Providence changes its mind.

The world is pale lilac, reminding me of the blooms I grew in Anchorage that the moose loved to eat. Soon the sun will burn off all color and the air will be bright and clear as crystal.

Taking a break from sleuthing, I toss out sunflower seeds from my back deck. Squirrels, chipmunks, and birds appear like woodland critters in a Disney animation. I raise the lid on the gas barbeque grill, jerk back, and swing it down.

Returning to the grill with my camera, I again lift the lid but slowly, then immediately snap three photos of the packrat among the beginning twigs and grasses of her nest. It's not the first time I've found a nest, which is why I periodically check, but I've never caught one in progress. Not exactly a bear at the birdfeeder, my little homemaker is a novelty nonetheless.

Packrats are amazing opportunists. They nest in anything. And they are tenacious. Last fall I moved a pair from the enclosed space surrounding the hot tub after they had gained access through a water hose hole in the wood paneling. I have no idea how long they had been inside that enclosure living the good life, but judging by what I had to clean up, I'm guessing a couple of years. Then there's the Gator and the hundreds of dollars in repairs because of chewed wires. Still, they are adorable, with round bodies, round faces, round ears and yes, huge, round, come-hither eyes.

Also called wood rats and trade rats, my packrats look nothing like the cone-head, beady-eye rats in horror movies or in sewers or in laboratories; in fact, they are **not** rats, but *voles*. Last August I stumbled across a naked newborn that had somehow escaped the nest. When I picked him up, he strongly objected in a high-pitched scream that could stop traffic. I held him in the palm of my hand and marveled at fragile eyelids seamed together with the delicacy of an Amish stitch, and pink, translucent ears flush to his head. That's when I noticed the nick, in the shape of a Cheshire grin, along the outside of his left ear. But he was beyond adorable; he looked like an incongruent mix of a mini-Winston Churchill and the sweetest puppy, but with an extra-long tail and hand-like feet that latched onto my finger. Totally blind, he nonetheless tried to wiggle away. I thought… *Where do you think you're going? You can't survive with your eyes closed...*

I don't know why nature is so cute. The squirrels, the chipmunks, the bunnies, the mice, the birds—especially the downy babies; the incredibly trusting fledglings that grip my finger as I climb the ladder to the rafters where I redundantly return them as they learn to fly. Even the tarantulas, snakes and toads have charm.

But I was talking about packrats…

When hot tubs, barbeques, and vehicles aren't available, packrats build the most incredible homes, mostly around fallen junipers. Called *middens,* they remind me of beaver dams—heaping mounds of sticks and natural debris, some rising three feet and spreading five feet. Inside is a maze of rooms used for food storage, nesting, and garbage. Behind the tractor barn, a midden has been created from a stack of leftover fireplace stones; atop this pile are horse apples applied like a roof.

Packrats, like ravens and women, love bling. They will decorate their homes with anything shiny and reflective—soda cans, glass, Mylar candy wrappers, aluminum foil. For little guys weighing less than two pounds, they have astounding construction skills.

Although packrats brilliantly use cactus to discourage trespassers, middens aren't Fort Knox and other animals, like snakes, invite themselves in. Which is why, given the opportunity, packrats would rather move into something akin to a luxury high-rise, such as a barbecue grill. Knowing life is uncertain, I hesitate to move someone out of a safe spot. But I have to set boundaries, or packrats will be swinging from the chandeliers and raiding the refrigerator.

Still, it's hard for me.

What I fear most, I think, is a life lived in vain. I look for fainting robins just to help them back unto their nests. If there's a breaking heart or an aching life, I am so there.

But it's exhausting living as if the world teeters on what I do. And I'm thinking… maybe I should stop…or at least, cut back. It's arrogant to think I am **that** important in the labyrinth of life, that I really make a difference. It's just plain craziness that I am forever following the Universe and straightening up after it.

I walk a tightrope between interfering and not. But, really, there's no such thing. It's simply a matter of degree and decision.

Holding blind baby *Winston,* I was tempted to raise him, thinking how much fun it would be to see a packrat grow up. Then I thought about the midnight feedings and the dirty bedding and trying to keep him safe from Alyx and Molly.

Common sense prevailed and I gently put Winston back where I found him—in the space below the passenger seat in the chassis of the Gator.

****

Before I begin my morning chores, I must tidy up the crime scene. Fortunately, it's only 5:30 in Anchorage; Brian is still asleep and nowhere near his office. In his e-mail *In* box, I open the new message from Bank of America notifying him of a passcode change.

After I hit delete—and go into his trash file and permanently delete—I take a gander at the new e-mails, opening the message from AT&T. I hit the link that takes me to his account. I've been here before, but my access was thwarted by the unknown password. I type in KateRene930…

Before all my sleuthing, I had one pretty easy password that, if you know me, could be guessed. Now I have one *hard* password.

The screen displays the long, long list of calls to and from Brian's cell phone during the last thirty days. My number is there, but most, like Michelle's, have a 907 area code—

I jerk back. My heart pounds at the number I know as well as my own. Searching for additional calls having the same number, I find another incoming, one outgoing. One call I might justify—and ignore—but three?

Courageous or stupid, I'm not sure which, I move out of this bill and click the link to prior months.

January 14

"This is Kevin Wright."

Driving home in the afternoon from Lowe's, I pull off the road, my heart pounding. "Thanks for calling, Kevin. I wasn't sure you would."

"Your letter said you had questions. I'm not sure I can help, but what do you want to know?"

I turn off the car radio, take a breath. "Well, what first comes to mind… Did you know about Brian…in the beginning?"

"Michelle and I were separated about eight months before she filed so I really didn't know what she was doing. But for the last three or four years of our marriage, she was sleeping around. You're not the first wife who's contacted me."

"I'm not the first wife…?"

"Michelle likes married men. I don't know what happened to her, why she wants to ruin lives, but this Michelle is not the woman I married. I tried to get her into counseling. I'm sorry she did this."

Odd that my only apology comes from a man who has nothing to apologize for. "It's not all Michelle's fault. Brian's not exactly a pillar of fidelity, either." I tell Kevin about Scottsdale. "Brian said he was perfectly happy and I was making *a big deal* out of it."

"It **is** a big deal—unless you don't care that he vacations with other women while you stay home."

Ouch. But, surprisingly, his bluntness helps.

"How old is Brian?"

"Fifty-eight."

"Really? Wow. I knew he was older—"

"He's a **young** fifty-eight."

"That's still a big difference. When Michelle and I were dating, she had a fling with a fifty-year-old. I don't know what that was about, but I guess I should've seen this coming."

I sense the nail in Kevin's heart and the pain he has stoically endured.

"I heard Brian has money."

Kevin's Achilles' heel. "Yeah, he does."

Kevin asks what kind of guy Brian is; if he'll be okay around his daughters.

"He'll be indifferent. We're all surprised that Brian is with someone who has young kids."

"Michelle is disconnected from the girls; they live with me during the school year. She makes a much better aunt than a mom."

"I figured something was amiss when she spent Christmas with Brian."

"She was supposed to have the kids for Christmas and then she asked if I would keep them. It worked great for me; I was feeling bad about not being with them. But it's troubling to see her put everything ahead of the girls. Brian. Her career."

I tell Kevin a little about me, about the Arizona ranch and Port Townsend.

Kevin knows Michelle was in Anchorage this past summer, but she didn't visit her daughters; he knows she spent time in Otter Bight.

"Come to think of it, I saw them in Moose's Tooth—" a very popular gourmet pizza restaurant in Anchorage; always crowded, always a wait. "—a few months ago. I didn't know who Brian was so I didn't make a connection. We were finishing dinner when they were seated."

"Are you sure it was Brian?" I imagine Kevin's shrug. Men don't pay attention to other men, unless there's a woman involved they're interested in. Then they compare.

"Older, in his fifties. Shorter than me, five-ten maybe. Heavier, kind of stocky. Brown hair."

It *could* be Brian even though his hair is more blond than brown and he's not really stocky—*Of course*, it was Brian. "Did they seem like a couple?"

Another shrug. "I'd say so."

I remember the touches, the kisses, the looks that made Brian and me "us," then I take myself out of the picture and put Michelle in.

But I push past the pain as I did when running a marathon, fearful that if I started lagging, I'd stop completely, lie down, and be sucked up by the street sweeper along with the litter.

"Another couple joined them as we were leaving," Kevin adds.

Which of our friends, I wonder, feeling drained. Yet, I still have questions—I just can't sort them out. They swim in my head like fish in a school. I ask if I can call again.

Kevin hesitates, but says yes. "I really don't want to spend time on this. I'm involved with a great woman now."

"That was quick."

"Relationships are important to me. And Michelle has been gone over a year."

I'm blubbering *One Less Bell to Answer*; he's crooning *Take a Letter, Maria.* And, yes, a year separates the loss we share, but still... "I can't imagine doing this again. Ever."

"Give it more time."

I thank Kevin for calling; we're about to hang up when something he mentioned jumps out at me, spawning one last question.

****

It took seven months for my parents' divorce to become final. All that time Ellie and I lived with our father. My mom's absence made little difference in our lives or my father's behavior; if anything, he hit less. But shortly after we moved in with our mother, I finally asked her the obvious question. Why, on that particular Saturday, at that particular clock tick, did she decide to leave?

Her answer was short and unemotional.

Daddy threatened to kill me.

****

"You're verboten," Jill tells me tonight. "Brian doesn't talk about you and none of the guys are allowed to talk about you."

I'm not surprised. When Brian divorced wife #1, he rarely mentioned her. He was angry about the settlement she got and he wanted her to take back her maiden name. Other than that, little was said.

I give details about my conversation with Kevin. We talk about the similarities between Brian and Michelle. Jill reports on their latest adventures.

I tell Jill about my upcoming hysterectomy and she volunteers to come down and stay with me. I quietly cry, hoping she doesn't hear. If she does, she ignores it.

****

Oh my God, what a wonderful shower! Robust, pulsating, enveloping! No more squeezing myself together to fit within a miserly stream of water.

Today, I bought a new showerhead. I unscrewed the old one, screwed on this one. All I needed was a wrench to loosen the original head and tighten the replacement. That easy, that fast. I can't believe I've lived with that wimp of a showerhead for six years, unrealizing I could simply buy a new one. And it only cost twenty-five bucks! Is this like the best-kept secret or what?

January 15

Three screeching beeps jolt me out of a sound sleep. I bolt from my bed before my brain wakes up. Standing, I prepare for the next round of obnoxious notes, but nothing repeats. It's 4:10. I can go back to bed, but I'll just be waiting for the smoke alarm to tell me again it needs a new battery.

The last time this happened, it was one in the morning and Brian was here, so as annoying as it was, it didn't seem so daunting. The failing battery is on a 13-foot ceiling. The ladder I need to reach that ceiling is down at the tractor barn.

Quivering from the screech, Molly joins me as I bundle up in fleece. She follows me into the kitchen where I put the kettle on for tea. I hope the alarm will behave until dawn when retrieving the ladder will be less of a hassle. Molly lies by my chair as I turn on Brian's computer for what has become a morning ritual. I look at yesterday's e-mails.

The subject line reads **Quick Claim Deed.** The sender is Michelle Wright. As my heart races, I open the message…

> *Thank you.*

That's it? *Thank you?* That's like having a confession without a crime. I allow myself a sense of superiority because of Michelle's incorrect wording of what should be **Quit**claim, not **Quick** Claim. But other than that, I've got squat. Has Michelle quitclaimed property to Brian or vice versa? Having seen the on-line evidence, I know Brian is the king of quitclaims, so is he passing this skill to Michelle, as an aid in her divorce, or is he hiding something from me?

I print this e-mail, along with a couple of others, and fax them to Beth.

Next, I write an e-mail to Brian telling him that a batch of unpaid bills are in the mail to his office. Then I give him the news that will put him on the first plane back to me.

****

I don't know if Mom seriously thought my father would kill her. But she wasn't willing to chance it. She had sacrificed her heart and soul for this man, but at least she drew the line at surrendering her life.

I never judged my mom for leaving her two daughters with a man she believed capable of such violence—violence even greater than what we had already experienced. I never made that connection until recently. Maybe I *couldn't* think about it or maybe I figured whatever it took to get my mom out that door was okay by me.

When I told Faith this story, she didn't judge my mom either, although I have to admit, I was kind of hoping she would be *a little* horrified. She simply said, "That was all your mother was capable of."

Put a different way—some moms are moose, some are bunnies.

****

Beth's first bill comes in the mail along with the book, *The Complete Idiot's Guide to Surviving Divorce.* She has used $3,349.61 of my $10,000 retainer and charged me $16.95 for the book.

I glance through the pages, but they depress me. And I'm really pissed that Beth billed me for this damn book I don't want!

Leaving my divorce on the kitchen counter, I fill the birdfeeders and hang them up. A dozen birds are waiting and more fly in.

Down at the barn, I feed the horses, wash their faces, brush their manes and tails, pick their hooves and wrap them in blankets, then I walk Molly to the gate and lock it. There's barely a flicker of daylight when I get back to the house.

I open a can of tomato soup but only *think* about a grilled cheese sandwich. Afterward, I nap on the couch under Mom's afghan with

Big Teddy while the television keeps me company. Waking an hour later, I bundle up for one more trip to the barn with Molly.

After picking up poop, checking blankets, and more hay, I turn off the lights and remind the horses, *I'm only a whinny away.*

****

It's easy to have limits that are never tested, convictions never challenged, faith without trial, courage absent threat. It's easy to judge, to *know* what you would or wouldn't do in situations that never confront you.

But no one stands in line to be crucified. There's more Judas in us than Jesus, I suspect, and that's okay, as long as we keep trying to be less sinner and more saint.

****

Before bed, I check my e-mails. Brian is responding to the one I sent this morning informing him about my hysterectomy. Finally, the moment I've hoped for, when everything *rights* itself.

> Sorry to read about your health but the smart thing to do is board the horses, move into town and take care of yourself.

January 16

Brian stopped loving me.

This is what really happened to our marriage; everything else is smoke and mirrors.

January 17

When *did Michelle change her plans?*

That was my last question to Kevin. I explained that Brian was coming here for Christmas; he had flight reservations into Phoenix, but on the 9th of December, he changed his destination to Seattle and broke the news that he wasn't coming home.

Kevin was very nice, but I could tell he didn't want to think too hard about this.

"I'm just trying to figure out what happened," I almost pleaded. Brian was going to be with me, Michelle with her daughters, then *something* changed that.

I've been mulling this over for three days now. It randomly pops into my head; wakes me during the night. I lie in bed, hours from dawn, my thoughts recycling, as if this one answer will explain why, on December 9th, Brian chose a different path.

Kevin thought about it, remembering that her call came the day of a school Christmas recital. *Friday.* Maybe three weeks before Christmas.

Maybe? Could it have been two weeks?

"Kate, you'll never have all the answers you think you need. And you might find out things you'll wish you hadn't."

Parked on the side of the road, cars speeding past, I listened to Kevin's advice. "I know you're not ready, but one day you'll let this go, and it'll be a relief."

****

When I was nine, my father did the extraordinary. Still with USAID, his tour in Laos was ending and Panama was his next assignment. For the first time, we, his family, would not go with him but would return to our home in Carbondale. My brother was in high school, intending to study medicine in college; my father wanted Taylor to attend the prep school run by the university. Mom, Taylor, Ellie, and I would stay in Illinois during the school year and spend summers in Panama and later in Ecuador for my father's final tour before retirement.

As we prepared to leave Vientiane, I worried about our mutt, Slim, whom we'd adopted a year earlier as a puppy. In a country where strays were trapped for dinner and puppies were sold at the market, Slim wouldn't last a week on his own. Then my father broke the news—he was flying Slim home. From *Laos* to *Illinois*—8500 miles!—Slim was coming with us.

If there was a moment I loved my father, this was it, and it's the second fond memory I have of him. For that one shining moment when he brought Slim with us, my dad was my hero.

Which makes what happened to Ben unforgiveable.

After that horrible Christmas, my father would periodically bring up Ben, and sometimes Carmen, too, reminding me that the blame lay with my mother and me, as if he was simply the executioner but *we* had committed the crime.

For two years, between my bachelor's degree and my master's, I was the director of that shelter where I abandoned Ben. Reviewing the donor list, I discovered that my father was a regular contributor, beginning shortly after I started volunteering when I was seventeen. By the time I left that job to finish my MBA, he had given $18,000. Since my father wasn't exactly a charitable giver, I consider his generosity proof of the monumental guilt he suffered because of Ben.

And it might prove something else.

My father knew what he did was wrong. Even as he was doing it.

Maybe his conscience dwelled in the same remote place as his

Little Red Dog stories, but it hounded him. He never asked my forgiveness—maybe he asked God's—but neither of us mattered. He couldn't forgive himself.

★★★★★★★★★★

In my old Paine Webber check register, about eight years ago, is an entry to Brian for $7,500. A year later is another entry for $25,000. Next to his name, I've written *AK Air Stock.*

I can't believe what I forgot. I gave Brian money to buy Alaska Airlines Stock. But, thumbing through the rest of my register, I don't see this money coming back to me. To be sure I'm not jumping to conclusions, I look through my other account registers, but find nothing. So what happened to the $32,500?

I go down the to-do list Beth gave me—items she wants me to research. On the list is "proceeds from house sale."

Shortly before I moved to Juniper Verde, we sold our 4-bedroom home in an exclusive hillside neighborhood. I remember Brian telling me that since he was now supporting me in Arizona, he should get the money from that sale. Honestly, that sounded fair. Other than that, I don't remember *anything*. I don't remember the closing or signing documents. What I do remember is staying up all night marking prices on items for the huge garage sale the next day and then being a zombie for the sale itself.

Of course, I was in the middle of moving out of our hillside house and into the new, smaller house closer to Brian's midtown office AND getting ready—two days later—to head down the highway with the horses to Arizona while Brian went hunting. So, I wasn't thinking about little things like where the proceeds were going, or even how much they were. Brian took care of that. But I'm thinking we netted $50,000, since we each put in $25,000 when we built the hillside house. Because the house was in both our names, the check from the sale would've been in both names, and it had to be deposited into our joint account.

There are two deposits recorded in our check register around that time, each for $5,000 and each in Brian's handwriting. Coinciding with those deposits, also in Brian's handwriting, are two checks,

#1703 and #1704, both noted as "VOID."

So, where did the "proceeds from house sale" go?

What I know for sure is that I don't have those ancient bank statements, not here, not in Anchorage. It's Saturday, so my sleuthing will have to wait until next week. Then I will call our bank in Anchorage and find out my karmic balance with the Universe.

Martin Luther King Day

"He's selling the property! I'm standing here looking at the *for sale* sign."

This past week has been very bad. I've hit *the wall*; I can barely put one thought in front of the last. Now this news from Ellie about our Port Townsend property.

I'm being dismantled, piece-by-piece. Brian is not only ridding himself of me, he's ridding himself of every memory and every dream, that's what this feels like.

"He must've just listed it," I say.

Ellie volunteers to ask her realtor friend, Eugenia, to look it up on the MLS. Then she rants, like so many times before, "I just can't believe he's doing this!"

However, now her outrage makes me suspicious. Is she furious at Brian for betraying me? Or betraying *her*? I close my eyes, wishing I had talked to Kevin and been given a chance to heed his advice *before* I opened that AT&T e-mail—and with it, Pandora's Box.

Ellie has a key to the gate. After the property was fenced, Brian gave it to her in case of emergency. When he visited our eighty acres on stopovers between Alaska and Arizona, Brian rented a car and spent the night at Ellie's house, midway between Seattle and Port Townsend.

Ellie always gushed about Brian's kindness—taking her and my niece to dinner, then leaving a couple of one-hundred dollar bills when he left the next morning for the airport.

He left money in my bananas, she told me one morning, laughing, as if she had shared a naughty secret. I *knew*, instantly, she had.

But what could I do with that information? After the screaming accusations and indignant denials, then what?

Of course, rather than imply, my sister might have confessed to their liaison, as she's done about my old boyfriends, and then I would've been screwed twice. Once that cat is out of the bag, you can't stuff it back in. And perhaps Ellie knows the difference between a boyfriend and a husband, and assumed—correctly—I would be less forgiving. Yet, she *wanted* me to know.

Ellie says she'll call me after she drives around the property.

The truth is, I never trusted Ellie. The irony is, I always trusted Brian.

"There's a new tractor sitting here." I hear rustling in the background as Ellie walks through the thickets. "There's a tag that says *Sold to Brian Willoughby.*"

I free my brain from the rubble. "There should be a metal plate, somewhere on the chassis, with a serial number…"

****

I remember that *first* moment, when Brian referred to me as his wife. We were boarding a plane, but our seats were apart. Brian asked the gentleman on the aisle to switch seats so that we could sit together.

"My wife doesn't like to fly," Brian told him.

My glow could've lit a city.

I think about *that* moment and wonder how Brian got to *this* moment. I wonder when I depreciated, when exactly Brian decided I was his back-up plan, when he realized he could store me in Arizona and hide my photographs in a drawer.

Because this much I know—every idea has a moment of conception that is then either nurtured or aborted. Moments like this don't just *happen.*

****

"He listed the property in June," Ellie's realtor friend tells me.

"**Last** June? Seven months ago?"

"Yes," Eugenia confirms. "It went on the MLS June nineteenth."

I get off the phone and confirm my memory.

Mile **619** Project.

June 19.

The same day Michelle filed for divorce.

Leaving no stone unturned, I'm back in Brian's e-mail; all the way back to January, going through his *Sent* file, looking at e-mails I've seen before, but passed without opening.

I stop on an e-mail from Laura that I remember from his *In* box. She appears to be an employee; she'll be out of the office and working with a client.

There's a response arrow...*Call me please.*

Three weeks later into February, there is a similar e-mail from Laura, telling Brian she is working out of the office and where. Brian replies...*Will miss you. I'll stop by to say hi.*

****

To be really, **really** honest, there is no *last to know* but there is *don't want to know.* Women have a sixth sense when it comes to their men. We're probably the *first to know,* the way a mammogram picks up those teeny little specks that otherwise go undetected. But they are so small and inconclusive that we take a wait-and-see approach. That speck may grow into something dangerous, but it might not.

I can look at Brian's response to Laura's first e-mail and **know** something personal is happening. Without even considering what I know now, if I had seen his e-mail when it was still in the present, I would've known. I know the way Brian writes, the way he talks; I know the difference between business and personal. I can sense it, feel it. I **know.**

Brian's response three weeks later is a no-brainer. That speck has grown into a lump anyone can diagnose. But I didn't have that e-mail. Or his credit card statement that has him spending $200 at an Anchorage restaurant on Valentine's Day, sandwiched between these two e-mails.

Of course, I could be jumping to conclusions.

Still, there were other specks I saw and ignored. Specks that grew into Michelle. And yet, I'm not sure you can prevent the Michelles in life. People find a way to do what they want. I decided a long time ago that a wig and sunglasses are not my style.

Before Garrett, there was Kyle.

He was a cop, a body-builder and *Oh-my-God*. I was a grad student, a runner, and *Thank you, Jesus.*

Although I travelled every hill and dale of Kyle, our relationship never went the distance even though we drove around for three years. I think most of the problem was Crystal, Kyle's girlfriend from high school, who was in the back seat.

Kyle once explained Crystal by telling me that they had been together *a long time.* I took that to mean he didn't have the heart to get rid of her. A man sensitive to another's feelings, even an old girlfriend's, is always endearing.

So I was patient. Really, really patient. And understanding. I rose to my highest self while poor Kyle wrestled with the burden of two adoring women.

Then I got impatient—about 2½ years too late—and I told Kyle to choose. He chose Crystal. But he said something so *revealing*, it has stuck with me for thirty years.

****

By now I've collected a banker's box of e-mails, going back a year, sorted by date and subject, including all deposits into the checking account of Willoughby Wickham & Steele. The business manager e-mails Brian a list of cash and checks that arrive at the office daily. Amounts have varied from a few hundred dollars to over a hundred thousand.

And every now and again, gold glitters in my pan, like the e-mail from Charles Schwab inviting Brian to open an on-line account. *Interesting.* Brian didn't include a Charles Schwab account on his financial declaration.

****

In the twelve years I've hung around horses, I've watched a lot of women. During this time, I've attended a few seminars in the fashion of Pat Parelli and John Lyons who are the John Gray and Wayne Dyer of the horse world.

Sitting in the audience, I've noticed that women far outnumber men who seemed to be there solely because of their attachment to the women attending. Otherwise, you rarely see men at seminars on relationships, unless it's with their golf clubs.

Women, conversely, are *forever* trying to improve relationships whether it's with their men, their kids, their horses, their dogs, themselves…

We are *tweakers*.

God knows, we exhaust our men, we exhaust our horses, we exhaust ourselves.

But if a woman wants to know, **really** wants to know, who **she** is, and how that impacts her relationships, she should hang out with a horse. Forget the therapist, the manuals, the seminars. A horse tells you pretty much at the first hello what your issues are.

Having observed women for all these years, I'm amazed by how many are afraid to leave the arena, go out on trail, drop the reins, or hardest of all, unhook the tether.

"He'll run off," is the common reason to keep a horse restrained. And yeah, he usually does. But surprisingly, he doesn't go far and he'll most likely stop at the first patch of grass. If you give him a few minutes to smell the wind, then tempt him with a carrot, he comes trotting back.

It was nerve-wracking the first time I let Chance go. I mean **really** let him go where there were no fences. Free of the rope, he took off—hooves thundering, mane flying, nostrils flaring. Convinced he was lost, I cursed myself for being so trusting, but then he made a wide arc and came back to me.

Now I do the same with Quinn.

Women fear *letting go*. Programmed to be caretakers and mommies, we're convinced all hell will break loose if we relax our grip.

Releasing our fears and accepting men for who they are—different relationship but same philosophy—seems a lot like giving them permission to be men, in what we assume will be their worst incarnation. It's true that some men will be their *worst self* and then blame us for allowing it. As Kyle revealed, "You sure made it easy for me."

But men will be men whether we *allow* it or not. Some will be selfish and hurtful; others will be generous and kind. Some men, neglecting to water what they have, will think that the grass is always greener elsewhere and will forever seek that sweet patch while others know that grass is grass, and *greener* is an illusion, but home is where the carrots are.

Trying to control a man is like trying to control a horse. No amount of bit, bridle, or crop will do it for very long and certainly not forever. They are with us because they want to be, out of love and appreciation, and if that changes, they will unseat us with ease. If our love and caring aren't enough, then it's best we let them trot on down the trail because our rides will be nothing but struggle and that's no fun for anyone.

Darla, who spilled the beans about Michelle to Jill, said to me a few years ago, "You need to come back to Anchorage."

Her tone was ominous, so I understood the warning, but still I asked her why.

"You just need to come back, that's all."

"If Brian's going to screw around, he's going to screw around," I told Darla. "And he's going to do it whether I'm here or not."

"But you're making it easy for him."

Ahhh-hmmm.

I decided with Kyle that I don't want to be a woman who polices her man, mostly because it's plain exhausting and, in the long run, impossible. I knew with Kyle as I know with Brian and every man in between that if you can't trust the man you've built a life with, then what the hell are you doing with him and what kind of life do you really have?

It's beautiful watching a horse run free and trusting that he'll never venture too far—or canoodle with the filly down the road.

But you can't know that until you let him go. When you do, magic happens; you get liberated, too.

I have made mistakes in my marriage. But my biggest mistake was **not** that I trusted Brian. My biggest mistake was trusting Brian when I knew he couldn't be trusted.

Unlike my horse.

January 21

I rush Molly into the hay room where she'll be safe. Then I address the boxer who has mysteriously arrived at the barn.

He's not friendly, but weirder still, he's aggressively standing his ground on ground that isn't his. Bared teeth, stiff hackles, frenzied bark. Every time I leave the barn, he threatens me and I **know** he'll attack if I allow it. As long as I stay inside, he relaxes, but one step out, he lunges at me.

He's afraid, but he has no reason to linger. He should flee, not fight. So why is he here? And why is he after me?

****

I was jogging down my neighborhood country road when the German shepherd darted off his property and sank his fangs into my left thigh. If that wasn't frightening enough, the dog's owner stood in his yard and watched. Just *stood* and *watched*.

The man didn't offer me a ride home or even a towel to stem the blood streaming down my naked leg, but he did suggest I have a doctor look at the wound. I turned around and limped a half mile home while the dog's owner went back to raking leaves.

Twenty-eight years later and that man's indifference still bites.

On a grander cosmic scale, I have never been attacked by any animal other than a domestic dog.

People worry about bears and moose and snakes and wolves and mountain lions and mice carriers of hanta virus, and God knows there might be a Grizzly at the end of *my* trail, but so far, the only animal who's sent me to the emergency room is a dog. Not a stray or a rescue or a dog at the shelter where you'd think I would be most in danger, but a dog like the shepherd, who was someone's pet.

In Anchorage, on my hillside walks, I carried pepper spray, not to repel bears, but to repel my neighbors' dogs. In spite of that, I was attacked twice, once by a black Lab and once by a Pyrenees. Both times, Nick came to my rescue, deflecting the attacks while, luckily, suffering little harm.

Still, it's really scary being on the receiving end of an unjustified and hateful attack. It's especially difficult when I consider all the years I've championed this same species that periodically wants a pound of my flesh for reasons I've yet to figure out.

In fact, it hurts my feelings that some dogs think I'm not worthy of kindness and trust. Or maybe, just maybe, there are dogs looking for a victim and I'm an easy target because love blinds me to their demons.

Is Felicity right? Do I love *too much*? Perhaps the twist is that I love too much the ones who don't value my love, those who harbor demons, those who do me harm.

****

I speak in soothing tones while walking slowly toward the boxer. I try to make myself small and nonthreatening, diverting my gaze, but the dog rages at me. I take a firmer stand with confident words and he rages even more. I back into the barn.

I can only imagine the abuse that torments this dog, making him so terrified. But I'm also scared. Alone, at the end of the road, I can't believe I'm being held hostage by a boxer.

I grab the pitchfork. Holding it like a lance, I walk out of the barn, uncertain if I could actually stab the dog with it. It's not in my nature to harm, certainly not to kill. But would I prefer having my jugular ripped out?

It worries me that I have to ponder that.

Three decades ago, I acted from the conviction that death should be delivered by gentle hands and a breaking heart. But seven years of heartbreak and death changed me. After my sweet hound by the side of the road, I put down the needle and became like Brother Cadfael, who was first a soldier, then a monk.

So now what?

I advance toward the dog who backs away. I narrow my eyes and tell him that I am not putting up with his shit. *No way, no how.*

When I stop, he barks and growls, quivering as if he might explode and take me with him. Ten feet out of the barn, I have 200 to go.

There has to be a better way.

I retreat and the dog comes after me. I swing the tines toward him and back into the barn.

As I tug and pull the heavy slider closed, the dog's angry expression melts into confusion. I open the other end of the barn then start the Gator to warm it. The last thing I need is the Gator sputtering and dying halfway to safety. If I make it to the house, I'll drive the Jeep back and get Molly who is safely hidden. But the only protection offered by the Gator is speed. Thinking of the movie *Cujo,* I wonder how crazy this dog is, if he'll chase me and jump inside, if the Gator can outrun him.

I floor the Gator and escape the barn, then speed up the hill and curl around the long drive toward the house. The boxer might take the 200-foot shortcut, but when I arrive the dog is nowhere in sight. I rush through the garage into the house. Grabbing the car keys, I'm in the Jeep then I stop. Back inside the house, I grab my 9mm Smith & Wesson from the nightstand… then leave it.

At the barn, I wait in the car; the boxer could surprise me from the rear. Cautiously, I open the door then dash into the barn. Taking Molly by the collar, I rush her into the Jeep.

Still no boxer.

Returning to the back barn door, I tug it open.

No bared teeth. No stiff hackles. No frenzied bark.

Venturing out with the pitchfork, I look around. I check behind me, through the barn aisle at the Jeep on the other end, but everything is as it was before the boxer.

This feels like a magic trick. The curtains open, the box is empty.

I breathe, relax, and put away the pitchfork. But I leave Molly in the car as I finish my chores. Then I drive to the house; maybe the vanished dog will reappear there.

No boxer.

An hour later, I walk Molly, carrying Brian's super-size golf umbrella, in case I need a defense. Our walk is uneventful.

So I'm trying to figure out the meaning of the boxer. I know there's a message because here's the back-story...

Maybe a half hour before my boxer showed up, I was feeling ambivalent about the divorce, wondering if I was on the right path, thinking I should follow Nina's advice and grab only my bowl and spoon and get the hell out.

I asked for a sign.

Along comes the boxer. Not a Dalmatian, not a collie, not even a shepherd. A *boxer*...

Did I mention—my boxer has balls.

So, this boxer, whom I apparently asked for, terrorizes me and holds me hostage *in **my** barn*. He makes me question my willingness to defend my life and territory; makes me wonder if I can harm those I love, those I've nurtured and protected—but who now threaten me.

Will I tuck tail? Cower? Roll over?

Or will I fight?

January 22

Maybe Brian never loved me.

January 23

I press the flashing message light.

"This is Annette Watters in the Archives Department at First National Bank in Anchorage. The statements you requested will be available for pick-up next week."

Okay...*really? Annette? Watters? In Archives?* Where, like in a *packrat* midden, stuff is collected and stored? Providence or Chance, Milton's message is clear. I still have a positive balance in my karmic account. Next week, when I'm in Anchorage, I'll know that balance in dollars and cents.

****

The jeweler held my bezel-set quarter-carat diamond earring between her left thumb and forefinger as her right hand touched the probe to the diamond. She glanced at the needle on the meter.

"Are these diamonds?"

My brows shot up. "I thought so."

"Well...they're not."

Rob, the mattress and intersection guy, had given me those earrings for my birthday. But I never liked the bezel setting, so a couple years after our break-up, when I was earning a good salary, I decided to put them into a prong setting.

I suppose I should've been angry at the truth, or even embarrassed, but the joke was too funny. I opened the clasp on my necklace where a quarter-carat diamond hung from a delicate gold chain. Her probe touched the faceted stone.

"Sorry."

That pendant had been a Christmas gift from Rob. I remember when I opened the box, I knew my eyes lit up. For three years, even after Rob was gone, I wore that necklace, rarely taking it off, believing it was real.

Now I was being told that what I valued, and proudly wore for all to see…was a cheap imposter.

"Do you still want to change the setting?"

I laughed. But, as I think about it now, she probably didn't see her question as ridiculous.

The stones hadn't changed, only my awareness. The truth is, I have CZ earrings that sparkle like the real deal and I wear them, knowing what they are.

But Rob's gifts were meant to deceive.

And they did, changing everything.

****

I tremble as my fax slowly reveals the invoice from the Sutter Tractor Company in Washington.

I cannot believe I had the chutzpah to request it. Just call and ask. High on moxie, I'm like the coyotes who stroll around the ranch—checking out the back deck, snooping in the barn—as if *they* hold the mortgage. I was absolutely sure that Cathy in the billing office would question my request and demand proof that I am Brian's wife.

Sure, I have all the pertinent information, thanks to Brian's back-and-forth e-mails with Dale, but I can't believe it was this easy. Cathy and I chatted about the weather in Arizona and Washington as she looked up Brian's file.

As an afterthought, I asked if she had a copy of the check that paid for the tractor. I asked her to fax that, too.

Now I have the invoice, *Sold to Brian Willoughby,* with his business address and telephone number, along with the specifics of the tractor—a loader, a cutter, a posthole digger—including the all-important serial numbers. They match the numbers that Ellie took from the tractor sitting on our eighty acres.

The second fax starts and I hover, impatient to see how Brian hid this purchase; anxious to compare numbers against the Anchorage bank accounts he listed on his disclosures.

But, holding the proof, I don't need to compare accounts. This check for $26,569.45 is from a bank in St. George, Utah. Check number 1922 suggests the account was opened years ago.

Gold weighs heavy in my pan; this is a joint account.

Brian has an accomplice.

****

Jogging on a trail by the lake, a woman comes across a sick and helpless snake. Recognizing a soft touch, the snake begs for help. The tenderhearted woman falls for the pitiful snake and takes him home.

She feeds him honey and milk, lays him by the fire, and then goes off to work—because she now has a snake to house, clothe, and feed. When she returns home, the woman discovers her snake has revived.

She is elated, as any woman would be, to see the happy result of her love and nurturing. The woman hugs the snake and strokes his beautiful skin and showers kisses, reminding him that, without her, he would have died.

The snake bites her....

Boys entered my life around the time Al Wilson first crooned this cautionary tale about *smart women, foolish choices* in the aptly titled song, *The Snake.*

The song always makes me smile. I think about it sometimes when I have a Diamondback in a noose at the end of my pole. But nature is clear. It's impossible to mistake a snake for a bunny. It's *human* nature that's ambiguous. Still, if you ignore the rattle, it's hard to blame the snake when things go south.

Getting back to the woman, she is, as any woman would be, bewildered and heartbroken at the snake's behavior. She loves him. She saved his life. And this is how he repays her?

The snake has no remorse and, as the woman lies dying, he cruelly reminds her, "Oh, please! You knew I was a snake before you took me home."

January 24

I'm *excess*. The third child of parents who already had my brother and sister. This thought popped into my head today after a twenty-four year absence.

When I was twenty-nine, my mom let slip that I was a surprise: *unplanned* and *unexpected*—her words—which is a tactful alternative for *unwanted* and *unneeded*—my words—and, most likely, what she really felt. Because, according to Mom, the only thing worse than being married to my father, was being married to my father while caring for a baby.

So there Mom was, relieved to be done with that miserable chapter in her life, and I made her do it again. Adding absurd to miserable, my father was angry with my mother for being pregnant in the first place, as if she had done it without input from him.

My father, as we know, didn't like crying. But, at least he knew that hitting babies was not going to quiet them, so whenever I cried, he threatened my mother instead. It's a wonder she didn't put a pillow over my face.

Hmmm...

But I survived and I learned to make myself useful by being what other people needed, having few needs of my own, or rather, my needs weren't important so why humor them. No matter how much love hurts, you bear it as my mother did, because the greater the pain, the greater the love. What are a few bruises compared to crucifixion? If Jesus suffered for humankind, surely she could suffer for one man. Which, I suspect, was my mother's rationalization.

Raised by missionary parents to be self-sacrificing, Mom stretched that to just shy of martyrdom. She said that staying in her marriage was her Christian duty. Yet, to her children, she condemned my father for his cruelty. Talk about a mixed message.

However, I don't believe my grandparents meant self-sacrifice to include bloody noses any more than my mother would today think it means being a doormat. She would wear a hair shirt in heaven if she knew how her example had imprinted on me.

So what's a kid to do? I embraced the message of her *actions*— *Love bears all things, believes all things, hopes all things, endures all things. Love never fails*—and I married Brian, who thinks *all* worlds spin on his axis. And nowhere in Corinthians does it say, *unless your spouse is a louse.* On my own since infancy, I would suffer almost anything to be taken care of, which Brian appeared to be offering. However, childhood is not like a bus; if you miss yours there isn't another to catch.

So, *of course*, Brian is now angry—and probably confused. Why am I not meeting his needs like I always have, including his need to have me gone without making a fuss?

Looking back on our marriage—and my life—I can't really be surprised by what's happening now. What does surprise me is me.

****

I struggle with the door handle on Brian's Corvette. Whoever designed this recessed handle—and it was definitely a man— intended to keep women out. No woman buys a car that breaks fingernails every time she opens the door.

Taking the claw side of a hammer, I wrap it in my glove and push it into the recess then leverage it up. The door unlatches.

Tomorrow I fly to Alaska. Bonnie and Sam, my former caretakers, will stay on the ranch. This afternoon, they're coming over for a job refresher.

Bonnie and Sam married after graduating from high school. Thirty-seven years later, it's obvious that neither can imagine life without the other. When I told them about the divorce and that I would be travelling back and forth to Anchorage, Bonnie immediately offered to care for the animals so I would have one less thing to worry about.

God bless Bonnie.

Sliding into the driver's seat, I breathe in memories that overwhelm. I really did fall in love with Brian in this car, and his *Tsar*-laced testosterone lingers. Looking in the back, I see Lisa and I return to that life-changing moment of being with a man who tolerated dog hair in his Corvette to make me happy.

Uh-huh.

I pull the hood release. Sam is giving me a lesson on operating the tractor and afterward we're going to rearrange the tractor and Corvette so there's space to park the gator in this barn at night. Before that happens, I want to know that nothing is nesting around the engine of the Corvette.

Hoisting myself out of the seat, I again question the design. Unlike on most cars, this hood separates at the windshield and hinges in front. Instead of three sides of access, there are only two.

I slowly raise the hood. Sunflower hulls are scattered about, along with little poops and…

"Oh my God… *Winston?*"

My packrat looks up from a nest inside the hollow created by the air filter casing, the thingamajig, and the whatchamacallit. Winston stares at me with big, dark eyes, then dives from the nest into a tangle of wires, hoses, and engine parts. He scurries from beneath the Corvette and out the door of the tractor barn, leaving behind two naked, blind, squirming babies. Since male packrats don't parent, there is only one conclusion.

We won't be moving the Corvette today. In about six weeks, these newborns will be grown and gone and then we'll rearrange the vehicles. But before I drop the hood, I pause to appreciate Winston's nest—the fur and hay and bits of paper in its construction, and the symmetry of its interior bowl—

Huh.

I look closer at the corner scrap of olive-beige paper jutting from the nest, the one with the "eye" printed on it. Gently wiggling it free, I expose another eye next to it, or what I now recognize as a stylized zero. *Two* stylized zeroes.

****

After my father died, Taylor, Ellie, and I sorted through his personal belongings. In a lower kitchen cabinet, in a shiny, lidded cooking pot, I found $23,000.

I'm sure there was a reason for my father's stash, just as I'm sure there's a reason a Corvette hood hinges in front. But I can't explain either one.

****

The horses are tucked in for the night and now I go to the tractor barn. I open the door and the outside lights fall across the concrete.

Movies and television have us believing that money takes up a lot of space, but, in large denominations, $50,000 is not much more than an inch in depth; it easily fits along the inside frame of a 1980 Corvette next to the plastic windshield-washer reservoir.

Winnie's nest is worth about $2,000 in partially chewed and shredded one-hundred dollar bills. I figure that's a pretty good split.

I leave a big piece of cheese under the Corvette for Winnie. Alongside the cheese, I leave a jar lid filled with water.

January 25

Two days ago, Brian sent me this e-mail…

> *I hired an attorney yesterday because there is no effective way to communicate with Beth. We now have tens of thousands of dollars going from us to the benefit of others. Let's both try to find a solution to the issue ASAP. I'm open to suggestions.*

I've spent the last two days writing a response.

> *I'm not any happier about this situation than you are, albeit for different reasons. Nonetheless, you want suggestions for stemming the flow of money to our attorneys? Stop doing stuff that requires attorney intervention. Like your power-play over the bills and the gator repair. Because of that, I've spent $3000 to draft a motion for interim support. What did you accomplish other than letting me know that you can make my life even more miserable than the divorce is already making it? I realize how badly I need an attorney to look out for my interests because you certainly aren't.*
>
> *Unfortunately, I'm merely playing the cards I've been dealt. While I am "economic" to you, you are still "personal" to me, and without Beth, I'd be at your mercy.*
>
> *While I may hate the way you chose to end our marriage, I don't hate you, and I'd prefer to get through this divorce without purposely inflicting pain. It may be a lofty ideal, but it's one I'm trying my best to live by.*
>
> *At this point, you are the only one who can make this divorce amicable (or at least, less hostile). I'm not suggesting we have to agree on everything, but your "bullying" approach*

isn't going to move anything forward. I would hope that we can remember the reasons we got married—and stayed married for twenty-two years—and maybe we can be less antagonistic and more cooperative. K

I have three hours before the shuttle leaves for Phoenix Sky Harbor airport. If I let myself, I could tweak this e-mail for two of those hours. I hit send.

Before shutting down the computer, I check incoming mail. I scan the new messages, repeatedly clicking the *trash* icon. But wedged among the certain deletions…I look closer, move the cursor to the message.

My heart pounds; I've been here before—one click away from disappointment. I take a deep breath.

Nine months after I sent my manuscript; nine months of drought without a drop of hope…

I lift my face to heaven and smell the rain.

****

From my first class window seat, I glance at the faces and expressions of Seattle-bound passengers as they file by. I look for couples, check hands for rings, wonder what stories are there.

Brian never wore a ring, although I bought him a gold band. Inside is engraved with *I love you more* followed by the date of our vows. I put it on his finger at the courthouse. Later that night, Brian returned the ring to its velvet box where it has stayed with his cards in my dresser drawer for twenty-two years.

Before Brian was in my life, my Anchorage therapist said that it's a bad sign when a man won't wear a wedding band. Why we were even talking about that, I don't remember. But I've known several married men who didn't wear rings and were nonetheless committed to their marriages and I've known even more husbands whose wedding rings didn't stop their ruts—or prevent women from hitting on them. So I don't think the presence or absence of a ring represents anything other than personal preference.

From day one, I wore a thin, gold band on my finger, 24-7. Over the years with horses and barn chores, my size 4 finger has increased a half size and the knuckle now presents an obstacle to a ring that small.

For the last year, it's been choking my finger, and finally a few months ago I managed to work it over my greased knuckle. But it remains there, an indentation around the base of my finger.

I still wear my diamond wedding set, but not because I'm sentimental. One of these days I will probably stop wearing the matching band, but I doubt I will ever stop wearing the wide, ruby and diamond band with the solitaire for three simple reasons: I designed the ring; I love the ring; and my money paid for the ring. But Brian always got credit. And I never set anyone straight.

The 4-carat center marquise gets a lot of attention, and not only from women. More than one man has speculated, "Someone must love you a lot."

Men understand what women don't. When a man spends his money on something he can neither use nor personally enjoy, he's seriously smitten.

While I know there are women who look at a diamond and think about the bedroom set they could buy, and while men praise these brides as practical, a point is being missed. If a man balks at spending three months of salary on something that will presumably last a lifetime for the woman he will presumably share that lifetime with…that lifetime may be short.

There is a reason fathers demanded cows for daughters. It might seem antiquated now to *buy* a wife, but really, it's basic marketing. People only value that which comes at a price. A garage sale purchase is always *less* valuable than a Nordstrom purchase, even if it's the same item.

Being men, fathers understood this truism. A suitor who puts his livestock where his mouth is, is usually a good bet for a husband.

Women think they're being noble and selfless by refusing a diamond, or some other cow-equivalent, but in fact, they're denying men the opportunity to value them, and to discover exactly how much.

Even though women don't like admitting to something so unflattering, and even though men prefer to keep this truth unaired, for most men, everything is relative to money, including love.

While no bride is thinking about the practicalities of the contract she's about to sign, especially when she's focused on gowns, cake, and happily-ever-after, the groom is calculating what he's gaining against what he's giving up—cost versus benefit.

I didn't ask Brian to buy me the ring I bought myself—I had a hard enough time getting him to spend $1500 on a diamond band. I thought it was wrong and selfish of me to expect him to part with $30,000 for something as frivolous as jewelry, even though I now know he well could have afforded it.

When I amortize that $30,000 over the life of our marriage, it comes to $1,368 a year. I contributed more than that in labor cleaning streaks off his skivvies. Instead, Brian spent a whopping $68 a year, or less than $6 a month. That's what? A couple of domestic beers?

Sadly, I'm not the only one selling herself short. For all the talk about equality in marriage, it rarely happens. Women contribute financially and then we have the lion's share of caretaking the home and anyone who might be in it, from pets to children to parents. We're the teenager who is *allowed* to have a job as long as she keeps making A's.

Women are *two-fers.* And we buy into that; in fact, we do it to ourselves. We take pride in doing it all while men reap the benefits. Men may pay for wives "up front" but women pay for husbands the rest of their lives.

We have come a long way, *Baby,* only to be worse off.

Yes, there are women who are gold-diggers and you can see them coming. But there are an equal number of gold-digging men whom you only see through the slamming screen door.

I always liked the idea that someone thought I was worth a $30,000 ring. I guess, instinctively, I knew the importance of cows.

And yet, I wanted to believe that love is greater than cows. I wanted to show Brian that cows didn't matter.

But the truth is, a man will never spend a cow when he can get a wife for free.

****

I hold my hand to the window and the sun strikes my diamond, shooting prisms into the cabin and along the wall.

The flight attendant interrupts my play, taking drink requests to be delivered once we are airborne. I order a bloody Mary; the gentleman next to me asks for white wine.

3C looks very familiar; very GQ; very successful; *very familiar*. Turns out he lives in Fairbanks. But I still can't place him. He says he is "picking up a wife in Seattle" before going back to Alaska.

"*A* wife? *Your* wife or someone else's wife?"

"*A* wife—I'm looking around." Then he laughs and says, "My wife."

There was a time when I might have found that chuckle-worthy. Now it hits too close to home. It makes me wonder what Brian's opening line was to Michelle…or maybe he had her at *hello*.

The thing is, there is always a kernel of truth in sarcasm and jokes. I suspect this man **is** looking—maybe not for a replacement, maybe just for *haggis* between flights. But I suspect he's looking.

I know there are men who aren't looking, men who joke without using their wives as a punch line. They're not looking; they're flirting.

But this man is looking and has probably found.

I listen intently to the flight attendant as she goes over the safety features on this Boeing 737-800. She reminds us to put on our own oxygen masks first, before we help others with theirs.

In other words, you're no good to anyone if you're dead. Maybe that's how Mom felt when she fled our house.

We taxi to the runway and the engines rev. We start rolling, picking up speed. The engines thunder through my chest; the cabin rumbles; the wheels bump against the concrete. We lift. The plane shakes and shudders as the wind pushes it around. A bump; a drop. Sweat coats my hands. We bank sharply right; the sun hits my face. I close my eyes then peek through cracked lids. I stare at blue heaven. Across the aisle, the windows frame the ground.

Slowly we level; the nose comes down. I breathe, filling my lungs. We bank left and I am face down into hills and mesas. Finally, mercifully, we level for flight.

The flight attendant delivers drinks. We climb through pillows of cumulus. I see what looks like a wisp of cloud then realize it's contrails from a jet.

Snow blankets the mountains below. Flagstaff?

The air has smoothed; the flight has smoothed. My heart and stomach react favorably. As long as everyone stays calm and no one upsets the balance, we will be fine.

From my carry-on bag beneath the seat in front of me, I retrieve my notepad and the stack of Brian's Visa statements. I'm still shocked by the numbers—his latest statement alone is over $14,000—and last year's charges total almost $79,000. But it's the individual purchases that shake me. So many restaurant and bar charges. And airfare between Juneau and Anchorage, again and again. I found all the charges for Scottsdale, including the hotel, and $3.61 at Wal-Mart for Michelle's birthday card. Then over Christmas, all the Port Townsend charges—hotel, restaurants, and The Seaside Gallery, which was undoubtedly a Christmas present for Michelle.

Brian's Lucchese cowboy boots are still wrapped for our anniversary and still hidden in our closet, along with his card and my sentiment…

Twenty-two years and counting, You still make my heart go pitter-pat. I love you most…

The plane drops; my insides rise. The clouds below turn to sheets pulled taut against the sky.

The flight attendant hands me my bloody Mary.

The bumps return, short and sharp like a washboard road.

****

I remember flying kites with Brian on Otter Beach when the summer twilight lasted until dawn. The simple paper diamond tugged against its string as it soared with the eagles in the lavender sky.

Then, when the air was still, roasting marshmallows over a driftwood fire—the crackling of wood, the smell of smoke, the taste of sweet, burnt sugar licked off my fingers.

Afterward, snuggling with Brian in bed, locked in the safety of his arms, the in and out of his breath like the ebb and flow of forever tide.

****

First class has certainly taken a tumble. Everything is in little bags...chocolate chip cookies, pepperoni strips, Almond Roca, cashew crunch. Thank God I had a croissant at the airport. I choose Almond Roca and cashew crunch.

Mrs. May's Naturals. Even my cashew crunch is married. I guess we don't trust sweets that come from an unmarried woman. *Miss Fields' Cookies.* Nope, doesn't inspire confidence.

I tug open the bag and discover three little squares of cashews held together with glaze.

This reminds me of trick-or-treating as a kid, going from house to house and taking only one or two pieces of candy from the offered bowl.

But I've spent $80,000 to get this *free* first class seat. I deserve more.

****

A few years back, Brian and I were traveling from Juniper Verde to Anchorage. We had seats in coach and when we got to the Phoenix airport, Brian was bumped to first class.

I couldn't believe Brian accepted the frequent flyer upgrade, leaving me in coach, without so much as a glance my direction. I was even more dismayed when my shock didn't faze him.

I think of this as a *Gift of the Magi* moment—an opportunity for each to be selfless in allowing what's best for the other.

It can be argued that I should've been happy for Brian's good fortune; that my need for his companionship—and his arm—should be secondary to his comfort.

Conversely, given that we were already apart about half the time, Brian could've chosen three hours with me over a comfy seat and free drinks.

But here's the thing. If the situation had been reversed and I was upgraded, I would've declined, *preferring* to be with Brian.

(Brian would've then said, "I'll take it.")

I suppose I was making a mountain out of a gopher hill, and, as it happened, at the boarding gate, I was bumped to first class, too, so it all worked out…I guess.

But the issue was never about first class. It was, and still is, about choices, and all those little gopher hills adding up to a whole lot of nothing.

****

After a bumpy descent, our plane lands in Seattle, but the bumps going down never bother me like the bumps going up. As we taxi to the gate, I look at 3C. "This isn't a come-on, but you look really familiar."

Clearly flattered, he smiles then tells me his name, which I immediately recognize.

3C served four terms in the Alaska House of Representatives.

****

In real life, I've yet to see a gopher hill become a mountain, and this ranch has a lot of gophers and gopher hills so I'm an amateur expert. One or two mounds aren't much noticed, but then one day, you look around and think… *Wow, there are **a lot** of gopher hills…* with even more popping up, but the threat isn't real because you can't see all the hollowing going on underneath.

Besides, the sun is shining and the ground is concrete hard and I've got mice in my attic to relocate, so I go about my business, ignoring how these little gophers and their little tunnels are undermining the very ground on which I stand, on which I build, on which I live.

Then one day it rains—like a jackhammer. Pockets of earth open revealing craters large enough to swallow a Gator tire, and in fact, one does. And here I am, pummeled by that Arizona shrew while I struggle to get the Gator into 4WD and out of the disappearing earth before the torrent sucks it beneath the barn and it's lost forever.

Finally, I get the Gator to safety and I stand here, drenched, but now in the shelter of the barn with the horses and the dog, watching the corral become gutted like a minefield. It's a really freaky thing to witness because I had no clue to all the devastating emptiness beneath the surface of those little gopher hills.

January 26

7:30 Monday morning, yet still night, brittle cold, with thigh-high snow everywhere.

God, I miss this!

My trail buddy, Paula, and I stake out the building where Brian has his office. It's a busy place with twenty-two stories of people arriving for work. Headlights sweep Paula's car and pass by on the way into the parking garage. Exhaust fogs the air. Fluorescent light rains down from above, illuminating sidewalks and steps, chasing away the winter darkness.

Drinking vanilla lattes, we watch from inside her car, the purring engine pushing heat into the interior, as we wait for Brian's Mercedes to show.

Last night after Paula picked me up from the airport, we drove to the house to see if there was anything to see. It was only 10:00, but the place was dark and solemn. It seemed weird not to have the glow of even a single bulb, but maybe Brian was elsewhere and hadn't left a light on. Without lingering, we drove to Paula's. Exhausted, I crawled into bed and slept soundly.

Before we parked here, we again passed by the house, and it was oddly still asleep. My plan is being thwarted by the unexpected.

Three days ago, as I cleaned out my travel purse, I discovered a key at the bottom. I wracked my brain trying to place it, trying to remember when I got it and what it fits. It looks like a house key, but it didn't fit any of our Arizona doors, and I'm thinking it belongs to a door in Alaska. But which door? Anchorage, Otter Bight, or the Alyeska ski condo? I'm hoping it belongs to our Anchorage home and that makes the most sense. But I misplaced my Anchorage key about three years ago; when I was last here, I borrowed an extra one from Brian without making a copy. Miraculously, I have a key that may be the one thought missing.

But, we've been sitting here an hour and still no Brian. Thinking he may have gone to work early, we drive through the parking garage, looking for his ML350. Using her cell, Paula calls his office and the receptionist says that Brian isn't in yet. Paula calls the house…

You've reached the home of Brian and Kate, Nick, Alyx and Chance…

"Maybe he went to Juneau to see Michelle," Paula suggests.

"Maybe." But I can't imagine Brian going to Juneau in January, even for sex.

"What do you want to do?"

The sun isn't up; the house is still dark when we return to it. We pull into the drive. A frosted newspaper lies on the walk leading to the front door.

"Keep the car running. I'll knock on the door and if no one answers, I'll try the key. If the alarm doesn't go off, I'll check the garage. If the alarm goes off, we're getting the hell outta here."

There is no response to my knocking so I try my uncertain key. It slides into the deadbolt… and turns over. Taking a breath, I turn the knob, and ease open the door.

Exhaling, I see shoes that look like they fit a little girl. From the landing, I look up the stairs into the hazy light of dawn peeking through floor to ceiling windows. On the upper level are the living room, dining, kitchen and master suite. Downstairs, cloaked in shadow, are two more bedrooms, a bath, and laundry room.

It's deathly quiet.

Leaving the front door cracked, I go to the door on this level leading into the garage. I slowly turn the knob…

"Go, go, go!" I tell Paula before I even get the car door shut. "His car is in the garage!"

We drive around the block, come back, park on the street. We watch the house as if we expect it to awaken and stretch.

"He must've gone somewhere," Paula says.

"Nothing came through in his e-mail." The house slumbers. "Should I try again?"

Ice crystals glitter the air as I make my way up the walk, past the frosted newspaper. I inch open the door, which I left unlocked in my escape. Sneaking past the shoes, I steal up the stairs, peering through the rails as I go. There is new light in the kitchen! Jerking back, I freeze, my heart pounding. I imagine coming face to face with Brian and maybe even Michelle…naked.

I wait, take a breath, then peer through the spindles again. The pale blue fluorescence in the kitchen is from a window. I take a few more stairs. Winter coats hang on the dining room chairs.

I tiptoe through the living room and up three wide, carpeted stairs. Passing between the kitchen and dining room, I'm now in the hall. I take one feline step at a time until I reach the open door of the bedroom. Thinking about the gun kept in the nightstand, I peek around the jamb…

****

If women stop taking the high road, maybe men will stop taking the low road.

The problem is, women are wusses and men know this too well.

Women aren't raised to fight, aren't expected to make waves. While many of us have the fortitude to stay in a bad relationship, we seem to run out of steam when it comes to break-up. We steadfastly stand beside undeserving men, yet our knees buckle standing up for ourselves.

Is fighting for marriage more admirable than fighting for self?

If so, what does that say about our worth as individuals?

Too often we are pacifists, expecting God to mete out justice while we avoid the trenches.

Philosopher Reinhold Niebuhr, a Protestant pastor and author of the *original* Serenity Prayer, offered this warning: "There's a difference between being a fool for Christ and a plain damn fool." Turning the other cheek is not always the answer. Sometimes power must be met with power.

I think back on Nina's e-mail and her fear that Harry could have "squashed her like a bug" if she fought too hard. I remember her advice to get on with life and to, essentially, leave behind what is mine the way a refugee flees his battle-ravaged homeland with only the clothes on his back and an empty bowl. I think about my sister who cowered during her own divorce. I think about my mother who accepted child support but "out of principle" refused alimony and a house offered by my millionaire father while I, at sixteen, got a job to help pay the bills.

I think about all the women taking the high road to impoverished martyrdom and all the men taking the low road to financial security.

Again and again, I've heard the lament, *I didn't have the strength to fight him*.

Why do women recoil at the emotional toll of a bad divorce when the emotional toll of a bad marriage sustains us?

And yet, if a burglar breaks into our home and steals our china do we let him keep it? Or do we fight to get it back?

Why do we lose resolve when love is involved?

****

The bed is made, sort of. Not my anally-retentive way with tucked-in sheets, plumped pillows and smooth spread, but made enough so it doesn't look like someone is coming right back.

I haven't been here in over two years but the bedroom hasn't changed except that my framed photographs are gone, and there is a sleeveless black dress on a hanger that is hooked over the top edge of the closet door. Three-inch silver heels are nearby which makes me think that Michelle is short, and in the corner on my side of the room are a suitcase and two duffle bags that I assume belong to my husband's girlfriend. Peeking out from under the bed are women's moccasin slippers edged in *real* fur. Costume earrings are on my night table.

I resist going through Michelle's stuff because I don't know where Brian is and when he'll be back. If he left for the weekend, he could walk through the door at any minute. Before that happens, I must find my check carbons and anything else that might help in my divorce.

Updating Paula from my cell phone, I head downstairs where I stored my stuff.

I pass the dining room; a self-portrait painting of me still hangs on the wall. I notice PG movie ticket stubs on the kitchen counter. There is a card from Michelle standing on end in exactly the way Brian displayed my cards.

Time breathes down my neck as I pick up the card.

On the cover is a heart. Inside...*the best thing to hold onto in this world is each other.*

I once gave Brian the same card.

I read Michelle's sentiment...

As always, I am at a loss for words to express how much you mean to me. Throughout these past months, you have been my happiness, my strength, my everything! Thank you for being you and for loving me & for taking care of me unconditionally. Always know that it is you I love most! You that I'm happiest with. Looking forward to loving you for many years to come... Happy New Year!

Taking care of me recycles in my brain like a familiar refrain. I compare my meager *You still make my heart go pitter-pat* to Michelle's sonnet.

How can *pitter-pat* compete with *my happiness, my strength, my everything* and then finished with an exclamation point like a perfect little cherry?

Now might be a good time to remember my redeeming qualities.

I take the card.

I pass through the living room where a bearskin drapes the sectional.

I never allowed dead heads and skins in my space. Instead, Brian's trophies stayed in his office or his plane hangar or in the Alyeska condo—there's a ram's head on the wall that eyed me every time I took the stairs to our bedroom.

Now his trophies are here, on the sofa, and hanging off the closet door.

Paula is in the house by the time I'm on the stairs to the lower level. In the larger of the two guest rooms, the double bed looks slept in. In the closet, my clothes are still in place albeit scrunched together on the pole so there is open space.

I ask Paula's opinion about taking sweaters and a lime green robe; she cautions me about the robe.

"That color is really bright and it's hanging in front. Someone might notice if it's missing."

In the other bedroom, where there are boxes instead of a bed, an air mattress is on the floor, with a pillow and blanket.

I don't dwell; Paula and I unstack boxes. I find the box where Brian has dumped all of our framed photographs. I look upon the jumble as I do a fallen bird. It's not my fault; I can't do anything about it; it's still sad.

When I spot a New Year's Eve photo of Brian and me, an idea strikes. Taking the 4x6, I turn for the door.

"What are you doing?" Paula asks.

"Planting seeds of doubt." I cryptically elaborate then rush up the stairs. I imagine how Michelle will feel finding a photo of me. I bet the feeling is similar to finding a note.

After opening Brian's underwear drawer, I lift one edge of the folded and stacked white t-shirts. But, instead of slipping my photo under, I pull out the 5x7 photo already hidden beneath the cotton. I recognize this professional portrait of me and Molly; I have its twin in Arizona. Framed in rosewood, this once sat only a few feet away on Brian's nightstand.

Like a boomerang, my unkindness has come back on me; doubts attack my resolve like weeds plague a garden.

I tuck the photo back in its hiding place, close the drawer, and retreat from the bedroom.

Looking up from a box, Paula glances at my hand, the New Year's Eve photo still in it; she cocks her head at me.

"It was a stupid idea," I say, returning the photo to the pile.

"Yeah. Michelle probably doesn't do his laundry anyway."

I did, and although it's politically incorrect—does Hillary do Bill's laundry?—that was one of many ways I loved taking care of Brian.

The next box contains little boxes of check carbons. Probably fifty boxes in all. Opening a few, I discover a hodge-podge: some from my personal account, some from our marriage, and some from our joint account *before* we were married. Beth is hoping for these. But they are mixed together and I don't dare sort through them here and now.

Inside the file cabinet is a disarray of records. What can I say— I'm a packrat. I throw the contents into the box Paula brought, where I've also put my check carbons, then we return everything else to its original place.

****

I was refilling the bird feeders one autumn afternoon when I saw him. Wedged among the rocks, he was a casualty of our living room window, his soft orange breast and black and white wings a silent testimony to the frailty of nature. With a heavy heart, I bent to pick him up lest the ants swarm and devour him, but as my fingers gently wrapped his silky feathers, he let out a deafening squawk that had me reeling back at his resurrection.

Out of my grasp, he scrambled across the rocks, managed to catch air, but clearly wasn't up to flying. Neither was he able to stand, and when he tried, his little legs stuck out rigidly behind him and he fell over like a defective toy. What began as a burial became a rescue. When I finally enclosed him in my hands, his beak clamped onto a finger with the intensity of a vise, tearing my eyes.

I felt sorry for the little guy who had lost some of his faculties and was now about to lose his freedom, but in his current condition he'd be an easy meal. Into my bucket he went, nested in a soft towel so he wouldn't fall over. If he thought he was in dire straits, he didn't let on. He took every opportunity to attack my fingers with his beak, just so I didn't get any ideas about him being grateful for my interference. He might fall over, but he wasn't about to *roll over* no matter how bleak his situation.

****

I simply cannot believe—*cannot believe*—what our statement from First National Bank reveals. I check the transactions while standing at the counter.

A deposit for $158,565.88 went into our joint account on 9/13 and *on the same date*, Brian wrote himself a check for $153,565.88—check #1704, one of the two Brian noted in our register as VOID. The difference between the two amounts explains the $5,000 he claims as a "deposit" into our joint account.

After paying off our mortgage, over $75,000 of *my* money from the sale of our Anchorage house went into *Brian's* bank account. Even if I want to give Brian the benefit of the doubt, want to believe I'm jumping to conclusions, it's a little hard to ignore this evidence.

Clearly I had no idea what the "proceeds from the house sale" were. Why else would Brian obscure his actions by noting this check as VOID? He knew I didn't know and he didn't want me to know.

What I don't know is…*why* I didn't know. With my name on the deed, the bank would've had to include me as payee on the check. Since I never signed the check, I have to assume Brian signed it *for me.*

Focused on my move to Arizona with the horses, I suspect I signed the closing documents where I was told to, without a glance at the net proceeds. Like most of my life with Brian, I loved, trusted, and believed.

The other quirky thing about this statement is the mailing address—Brian's office. Which might make sense since we were moving. I try to remember the last time I looked at any of our bank statements. Pretty much from day one of our marriage, Brian reconciled our account. The clerk goes through the records until she finds the address change, *six years before we sold the house.*

Was this *diversion* of money from our bank account into his an isolated incident? Or a regular activity? Over the fourteen years I contributed equally to our joint account through paychecks and inheritance, was Brian syphoning money into his pocket? $500 here, $1000 there. Over the years, what might that add up to? $20,000? $50,000? $70,000?

My MBA courses taught me squat about wisely choosing a husband; however, they did teach me how to catch an embezzler. I never dreamed one would be the other.

****

That first night, my handsome bird ate dampened rice bran from tweezers and accepted water from a syringe. The next day, I took him to Louisa, a vet tech at a local animal clinic. Last spring, she advised me on raising a young finch that had fallen from its nest in the cupola of the barn.

Louisa extended his black and white wings then felt his body; he squawked and attacked her fingers with the vigor of a hawk. Her diagnosis was "concussion." His little brain was swollen and on temporary hiatus, but the rest of him was fine. A full recovery could take days, even weeks. **IF** he recovered.

Back home I consulted my bird book for a feisty orange and black bird with a strong beak. However, my book didn't categorize birds by any of those attributes. Thumbing through the pages, I finally found, on page 400, a picture that matched my patient.

I was keeping company with a black-headed Grosbeak, eight inches from beak to tail, and based on his muted orange coloring, an immature male.

****

Sitting on the floor in Paula's guest bedroom, with records from the house strewn on the carpet, I find the agreement I told Beth about, the one before we decided to marry. Brian and I were going to build on hillside, move out of my house, then live together in "our" house as an unmarried couple. Instead, we married and stayed in my house for five more years while Brian recovered financially from his divorce and real estate losses.

I also find check carbons from Brian's and my *pre-marital* joint account, with checks written by his hand as well as mine.

But the real treasure is in the two checks from this same joint account, written to ***our*** attorney who drafted our agreement for sharing the house purchase and living together unmarried. The same attorney who produced the pre-nup. This helps counter Brian's assertion that both the attorney and pre-nup were mine and all Brian did was sign. Brian must be considered, at least, a partner in the pre-nup, or it will be nearly impossible for me to void it.

I marvel at my husband's genius even as my stomach turns at his dishonesty. Although Brian authored the pre-nup, he had me take it to "my" attorney who essentially copied Brian's draft and created the final notarized document. Now it can't be linked to Brian. I kick myself for not keeping a copy of Brian's draft, but I simply knew too little and trusted too much.

I pick up the stack of twenty bank statements from our joint account I randomly selected from the bank's archives. Auditing is about percentages; only a small sample is needed for confidence in your findings. If embezzlement is ongoing, even if it's not monthly, it can be found.

Before all this, I didn't know how literal "a heavy heart" could be. But there's an anvil in my chest, pulling me down. I imagine falling through Paula's floor into her basement, cracking and spreading the concrete, then lying in the cold, barren dirt that never feels the sun.

January 27

"*Michelle Wright will be out of the office from January 24th to February 2nd; she'll be back in the office on February 3$^{rd...}$...*"

"Now call Brian's office," I tell Paula.

The receptionist tells Paula what she told her yesterday and asks if she'd like to leave a message.

"I left a message," Paula complains. "And he hasn't called me back."

The receptionist confides that Brian won't be back in the office until next week.

Half an hour later, we're parked in the house driveway, checking out the neighbors. By now, everyone who works a day job is gone from their homes. Even if that weren't so, I doubt anyone would view as suspicious a car in Brian's driveway. Unlike me, always telling the neighbors when I'm gone, Brian never tells anyone his business.

Paula and I go to the front door, passing yesterday's newspaper on the walk. There isn't another for this morning. I slip the key into the deadbolt.

Taking off my coat along the way, I make a beeline for Michelle's bags while Paula snoops in the kitchen.

I leave the first bag in its place on the floor and unzip. Looks like work stuff: manuals, notebooks, papers. Then I find three cards along the side.

The first card, inside a tattered yellow envelope, is long and narrow. Brian has written Michelle Wright on the envelope.

Here you are another year older and it's obvious
you'll never change...

But then, why should you? You're great just the way
you are!

This must be the Scottsdale birthday card. On the inside left is
Brian's note.

Thank you for being you and being with me.

I compare this to the messages he has written to me for twenty-
two years. Although he has put *love* before his name, this offering
to Michelle seems a little shallow. But maybe that's what I want to
see; Brian doesn't love her as much as he loves me.

The next card is for Christmas, a cute, generic money holder
that asks why Santa's reindeer are so excited—they can always tell
when there are a few "bucks" around. Brian probably bought an
assortment to give to his kids and grandkids...his housecleaner,
his girlfriend, his wife...

Again, Brian has written a note on the inside.

*Naked or dressed, YOU make ME excited! (But naked
is more fun!)*

Maybe my skin is getting thicker, but his words barely scratch.

The last card is another for Christmas—a Hallmark musical
moment with Louis Armstrong croaking *Winter Wonderland*.
Below the printed sentiment is Brian's sentiment, but again lacking
the depth I'm used to—until the last two lines...

Let's spend every Christmas together. Is it a date?

He once penned those words to me.

"Are you finding anything?" Paula calls from the bathroom.

"Not yet."

Searching inside the bag, I pull out a small notebook and start
flipping through.

"Brian and Michelle are in Hawaii," I shout to Paula who comes
quickly to the bedroom. "And they took her kids."

The compact pages detail the trip—dates, flights, travelers, hotel reservations, and confirmation code. I write the information down in my own notebook; later, I'll print it from the Alaska Airlines website to include in my divorce file.

Paula sees the trophy dress. "Do you think she wore that for New Year's?"

"Probably. I'd freeze if I went sleeveless in winter. Check out the shoes."

"Those are pretty. Is Michelle short?"

"Shorter than me, obviously. Or she doesn't care if she's taller than Brian."

From inside the closet, Paula announces, "Her dry cleaning is hanging up."

I flip the next page in Michelle's notebook and the next and…

"Oh-my-God. Oh-my-God. Oh…my…God!"

****

When I was twenty-four, I had a laparoscopic tubal ligation.

I did it spring break during the last semester of my MBA program. My friend, Didi, who was also an MBA candidate, drove me ninety miles to a clinic in St. Louis where "procedures" were performed, mine being one of the less common. Usually women went there *after* they were in a pickle, and wanted an immediate fix but, unlike me, didn't want a permanent solution.

I was groggy, but awake. Gas was pumped into my abdomen so that my internal organs floated away from each other and my tubes were easier to find. A tiny incision was made near my navel and a scope inserted. *Snip-snip.*

On the way home, Didi and I stopped for dinner at Red Lobster.

****

Paula shoots her head out of the closet. "What?"

"Look at this. **Look at this!**" I hold the notebook toward Paula so she can see the writing on the page. "You're a nurse. What does that say to you?"

"Huh. That's…unbelievable."

"I'll tell you what's unbelievable. Brian got caught by the oldest trick in the book."

"You think Michelle planned this?"

"Duh. What better way to force a decision? She probably gave Brian the news right before he decided not to come back for Christmas—" Which now makes sense. "I can just hear her, *I'm so surprised. I haven't used birth control for **years**. You must have really strong sperm…* Men are idiots."

"Y'know, this could be for someone else."

"Like…?"

"A student, maybe?"

"I doubt this falls under her job description. But even so, there's something else. The dates for the *procedure*? January 11 and 12? In **Seattle**?"

"Yeah?"

"Brian was in Seattle on those same dates."

✶✶✶✶✶✶✶✶✶✶

The few people who knew about my tubal thought I didn't want kids; they assumed it was about career and independence. Maybe there was some of that, but mostly I was haunted by my past and feared my future would see its repeat.

I was so afraid of my father's DNA—so afraid that I would inherit even half his demons—that I didn't want to risk putting an innocent soul through my childhood.

It can be argued that I worried for nothing, that I knew better, that I was aware and wouldn't do such horrible things. But my father knew better, too. He *knew* what he did wasn't right. He may have had a tough childhood, but he grew up, was an Air Force colonel, earned a Ph.D., travelled the world and saw a different way to live other than by anger and cruelty, and *still* he did what he did.

So I cut the connection.

Turns out, I was worried about the wrong DNA.

****

With the information on Michelle's procedure tucked in my purse, I go through the rest of her bag, finding a stash of personal information. I take notes on everything. Her social security number, her maiden name, her middle name…

Michelle Joy. A good name for a boat—unless you believe the sea farers' warning that bad luck follows a name change.

I open her checkbook, write down her address. I discover the year she was born.

Michelle is twenty-one years younger than Brian, three years older than Brian's oldest, a daughter, but a year younger than his daughter's husband.

I imagine the family sitting down for Thanksgiving dinner.

I open a file and find Michelle's divorce papers, yet to be finalized. Kevin and Michelle have been married thirteen years. I find the names of her daughters and their ages. Brian has grandkids the same ages—and older. According to the child custody arrangements, Kevin has the girls during the school year; she gets them summers.

I thumb through loose papers—

"Oh-my-God, oh-my-God…oh…my…God!"

Paula pops her head out of the closet. "What now?"

"A quitclaim deed. To Brian."

"For what?"

"It looks like Michelle has property in Colorado she doesn't want Kevin to know about."

"What does that mean?"

I set the paper aside. "It means Kevin is about to get property in Colorado."

Paula returns to the closet while I put everything back, zip this bag, and go to the next. Nothing but clothes, neatly folded. Michelle wears size 10 jeans and a 36D bra.

I fit in her shadow.

Finding nothing else interesting, I close the bag and check the rest of the house. In the master bathroom, tampons are in the cabinet. I think about my upcoming hysterectomy and the irony.

Brian always hated my monthly inconvenience and now that my inconvenience is about to be gone, he's gone, but with a new inconvenience.

I turn for the door. Behind it, a white negligee hangs on a hook.

I look around the kitchen. The refrigerator is barren of food. Only a few condiments sit on the shelves along with a couple of cardboard containers holding restaurant leftovers.

Adding it all up, I think how different Michelle and I must be.

In the garage, Paula and I find four small boxes of kid stuff, like school records and medical files. I find Michelle's photographs—before Brian. Photographs of Michelle and her handsome husband, now in the past; of Michelle and her cute daughters; of just kids; of the family. Photos when the girls were still stroller-size and then older photos. Photos on vacation, photos at home, photos with, I assume, grandma.

I think how similar Michelle and I must be.

Putting everything back, I close up the boxes.

I look inside the Mercedes. Brian has a jacket in the rear seat but not much else. And now I see it, in the cup holder between the driver and the passenger seats—a navy-blue hair Scrunchie.

January 28

Snow crunches beneath my boots. Paula and I walk the same wooded trail we rode our horses on a lifetime ago.

We're here after a good cry on Paula's couch.

The waning mid-day sun steals between the trees the way light leaks into an old barn between the seams of its weathered planks. The air glitters. Walking in the silence of insulating snow, we cross patches of light and shadow. We breathe out white puffs as if sending signals.

This takes me back to moments I never imagined leaving; moments I count as the happiest in my life.

But with each frozen step, I am more convinced that I can't bring Quinn here and warehouse him in a snow berm for five months each year. But if the horses can't come to Alaska, where will we go?

"Are you keeping your name?"

Paula's question seems premature. "I don't know. I've been Willoughby a long time and I remember what a pain it was to change my name. I hate the thought of doing that again."

But what I really hate, and keep to myself, is losing my identity, of not being Brian Willoughby's wife. It's so weird, if not unacceptable, to *want* to be identified with my well-known husband.

In Illinois, long before any of this, I was often identified with my well-known father…*Are you Bill's daughter?* And I have to say, I didn't mind that either. It was one of the few upsides to a life of downsides.

It's nice to *be somebody*, as Andy advised Opie, with the foundation laid. All I had to do was build on it.

But Brian not only had the foundation, he had the house. I moved in and together we built a second story. So giving that up makes me *homeless* in a different, more pathetic sort of way.

"Well, you have two pretty good last names to choose from," Paula says. "Not like my last name."

I don't pretend that Paula *Hurlbutt* is a good name. "It's not like either of my names are mine. One belongs to my father, the other to my husband. Maybe I should come up with a name just for me."

"You mean, make one up?"

"It wouldn't be made up like…Huckleruffmop. It would be a real name, but one I choose. Like Selleck."

Paula laughs; she knows my Tom Selleck fantasy. "Living the dream."

I laugh, too, but…*why not* live the dream? How many opportunities does life give you to change not only your future, but your past as well? *Why not* correct my DNA and journey forward, not with blue face, but most definitely with *brave heart*…

✶✶✶✶✶✶✶✶✶✶

The bird book said that Grosbeaks eat seeds, nuts, fruits, and Monarch butterflies. Since my cupboard was empty of Monarchs, I surveyed other possibilities.

Apples—too hard. Nectarines—too stringy. Bananas—soft and mushy.

I don't know if Grosbeaks ever stumble onto bananas in the wild, but since bananas are "brain food…"

My Grosbeak LOVED bananas. And he did not eat like a bird. He devoured his banana with the appetite of a gorilla. And for once, he stopped attacking my fingers.

But after three days of bananas without much brain improvement, I feared my Grosbeak's rehabilitation might take weeks and not days. And I was getting tired of referring to him as "the bird."

Grosbeak is German for "large beak." It seemed logical, then, to consider the Hun side of my family for his name, but truthfully, I've always felt a greater affection for the Celtic limbs of my tree.

My great grandfather was born on the Emerald Isle but migrated to the Lone Star state. Except for his name, *Phineas Clairborne,* I don't know much about him other than he played the fiddle and fathered my grandfather whom I know only by the initials E.E. But the Irish have a reputation for being independent, proud, and good fighters, which summed up my bird.

By day four, *Phineas* finally showed improvement. He could tuck his legs beneath him and was able to maintain his balance for several seconds before tipping over. And his little feet had a grip like Velcro on wool. Periodically he would stretch and flap his wings. Along with bananas, he enthusiastically ate sunflower seeds and was less inclined to attack my fingers when I set him upright. By sheer will and ignorance, he was overcoming his challenges.

A bucket was no place for such a determined bird.

January 29

I guess this has been a productive trip.

I meet my attorney, Beth, and she's pretty much what I expected—grounded, supportive, witty—and outraged by Brian's Hawaiian vacation with his girlfriend. Sadly, I suspect I'm what she expected, too. What I didn't expect is the Fisher-Price play castle on her office rug.

"For my grandkids," she told me.

Beth, the legal pit-bull and Bubby, is delighted with all my evidence. But she merely rolls her eyes and breathes *Oh my God* when I show her the information about Michelle's "procedure" two weeks ago in Seattle.

In an age where a California governor fathers a child with the family housekeeper, and then raises their son under the same roof with his unsuspecting wife, and the US President pays for hookers, my stuff is tame, mundane, really. It's just sourdough to accompany my husband's haggis. No one, especially the court, cares about this.

Yet, oddly enough, I think about how adorable Brian and Michelle's child would've been. I see a little boy…on Santa's lap.

On the heel of that vision is an unbidden spark of compassion for Michelle, a woman more desperate than I. Maybe one day I can fan this spark into a flame of forgiveness, but right now I wonder… *Would Brian have come home for Christmas had Michelle not delivered her news?*

But she did and he didn't and now we are here, beyond going back, so what does it really matter?

Well, it matters to me. It feels like Michelle *won* and I *lost* because of a really bad call.

It's as if Providence was looking the other way when Michelle sucker-punched me, and it seems *unfair.*

But Providence is **not** unfair. It may not be *equitable,* but it **is** fair. Sometimes brutally fair. We don't necessarily see that because we aren't often privy to before and after, but I've always felt the presence of a cosmic Solomon.

So maybe we **aren't** *beyond going back.* Maybe if I tell Brian that I know about *everything...* maybe it's **not** too late...for us.

Maybe there's a reason I unwittingly came to Anchorage the same week Brian and Michelle—and her kids—went to Hawaii.

What if this is the plan?

What if I'm *supposed* to discover secrets and hidden photos?

What if I'm meant to defeat the demons and win back my husband?

And this is what I think when I conveniently forget everything else.

****

"You've been a busy bee," Beth says, perusing the bank statements, check registers and credit card charges. "I'm sure Brian doesn't expect you to use your brain to figure anything out."

I *think* this is a compliment. But I have to weigh that against all the years I **didn't** use my brain, which Beth kindly doesn't mention.

Yet, in spite of all those years of brain atrophy, I've revved up my little grey cells and built a case with legal sting—the years I supported Brian; the $10,000 cashier's check; the Otter Bight quitclaim deed; the pre-marital joint account; the checks to *our* attorney; the pre-nup signed on the day of marriage; my $32,500 for Alaska Airlines Stock that *disappeared* into Brian's cache; the incriminating e-mails, undisclosed assets, and the Utah bank account held jointly with his stepmother, Dorothy Willoughby.

But it's Brian who has done the most damage to the pre-nuptial agreement. He *co-mingled funds* when he wrote a check to himself from our bank account—stealing my $75,000 from the sale of the house—and put that into **his** account, thus *transmuting* his assets into **our** assets.

All in all, this has been a productive trip. I should be soaring. So why do I feel like I've lost a wing?

"Are you ready for his settlement offer?" Beth sets aside the pages I gave her and hands me a copy of a letter she received this morning from Brian's attorney. As I read, Beth paraphrases.

"He'll give you $100,000 within ten days of acceptance and a note payable for $200,000 which he'll pay off at $1,000 a month with a 5-year balloon payment."

I look up. "He's offering me $300,000…after twenty-two years?" I do the math. "That's what, four or five percent of the assets?"

"That we know about. We don't know how much money is in the Utah bank or the Charles Schwab account, or whatever other accounts he has. But now that we know he's hiding stuff, we can petition the court to look at tax returns beyond the three most recent years."

"But tax returns don't show everything." My annuities were only visible when money was coming out of my paycheck. They're nowhere on the returns now. And God only knows how many *Corvettes* he has. "Brian could have money stashed in all sorts of places. Bank accounts we don't know about; real estate outside Alaska and in other people's names."

"But all we have to do is prove that he's not disclosing his assets and the judge will view our side favorably in the property settlement, especially since Brian has co-mingled funds. There's no way Brian can separate your money from his money or even the money from his law practice. It's all *joint* money now."

"You'd think he would know better."

"He does," Beth says. "But he's greedy and he didn't think you'd question it, let alone *find* it. Honestly? **I** can't believe you have the check he wrote for the tractor. What are the odds we'd find that Utah account? It'll be interesting to see what's going in and out. I suspect the checks he writes to Dorothy Willoughby for loan payments—" She puts air quotes around *loan payments*. "—are actually deposits into that account. His stepmother probably reports the interest income on **her** tax return so Brian doesn't have to worry about discovery. I bet he's been doing this for years."

Dottie's participation is understandable. Her career has always been husband and family. She trusts Brian implicitly and doesn't realize what she's helping him do. *Or maybe she does.* Maybe she believes, and the rest of his family, too, that I've been a leech on Brian's butt for twenty-two years.

"By the way," Beth segues. "Why would Brian buy a tractor if he's selling the Washington property?"

I shrug. "I'm guessing he wants to keep the roads maintained and the weeds cut and the pastures mowed so it will show better."

Beth cocks her head at me. "What's the smile for?"

"I'm remembering when Brian mowed a lawn."

"I don't understand."

My smile fades. "You had to be there." I ask her if Brian's clients would pay him cash.

"Are you thinking he has unreported income going into Utah?"

"Just asking the question."

"Over the years, probably. But it's unlikely he gets very many cash payments, not like a criminal defense attorney. But we can't look at that. How an attorney gets paid is confidential."

Hmmm.

"Brian isn't dumb," Beth adds. "His ego just got the better of him. He can't imagine that this divorce will be any different from all his other cases. He plain underestimated you."

I go back to the letter… *Ms. Willoughby would need to vacate the ranch no later than June 30…Each would be responsible for his or her own costs and attorney fees…The horse, Teena, care and lodging would be transferred to Mr. Willoughby by June 20.*

"I've added the Colorado property to the list of Brian's *undisclosed* assets. Do you want me to do *something else* with Michelle's quitclaim deed?"

I lower the letter into my lap and look at Beth; she obviously wants to do *something else* with Michelle's quitclaim deed. "Send a copy to her husband's attorney."

Poor Kevin—he's about to learn more crap about his wife that he doesn't want to know. I fold up the settlement letter, put it in my purse, and reach for my coat, feeling with every effort, the weight of this divorce.

"Y'know, Kate, sometimes the best revenge is the other woman."

I stop at her office door leading into the hall. "Do I act like I want revenge?"

"No—amazingly not—I'm just saying, given what we know about Michelle, Brian may one day get a dose of his own medicine."

"I hope not. I hope Brian and Michelle have a long and happy life together. I hope she takes care of him. I hope she loves him. I hope she's there until the bitter end… "

Beth looks at me as if she thinks I'm vying for sainthood.

"…I don't want Brian to be alone. I don't want to think about him. I don't want to worry about him. I want him to be happy so I can be free."

Downstairs, the receptionist with the dreadlocks hands me an unsealed envelope before I escape the 1940's house that is home to Beth's law practice.

Outside, the air glitters and the shadows are long. It's 3:00.

Waiting for Paula to pick me up, I pull out the folded papers from the envelope and flip through the details of the legal services provided by Beth and her staff. The last page delivers the bottom line.

My $10,000 retainer has been gobbled up by the divorce monster. I now owe Beth an additional $3,483.07. I stare at the dollars. *Seven weeks.*

Back inside the house, the receptionist with the dreadlocks raises his eyes to me. I flutter my bill at him.

"Do you guys take cash?"

∗∗∗∗∗∗∗∗∗∗

The closest thing I had to a birdcage was a small, old-fashioned cat carrier with five solid sides and the remaining one in mesh; with a few modifications, it worked fine.

I put a sheet of foam on the bottom, covered that with a towel, and lodged a small branch inside for a perch. In went Phineas who seemed happy to be out of that bucket and into a room with a view.

A quick learner, he was on the perch—and falling off—like clockwork. But he never gave up, exhibiting the same spirit he'd shown from his first attack on my fingers.

Slowly his time on the perch stretched into minutes before he would slowly fall backward, as if a weight dragged his tail, and then, *plop* onto the towel. My heart sank with each failure, but Phineas would have none of my pity. Back onto the branch he climbed, determined to be a bird again.

By day six, Phin was on the perch more than he was on the towel, but his balance wasn't perfect. He compensated by being excellent at wing flapping. I put the carrier with him in it on the back deck and in his quieter moments, he sat on his branch, basking in the sun… until he fell off.

Other times, he beat his wings madly and flung himself at the mesh, tempted by the freedom beyond. When I tucked Phin into bed, I told him, *one more day.*

When day seven came and went with his balance still not 100%, but his wings more determined, I told him again, *one more day.*

****

Sea Galley is the same as I remember, right down to the table where we always sat.

I'm here to make a statement—and to maybe get a little drunk. But not too much as I'm on the red-eye back to Arizona in just a few hours and flying while drunk is not fun. Mostly I'm here to make a statement.

I'm okay.

It's not Winston Churchill, but sometimes *okay* is a miracle by itself.

Isn't that what's asked after a car crash…*Is everyone okay?*

After a bad diagnosis…*Are you okay?*

After *Dear Brian*…

Okay is the barometer by which everything is measured. Either you are or you aren't. And I want everyone to see that I am…*okay*… even if I'm not.

****

Sometimes you must forge ahead even if things aren't perfect; aren't the way you wish they were. Sometimes you have to jumpstart life.

Maybe I underestimated Phineas. Maybe Phineas already had what he needed most to soar—the unshakeable conviction that he could.

****

Jill and Shawna, the significant-other of Dwight, another decades-old friend of Brian, escorted me here along with Jill's husband, Archie, who is being a gentleman and springing for my Margaritas.

Jill and Shawna haven't been here in ages either, but they agreed to circle their wagons while I make my statement.

So now we are sitting at our table with other members of the old gang, on a busy night, and I can't believe how alone I feel. I imagine this is what amputees experience when they still have the sensation of the phantom limb.

Any moment now, Brian will walk up behind me, put his hand on the small of my back, lean into me with a kiss and say… "Hi, Hon."

This doesn't happen, of course, because my phantom husband is in Hawaii with his very real girlfriend and her kids.

Archie sits across the table from me, beside Jill; Shawna is on my left; Sheila, a former colleague of Brian's, is on my right. There are others down the table both directions, some I know, some I don't.

Sheila is sympathetic; her first husband left her for *the other woman*. She tells me that the kindest thing her ex did was offer no hope. She feels bad for me, really, really bad. And her second husband, sitting across from her, echoes Sheila's sympathy.

Finally, I see the advantage in being a throwaway. No one asks for an explanation; no one looks accusingly at me as if I somehow caused this mess. It's understood, and accepted with a shrug. Trapped packrats, Premarin mares, inconvenient life. This just happens.

I think about the daughters and the shallow waters we share.

For a split second, it feels real.

Sheila finishes her story, telling me that her husband did marry his haggis, but came back with regrets a few years later, wanting another go with her. As her ex tried to kiss her, Sheila tells me, she stopped him and said, *the grass is not greener.*

Then, out of nowhere she says, "You're prettier than Michelle."

I stare at her, unsure how to react. Should I thank her? Is it a compliment or a consolation? Michelle has Brian but I have looks? Or is she suggesting that Brian chose poorly because I'm prettier?

Surely, I have other, more laudable attributes that make me a better choice than Michelle. Because, I can't possibly be prettier. To begin with, I'm sixteen years older and I haven't eaten in ten weeks so unless Michelle has recently been hit by a Mack truck, two or three times…

Then again, her comment could suggest I am so devoid of redeeming qualities that Brian would rather be with someone of inferior looks than suffer with me even one more day.

But I know Sheila was merely trying to say something *inspiring*, as I would want to if I were sitting next to poor, pitiful, discarded me.

So, I kind of shrug and mumble *thanks* and then Archie asks if I want another Margarita and the woman on Sheila's right nabs her attention and next I'm talking to Archie about Brian and somehow we get to Rae-Lynn.

The tequila has relaxed my brain and loosened my lips, and though I vowed I wouldn't talk about Brian to any of his friends, I tell Archie about the *Cosmo* I found at the cabin with Rae-Lynn's name on it. I tell him the whole story about how Brian claimed that Rae was a buddy's girlfriend. I tell Archie that I should've paid attention to my gut back then.

Archie confesses that he knew Brian was juggling, but then he says that Rae found out about me and she broke up with Brian so it all worked out—

"Wait a second. Rae broke up with Brian?"

"Yeah…"

"So…I got Brian…*by default*?"

Archie kind of smiles. "Well, yeah, I guess you could look at it that way."

"How did Rae find out about me? Did someone tell her?"

Archie gazes across the crowded bar then comes back. "As I remember it, Rae found a card you had written to Brian…"

January 30

I suppose there's something to be said for being surprised after 22 years. I mean, REALLY surprised. And right when I thought I couldn't feel any dumber. I wonder—did Brian's first wife find a note from Rae-Lynn? How many times has Brian let someone else do his dirty work? And, of course, the inevitable question...

"Would you like something to drink after take-off?"

Looking up from my journal, I smile at the flight attendant, but decline a drink. Although it's been a few hours since my second Margarita, the residual effect, plus a recent lorazepam, will let me sleep the rest of the night to Seattle. Even now, I'm starting to bob.

While I still have my thoughts, I put pen to page.

What else is lurking in my woods?

I glance up as 4D takes the seat next to mine.

****

Eight days into his convalescence, Phineas was beating his wings so violently against confinement I feared he was worse off inside the carrier than out. Near the birdfeeders, I unlatched the carrier door.

In a flutter, Phineas reached the nearest juniper. He landed a bit rough and teetered on the branch—stopping my heart—but he didn't tumble. After a few fortifying breaths, he flitted to a higher branch, and then another and another, until he was at the top of the juniper, surveying his freedom.

Then I heard it—the crystal-sharp melody of his flight call.

He sailed to the next juniper and repeated his awkward landing. He slowly made his way to the top, sang to the wind, then spread his wings…and let go.

I watched him for an hour, following in his wake until his last launch took him from my sight. And then I watched a little longer.

****

4D is an assistant manager with our summer league baseball team, the Anchorage Bucs.

You'd think there would be a "k" with that, like the male deer, but Anchorage doesn't have deer, not even reindeer. Apparently, however, Anchorage has at least two *Buccaneers*.

4D is young; he looks maybe twenty-eight, with all that boyish exuberance you can't fake. He's big like an athlete, the kind of man to whom women give a second look.

No, he's not flirting; he's courteous, talking to me as if I'm a person who might be interesting, probably because his mother taught him to be kind to the elderly.

I try to be interesting. I tell him that I'm a romance writer and last week my agent broke the news that a publisher wants my romantic comedy, *Spooning Daisy*. I think I exceeded 4D's expectations.

He tells me about his job; he loves being a baseball scout and working with kids. I listen to this man who is a kid himself.

I don't know him at all, but he seems like the real deal—a man who will keep his penis in perspective and his promises intact. Maybe he represents the countless men we never hear about who are happily nesting like Albert, devoted to their mates and raising families.

And I like to think I'm the last of the women we always shake our heads at. But, when it comes to relationships, we keep reinventing the wheel.

As the plane taxis, 4D tells me that he's on his way to Phoenix for his sister's wedding. He asks where I'm going.

"Phoenix. I have a ranch, three hours north, outside of Juniper Verde."

"Would that be *Forget-Me-Not* Ranch?"

That wakes me up.

"It's on your shirt," 4D tells me.

I glance at my heart where *Forget-Me-Not Ranch* is embroidered in an arch over two running horses.

The cabin lights dim and our conversation stops, but not my smile, which stretches into quiet laughter. Outside my front gate, a sign hangs that matches my shirt. In keeping with western tradition, naming the ranch was about the first thing I did after landing in Arizona.

The engines thunder. I hug my pillow as we leave earth and push toward the Big Dipper. We bank right, climbing higher and higher into crystal night, and circle Anchorage heading south.

I gaze out my window at the oasis of lights, made even brighter by the reflection off snow.

So much of my life happened here…even when I wasn't. And yet, it's where my needle points.

I watch from my window as the lights fade to a glow and then I watch a little longer until the glow disappears.

A star winks at me. And now another.

It's funny how things sneak up on you. Even when they were here all the time.

I offer a blessing for Brian's journey, a prayer of letting go for mine.

The bucket tips.

About the Author

KATE RENÉ MACKENZIE spent her childhood overseas, the daughter of US diplomats. Attending college in Illinois, she volunteered at the local humane shelter, eventually becoming director. While earning a BA in Art and then an MBA, Kate worked at various jobs including go-go girl, bartender, artist, and teaching assistant. At 26, she sold her 280Z, packed her dog and cat into a Ford truck, and drove the Alcan Highway to Alaska, where she spent 24 years exploring The Last Frontier in a single-engine Cessna. A vegan and animal rights advocate, Kate provides a sanctuary on her Arizona ranch for all creatures great and small. Every year, like the gray whale, Kate returns to Alaska. Visit Kate's website at *KateReneMacKenzie.com*.

Made in the USA
Columbia, SC
14 March 2023

13784987R00174